"I have read many of Karen's bo╌╌ and I cry with every one. I feel like I actually know the people in the story, and my heart goes out to all of them when something happens!"

—Kathy N.

"Novels are mini-vacations, and Karen's are my favorite destination."

—Rachel S.

"The best author in the country."

—Mary H.

"Karen's books remind me that God is real. I need that reminder."

—Carrie F.

"The stories are fiction; their impact is real."

—Debbie L. R.

"Every time I read one of Karen's books I think, *It's the best one yet*. Then the next one comes out and I think, *No, this is the best one*."

—April B. M.

"Whenever I pick up a new KK book, two things are consistent: tissues and finishing the whole book in one day."

—Nel L.

"Karen Kir╌╌╌ ╌╌╌time."

—╌ren W.

More Life-Changing Fiction™ by Karen Kingsbury

Angels Walking Series
Angels Walking
Chasing Sunsets

Stand-Alone Titles
Fifteen Minutes
The Chance
The Bridge
Oceans Apart
Between Sundays
When Joy Came to Stay
On Every Side
Divine
Like Dandelion Dust
Where Yesterday Lives
Shades of Blue
Unlocked
Coming Home: The Baxter
    Family

The Baxters, Redemption Series
Redemption
Remember
Return
Rejoice
Reunion

The Baxters, Firstborn Series
Fame
Forgiven
Found
Family
Forever

The Baxters, Sunrise Series
Sunrise
Summer
Someday
Sunset

The Baxters, Above the Line
    Series
Above the Line: Take One
Above the Line: Take Two
Above the Line: Take Three
Above the Line: Take Four

The Baxters, Bailey Flanigan
    Series
Leaving
Learning
Longing
Loving

9/11 Series
One Tuesday Morning
Beyond Tuesday Morning
Remember Tuesday Morning

Lost Love Series
Even Now
Ever After

Red Glove Series
Gideon's Gift
Maggie's Miracle
Sarah's Song
Hannah's Hope

www.KarenKingsbury.com

Chasing Sunsets

Book 2 in the Angels Walking Series

KAREN KINGSBURY

SIMON &
SCHUSTER

London · New York · Sydney · Toronto · New Delhi

A CBS COMPANY

First published in the US by Howard Books, an imprint of Simon & Schuster Inc., 2015
First published in Great Britain by Simon & Schuster UK Ltd, 2015
A CBS COMPANY

1 3 5 7 9 10 8 6 4 2

Simon & Schuster UK Ltd
1st Floor
222 Gray's Inn Road
London WC1X 8HB

www.simonandschuster.co.uk

Simon & Schuster Australia, Sydney
Simon & Schuster India, New Delhi

A CIP catalogue record for this book is available from the British Library

TPB ISBN: 978-1-4711-4325-0
Paperback ISBN: 978-1-4711-4324-3
eBook ISBN: 978-1-4711-4326-7

Printed and bound by CPI Group (UK) Ltd, Croydon, CR0 4YY

To Donald:

Well, my love, the nest isn't empty just yet, but it's getting there. The years have picked up speed and now most of our boys are out of the house and caught up in the wonder of college at Liberty University. Kelsey has been married to her wonderful Kyle for nearly three years and Tyler is about to graduate from college. Where in the world has the time gone? Wasn't it just yesterday that we were taking the kids to the zoo for a Super Surprise Saturday? Or bringing home three wide-eyed orphans from Haiti? So much laughter, so much fun, and always you at the center, leading the way. I remember once writing down the ages the kids would be as the years ahead unfolded. The years sounded almost futuristic—2014, 2015, 2016. A million miles away from my comfortable place at the turn of the century. I would try to imagine life without the noise and homework and music and childlike laughter. Life without six sports and theater and dance schedules to somehow balance. I couldn't picture it. But now that we're here I can see something I didn't see back then. I see you, my love, ever so much more clearly. You and me, holding hands and having more and more time together, the two of us rejoicing over the goodness of God, the faithfulness of Him. The lesson we're learning is this: It's all wonderful. Every amazing season back then and now and yet to come. It's been said the best is yet to be. And so it is, especially with you by my side. Let's play and laugh and sing and dance, and together we'll watch our children take wing. The ride is breathtakingly wondrous. I pray it lasts far into our twilight years. Until then, I'll enjoy not always knowing where I end and you begin. I love you always and forever.

To Kyle:

Kyle, our newest son, who so beautifully leads and loves our only daughter. I think of Don and me, standing on the beach in Mexico on the last day of our honeymoon, praying for the next generation—kids that God might bless us with and their future spouses. That day as we prayed on the beach, thousands of miles away, you were born. While we were praying. Amazing how God works out His plan and how faithful He is to answer prayers. Kyle, your heart is beautiful in every way. You cherish simple moments and are kind beyond words. You see the good in people and situations and you find a way to give God glory always. Your music is taking wing and now everyone knows about Kyle Kupecky and your gift of singing for Jesus. God is doing such great things with you and Kelsey and your ministries, your love for people. I thank God for you and look forward to the beautiful seasons ahead. Love you always!

To Kelsey:

My precious daughter, how wonderful that our dream of making a mother-daughter card and gift line has come true. Possibilities by DaySpring/Hallmark is now in stores everywhere . . . and we are hearing such beautiful things about how this line is bringing people closer. It's all just a dream come true—something I couldn't have seen coming. But God did . . . and He continues to surprise us, doesn't He? Also, I'm so happy for you and Kyle. Your first book comes out soon and girls everywhere will want to read *The Chase: When God Writes Your Fairytale*. I pray it will change the hearts of this generation. I've never known you to be so happy, and time and again I point to you and Kyle as proof of God's faithfulness. Now, as you two move into the future God has for you, as you follow your dreams and shine brightly for Him in all you do, we will be here for you both, praying for you, believing in you, and supporting you however we best can. In the meantime, you'll be in my heart every moment. I love you, sweetheart.

To Tyler:

It's hard to believe you're so close to college graduation. The time has moved along faster every year and now here we are . . . knocking on the door of all that is ahead. All that God is still revealing to you. I'm so proud of the lead roles you've had in your college musicals. To think your papa told you he could see you as Tony from *West Side Story* one day . . . and that this past year you were Tony—it's further proof of God's love. But most of all I am proud of the example you have been to your friends—day in, day out. People around you are stronger because of you, and they are closer to God because of your example. I love that most of all about you, Ty. I'm so excited about your future. You are such a talented screenwriter, songwriter, director. One day the whole world will know! However your dreams unfold, we'll be in the front row cheering. Hold on to Jesus, son. Keep shining for Him! I love you.

To Sean:

You're finishing your first year at Liberty University with the dream of playing football. No one has worked for it harder than you, and we're so proud of your effort. But more than that, we are proud you want to be at a school that puts God first. In every sense of the word. He has such great plans for you. Sean, you've always had the best attitude, and now—even when there are hard days—you've kept that great attitude. Be joyful, God tells us. Be honest. Be a man of character. Keep working, keep pushing, keep believing. Go to bed every night knowing you did all you could to prepare yourself for the doors God will open in the days ahead. You're a precious gift, son. I love you. Keep smiling and keep seeking God's best.

To Josh:

What changes you've gone through in the last year. You're at Liberty University now, working on becoming a champion for Christ! Whether on the football field or soccer field, you play with everything in you, leaving everything you have in the moments between the whistles. I'm so proud of you! This we know: there remains a very real possibility that you'll play competitive sports at the next level. God is going to use you for great things, and I believe He will put you on a public platform to do it. Stay strong in Him, and listen to His quiet whispers so you'll know which direction to turn. I'm so proud of you, son. I'll forever be cheering on the sidelines. Keep God first in your life. I love you always.

To EJ:

EJ, it's hard to believe you're finishing up your first year at Liberty University! As you continue to walk into this new season, I'm so glad you know just how much we love you and how deeply we believe in the great plans God has for you. With new opportunities spread out before you, keep your eyes on

Jesus and you'll always be as full of possibility as you are today. I expect great things from you, and I know the Lord expects that, too. I'm so glad you're in our family—always and forever. Thanks for your giving heart, EJ. I love you more than you know.

To Austin:

Austin, what changes God has brought about in your life this past year. First the devastating blow that you could no longer play football, that you would never suit up for your junior year or ever again, for that matter. The heart defect you were born with finally caught up with you in ways we didn't see coming. And though you are so very healthy, as the doctor told you that very sad day, his job is to keep you alive. And so we have watched you cry and call out to God, but also we have watched you embrace this next stage of life like a quarterback, fourth and twelve. Like everything about tomorrow depends on it. We've always known there's no quit in you, and now we can see that happening. God has great plans for you still, son. What they are? Well, that's still taking shape and it has all of us more excited than ever! God saved you at birth and again when you gave your life to Jesus. Now He has saved you a third time by taking you off that field before the unthinkable might've happened. Whatever He has ahead, I pray you will change the world for the better. I am completely convinced. But through it all I pray you remember you are only as strong as your dependence on Jesus. Only as brave as your tenacious grip on His truth. Your story is a series of miracles and this next chapter will be more of the same. Along the way, your dad and I will be in the front row cheering you on—whatever you play.

Whatever you do. Sky's the limit, Aus. The dream is yours to take. I thank God for you, for the miracle of your life. I love you, Austin.

And to God Almighty, the Author of Life, who has—for now—blessed me with these.

Prologue

Town Meeting—Heaven

JAG WAS GOING TO volunteer.

He had decided long before he walked into the meeting. It had only been a matter of convincing his still-broken heart. He moved into the room as the others took their seats. A spot at the back was still open. He slipped in and waited.

At the front, Orlon rose to face them. "You know why we're here." His voice sounded somber. "It's time for the next part of our mission." He set his shoulders back, strong, determined. "This time the task ahead is very serious. Life or death."

Jag closed his eyes. The feel of the moment, the electricity and sense of expectation—all of it was familiar. Just like last time. *Am I wrong? Wrong to think I can make this journey when I failed last time?*

No answer whispered to him, but Jag knew what God

would say. The Father had already told him after his last Angels Walking mission. What had happened, the tragedy of it all—it wasn't Jag's fault. Earth belonged to the ruler of the kingdom of the air. Darkness would often prevail among men.

Until the trumpets sounded. And the Father would defeat evil for all eternity.

But that truth didn't lessen the weight of Jag's decision this time around. He had been told he would work again, that the day would come when another Angels Walking mission would require his skills. The time was now. Jag was convinced.

He opened his eyes.

Orlon was explaining the situation. "This time our mission involves Marcus Dillinger, the pro baseball pitcher."

Around the room the angels nodded. They had all shared a window to the work of the last Angels Walking team. The way Marcus Dillinger was used by God to bring his childhood friend Tyler Ames to Los Angeles.

"Marcus was MVP for the World Series win a few months ago." Orlon smiled. "On earth this is a big deal." His smile faded. "But now more than ever, Marcus is searching for meaning. Not only in life, but in love."

Of course he is, Jag thought. *Man's trophies and titles, his fortune and fame, could never satisfy.* Deep in the depths of any human heart that much was understood. Chasing after such meaningless things resulted in emptiness every time.

Orlon went on. "Marcus is a good man. He will not let darkness satisfy the longing in his soul. He wants the plans of God. This will work in our favor." His voice fell. "Even when everything else in Marcus Dillinger's world will seem to work against us."

He explained that Tyler Ames and his longtime love, Sami Dawson, would be part of this mission, as would Mary Catherine—Sami's friend and roommate. "The success of this mission will come down to Mary Catherine." Orlon narrowed his eyes, his shoulders set. "Our team will work in the inner city of Los Angeles, where survival is key. I'll be clear with you. The enemy wants to cut short several lives—especially the lives of Marcus and Mary Catherine."

Orlon hesitated. "You remember the ultimate goal." It wasn't a question. Of course they remembered. All of heaven was mindful of the near-impossible goal for this angel team, the way each mission would require victory before the next could begin. How only at the end of these missions would they know if they were ultimately successful.

That success would come with the birth of a baby named Dallas Garner.

"As I've told you"—Orlon moved along the front of the room—"if the child is born, he will grow to be a very great evangelist, a teacher who will help turn the sons and daughters of Adam back to knowledge of truth and love. Back to a foundation of Scripture. Dallas will offer a revival, especially for the United States. A nation that once trusted and revered God."

Orlon had never looked more serious. "We have one successful mission behind us. We have several more ahead. But this one . . . this one will be dangerous for everyone involved. Even our team of Angels Walking."

The angels shifted in their places, as if the heaviness in the room had taken up residence on each of their shoulders. Jag felt it most of all. Angels were never in physical danger, of course. They were eternal. But they could lose a battle with man, and certainly they could be detained by the enemy. When Jacob of the Bible wrestled an angel, Jacob won. And when an angel was sent to Daniel in Babylon, the angel was prevented from his mission—blocked—by the prince of darkness.

Orlon checked the notes on his mahogany podium. "Michael tells me the baby has only a two percent chance of being born. The enemy has orchestrated a number of very dangerous circumstances. Health issues, relationship struggles, discouragement." He looked around the room again. "Our Angels Walking team will be very busy."

Jag ran his hand through his wavy blond hair and flexed his muscles. The tension in the room was building. It was time to choose the angels. Everyone could feel it.

"I need experience on this Angels Walking team. Veterans." Orlon searched their faces. "Who would like to go?"

Jag didn't hesitate. He rose to his full height. "I volunteer."

Orlon paused but only for a moment. His eyes spoke volumes, for he knew Jag's history, his heartbreaking past. "Jag." A smile tugged at Orlon's lips. "I was hoping you would consider this. It's time."

Once more Orlon looked around the room. "Who will take this Angels Walking mission with Jag?"

From the front of the room a willowy black angel rose from her seat. Her eyes shone like emeralds as she looked back at Jag and then at Orlon. "I volunteer."

Aspyn.

If Jag could've chosen any angel in the room, he would've chosen her. The two of them had succeeded at a dangerous Angels Walking mission a hundred years ago in Germany.

Aspyn was skilled at intervening in battle, practiced at working with people who lived angry, violent lives.

Orlon looked satisfied. He drew a deep breath. "Very well." He motioned to the others. "Our job will be important also. We will watch and we will pray. Beginning now."

In a rush the other angels surrounded them. And with that their voices rose to the Father on behalf of the mission ahead.

Never mind the danger. Jag had a decade of defeat to put to an end.

He was practically desperate to begin.

1

THE JANUARY SUNSHINE CAST an array of shimmering diamonds across the Pacific Ocean that early morning as Mary Catherine kicked off her sandals and headed for the water.

"We'll freeze. Even with our wetsuits." Sami Dawson, her best friend and roommate, was right behind her, laughing at the insanity of their decision.

"Only for a few minutes." Mary Catherine's long golden red hair was caught up in a ponytail and it flew behind her as she ran. She was laughing, too, but more because she loved starting her Saturday like this. "Once we're in we won't feel a thing."

They carried their boogie boards as they ran through the shallow surf and then jumped over the frigid foamy breakers. In no time they were in up to their shoulders, past the foam and ready to ride the next set of waves.

Mary Catherine shook the water from her hair, breathless. "See? It isn't terrible!"

"Sure." Sami shivered. She nodded to the wave headed their way. "Come on. Keep moving."

They caught the first one and rode it all the way to shore. The spray of cool seawater in their faces, the rush of the powerful ocean beneath them. Mary Catherine loved everything about this. She felt alive and whole and connected to God. A thrilling diversion from the news she'd received last week.

The news that her heart didn't have long.

Sometime today she would tell Sami the truth about her health, come clean about the things she'd been hiding. But for now she would enjoy this moment. And she would remember what her mother told her years ago. Life could never be measured in the number of days a person lived, but only by the beautiful, brilliant life that had colored those days.

Mary Catherine paddled back out alongside Sami. Her friend's eyes were wide. "I think I saw a dolphin." She pointed behind the waves. "Like fifteen feet that way."

Mary Catherine scanned the distant water. "I hope it wasn't a shark."

"What?" Sami let out a quiet scream. "Don't say that!"

"I'm kidding." Mary Catherine laughed again. "I saw it, too. A few of them. Definitely dolphins."

Another swell came and again they caught the ride all the way in. They took their boards and sat on the wet sand, trying to catch their breath. Sami shook her shoulder-length dark hair. "Thank you for making me do this. I'm not cold."

"It's perfect out here." Mary Catherine headed back out. "Come on. A few more."

They pushed through the white surf to the smooth area and waited. Sami wiped the water from her face. "I can't wait for tonight. I really think Marcus is onto something with this youth center."

"Me, too. I'm glad we're going early." Mary Catherine felt it, the way she always did at the mention of Marcus's name. A feeling that started in her heart and made its way down her arms and up the back of her neck. She hated the reaction. The last thing she needed was a crush on Marcus Dillinger. "Is he still dating his coach's niece?"

"He is. We're double-dating with them next week." Sami wrinkled her nose. "I don't think they're a good match." She shrugged. "I don't see it."

Between her heart condition and half a dozen charities she was involved with, Mary Catherine certainly had no time to worry about a professional baseball player. The guy could never be her type.

They rode a few more waves and then Mary Catherine nodded to the shore. "Let's dry off."

"Good idea. I still have to do laundry before we meet up with the guys."

Their towels were ten yards up the beach, and after a few minutes they pulled on sweats and sat on the sand facing the water. Mary Catherine turned her face to the winter sun and savored the way it melted through her. How could anything be wrong with her heart? She felt too good to be sick.

The quiet suited them. Since rooming together a few years ago they'd had the sort of friendship that could erupt into laughter or feel comfortable in complete silence. They were very different, she and Sami. Mary Catherine broke the silence. "Did you and Tyler have fun last night?"

"We did." Sami's smile lit up her face more than the morning sun ever could. "I can't believe how good things are. I think he's going to ask me to be his girlfriend. Officially."

Mary Catherine jumped to her feet. "Really?" She danced around in a circle. "Yes!" She raised both fists in the air. "Yes, yes, yes!" Then just as quickly she dropped back to the beach. "What in the world is taking so long?"

"Well . . ." Sami shrugged, sheepish. "It's more me. Like I told you." This time her laugh sounded more nervous. "I needed time."

"Come on." Mary Catherine leaned back on her hands and grinned at her friend. "You've been in love with him since you were in high school."

"But I was practically engaged to Arnie." Sami's tone held a mock protest, nothing serious. After a few seconds she burst into the sort of laughter she and Mary Catherine shared so often. "Okay, okay! You're right. I don't need much more time."

"Oh, come on." Mary Catherine leaned forward and crossed her legs. "How long before he'll ask you to marry him?"

"Seriously?" Sami looked shocked. "Let's not rush things!"

"It won't be long." Mary Catherine raised her eyebrows. "You heard it from me first."

"You're crazy."

"But in this case, also right." Mary Catherine let her silliness fade, let the breeze off the ocean frame the moment, the significance of it. "Was it beautiful? Your date?"

"It was. We were at Disneyland, as you know." She looked so much happier than before, back when she was dating Arnie. "When it was dark he took me to the bridge in front of Sleeping Beauty's castle." Sami was sitting cross-legged now, facing Mary Catherine. "He told me he never stopped adoring me, never stopped thinking about me. Even with every bad decision he made back then."

"That's sweet."

Sami's smile held a contentment that hadn't been there in the beginning, back when Tyler first returned to Los Angeles. "He says he has just one regret now. One that still haunts him." She paused and lifted her face toward the sun for a few seconds before looking back at Mary Catherine. "That he ever left me at all."

The story touched Mary Catherine. She couldn't be happier for her friend, for the love she'd found. "I want to be maid of honor." She held up both hands in a teasing surrender. "That's all I'm saying."

"Seriously, though . . . you could be right." Again Sami's joy was tangible. "I love him so much. This new Tyler, the one with lessons learned and a faith that gets stronger every day . . . I just never dreamed we would have a second chance."

"I did." Mary Catherine gave Sami a knowing look. "Remember?"

"True." Sami's laugh mixed with the disbelief she still clearly felt. "You told me I couldn't leave Florida on that business trip, unless I spent a few hours with him."

"Let's just say I'm a very good friend." Mary Catherine grinned.

"Definitely maid of honor status."

The sun was higher in the sky, temperatures heating up. Mary Catherine allowed the silence again. She needed some kind of buffer before she could tell Sami the truth about her health. The one thing they'd never talked about. She checked her phone. Nearly eleven o'clock. They needed to be at the newly renovated youth center by three that afternoon to help with last-minute details for the grand opening.

Finally Mary Catherine shifted on her towel so she was facing Sami. "You ever wonder why I changed my eating habits lately? No more frozen pizza?"

Sami's smile came easily. "The whole no sugar, no gluten, no grain thing?" She uttered a quick laugh. "Because you're amazing and you like feeling good enough to climb walls and jump out of planes?" She laughed again. "That's what I always figured. I sure couldn't eat that clean."

Mary Catherine hated what was coming. She wanted everyone in her world to go on thinking she had switched up her eating because of her zest for life. Nothing more. She hesitated.

Finally Sami's laughter faded. "Isn't that why?"

"No." Mary Catherine's smile remained, but she could feel a sadness filling her eyes. "I'm diabetic. Type two."

"What?" Sami put her elbows on her knees and leaned closer. "Since when? How come you never told me?"

"I only found out last month, and my eating keeps it under control." She angled her head, willing her friend to understand. "I don't like thinking about it. Obviously. And, well, the way I eat I don't need pills or shots. I check my blood sugar every morning. So far, it's controlled."

Sami hesitated. "Okay, good. You scared me for a minute."

"There's more. Diabetes runs in our family." She paused. "Just like congenital heart defects. My uncle died because of his heart disease when he was in his late twenties. My mom never had any problem, but the gene passed on to me."

Again Sami looked beyond confused. She stared at Mary Catherine. "You're saying . . . there's something wrong with your heart?"

Mary Catherine took a slow breath. "I was born with a coarctation of the aorta, and a bicuspid aortic valve. I had emergency surgery when I was a few weeks old and since then I get checkups every year." She forced her smile. "No big deal."

"You should've said that first." Sami looked like she wasn't sure whether to relax or expect more news. "So . . . you're okay? Like long-term?"

"Not really." She hadn't talked about this with anyone. Not even her parents. "I had a checkup last week. My heart's enlarged—which isn't good. And my valves are deteriorating. I'll need a transplant sometime in the next year."

Sami pulled her knees up to her chest and hung her head for several seconds. When she looked up, there was no mistaking the fear in her eyes. "What does that mean?"

"The valve transplant isn't the worst thing. People survive those—though mine will be trickier for a lot of reasons." Mary Catherine looked to the sky; the California sun filled the morning. "It's my enlarged heart that's the real problem. Even with a transplant I may not have more than ten years. Maybe less."

The color left Sami's face and she simply stared, like she couldn't begin to believe the news. "That's . . . awful."

"You're the only one who knows." She reached out and gave Sami's hand a brief squeeze. "You're my best friend, Sami. I've been looking for a way to tell you."

Sami hung her head for a long moment again. When she

turned to Mary Catherine, there were tears in her eyes. "There must be something they can do. Your parents know the best doctors, right?"

"They do. But this . . . well, you can't fix an enlarged heart like mine. There are drugs that can slow the process. But that's about it."

"I can't believe this." Sami stared at the sky. A minute passed before she lowered her arms and faced Mary Catherine again. Tears fell down her cheeks. "We have to find another opinion."

"I've done that." She looked straight into Sami's eyes. "Look, the reason I'm telling you is so you'll pray. God can do anything—even with this." Again, she worked to keep discouragement from her voice. "That's why I care so much about living. Why I'm always talking about only living once. Because I don't have as long as most people."

Sami wiped her tears with her fingertips. "It's not fair."

"It is." Mary Catherine sat up straighter. "God's given me all these years of life and probably many more. I still have lots to do—like get that youth center up and running tonight. And maybe move to Africa for a year and work with orphans."

"You always say that."

"I'll do it one of these days." Mary Catherine found her smile again. "Of course, I'll probably skydive another dozen times at least, and look." She turned her face toward the ocean again. "I have mornings like this, with you." She felt a familiar peace fill her soul. "God has been far more than fair with me."

"Are you in pain? I mean . . . like, does it make your chest hurt?"

"Not at all." She raised her hands and dropped them again. "I feel perfect."

"Good." Sami looked off, her expression marked with sorrow. "What about love?"

"What about it?" Mary Catherine felt her heart sink.

Sami stared at her. "You deserve love."

"No." She shook her head. "I won't have time." Mary Catherine felt tears sting her own eyes. "But I'm okay with that."

Sami looked into her eyes again. "You were going to find someone real, remember? Someone like you, with faith like you and a love for life like you." Sami shook her head. "That was supposed to be the miracle of your life." She exhaled hard. "I can't believe this."

"Sami . . . it's all right." Mary Catherine put her hand on her friend's shoulder. "God's going to give me a different kind of miracle." She stood and reached out her hand. "Come on. Let's go find those dolphins."

Sami waited several seconds before she took Mary Catherine's hand. "Really?" She shaded her eyes so she could see better. "Can you do this? Swimming in the ocean? Is that good for you?"

"It's all good." She slipped back into her wetsuit and ran a few steps ahead. "The more life in my days, the better. Then it doesn't matter how many days I have. Just that I really lived them."

"I hate this." Sami climbed into her wetsuit and caught up to her. "You're probably supposed to be home resting."

"Never." Mary Catherine grabbed her boogie board and ran through the surf. Her laughter mixed with the sound of the waves. "God wants me out here."

Sami paddled alongside her. The moment they reached the calm area before the swells, they spotted the dolphins. Three of them, playing in the water a few yards away.

"See!" Mary Catherine's joy was as genuine as the sun on the water. "I don't want to miss this."

For the first time in many minutes, Sami smiled again. "I don't know anyone like you, MC."

"I'll take that as a compliment." Mary Catherine looked over her shoulder as the perfect wave came straight for them. "Here we go!"

And with that they both caught the wave and started to ride it in. The moment they did, Mary Catherine spotted two of the dolphins riding alongside them. "Look!" she shouted.

Sami turned her head and saw what was happening just before the dolphins kicked out of the wave and headed back out to sea. "Wow!"

"That never happens!"

"So beautiful." Sami was laughing now, too.

Mary Catherine turned her attention to the shore as the ride continued. Tears filled her eyes and mixed with salt water and a happiness that knew no limits. The heaviness from earlier was gone. No matter how many years she had or where God would lead her from here, one thing would always be true.

As long as she drew breath, she would spend her days living.

2

DWAYNE DAVIS WAS HER life now.

Lexy watched him behind the wheel, his face twisted in an angry look. He was determined . . . this time he was really going to do it. Which was crazy, because a daytime robbery was the stupidest thing ever. They could both get caught and Lexy would wind up in prison just like her mama. How was she going to tell her grandma something like that?

Dwayne jerked the car into the parking lot of the Shell gas station. Lexy couldn't breathe, couldn't talk. What if the guy behind the counter had a gun? What if Dwayne got shot?

"I'm not sure if we should . . ." She couldn't think of anything else to say.

Dwayne slammed the car into park and glared at her. He left the engine running. "Shut up." He looked over his shoulder. "Stay low."

She did as he asked. Her heart pounded against her thin

T-shirt. Dwayne was her man. She wasn't ready to lose him. If the store guy had a gun then this could end bad. Really bad. Lexy closed her eyes. She was only sixteen. But they would throw her behind bars. She could already feel the cold metal handcuffs on her wrists.

If he could do it, if Dwayne could pull off the robbery, he'd be leader of the gang. Which would make her the girl everyone wanted to be. That girl. Gang leader's girl. She opened her eyes. Her heart was beating so hard, the noise was all she could hear. Where was he? What was taking so long?

For a quick second she caught her reflection in the mirror. Her dad was black, mom was Hispanic. She had long, straight hair and light brown skin. Guys thought she was pretty. She'd been sleeping around for a year, but the last few months she'd belonged to Dwayne. Him alone.

He made her feel special. Like she was someone.

Lexy peered through the window. She couldn't see the cash register, but she could hear yelling. Probably Dwayne. He was so angry today. Like he could shoot someone without thinking about it. He was actually scaring her.

Suddenly Dwayne burst through the door with a paper bag, probably full of money. He stopped, aimed his gun back toward the store, and fired. At the same time a bullet whizzed past Dwayne's head, barely missing him. "Dwayne! Hurry!" she cried out.

Dwayne turned and ran for the car. He jumped in and sped out of the parking lot. He didn't look at her or say anything. His eyes were like black steel.

Lexy felt like she was going to throw up. The wheels spun

as they turned left and peeled down the street. She tried to understand. "Where you going?" Her voice was loud and frantic. She hated this. Why couldn't he talk to her? She could hardly breathe. "Dwayne, where?"

"I'm thinking." He was breathing hard. He looked into the bag as he drove and let out a victory shout. "We did it, Lex . . . we got this thing. Gotta be a couple hundred dollars here."

"Did you . . . did you kill him?"

Dwayne glared at her. "I missed, okay?" He kept one hand on the wheel and lunged at her like he might slap her. Instead he shoved the bag onto the floorboard.

Lexy didn't dare ask where they were going again. Dwayne was eighteen—he would think of a plan.

Sirens sounded in the distance. Dwayne rattled off a bunch of cusswords. He leaned forward, like he was looking for a way out. The car's steering wasn't the greatest, so he took a turn on two wheels and sped halfway down the street before he pulled over.

Dwayne dropped down in the seat and pulled his baseball cap low over his eyes. "Don't talk."

Lexy wanted to yell at him that she wasn't a baby. She could talk if she wanted to. But then Dwayne might tell her to get out and walk home. If she wanted to belong to him, she needed to do what he asked. She crossed her arms and kept her mouth closed. At his house, when they were in bed, he was the nicest guy in the world. One day he'd quit getting so angry. Maybe if he became leader of the gang. That would make him happy.

Dwayne's phone rang. He was shaking, looking at the

money and then checking the rearview mirror. He took his phone from his pocket and answered it. "S'up."

It was a guy's voice on the other end. Lexy could hear that much. But she couldn't make out what he was saying.

Dwayne cussed at the guy and then lowered his voice. "You can't keep changing the rules."

Lexy felt sick again. Must've been someone from the committee, the guys who would decide the next leader of the gang. So far Dwayne was only supposed to hit up a convenience store in the middle of the day. Nothing more. But it was never that easy, not with the WestKnights.

Dwayne shook his head and then smacked his hand on the dashboard. He cussed under his breath this time. "Fine. Tonight." He shook his head, angrier than before. "Later."

Lexy knew better than to ask. Instead she looked straight ahead, her arms still pressed against her stomach.

He slammed his hand against the dashboard again. "Gotta kill three EastTown thugs or Marcus Dillinger. Tonight."

"The baseball player?" Lexy stared at him. "You can't kill him."

Dwayne made a fist and then relaxed it. "Marcus is an easy kill." Dwayne laughed, but the sound seemed dark. Almost evil.

Lexy's heart raced faster than before. Dwayne couldn't be for real. He couldn't kill Marcus Dillinger. The guy was a hero. MVP of the Dodgers. The opening of his youth center was tonight. Killing Marcus? Lexy wanted to scream. Marcus was the hottest player on the Dodgers. From everything she'd

seen on TV he seemed like a great guy. Why would the committee want Marcus dead? None of it made sense.

Dwayne picked up his phone and made a quick call. The
voice on the other end sounded like the same guy. "Yo. I made
up my mind. I got Dillinger. Tonight."

Dwayne took off his baseball cap and rubbed his head.
He looked over his shoulder behind them. "Police missed us."

This time, Lexy wanted to say.

He tossed the bag of cash at her. "See what your man did
for you, baby? This is only the beginning." He peered at her as
he pulled the car back onto the street. "Now put it down. You
don't touch my money unless I tell you."

He drove down the street and turned right toward the
freeway. With every mile he seemed to relax a little more.
"Gonna be a bloody night, baby. Gonna make you proud."

"You should get the EastTown guys. That'd be better."

He glared at her again. "Maybe I'll start with you."

"I'm just saying you can't kill a professional—"

"Shut up!" He cussed at her again. "You take orders from
me. You got that?"

Lexy felt her anger rise up, but then it fell away. She was
here by her own choice.

They drove ten miles south before Dwayne pulled off the
freeway and headed north again, toward home. Toward the
streets just a few miles from Dodger Stadium.

Lexy felt tears in her eyes. The feeling wasn't something
she was used to. Gang girls didn't cry. Too much going on.
Still, Lexy wished they could take a week off from stealing
and killing and claiming territory. The whole thing was ex-

hausting. And now Dwayne was going to kill the city's favorite baseball player. She should've demanded he pull over so she could get out, demanded to be done with this life, but she couldn't. It was the only life she knew. Besides, she had everything she'd ever wanted.

She was Dwayne Davis's girl.

3

COACH OLLIE WAYNE WALKED into the bathroom where his wife, Rhonda, was finishing up her eye shadow. Ollie came to her and kissed her neck. "You look beautiful. Prettiest coach's wife ever."

She cast him a teasing look. "Coach's wife?"

Ollie loved her spunk. He gave his own forehead a light smack. "What? Did I say coach's wife?" He did a humble bow. "Forgive me. I meant you're the prettiest woman in all the world. Wife or not. Forget about just us coaches."

"Thank you." She gave him a flirty grin and returned to the mirror. "Will Tyler be there today?"

"Yes. Tyler and his girlfriend. A few other friends of Marcus and the volunteers from the neighborhood."

Rhonda smiled. "I'm proud of Marcus. What he's done, it's really something."

"He and Tyler have worked on it around the clock." Ollie

sat on the edge of the tub. "He requested that the media not be there tonight. Doesn't want it to be a circus."

"See! That's what I love about him." Rhonda was putting on her lipstick. "This isn't about getting another headline."

"The exact opposite." Ollie stood. "I'll bring the car up."

"Okay." She grinned at him and returned to the eye shadow. "Five minutes tops."

Ollie chuckled as he left the bathroom and walked downstairs to the garage. They lived in Silver Lake, in the shadow of Dodger Stadium, an area recently voted the number one most hipster neighborhood in the country. Of course, that wasn't why Ollie and Rhonda and their family lived there. They'd moved to Silver Lake fifteen years ago when Ollie was hired by the Dodgers. He'd been the head pitching coach for the last decade. They didn't plan on going anywhere.

Besides, the neighborhood suited them. Organic food and farmer's markets and the new Whole Foods down the street. People were friendly and the coffee was the best in all of Los Angeles. Ollie and Rhonda loved being with their neighbors and sharing their faith whenever possible.

Ollie climbed in the family's Suburban and pulled it up the driveway and around to the front of the house. As he waited, Ollie thought about the goodness of God. He and Rhonda were about to celebrate twenty years of marriage. Their three kids were healthy and finding their way through life with a faith that was increasingly their own. Shane was eighteen, a senior shortstop at nearby La Mirada Academy, and at eleven, Tucker was finishing up fifth grade and excited about middle school next year.

The only one Ollie worried about was Sierra. Their pretty

brunette was sixteen, a sophomore at La Mirada. All her life Sierra had been close to Rhonda. The two of them shopped and shared coffee dates and spent Saturday mornings hiking around Silver Lake. But this year things had changed. Sierra had started to hang out with a rougher crowd, and before Christmas break a school monitor caught her in the parking lot with a group of shady kids, ditching class.

More prayer, Ollie told himself. They wouldn't lose Sierra without doing everything in their power to keep her from straying. She was inside now, up in her bedroom studying for a biology test. Ollie almost wished she was coming with them to the youth center instead. Serving someone else might help Sierra remember who she was and the family she belonged to.

Part of the problem was his niece, Shelly. She was nineteen, a fashion design major at USC. Shelly didn't share the same faith as the rest of the family, but Sierra looked up to her. The two would go for coffee or shopping every few weeks. Shelly figured herself too smart to need Jesus, too gifted and financially secure to need redemption. That attitude was rubbing off on Sierra.

Her father—Ollie's brother—was a neurosurgeon. He'd lost control of Shelly long ago. Even before her freshman year at USC, when she moved in with a grad student she was dating at the time, she'd told her parents she didn't share their beliefs or their values.

And now Shelly was dating Marcus Dillinger.

Rhonda came hurrying out and jumped in the passenger side. "Let's do this." She smiled at him as she set her purse on the floor.

"We're picking up Shelly?" Ollie assumed as much.

"Yes." Rhonda gave a careful nod. "Your niece wouldn't miss this."

"Amazing. She's found this sudden desire to help others."

Rhonda gave Ollie a polite smile. "She would pick up trash in the gutter if it meant being close to Marcus."

"I know." Ollie sighed. "What does Marcus see in her?"

This time Rhonda cast Ollie a wary glance. "Really?"

Ollie thought about his niece for a long moment. Tanned, bleach blond, with a body that bore the proof of her twice-daily yoga. She had confidence, a career ahead of her, and money. She was the kind of girl Ollie was used to seeing on the arms of his ballplayers.

But Marcus Dillinger?

His star pitcher had changed so much in the past year. Ever since Tyler Ames arrived, the two of them had shared a quest to change life in the inner city. He had watched Marcus's faith in God grow every week in every area except one: Marcus's decision to date Shelly.

Ollie could only pray that in the next six weeks before spring training, Marcus would see the light about Shelly. Sooner than later. Before things got more serious. He'd seen some very good men brought down by the wrong women.

Marcus was a great guy, but he wasn't bulletproof.

4

Marcus PULLED HIS HUMMER off the freeway and turned right toward the brand new Chairos Youth Center. The afternoon sun was even warmer than expected. Marcus had the windows down and now he turned the radio off and breathed. Just breathed.

God, you did this. You gave me a dream to change things on the streets and now, well . . . here we are. It's all You, Lord.

My son, you will do even greater things in My name. I have chosen you for such a time as this.

The words came like the softest whisper, so real and clear Marcus jerked around to make sure no one was in the backseat. Chills ran down his arms and legs. Was it his imagination or was that really God? Talking to him right here in his SUV?

He felt the adrenaline begin to subside. God was with him. There was no question about that. The whispered words echoed in his head. Marcus wanted to do great things for

God. It was the reason he was excited to get up in the morning. This new adventure of faith.

But the idea that he might've been chosen for such a time as this? That thought had never occurred to him until now.

Marcus took a deep breath and focused on the streets ahead. Tyler Ames liked to say he'd spent his life chasing sunsets across the country for baseball. Always heading into the sunset but never really finding it. The elusive happy ending.

Now Tyler agreed with Marcus. The happy ending wasn't in baseball. It was right here—helping other people.

Marcus was five minutes from the center. All he could think about was that early morning when he ran the stairs at Dodger Stadium after Baldy Williams died of a drug overdose.

That morning everything had felt meaningless. The pitching, the fame, the money. All of it. What did a life in pro baseball matter if it could all end in a cold hotel room with a needle in your arm?

So he'd made God a deal. He would believe in Him, if only God would give Marcus's life meaning. Days later Marcus heard from a woman he had once rented a room from, a woman who was calling looking for help for Tyler Ames.

The same Tyler Ames that Marcus had grown up with.

Marcus remembered picking up Tyler at the airport and bringing him back to the stadium. Tyler needed shoulder surgery, and Marcus wanted to pay for it. But Tyler struggled to accept the gift. *This isn't your problem to fix*, he had told Marcus.

But Marcus had only smiled, his heart full. "No. It isn't my problem, Ames. It's my miracle."

And so it was. The answer Marcus had asked for, the

meaning he had wanted, started with finding Tyler Ames again and helping him with that surgery. Since then the two of them had worked together to convert an old warehouse into a youth center. A center they believed would make a difference for lost kids in the inner city.

The World Series win and the MVP trophy sitting back home on his bookshelf meant nothing compared to this day. The grand opening of the youth center. A crew of contractors had worked practically around the clock to meet today's deadline.

Marcus pulled his Hummer into the back parking lot. Inside he met up with Officers Joe West and Charlie Kent, along with the mayor. One of the parent volunteers made the introductions, and Marcus thanked them for being part of the celebration. "A year from now," he told the officers, "I hope we can celebrate a drop in crime around here. Kids staying in school. Drug dealers leaving the area. Gangs broken up."

The officers exchanged a look and the older of the two, Officer Kent, stepped forward. "We'd love that." He looked back at his fellow officer and at the mayor. "But, Marcus . . . we're not there yet."

Marcus recognized a heaviness in the man's words. "Did something happen?"

"If you have a minute, we'd like to talk to you in private before things get started."

"Sure." Marcus followed them into a small room. Every part of the building was freshly painted. Three new basketball courts had been built at the front of the center.

When they sat down, Officer Kent took the lead. "You live in Silver Lake, not far from Coach Ollie Wayne's family, right?"

"Yes." Marcus felt his heart drop to his knees. He had no idea where this was going.

"You obviously know things are bad in this part of town." He hesitated. "I'm not sure you understand just how bad."

Marcus felt himself begin to relax. This was a warning speech. He could handle that. He leaned back in the chair and listened while Officer Kent explained the statistics here in the projects.

"Few of these kids survive. Half of them don't make it to their twenty-first birthday. The gang activity here is at an all-time high."

He told Marcus about the WestKnights and the EastTown Boyz—rival gangs that would kill for status and recognition. "We've got kids turning tricks, dealing drugs, and killing rival gang members because that's what their dads and granddads have done for years."

The weight of the situation settled in around Marcus's shoulders. "We need to change that."

"Yes, well, first you need to know something. We've gotten reports of some gang activity planned for tonight. Probably right here on this block." The officer went on to explain that the leader of the WestKnights had been shot and killed last week. "A new leader has to be chosen by committee."

"Committee? They're organized?" Marcus had no idea.

"Definitely. They set up challenges for guys trying to lead."

The other officer nodded. "The challenges usually involve killing. Rival gang members, or innocent people walking by or sitting on their front porch."

Anger began to build in Marcus. He had been raised in the suburbs of Los Angeles, in Simi Valley, where gang activity was rare. It was impossible to live in Southern California and be ignorant of the gangs in their midst. But Marcus hated that things in this very neighborhood were so bad. He looked from one officer to the other and then to the mayor. "What can we do about it?"

"Not a lot. We arrest them, of course, but they don't care. There're six young boys ready to join the gang for every one that gets killed or locked up."

Marcus didn't want to feel defeated. "What about educating the kids, helping them find a different way to live?"

"That's possible. It takes money and time. A lot of commitment. There will be setbacks." The mayor straightened his tie. "It's very dangerous trying to make a difference down here. Tough to find volunteers."

Marcus thought about Tyler and Sami and Mary Catherine. The Wayne family and his girlfriend, Shelly. They were committed to the youth center. "Maybe no one's ever really tried."

The three men nodded, but none of them looked encouraged. Officer Kent studied Marcus. "We're just saying be careful. It's not easy coming into an area like this and trying to change things."

Marcus thought for a moment. "What about the Scared Straight program?"

"We used to have it." The other officer nodded. "It didn't work as well as people thought. The recidivism rate was actually higher than for kids not involved in the program."

Images filled Marcus's mind, scenes from the TV show *Beyond Scared Straight*. "I thought it always worked."

"That's just for TV." Officer Kent's expression remained

serious. "These kids might not like the idea of prison, but they don't know anything different. In most cases they have a parent there."

A heaviness hung over the small room. Marcus thanked the men for their time and warning. "No matter the danger, I'm supposed to be here. I believe that. We already have local volunteers willing to staff the center around the clock. So that kids will always have a place to get away from the crime and gang activity."

"Yes." Officer Kent smiled, but it didn't reach his eyes. "I'd love to see a change." He looked at the other men. "We all would."

Marcus stood first. "My friends will be here soon." He shook each of their hands. "Will you stick around?"

"Absolutely." Officer Kent rose to his feet and the others joined him. "We plan to keep a few patrol cars circling the center. Gangs like to take over a place like this. If that happens, every bit of money and work has been wasted."

"That's why the patrol cars. So that won't happen this time, right?" Marcus waited. He wanted more than hope here. He wanted a promise.

"You have our word." The mayor nodded. "This center will be for kids looking for a way out."

"Great." Marcus led the way to the door. He couldn't get out of this meeting fast enough. Yes, of course, he knew the streets were tough. They were dangerous to anyone in this part of town. But if someone didn't offer these kids hope, then nothing would ever change.

So maybe that's what the whispered response meant while he was driving in. Maybe this was exactly what God had chosen him to do—to give kids hope where currently they had none. If things had never been worse, like the officers said, then the rest of the whisper made sense, too.

He had been chosen for such a time as this.

JAG AND ASPYN stood in the corner of the room, invisible to human eyes. The news was troubling but not surprising. They had been told from the beginning that this mission would be dangerous. And so it would be. The officers had no idea how serious the gang activity would be that night.

But Jag and Aspyn knew.

They knew about Dwayne Davis and his plan to kill Marcus Dillinger. They knew about the trap Lexy was in and the desperation that filled every home along the streets of this neighborhood. That's why they were here.

It was time to decide where they would take their stands.

"I'll be a police officer." Jag spoke first.

"Good." Aspyn looked serious, her mind working. "I'll be a volunteer. A local parent."

Jag liked the idea.

"We need to break up the gang activity tonight. EastTown plans to kill Dwayne. They know he's pushing to be the leader of the WestKnights."

"Such a waste." Aspyn stayed in place. "Why do they want to kill each other?"

"Sons and daughters of Adam have strange ways of finding identity and power." Jag watched the two police officers, the mayor, and Marcus Dillinger. "The offer of love and salvation is available for any of them." He felt the pain of earth. "But they choose this."

They needed a plan for tonight. Aspyn was small but capable. Jag believed in her. He steadied himself. "The biggest danger tonight is Dwayne Davis. One of us has to stay here at the center. Distract Marcus. Keep him from going out front. No way Dwayne's coming inside the center tonight. Not with the police here."

"I'll stay. I can distract him." Aspyn's confidence was unwavering. "All of heaven will be praying. Don't forget that."

"Exactly." Jag thought for a moment. "I'll deal with the EastTown gang . . . and keep watch over Dwayne."

Aspyn must've seen the look in his eyes. She put her hand on his shoulder. "You have nothing to avenge, Jag. Nothing to prove." Her smile was weighted with understanding. "This is a new mission."

"I know." New mission or not, Jag had a score to settle with the enemy. He needed to succeed at this Angels Walking mission. "I'll be fine."

"Okay." Aspyn knew Jag's past, the reasons he hadn't been on a mission in ten years. "Remember how this works. You can't have the assistance of heaven unless you follow the rules."

"Of course." He reached out to her. "Let's pray."

They held hands and asked God to guide them, to give them wisdom and vision, and to help them prevent any loss of life—one of the directives of those angels who walked among the sons of Adam.

Jag turned to Aspyn. "Godspeed."

"You, too."

And with that they were gone.

5

Jag HAD NO TROUBLE finding the alley where the EastTown Boyz hunkered down, waiting for nightfall. He could see the enemy gathered in the shadows up and down the passageway. He could feel the presence of darkness.

You're not winning this one, he thought to himself. "Jesus has already defeated you." He uttered the words out loud and smiled when the demons in the shadows cringed, when they shrank back in fear.

The name of Jesus. Scripture was clear about the power of that one name. At the mention of Jesus the demons had no choice but to obey. Every time.

But that didn't mean the enemy would run from a fight.

As soon as they gathered themselves, the dark beings lunged toward Jag, hissing at him, trying to scare him from their gathering. "This is our territory."

But Jag wasn't about to move. "I'm here in the name of Jesus."

Again they twisted, writhing in pain at the sound of the name of the Savior.

Jag felt a holy satisfaction. How dare the enemy send his evil army to destroy the sons and daughters of God, His chosen ones, His creation? Moments like this made Jag impatient for the time when all angels would be unleashed and the enemy would be overthrown once and for all. When time ended and eternity began.

Until then, Jag wasn't backing down. The scene about to play out tonight was all too familiar. He'd already failed on a day like this one.

While the demons hissed and spat at him, Jag remembered. The years faded and Jag was there again. That Angels Walking mission had also been in Los Angeles. Jag had been assigned to protect a man of great faith, a police officer. Terrance Williams was his name. He had been called to testify against one of the city's most notorious drug dealers.

There had been only two days left in the trial when Jag failed.

Up until that point Jag had kept Terrance Williams safe at every turn. Two hit men had been assigned the job of killing the officer. In the weeks that led up to that fateful day, Jag had found ways to distract Williams, ways that had saved his life. Jag had also created obstacles for the killers, delays that had kept the men from carrying out the murder.

The whole time Jag knew the situation. The murder was the bad guys' only hope to avoid a guilty verdict. If the trial reached a guilty verdict before the hired guns could kill Williams, then the deal was off. No hit, no payment. No point.

With only two days left in the trial, Jag was hovering behind Officer Williams's car when the man stopped at his son's school.

This was not part of the plan.

Jag hadn't known that on that day the man's son was in a class play, or that the boy had invited his father to watch. Jag had missed that. Even now, with a host of demons threatening him, Jag could see what had happened that day. Terrance Williams had parked his police car across the street from the school and gone inside. Jag had been nervous, his instincts on high alert. His Angels Walking partner had been across town, working behind the scenes at the courthouse.

So Jag was alone.

He stayed in the auditorium with Officer Williams for the entire hour-long school program. It was an hour Jag could still remember, every detail. The boy attended a Christian school and that day he sang a solo from the front of the stage. "How Great Thou Art." Halfway through the performance Jag saw Terrance Williams wipe tears from his eyes.

The boy was ten years old and everything to the man.

Which created a problem. What if Terrance decided to take the boy home with him early? For weeks, when Terrance picked his son up, Jag had his Angels Walking partner with him. Together they had been able to protect both father and son.

But that day Jag could feel the demons, same as he could feel them now. Without his partner he would be outnumbered if a battle ensued.

Long before the program was over, Jag knew the hit men would be waiting for Williams, their guns trained on him from the moment he left the school. They had followed him here. Jag knew he would have to appear like one of the parents picking up their child at school.

But he had wondered if his efforts would be enough.

As the program ended, Jag had materialized in a hallway outside the auditorium. He looked like any other parent as he walked into the crowded room. Quickly he found Terrance Williams and his son, Ryan. Jag had walked up and put his hand on Ryan's shoulder. "Hello. You're Ryan Williams, right?"

The child looked startled. Same with his father. Officer Williams stepped forward. "I don't believe we've met."

"I'm Jag. My nephew Billy Goodall is in Ryan's class." Jag smiled. But he could see the confusion on the officer's face.

"How do you know Ryan?" The man pulled his son close.

"Ryan's been a good friend to my nephew." It was true. Information Jag had picked up during the mission. "Billy gets picked on by the other kids, but Ryan . . . he stands up for Billy."

Ryan smiled and looked at his dad. "Billy's my friend."

Jag remembered feeling desperate. He was out of ideas. He needed time to figure out how to get between Terrance and the hit men. If Jag could delay the officer long enough, the hit men would leave. They needed the cover of a crowd to pull off their deed without getting caught.

"Okay, well . . . thank you for saying so." Terrance Williams took a step back. "We need to go."

Jag could still feel the way his heart had fallen. If only they could've stayed in that moment. He would've begged God to freeze time so that the father and son might've stayed there, safe in the auditorium.

But freezing time was not something angels could do.

"See you." Terrance Williams waved and then he smiled at his son. "Mom made lasagna!"

"Hold on!" Jag had followed him. For five minutes he tried stalling by asking the officer questions. But in the end, it wasn't enough. As they left the school, Jag stayed behind them. He saw the hit man across the street behind the wheel of his car, saw him lift his gun, aiming for Terrance Williams, and in that split second Jag tried to knock both of them to the ground. "Look out!" Jag had shouted.

But years of police training kept Terrance standing on his feet even as his son hit the grass face first. The bullet was through Terrance's chest before Jag could say another word.

"Daddy!" Ryan screamed, and ran to his father's side. "Daddy, no!"

Demons celebrated in the air above them as Jag rushed up to Terrance. A crowd gathered quickly, but Jag kept them at bay. "Give us room. I know CPR."

But even as Jag began administering chest compressions, he knew it was too late. The gunman had been too accurate. Ryan stayed near his father's head, patting his hair and crying. "Please, Daddy, wake up! Please, God!"

That afternoon Jag tried for twelve minutes until the paramedics arrived. Only then did he stand up and disappear into the crowd. He watched the rest of the scene from a few feet away, hovering over the fallen officer and his brokenhearted son.

Please, God, he had prayed. *Don't let him die.*

Paramedics finally helped Ryan away from his dying father. Even then the boy stood as close as he could, reaching out both hands and crying for his daddy. It was a scene etched forever in Jag's mind. They didn't officially declare Officer Williams dead until an hour later at the hospital. By then Ryan's mother was with him, along with half the officers from Terrance Williams's precinct.

But none of that changed the truth for Jag.

He had failed.

The loss of Terrance Williams made Jag doubt his very purpose. He had been given one task—protect the life of Terrance Williams. Yes, God knew the number of a man's days. But sometimes that number was small because the enemy had cut it short.

The demons in the alleyway hissed at him again, grabbing for him.

"Jesus will win this battle."

Screeches filled the air, the demons recoiling in painful fear.

Jag remembered what happened after his last failed Angels Walking mission. The other angels had tried to comfort him. Failure was always possible. The enemy would win some battles—but not the war. The other police officers would care for Ryan Williams now. He would never be without the love of a father figure.

Jag had appreciated their efforts. Their words were true.

But none of that would ever give Ryan Williams his daddy back. Jag had failed. He would always believe the failure was his fault. He should've found another way to protect Terrance.

It had taken every one of the past ten years to believe he could be used by God again. When he learned of this mission, of the danger it entailed, he knew it was time. His chance—

not only to find victory in this mission, but to make right the one he'd failed at a decade ago.

The sun was setting. Darkness gathered in the alleyway. The demons continued to hiss and scream. If they had it their way, someone was going to die tonight. Several people, maybe. And somewhere on the other side of the new Chairos Youth Center, Dwayne Davis was feeling the same way. Ready to kill Marcus Dillinger.

Jag wasn't afraid.

This time he had a plan that would work.

6

MARY CATHERINE AND SAMI walked into the new youth center just after three o'clock. She felt more like herself again. Now that she had told Sami the truth about her heart. At their apartment earlier Mary Catherine had made Sami promise she wouldn't treat her any differently.

"I'm not dying," Mary Catherine had said. "Not yet."

"But you will . . . too soon."

Mary Catherine had held up her finger and shook her head. "None of us knows how long we have."

Eventually Sami had agreed. "God wants us to live today, that's what you're saying? He'll handle the rest?"

"Yes. Exactly."

Since then they hadn't talked about it. Sami was a little quieter than usual, but nothing the guys would notice. Mary Catherine was only glad the discussion was behind them. As difficult as it was to share the news with Sami, Mary Catherine had wanted her best friend to know.

They headed through the triple gymnasium into the Virginia Hutcheson Hall, the place where tutoring would happen every school day afternoon and evening. Today, though, tables were set up around the perimeter for the grand opening. Marcus was carrying a box of plates to one of the tables.

Mary Catherine felt it again, the way her dying heart came fully alive in his presence. She chided herself to keep tight control over her emotions. Marcus wasn't interested, anyway.

"Sami!" Tyler was at the opposite side of the room setting out plastic cups. She hurried to meet him.

Mary Catherine made eye contact with Marcus. At the same time, the box he was carrying broke open and plates started to fall to the ground a few at a time.

She hurried over and began picking them up. "Perfect timing."

"So you were late on purpose?" Marcus set the box down and helped her gather the plates from the floor.

"Late?" Mary Catherine hoped he couldn't see the heat in her cheeks. "It's not fashionable to be exactly on time. You should know that."

Mary Catherine and Marcus always slipped into this teasing type of banter. Sarcastic and even a little flirty. Nothing too deep. The two of them held the box together long enough to get it to the table.

"Seriously. How can I help?" Mary Catherine kept her tone light. She probably should've gone to the other room and helped Sami and Tyler. It did her no good being around Marcus. Not when he had this magnetic pull on her. Like being in his presence caused the oxygen to leave the room.

"I still have to wash down half a dozen tables in the back." He winked at her. "You can help."

Mary Catherine looked over her shoulder. "I thought the Waynes were coming."

"They are." He grinned. "Even more fashionably late than you and Sami."

Before they could head to the back for the dirty tables, Coach Ollie Wayne, his wife, and his niece entered the room. "We're here!" Rhonda Wayne led the way. "Ready to help!"

Mary Catherine took a step back. As she did, Shelly set her eyes on Marcus and came to him. She looked like a hunter eyeing her prey. Mary Catherine felt her frustration rise. *Don't be catty*, she told herself. *You have no reason to be jealous. Just walk away.*

Shelly reached Marcus and gave him a long hug and a kiss on his lips. Marcus looked surprised, and maybe a little embarrassed. He chuckled. "Well, hey there."

"Help can mean a lot of things, right?" Shelly spoke loud enough for everyone to hear.

Mary Catherine was ready for a new location.

She crossed the room to where Rhonda Wayne was helping Sami with the cups. Rhonda was explaining that they'd brought six flats of water bottles. "I'd like to get them in the fridge."

"That's another project." Tyler was bringing in empty jugs. "Someone donated three additional refrigerators a few hours ago." He made a face. "They work, but they're filthy."

"Perfect." Rhonda clapped her hands and looked at Mary Catherine. "You up for some refrigerator cleaning?"

"Definitely."

On the way back to the kitchen, Rhonda introduced herself. "I've heard of you. Sami can't stop talking about how you taught her how to live." Rhonda smiled. "You're her hero."

"That's sweet." Mary Catherine felt the compliment to the center of her soul. She had no idea Sami talked about her to other people. God was letting her help other people learn how to live—even while she was dying. "I hear a lot about your family, too. I guess yours is the hangout house."

"Marcus lives in the neighborhood, and you probably know Tyler's staying with him for now. They come over for dinner, and then a game of pool breaks out and the two of them stay till midnight. Happens all the time."

Mary Catherine could picture that. Sami had been there many times with Tyler. Apparently, Shelly was usually there, too. "You host a house church, right? That's what Sami told me."

"Yes." They reached the refrigerators and found a few empty buckets. "Our pastor stepped down so our main church is in transition. For the next few months the staff encouraged us to meet in our homes. Invite neighbors, that sort of thing. Tyler and Sami have been joining us for a while now." Rhonda found a few rags and she and Mary Catherine filled the buckets with hot soapy water. "Do you have a church?"

"I do. It's an hour away."

"Well, then join us tomorrow. We'd love to have you!"

The invitation was tempting. "Thank you. Maybe some other time." Mary Catherine couldn't attend. Not when Shelly would be there fawning over Marcus. In that setting it would be almost impossible to focus on God. Besides, the hour drive each way was good for her. Time to pray and sing and remind herself that true happiness could only come if she busied herself with things that mattered.

Things like this.

She and Rhonda worked for an hour cleaning the refrigerators, until the mold and the mildew were gone. They even found a box of baking soda in the pantry and after a few rinses the shelves actually smelled clean.

The whole time they talked about family and faith, how Rhonda and Ollie liked to think of their home as a church in more ways than one. "We ask God to fill our home, and then He does. Every time." Rhonda's laugh came easily. "Not saying it isn't crazy around the dinner table sometimes, but it's worth it."

Mary Catherine tried not to feel jealous. That was the type of home she had always wanted. Instead she'd been an only child raised by wealthy parents. Parents too busy with their social clubs and charities to notice their daughter's loneliness.

Maybe someday she would take Rhonda up on her offer and attend home church at their house. Whenever Mary Catherine stopped reacting every time she saw Marcus Dillinger. However long that might take.

When they finished, Mary Catherine and Rhonda joined the others in the hall. The place had filled up. Volunteers from the neighborhood had flooded the place and half the tables were full of cookies and cupcakes. In another room, neighbors were helping set up games and filling bowls with candy.

Marcus and Tyler hadn't missed a detail.

Mary Catherine found Sami working on one of the dessert tables. Shelly was helping Coach Wayne at the other end of the room. "Where's Marcus?"

"The police wanted to talk to him and Tyler." Sami didn't sound worried. "Probably just figuring out logistics for tonight. They're expecting a ton of people."

A few minutes later Marcus and Tyler returned, their expressions concerned. Tyler motioned to Sami and Mary Catherine. "We need to talk to you." He pointed across the room. "Mary Catherine, could you get Rhonda and Ollie Wayne? They need to be there, too."

Something was wrong. Mary Catherine could feel it. In this part of town, there was no telling what had happened, but whatever it was the guys were deeply concerned. She found the coach and his wife and they headed to the small room with the others.

Once they were in the small room, Marcus took over. "The police have warned us." He looked alarmed and more than a little frustrated. "The two largest gangs in the area, the WestKnights and EastTown Boyz, are planning a confrontation tonight. Here. In front of the youth center."

For several seconds, no one said anything. Coach Wayne was the first to talk. "They should call in backup. You can't let a bunch of thugs ruin this for everyone else."

"It's their way of resisting change." Marcus pinched his lips together. "That's what the officers said."

"Well, that's not right." Rhonda stood at her husband's side. "I agree with Ollie. Let's get more police out here. Until they figure out that this isn't a place for gangs."

Sami stood next to Tyler. She looked terrified. "Maybe we should call it off. We can do this next week, right? Let the police figure it out and try again when the gangs aren't threatening."

"We can't do that." Mary Catherine's words came before she could stop them. "We need to pray. God will keep us safe. We just have to ask Him."

Marcus looked at her and his eyes softened. "I like it." He held his hands out to the others in the room. "Let's pray. The police will keep a watch out front, and here on the inside we'll just love on whatever kids come through the door."

A quick discussion broke out about whether they should cancel, but in the end everyone agreed on moving forward and praying for protection. God was with them. Who could come against them? As they formed a circle, Mary Catherine realized too late that she was standing closest to Marcus. He reached for her hand. As he did, he whispered, "Thank you."

She smiled and gave him the slightest nod.

Then it happened. His hand was around hers, his fingers warm and strong. Something about the feeling felt familiar and breathtaking all at once. *Dear God, help me think. Help my heart get back in line. Please.*

Coach Ollie was praying, asking God for protection, asking that He place His angels around the building to keep them safe at tonight's open house.

Mary Catherine could barely concentrate. When the prayer ended, Marcus gave her hand a slight squeeze. He smiled at her. "Seriously. Thank you." He allowed a brief laugh. "I can't believe no one else thought to pray."

"No big deal." She needed to get away from him. Falling into his gravity wasn't going to do her any good. "I'm going to check on the game room."

"Okay." He looked like he might ask her to stay. But instead he hesitated and then he turned to Coach Wayne and his wife.

Moving as quickly as she could, Mary Catherine returned to the game room. A new volunteer had arrived, a willowy young black woman who didn't seem to have come with anyone. Mary Catherine came up to her. "Hi. I'm Mary Catherine."

"Hi." The new woman held out her hand. "I'm a parent in the neighborhood. Aspyn. Thought you could use the help."

"Aspyn. That's pretty." Mary Catherine checked the time. It was close to five o'clock. The pizza would be there in an hour. "Let's work on the corn hole boards."

They walked over to a part of the room where six corn hole games needed to be set up. Someone had left a set of directions, so together she and Aspyn got to work. "How long have you lived in the neighborhood?"

"Not long, actually." Aspyn smiled. She had the greenest eyes. Something about them looked almost otherworldly. "I figured no time like the present to jump in and help."

"Do you know Marcus?"

"Not well." Aspyn smiled. "I know he plays ball."

"Yes. That he does." They both laughed and Mary Catherine was grateful to talk with someone new.

Across the room, Marcus and Shelly set up a small plastic basketball hoop. Mary Catherine tried not to watch, but it was impossible. The girl was hanging all over Marcus.

Aspyn seemed to notice. She looked that way and then turned her eyes back to Mary Catherine. "She's not his type."

"Who?" Mary Catherine wasn't sure what her new friend meant.

"Shelly Wayne. She's too young. Too much growing up to do." Aspyn smiled. "If you ask me, Marcus Dillinger needs a girl like you."

The heat was back in Mary Catherine's cheeks. "How do you know what he—"

"Be right back." Aspyn dusted her hands off on her jeans. "I'll get us some water."

Mary Catherine watched her go, confused. Aspyn said she didn't really know Marcus, but then . . . how could she have known whether Shelly was right for him? And what would've made her say that last part about Marcus's needing a girl like her? Mary Catherine could've been married for all Aspyn knew.

For a moment she watched Marcus and Shelly across the room. Marcus worked on the hoop and Shelly mostly flirted with him. Truthfully, Marcus didn't really look interested.

After a few seconds, Marcus turned her way and their eyes met. Mary Catherine looked away, embarrassed at having been caught. What was she doing? Even if Marcus had been single, she wasn't interested. He wasn't her type. Besides, she had no time for love. Just as well that God didn't bring along the sort of guy who could really turn her head.

Still, as Aspyn returned with their water, and as they worked on the boards, Mary Catherine couldn't quite shake her new friend's words. The idea that Marcus might actually need a girl like her. Or vice versa. The possibility defied her mind and filled her heart.

More than a couple of times she caught herself looking

for him, watching the kind way he had with the volunteers, the humility in his eyes. Finally, she stopped herself and focused on the task at hand. She wasn't going to waste the hours dreaming about a guy she could never have. Life was too short.

Especially hers.

7

Lexy sat in Dwayne's passenger seat, once more slumped down in the shadows. They were parked half a block down from the new youth center.

Any minute Marcus Dillinger was going to walk outside and get the pizza. That was the big draw tonight. Free pizza. Lexy felt sick to her stomach. She wanted to be Dwayne's girl. Wanted her spot beside him. But she didn't want Dwayne to shoot the Dodgers' pitcher. *Don't come outside, Marcus.* Lexy silently begged the baseball star. *Stay inside.*

Beside her Dwayne tugged at his baseball cap. He had one hand on the wheel, the other on his loaded revolver.

Lexy didn't dare say a thing. She looked at her shaking fingers. She looked toward the youth center. If only she could defy Dwayne, take a stand for herself. Find her own way. But she couldn't. Being Dwayne's girl was the biggest thing that had ever happened to her.

Lexy thought about the rest of the guys in the gang. The WestKnights were on a drug run tonight. At least they were supposed to be. Dwayne made a call. His words were short, but Lexy got the idea. The gangs were going to fight in the alley across from the center. Dwayne needed to kill one of them before he could take a shot at Marcus.

Her teeth began to chatter. So many rules. She wanted to open the door and throw up. What if they got caught? And why did Marcus Dillinger have to die? He was only here because he wanted to be nice. She kept her mouth shut and waited.

Dwayne had shaved his head. He didn't look as hot now. His face was meaner. Scarier. Beneath his baseball cap he had a blue bandana around his forehead. He told her he had to look the part. More gang leader than gang boy.

Five minutes passed, then ten. Dwayne made another call. If the EastTown Boyz didn't show, the killing was off. When the call ended, a pizza delivery car pulled up in front of the youth center. Dwayne started the car and pulled out onto the street.

No! Not Marcus. Lexy put her hand over her eyes. This was terrible. She couldn't watch. Through the cracks in her fingers she saw Dwayne drive slowly up to the youth center. So far no one was coming out for the pizza.

Through the windows they could see kids playing basketball and what looked like maybe carnival games. For a moment Lexy wondered what it would be like to be inside. Playing games. Being a kid.

Dwayne laughed, and the sound rumbled deep in his throat.

Lexy stared at him and then looked down at her lap. What was so funny? Had he seen Marcus? Was the baseball player about to come outside? How could he laugh at killing Marcus Dillinger?

Dwayne hit the steering wheel. He looked down the alley, down the street. Suddenly Lexy realized something. The East-Town Boyz were nowhere to be seen. At the last second Dwayne sped up and squealed down the street. If the East-Town Boyz weren't going to show up, the fight would happen another night. She had never been so scared in all her life but now Lexy felt like she could breathe again.

Later, back at her grandmother's house, Lexy sat alone in the dark. Just sat there staring at the picture of Jesus on the wall. She sort of wanted to wake her grandma up and tell her what had almost happened. What was about to happen. Maybe her grandma would have some advice. Some way she could get out of this crazy life.

Last thing Dwayne had told her before she got out still made her feel sick. He told her he was still going to kill Marcus. But more than that, he would kill her if she said anything. If she told anyone what he was about to do.

Lexy clenched her teeth.

For a year all she had wanted was to be Dwayne's girl. But now she was afraid of him. Like for real. She couldn't tell her grandma. The woman was old. She still missed Lexy's mom every day. Her grandma would be so disappointed if she knew Lexy had joined the gang.

No, there was no one to talk to. Nowhere to turn. She needed to go to bed. There was only one reason she could bring herself to walk to her bedroom and fall into her bed.

Marcus Dillinger had not been killed.

Not tonight, anyway.

JAG WAS A police officer again, all six feet five inches of him. His blond hair framed his face, but it did nothing to lessen the fierce look in his eyes. He had distracted the EastTown Boyz, kept them away from the youth center. Now he shouted just once at them. "Leave!"

The EastTown Boyz—twenty or so of them—sauntered into a cluster. One of them pointed a gun at Jag and laughed. "You talking to us, pig?"

Jag knew how to respond in a situation like this. The kids were just that—kids. They weren't the ones at fault. This was all they knew. It was all their parents knew, and their parents before them. The kids gathered before him were not the enemy.

But all Jag could see was the gun. The same type of gun the hit men had used against Officer Terrance Williams. He felt fire in his veins. Without a single hesitation he walked toward the gang members. "I said leave!" He boomed the words like so many gunshots.

"We ain't 'fraida you, man!" One of the guys flashed a gang sign at Jag, taunting him. Another fired his gun toward the sky.

"Hear that, big guy? That's you if you come another step closer."

Jag kept walking. "You will leave this place in the name of Jesus."

The guy with the gun aimed it at Jag.

"I said leave! In the name of Jesus!"

The one with the gun waved it in the air. "We don't care about your Jesus." He aimed the gun again. "You're dead, pig. Don't come any closer."

Jag had taken enough.

In a fraction of a second he disappeared and reappeared at the opposite side of the alley.

The EastTown Boyz shouted expletives, turning this way and that looking for him. "How'd he do that?"

"You see that, man? He disappeared!"

"Yeah . . . like a ghost."

Jag appeared again, this time a few feet from the guys. With a voice that echoed through the alleyway, Jag shouted, "I . . . said . . . leave!"

The guy with the gun aimed again. "That's messed up, man." His hand was shaking. "No one plays with the East-Town Boyz."

Jag simply put his hands on his hips and stood there, legs a few feet apart. "Go home."

This time his booming voice made the boys back up, slowly at first and then faster until finally they took off running.

Jag felt the deepest sense of satisfaction. He hated violence, hated the way the sons of Adam loved to hurt each other.

They aren't the problem, he told himself. But they felt like the problem. They felt like the enemy, if Jag were honest with himself. He searched the alleyway. The demons were gone. They had scattered with the gang. Now that he was alone, Jag exhaled. For today, he was successful. He felt the unfamiliar adrenaline rush, the feeling that only came when angels were in human form. And something else, something angels weren't supposed to feel. Something he would have to pray about if he were to be successful in this mission.

The feeling was rage.

8

MARCUS LOOKED AROUND THE packed youth center and silently thanked God for the success and safety of the night. Everything had gone perfectly. Whatever gang violence was supposed to materialize, it hadn't happened yet. In fact, the whole night had been one unforgettable series of amazing moments.

And it had all started with Mary Catherine's suggestion that they pray.

He hadn't talked to her since then. Of course, Shelly hadn't left his side once, so he didn't blame Mary Catherine for keeping her distance. Still, he had seen her look his way a couple of times throughout the night.

The girl intrigued him.

She didn't care what anyone thought. Her allegiance was to God and her friends and helping others. There wasn't an ounce of pretense or showiness—qualities that practically defined Shelly.

The night was winding down, and he stood in a corner of one of the basketball courts signing autographs for the kids. Across the room, Mary Catherine read to the littler kids. Everything about her was real and genuine. The way she laughed and held the hands of the toddlers.

A woman came up next in line. She had a small boy with her. "Hi." She seemed shy. "My name's Shamika."

"Hi, Shamika." Marcus smiled at her. He was signing press photos of himself pitching. He picked one up and stooped down eye level with the boy. "What's your name?"

"Jalen." The boy grinned. "My mom says you're a hero."

Marcus gave the boy's mother a quick smile. "Well, I think the real hero is your mama. She takes care of you, right?"

"Yeah." The boy giggled. "Seems funny having a mama for a hero."

"Not at all. My mom and dad are my heroes." Marcus held the photo up. "Want me to sign it to you?"

"Yeah." Jalen grinned.

"'Yes, please.'" His mother put her hand on the boy's shoulder. "Use your manners, Jalen."

"Sorry." He looked down for a beat and then back at Marcus. "Yes, please."

Before they left, Shamika looked deep into Marcus's eyes. "We're about to be kicked out of our apartment." She kept her voice low. "I need another job and no one's hiring." She looked down at Jalen. "I'm all he has. So maybe . . . would you pray for us?"

"Of course." Marcus had never been asked to pray out loud before. He wasn't even sure he could manage it. But he had to try. Coach Wayne prayed out loud all the time. Just talking to Jesus, that's what Coach said. Marcus put one hand on Shamika's shoulder and the other on Jalen's. "Dear God, I know You're here and I know You're listening. Could You please help my friend Shamika? She's up against it pretty bad, and she loves her boy so much. If You could just give them a reason to believe again. The way You did for me. Thanks, God. Amen."

Shamika had tears in her eyes. "That's why I came here tonight. So I could see for myself that someone like you really exists." She looked around. "Thank you. For doing this for all of us. And thanks for praying."

She leaned in and gave Marcus a quick hug. "At least now I know you're real and not some imaginary angel."

Marcus watched Shamika and Jalen head toward the junior basketball hoop. The image of the two stayed with him as he finished signing autographs and as he took the microphone and thanked everyone for coming. More than two hundred people had stayed for this moment. They gathered around, their attention on him. Most of the adults looked despondent. Defiance flashed in the eyes of half the teens.

Marcus understood. They had come out of curiosity, hopeful for free pizza and candy and wondering what sort of difference a pro ballplayer could ever make on streets this rough.

He held up the mic and took a slow breath. "Good evening. Thanks for being here. For sharing in our grand opening." He looked at the back of the room to Tyler and Sami, the Waynes and Mary Catherine. "A special thanks to my friends, who have been here most of the day."

The crowd was quiet, shifty. "You gonna have free pizza next week?" one of the teens yelled out.

"Maybe." Marcus felt himself relax. "In life, you gotta have vision, man. If your vision is free pizza every week, then talk to me after. Maybe we can figure out a way to make it happen. Do a little fundraising."

A nod came from the teen and his eyes showed something he didn't have when he blurted out his question.

Respect.

Marcus looked around the room. "That goes for all of you. We all have to want something better for ourselves. Better than kids joining gangs and dropping out of school. Police tell me half the kids on these streets don't live to be twenty-one. That's insane." He felt the passion in his voice. "You gotta have a bigger vision if you're going to have a different life."

He talked a little about his own vision, how he pictured kids coming to the youth center after school and getting help with their studies. "I'd like to have counselors here, too. You got problems, you should have someone to talk to."

His speech was winding down, and really he had just one thing left. "Six months ago my life didn't have meaning. Sure, I play for the Dodgers. Pro ballplayer with the big contract. But that doesn't give a man meaning."

The kids were listening.

"I gave God a challenge. Told Him I'd believe if He would give my life meaning. Something that lasted. And guess what? God did exactly that. So now I give that challenge to you." Again his tone picked up intensity. "Every one of you. A youth center isn't a reason to live. God's the only one who can give us that. So tonight before you hit your pillow, talk to Him. Ask Him to give your life meaning." Marcus took off his baseball cap. "Pray with me."

Then, for the second time in his life, Marcus Dillinger prayed out loud. He could hardly believe it, but he was getting the hang of this. He asked God to bless the people there that night and to bless the efforts of the youth center. "We need a purpose, God. So give it to us. Make us a community. Thanks for tonight, God. Amen."

When he was finished, the crowd gradually dispersed. Several parents came up and thanked him for his commitment to the center and the community. The teens mostly kept to themselves. Marcus wondered how many of them were already in one of the local gangs.

The volunteers stayed to clean up. Most of the games had been borrowed from a local church, and plates of the leftover food had to be wrapped up and saved for whatever kids would come by the center in the coming week.

Marcus and Tyler were washing down tables when Sami and Mary Catherine found them. "We wiped down the water coolers." Sami brushed her hands together. "You guys must be exhausted."

"Exhausted, but happy." Marcus shot a smile at Mary Catherine. "That idea of yours . . . that we all pray before everyone got here? It was the perfect choice." He looked at Tyler. "Ty was saying he could almost feel the hand of God over this place. Like we had divine protection."

Mary Catherine smiled, but she looked more at Tyler and Sami than at Marcus. "Prayer makes a difference."

Marcus thought about Shamika and little Jalen, and then

the talk with the people at the end. He aimed his next words at Mary Catherine again. "You've made me a believer."

She didn't seem to know what to say. Instead of responding to Marcus she turned to Tyler. "Where's the Wayne family? I didn't see them leave."

"They needed to get back to their kids." Marcus looked at Mary Catherine, but she wouldn't make eye contact with him. "They invited us back to the house for coffee whenever we're finished."

"What about Shelly?" Sami looked at Marcus. "She didn't say goodbye."

"She had plans with her friends." Marcus wanted a moment alone with Mary Catherine. Why was she acting like this? Like she didn't want to talk to him? "Anyway, we're almost done here."

He was about to ask her to join them for coffee back at the Waynes' house when Officer Kent walked through the door. He stopped when he saw the group. "Marcus, you got a minute?"

"We can talk here. My friends know about the gang stuff."

"Okay." He came closer. "Something happened tonight I can't really explain. We learned the fight here was supposed to be a big one. We had a few leads that everyone was talking about it. Supposed to have been a few killings, as well."

"That's what I told them." Marcus turned his eyes to Mary Catherine again. "But then my friend MC here, she suggested we pray." He looked back at the officer. "I'd say God answered our prayers."

Officer Kent ran his hand over his dark hair. "Definitely." He paused. "Apparently some officer from another precinct showed up in the alley where the EastTown Boyz were gathered. Just one guy. By himself. No backup. No one knows who he was." He hesitated again. "Anyway, whatever went on between the officer and the gang, the boys came running out of the alley like they were being chased by a pack of Dobermans."

Marcus chuckled. "I like that picture."

"He was probably an angel." Mary Catherine looked serious, the light in her eyes brighter than before. "They're real, you know."

Officer Kent shrugged. "After tonight I'd believe anything." He nodded to the group. "Be careful leaving. We'll be outside until you go." He looked around. "I'd say tonight was a huge success. Keep up the good work."

When they finished cleaning, Marcus asked the others back to the Waynes' house for coffee. It was after ten o'clock, but he still wanted to be with them, maybe share stories from the night.

"You coming, too?" Marcus walked next to Mary Catherine as they headed out to their cars.

"I think so. I really liked Rhonda Wayne."

"She's everybody's mama." Marcus grinned and as they reached their cars, he waved once. "See you there."

Tyler drove with Marcus. When they were on the freeway headed to Silver Lake, Marcus looked at his friend. "What do you think of Mary Catherine?"

"Sami's friend?" Tyler turned so he could see Marcus better. "I thought you were into Shelly."

"I was. I mean, I am . . . sort of." He narrowed his eyes, his attention on the freeway ahead of them. "Mary Catherine . . . she's different. You know what I'm saying."

"She's one of a kind. That's for sure."

"Exactly. I got that tonight." He glanced at Tyler. "What do you think of her?"

"Mary Catherine?" Tyler smiled. "She's crazy and fun and full of life."

"She has beautiful hair." Marcus heard the distraction in his voice.

Tyler raised his brow. "Not that you're interested."

"I like her spirit." Marcus could still see her, the way she looked tonight surrounded by the younger children. "The girl loves God more than anything or anyone."

"That she does." Tyler smiled. "Sami says Mary Catherine's the real deal."

"Yeah." Marcus felt his laughter die off. "Maybe that's it."

The conversation switched to spring training and the fact that pitchers, catchers, and pitching coaches had to report earlier than everyone else. Marcus didn't bring up Mary Catherine again the rest of the ride, but he was glad Tyler did most of the talking. It was all Marcus could do to stay partly interested. His mind was too preoccupied with the one thing he couldn't stop thinking about.

The light in Mary Catherine's eyes.

And the fact that in a few minutes he would see her again.

JAG AND ASPYN watched from the back of Marcus's Hummer as he headed back to Silver Lake. They were exhausted, but they weren't about to leave Marcus. Not with so much at stake.

Jag felt the strength of God fill him, renew him. "We succeeded tonight."

"Yes." She gave him a concerned look. "You were angry, Jag. I could feel it when we met up at the youth center."

"Of course I was angry." He was calmer now. "Those kids wanted to kill someone. There's enough killing on earth without kids killing each other."

"It was more than that." Aspyn had an uncanny way of reading other angels. Him in particular. The skill made her a great partner, but a meddlesome one at the same time.

There was no getting around the truth. Angels were honest. Period. "One of them pulled a gun on me. Same kind of gun the hit men used when . . ."

"Terrance Williams died." Aspyn's tone was rich with sympathy. "I'm sorry."

"This . . . rage. It came over me." Jag was completely himself again, full of peace and purpose. "I've only felt that one other time. In the minutes after Officer Williams was shot." He could barely describe it.

"I understand." She touched his shoulder. "Just be careful, Jag. Anger does not bring about the righteousness God desires. You know that."

"Yes."

"This is only the beginning. Things will get rough again on Tuesday night."

"I know. I need to be in control." Jag nodded. He appreciated Aspyn's wisdom.

"Exactly."

Jag pictured the gang gathered in the alley, the way they taunted him and flashed the gun at him. He let the images disappear from his mind. "Thank you, Aspyn. I'll be ready."

He had a feeling Aspyn was right. The worst of the violence was days away.

9

From the moment she walked inside, Mary Catherine loved everything about the Waynes' house. The smell of fresh coffee came from the kitchen, and something else, something warm and rich with cinnamon.

"Come in!" Rhonda welcomed them inside. "I roasted a batch of organic almonds. A little coconut oil and cinnamon and they're delicious."

"Mmmm." Mary Catherine flashed a grin at Sami and then back to Rhonda Wayne. "I knew I liked you."

"We don't do sugar. At least most days." She grabbed a potholder and pulled the pan of fresh roasted almonds from the oven. They smelled delicious. "I whipped up a pint of organic cream."

Rhonda went on about how organic cream from grass-fed cows was actually healthy. "Full of omega-three acids. The good ones."

Mary Catherine knew all about that. She could've written

a book on the foods that healed as opposed to those that caused inflammation. Low carb, high fat. Moderate protein. "I love that kind of cream."

Sami looked lost. "You two are speaking a different language."

"Here." Rhonda put a spoonful of the almonds in a bowl and topped it off with a dollop of whipped cream. She handed it to Sami. "Try this."

From the first bite it was clear Sami loved the dish. "This is amazing. What's in it?"

Rhonda laughed. "Nothing. Pure cream and organic vanilla. I whip it myself so it's just the right kind of creamy."

"I don't think I could ever go back after this. I don't miss the sweet taste at all."

"Sugar fuels illness."

"Exactly." Mary Catherine pulled up a chair and grinned at Rhonda. "I've been telling Sami that. She eats way too much chocolate."

"I'm an addict. What can I say?"

Mary Catherine took a bowl of the almonds and cream as the guys walked in. Tyler led the way. "How'd you beat us?"

"Better driver." Mary Catherine looked over her shoulder, teasing him. "Nah, you got stuck at the light before the freeway."

"I was gonna say . . ." He laughed and looked back at Marcus. "Also, we took it slow on purpose. Us guys need our bonding time."

"Oh, I'm sure." Sami went to Tyler and the two of them shared a quick kiss. "You have to try Rhonda's almonds and cream."

Ollie had been checking on the kids. He joined them now and smiled at Mary Catherine. "So you're a health nut like my wife?"

"You could say that." She shared a look with her new friend. "We're trying to convert Sami."

The conversation continued, and Mary Catherine held onto every moment. This was what family love should feel like. Fifteen minutes later, Sam came down for water. Rhonda was kind and tender with him, kissing him on the cheek before he returned to bed.

And when Shane came home from a movie with friends, Rhonda and Ollie took time talking to him, hearing details about his night. Only their daughter, Sierra, wasn't home. She had spent the night with a friend. But Mary Catherine had seen enough to know that if God by some miracle blessed her with more time, with a man like the one she used to talk about finding, then this was the sort of family she wanted to have.

A family who lived out their faith as easily as they breathed.

They talked for a good hour before Sami and Tyler decided to head out. "We'll be here tomorrow for church!"

Mary Catherine had planned on leaving now, too, but as she found her purse Marcus approached her. "Hey . . . why don't you stay? I can take you home in a bit." He grinned at Sami and Tyler. "You know, give them their space."

"Marcus!" Sami sounded disappointed, but she was teasing him. "We don't need our space." She motioned to Mary Catherine. "Come on, MC. We want you to come with us."

"No, really." Marcus seemed like he was trying to keep

things casual. "Stay and walk around the block with me. I want to hear your story." He patted his stomach. "Plus I have to walk off these almonds."

Mary Catherine could feel it again, the heat in her cheeks, the way her heart beat faster around him. Was he serious? Did he really want to take a walk with her? In her peripheral vision she thought she saw Tyler give Sami a light elbow. Whatever the signal meant, Sami was suddenly quick to change her mind.

"Actually, it might be nice to have a little time with Tyler." She leaned up and kissed him again. "We have a lot to talk about."

Like that they were gone, and before Mary Catherine could argue, Marcus was ushering her outside for the walk. Never mind that it was nearly midnight or that Mary Catherine had intended to avoid anything even remotely like this. Marcus couldn't help himself. Every time they shared a moment together, the world around him turned to summer. The hillsides and skies of his heart came alive with new life.

They were still in sight of the Waynes' house when Marcus laughed. "Sorry if that felt a little forced."

"Just a little." Mary Catherine had no idea why he wanted this time with her. Whatever his reason, she had to be careful. She couldn't stop herself from feeling attracted to him. But she could at least keep her distance emotionally.

"I don't know . . . it's like I sensed something earlier, when we were cleaning up. Like you didn't want to look at me." Marcus slowed his pace so he could see her. "Or was that just my imagination?"

Mary Catherine was glad for the cover of night. She uttered a single laugh. "Well, Marcus. I mean, you have Shelly. I wouldn't want to be too friendly."

He nodded slowly. "Okay. If that's all it was."

"Tell me about her. You and Shelly." Mary Catherine was proud of herself. This was a good way to turn the conversation.

"There's not much to say." He stayed quiet for a few minutes while they walked. Then he turned to her. "So what's your story, Mary Catherine? Tyler tells me you grew up in Nashville. Why'd you leave?"

"Good question." There had been times when she tried to tell herself Marcus was shallow. He was a pro ballplayer, after all. But that simply wasn't the case. His tone was kind and tender, and she sensed a depth in him that surprised her.

"Didn't you like the South?" Their pace was easy, relaxing.

"Actually, I loved it." She laughed lightly and looked up at the stars. "I guess I was too comfortable. Everything felt predictable and safe."

"Hmm." Marcus laughed, but barely hard enough to be heard. "Sounds like you. Sami says you like jumping out of planes and riding your bike down Santa Monica Boulevard."

"And swim with dolphins." She laughed. "That actually happened right here."

"Really?"

"Yes. It was amazing." She cast him a look. "I like feeling alive." She walked a few more steps and shrugged. "That's just me."

"Now we're getting somewhere." They turned a corner

and kept walking. "Were you like the oldest of six kids or what? Locked in the house till you were eighteen?" He chuckled. "Why live life on the edge?"

"Actually, I was an only child. My parents did well for themselves. The right house in the right neighborhood, the best social clubs and affiliations." She smiled. "They loved me, but . . . they didn't stay together." This was the part of her story where her health came into play. Both of her parents worried about her, wanted her close to them, where she could be safe.

Mary Catherine wanted adventure.

She skipped that part. Marcus didn't need to know. There would be no reason.

"Okay. Why Los Angeles?" He seemed genuinely interested.

She grinned. "It was everything Nashville was not. Wild and loud and crowded and godless." She nodded once. "In LA, I don't go an hour without knowing how desperately I need the Lord. I like it that way."

"So did you break some poor guy's heart back in Nashville?"

"Hardly." She laughed out loud. "I dated a few guys, but I never found *that* guy. You know . . . the one I could be real with." She thought for a moment. The last guy she dated was a good one. They loved to laugh together. But in the end, he wasn't the right one. Just as well, given the news about her heart. "I guess I'm picky."

"I could use a little more of that." He grinned at her.

He had to be talking about Shelly, but Mary Catherine didn't want to push the issue. She slowed her steps. "Another thing . . . have you noticed how selfish everyone is? We're all about our own social media, our own platform, our own interests. I still haven't found a guy who can be in the moment. You know, carry on a conversation without checking his phone halfway through."

Marcus stopped walking and looked down. He checked the ground in front of him and behind him, and then reached into the pockets of his jeans. When he found them empty, he patted his other pockets. Then he shrugged.

"You lost your phone?" Mary Catherine glanced at the sidewalk behind them.

"No." He slipped his hands in his pockets and looked straight into her eyes. "I didn't bring it. Figured I'd rather be in the moment."

Touché. Mary Catherine felt something strange and unfamiliar in her heart. He was right. Where so many guys were too distracted to pay attention, Marcus had asked for this time with her and he'd remained truly present. "Thank you." She felt her smile soften.

They started walking again. "For what?"

"For being in the moment. That's one of the greatest gifts people can give each other. It's like a lost art. Listening. Caring enough to look into someone's eyes." She couldn't fall for him. Absolutely not. But she would be wrong not to express her gratitude. "Just . . . thanks."

"You're welcome." He looked happy with himself. "Maybe next time we have a conversation among friends you'll look *me* in the eyes. The way you didn't do today."

"I told you . . ." She giggled, not really frustrated.

"I know . . . you didn't want to seem too friendly. I'm dating Shelly. I get it." He gave her a knowing look. "Let's just say today at the center no one would've thought you even knew me."

"Good." She kept a straight face. Much as she wanted to laugh, she needed him to know how serious she was. "I didn't want to overstep my bounds."

"Obviously." The quiet between them for the next few steps felt comfortable. Marcus looked at her a long time before his next question. "So is it a faith thing, your living dangerously? Jumping out of planes and swimming with sharks?"

Her laughter felt wonderful. "Not sharks. Dolphins."

"Whatever." He chuckled. "Really, Mary Catherine. Why?"

The truth wasn't something she was willing to talk about. Her doctor had told her anything that released too much adrenaline was bound to be hard on her heart. A quiet life, they told her. Keep to the house, the daily tasks and chores. Learning and reading were fine. A desk job, maybe. Anything out of the box would knock days off the life of her heart.

Her mother had begged her to follow her doctor's orders.

Mary Catherine would rather have died young. She took a deep breath and imagined a way to explain all that without talking about her health. "There's a Bible verse in John, chapter ten, verse ten."

He shook his head. "Don't know it."

"Jesus is talking. He says, 'I came that they may have life and have it abundantly.'" Her tone held a passion never far from the surface. "I figure if Jesus came to give me that sort of life, well, then . . . I might as well live it."

"Hmmm." Marcus nodded. "Fair enough."

"How about you, Marcus Dillinger? You ever jump out of a plane or swim with dolphins?" She loved this, walking with him at midnight. This far up in the hills, the stars shone bright overhead, the moon a sliver in the sky.

His laugh was quiet again. "Hardly." He sighed. "For me it was baseball, baseball, baseball. My dad was a blond, blue-eyed ballplayer for the Giants back in the day. Played a few years and then got cut. He moved to the Bahamas to try to figure out his life and met the most beautiful woman he'd ever seen." He smiled. "That's how he tells the story. My mom was just eighteen, six years younger than my dad. Born and raised in the Bahamas. They fell in love and got married six months later at a little white church in downtown Nassau. Right in the heart of the city."

Mary Catherine had figured one of Marcus's parents must've been white. His light skin and eyes told her that much. But she had never heard his parents' love story. "That's beautiful."

"It was. My dad got a job in San Diego in computer engineering. He and my mom had me and two girls. Dad and I played ball all the time. He was one of my coaches. Believe it or not, I had a choice about playing baseball. He wasn't one of those fathers." Marcus grinned. "I just loved the game."

"So no time for planes and dolphins?" She could feel her eyes sparkling as she looked at him.

"Exactly."

Their teasing made her feel like she'd known him all her life. *He has a girlfriend*, she told herself. *Don't let yourself fall.* "Hey, wait!"

"What?" He looked intently at her. He had definitely perfected the art of being present.

"I know that little white church. The one in Nassau. Is it on the main street, right past the pink government buildings?"

He looked surprised. "Yes. That's the one."

"I went there once on a mission trip." She laughed. "I know. Not the roughest place to do mission work. Anyway, on Sunday most of our group went to service there. It was super colorful. They passed out tambourines and percussion instruments." She nodded. "I loved it."

"You and my mom should meet." His tone remained genuine. "She grew up in that church. She'd love to hear that story."

They had turned around and now they were nearly back to the Waynes' house. Mary Catherine wasn't going to bring up Shelly again, but this time Marcus did. "You asked about Shelly. She's interesting. A little aggressive." He raised his brow. "It's awkward, her being Coach's niece."

"Mmm." Mary Catherine didn't want to say too much. "You think Coach Ollie is in favor?"

"I'm not sure." His laugh sounded nervous. "Just feels awkward. I kind of fell into the whole thing before I knew what was happening."

Up until then, Mary Catherine wondered whether Marcus had a chink in his armor. She had assumed the guy was a typical pro ballplayer, but her assumptions had been wrong.

Until this.

She considered her words before she spoke. "So . . . are you pursuing her?" She was careful not to sound mean. Just curious. "Or the other way around?"

"I asked her out, if that's what you mean. But more to kind of see if we were compatible." He was quiet for a long minute. "Actually, I guess she asked Coach if I was interested. I didn't really know about her until a month ago."

Mary Catherine didn't respond. Maybe it was better if Marcus was allowed to sit with his own thoughts for a bit.

"Yeah, maybe she's doing the pursuing." He looked troubled. "To answer your question. I guess I hadn't thought about it."

They were back at the house. Mary Catherine smiled. "The Waynes are great. I love the way their home feels." She was finished talking about Shelly. Marcus could figure that out later.

"They're my second family." He looked to the front door. "They seriously always have a light on." He chuckled. "Like that old motel commercial my dad used to like."

They both laughed and headed inside. Mary Catherine said goodbye and thanked Rhonda and Ollie for having her.

"Come anytime. Seriously." Rhonda hugged her. "We health foodies need to stick together."

"I'll be back." She grinned from Rhonda to Ollie. "I want to meet your daughter next time."

The only thrill greater than jumping out of a plane or bungee jumping off a bridge was investing in people. Mary Catherine worked with the youth group every Sunday at church. She didn't lead it, but even as a volunteer, girls were always talking to her. Telling her their struggles.

It was another wonderful reason she loved being alive.

Marcus walked her out and opened her door first before he slid behind the wheel. The whole way back to the apartment, Mary Catherine couldn't stop from dreaming. Even just a little. And in the time it took them to reach the freeway, she allowed herself to imagine the greatest possible plans ahead. If she could, she would walk that way whatever the cost. However many steps the journey might hold.

For tonight, she could dream about the possibilities. As if for this one moment she might pretend Marcus was *her* boyfriend and the two of them were facing life together. Head on.

She looked out her side window. *Don't be ridiculous*, she chided herself. *There are a hundred reasons why it could never happen.*

Because Mary Catherine had no time for a relationship. If God was going to give her more than thirty years—the way she truly believed—then she would spend it living and serving and loving people.

Just not the sort of love her wayward heart had dreamed about tonight.

10

MARY CATHERINE HATED SEEING her time with Marcus come to an end. He parked in front of the apartment and walked her to the front door. She hoped he couldn't hear how hard her heart was beating. The rush she felt had nothing to do with her health. Something about being with him stirred feelings she'd avoided most of her life.

He stood closer than she liked. Or maybe she liked it more than she wanted to admit. Either way, he looked deep into her eyes before he spoke. Like he had all the time in the world. "I had fun tonight."

"Me, too." She folded her arms in front of her. "Thanks again . . . for not bringing your phone."

He chuckled lightly. The sound sent chills through Mary Catherine, and she could do nothing to stop them. "You, too. Looks like we're both good at being present."

"Yes, sir."

"'Yes, sir'?" He angled his head. The look in his eyes took

her breath. "You had that Southern thing in your voice just then."

She giggled. "Blame it on the upbringing. You can take the girl out of the South . . ."

He grinned at her, as if he wanted to stretch the moment as badly as she did. "But you can't take the South out of the girl."

"Exactly."

"I love it. And you still have an accent, by the way."

"Maybe." She was enjoying herself more than she wanted to admit.

"Anyway . . . I'll say this, Mary Catherine." He paused, searching her eyes. "Sami was right about you."

"About how wild I am?" She blinked a few times. Under his gaze, her walls didn't stand a chance.

"No . . . that you're one of a kind." He looked up at the sky and then back into her eyes. "I had to find out for myself."

"I'll take that as a compliment."

"As it was intended." She wondered if he was going to hug her. Instead, he did the slightest bow. Like a knight from a long-forgotten era. "It's been a pleasure, m'lady."

"Oh, now look." She laughed softly. "Southern gentleman, are you?" The sound faded and she looked deeper into his eyes, all the way to his soul. "Marcus Dillinger . . . you're not who I expected."

"Now, now . . ." A twinkle lit up his eyes and he waved his pointer finger at her. "You thought us ballplayers were all the same."

"I did. I confess." No matter what she'd told herself up to this point, she didn't want the moment to end. She could've stayed out here beneath the stars with Marcus Dillinger, being far too friendly, until daybreak.

"Well"—he took a step back—"happy to prove you wrong." His teasing lifted like morning fog and for several seconds he stood there, just watching her. Again she had the sense he didn't want to leave any more than she wanted him to go. "See you later, Mary Catherine."

"See ya." She put one hand on the door, but she didn't turn around until he did, until he jogged to his Hummer, climbed inside, and pulled away.

Inside, she was grateful Sami was already asleep. She didn't want to answer questions about the night or her walk with Marcus or what she might be feeling. She stood at the window and peered through the crack in the curtains. Her heart was giddy with love and life and every wonderful thing. Springtime reigned in her soul and sunshine followed her into the apartment despite the dark of night outside.

Had the last few hours really happened? Had Marcus really just driven off at one thirty in the morning after spending the most wonderful time with her? And what was she thinking, allowing herself to feel this way?

Mary Catherine had no answers for herself.

For once she didn't care about her sensibilities, about her determination to keep herself unattached, to never fall in love. She always thought she could find a grander purpose outside of love. Learning to fly, or feeding children in Africa, or sneaking Bibles into North Korea. She had believed her wild side was enough to soak all the life she could out of the time God gave her.

But she would never have this night again and right now

she would've given up every adventure ahead for the chance to be loved by Marcus Dillinger. Something that would never happen. She drew a shaky breath.

Right now she didn't feel wild. She felt scared and unsure and lonely. Just for tonight, she wished for the freedom to fall in love if she wanted to. She wished she wasn't sick and that tonight wasn't only a dream. And something else.

She wished she had a hundred years.

IT WAS A half hour back to his house in Silver Lake, and Marcus was pretty sure he'd need every minute to sort through his feelings. The ones that had made it hard to feel the ground beneath his feet a minute ago.

Mary Catherine had filled his senses for the past two hours like no girl ever had. Yet, he was pretty sure she wasn't available. She didn't have a boyfriend—at least he didn't think she did. But she gave off no real proof of being interested, either.

Marcus gripped the steering wheel and gritted his teeth. What was he thinking? Of course she wasn't interested. Hadn't she said that at the beginning? Sure, she'd opened up to him tonight. But in front of their friends she'd been just short of rude. Too concerned with offending his girlfriend. Which was another problem.

He had never intended to have Shelly be his girlfriend.

The thing with Shelly just sort of happened. She was relentless when they were together, and when they weren't, well, she texted him constantly. Always her texts were forward and laced with innuendo. He came to a stoplight and checked his phone.

Another two texts had come in from Shelly while he was saying goodbye to Mary Catherine. The light was still red, so he glanced at them. The first was short. *Miss you.* The second was longer. *All I can think about are those long legs of yours and . . . well, you know. See you soon.* Each text was punctuated by half a dozen emojis.

Of course he hadn't brought his phone on the walk with Mary Catherine. Her texts came in like clockwork.

He tossed the phone on the passenger seat as the light turned green. How had things gotten this way so fast? The two of them hadn't been alone except for their goodbyes— which was a good thing. Even when he took her home, she was all over him, kissing him and asking him to park further down the street. "Let's take our time," she always told him.

Mary Catherine had asked the most profound question of the night. Who was pursuing whom when it came to Shelly? Marcus sighed, and the sound rattled around in the empty Hummer. He knew so little about being a Christian. Sure, his dad had been a good man. He'd met Marcus's mom in church, after all. But as far back as Marcus could remember there had only been baseball.

A good life, a nice family, and baseball.

He thought about how easily Mary Catherine had rattled off the Bible verse. What was it? John something. Marcus had never even read the Bible, at least not as far as he could remember. It wasn't something he and Tyler had talked about, either.

Mary Catherine's face came to his mind, consuming his

senses. She was the sort of girl a guy could pursue. No question. But if they'd had another hour, if their walk had gone on longer, eventually the questions would've turned to him and his past.

He had basically told her everything there was to know—at least from his high school days. He had played ball. Period.

But his time in college and the pros? Those years, there was much more to his story. A sick feeling came over him. There didn't seem to be enough air in the SUV, so he rolled down his window. Pitching for the Oregon State Beavers came with certain expectations. Different girls every weekend. Others on the road and still more midweek on campus. It was all part of the game.

Marcus liked to think he was better than some of his teammates. He didn't drink, didn't party. But he couldn't remember the names of all the girls he'd been with.

Shame burned through him, so that even the skin on his hands felt hot. He could never tell Mary Catherine about his past. She wouldn't want another conversation with him. He squinted at the freeway ahead of him. *Dear God, what sort of pathetic, wretched man am I? How many girls do I owe an apology to?*

He rarely thought about this. Especially in the last few years, when he'd cleaned up his act and stayed away from women. But if he was honest with himself, things only grew worse after the draft.

Los Angeles was a place without values or morals. Everyone was out for themselves, on the hunt for money, fame, sex. The thrill of the one-night stand worked both ways in LA. The girls Marcus hooked up with hadn't wanted a commitment any more than he had.

People using people. Until recently, that was Los Angeles for Marcus.

He tried to imagine what Mary Catherine would think about that. If she were telling him the whole story, the girl hadn't had a serious boyfriend. Maybe not ever—though he found that hard to believe. One thing was for sure—Mary Catherine wasn't going to settle. Not in life, and not in love.

The weight of his past pressed in around his shoulders. Sure, he'd made a deal with God, and God had come through. But where did that leave him? The question that had plagued him after Baldy's death suffocated him again. Here in his Hummer. If he didn't make it home, if a drunk driver drove the wrong way onto the freeway and he never saw it coming, where would he be at night's end?

Heaven or hell?

Yeah, he needed to talk to Ollie Wayne. The family opened their home week after week. They hosted church every Sunday, but Marcus had never talked about his past, about what to do with it.

Let me just say this, Lord . . . I'm sorry. If I could do things over again, I'd avoid every bit of it. The girls . . . they were nothing to me. But . . . it was something to You. I'm sorry.

The breeze through the open window brushed against his face and the pressure on his shoulders eased. He didn't hear any response, the way he had earlier on the way to the youth center. But he felt something. Hope, maybe. Yeah, that was it. Hope.

He would talk to Ollie and Rhonda and he'd start reading the Bible. He'd start with Mary Catherine's verse in John.

Her name brought him back to the moment.

Tonight was a dream. He could've talked to the beautiful redhead all night. She carried with her a childlike joy, the kind that could warm an entire room. Her very presence was intoxicating. But he didn't dare dream about her.

God might forgive him for his ugly, sordid past. But Mary Catherine would never even have the chance because he could never tell her. If he ever did, the magic of tonight would be gone as soon as he said the words. The simple truth was this:

A girl like Mary Catherine deserved better.

11

LEXY FELT A HUNDRED years old as she walked into her grandma's house. It was only nine thirty, but already the woman was asleep. Her grandma didn't belong in this generation or this neighborhood. She was a God-fearing woman who had nowhere else to turn.

Lexy crossed her arms and stared out the window. A kid had died tonight. One of EastTown's youngest. Dwayne had no choice—that's what he said. The rules had changed. Now if he wanted to be leader of the WestKnights he needed two murders. A kid from EastTown and Marcus Dillinger.

He was halfway there.

Vomit rose in Lexy's throat. Sure, she'd been around a lot of killing. Still, tonight was different. Dwayne hadn't been able to find one of the EastTown Boyz. They were headed home and he was cussing at her. Like it was her fault.

Dwayne didn't have to treat her like that. Lexy was his, heart and soul. He could at least be a little nice. That's what she was telling him when all of a sudden he slowed the car down.

"There." Dwayne had cussed under his breath. "Two-bit punks. Say goodbye to life." He had rolled down his window.

Lexy had heard him cock the gun, but she didn't want to look. For all her time on the streets she'd never actually seen someone shot and killed. Not close like this. But at the last second she looked. She turned and everything happened in slow motion.

The two EastTown Boyz had been sitting on trashcans, their backs to the street, red bandanas proudly wrapped around their heads. And Dwayne had started cussing again, saying something about getting the younger one. Then before Lexy could take another breath, Dwayne fired at the smaller of the two guys.

And both boys had turned and looked right at them and Lexy had gasped. Because they were young. Too young. Twelve, maybe thirteen. Both of them. And she watched the kid's eyes grow wide, watched the fear as Dwayne's bullet ripped through his head.

And the blur continued as the other kid screamed and the one who'd been hit fell to the ground, and the screaming . . . the screaming echoed in Lexy's heart and mind and soul and Dwayne had sped away and that was it.

Her boyfriend had met the challenge.

But Lexy hadn't been able to speak or breathe. All she could see were the boy's eyes as he fell to the ground. And terror shook her body, her knees, her hands. And Dwayne had said, "Don't get soft on me now, baby."

She had turned and looked at him. Dwayne still had the

gun in his hand. She said nothing, but she had one thought. The thought she still had now sitting here in her grandma's house.

Maybe she didn't want to be Dwayne's girl.

Anyway, the police would be looking for them by now. The other kid would say it was one of the WestKnights. The chase would be on. It was only a matter of time. Dwayne must've figured that out because right after the shooting he drove her back here. "Don't need no other witness hanging around." He nodded for her to get out. "If you hear a tap on your window later tonight, be ready. I still need to celebrate."

Lexy's breath was still shaky. She turned away from the window and sat in her grandmother's rocking chair. The darkness felt heavy around her. She could already feel the prison bars. There was no way out of this life, not if she wanted one. And where would she go if she did want out? She might as well run in front of a moving train.

The gang would destroy her—one way or another. Behind bars or on the streets.

Being part of the WestKnights was all she knew.

And Dwayne was about to be leader of the gang. The rocking chair creaked in the dead of night. Something moved a few feet from her. Lexy turned but nothing was there. Her heart beat harder. One time she and her friends had watched a movie about demons. Lexy walked away believing they were real. You could feel them even if you couldn't see them. A skin-crawling feeling of horror and evil.

Which was what she was feeling now.

Lexy folded her arms tight around her chest. She could text Dwayne and tell him how scared she was. She was his.

She tried to remember that. But all she could see were the kid's eyes as his body fell off the trashcan. As he took his last breath.

She needed a light on. Even if it woke up her grandma.

Another sound over her other shoulder. Lexy put her hands to her face. She didn't want to stand, didn't want to move. But she needed light. Needed it in the most desperate way. Finally she stood and braced for an attack of some kind. From whatever was here with her, whatever was hunting her.

Somehow she made it to the light switch and flipped it on. There. Her breathing resumed, fast and shallow. There was nothing there, no one with her in the room. The sounds must've been her imagination. Demons weren't real. She was just freaked out by the shooting.

Lexy waited until her breathing relaxed a little. The house was small, two rooms and a kitchen. Nothing more. But it was always clean. Her grandma saw to that. The heaviness in the air remained—even with the lights on. Lexy walked to the kitchen and there on the broken table against the wall sat her grandma's Bible. It was open, like maybe her grandmother had been reading it before she went to bed. Lexy came closer and looked. A section was highlighted, but Lexy couldn't read half the words. Her grandma had tried to teach her, but Lexy had long ago stopped learning. School meant nothing to her.

She sat down, weary and sick from the killing. The Bible was ancient looking, the letters so small her grandmother used a magnifying glass to read it. The letters at the top spelled R-O-M-A-N-S. Lexy had no idea what that meant. She pulled the Bible closer and looked at the yellow part. She could read a few of the words.

Hate what is evil . . . cling to what is good.

A strange feeling came over Lexy, like someone was watching her from the shadows. Hate what is evil? Did the Bible really say that? She looked at it again and read it more slowly this time. Yes, that's exactly what it said. Cling to what is good. Lexy wasn't sure what *cling* meant. Dwayne always told her not to be clingy in front of the guys. Not too much hand-holding and hanging onto him.

She let the idea sink in. So then . . . according to the Bible people were supposed to hate bad things and hold on to good. Lexy dropped slowly to the hard wooden chair and stared at the wall, at nothing, really.

Demons or not, her whole life was built around evil. She didn't think about it that way most of the time, but tonight? Watching the kid from the EastTown gang die right in front of her? That was evil. No one could say different.

But what about the good? Lexy felt ice in her veins. Anger came around her and made the muscles in her face tight. Who was she kidding? There was no good, none at all. Her grandma was good, but no one else. Lexy stared at the Bible and then, in a rush of frustration, she slammed the cover shut. What good could come from an old book, anyway? People had to believe it; they had to read it for it to make a difference.

She stood and thought about going to bed, but she couldn't. She couldn't stop looking at the Bible and thinking about the words her grandma had colored in yellow. Hate evil. Cling to good.

And suddenly she remembered.

There was someone good out on the streets, someone trying to make things better. Someone who cared about the broken kids and homes without mamas and dads. There was someone willing to put his own money into giving all of them a better way.

His name was Marcus Dillinger.

And tomorrow night at this time Dwayne would be leader of the WestKnights and Marcus would just be another victim. Another guy in a body bag. Tears stung her eyes. She could stop it. Never mind the evil around her, Lexy could cling to good—even if only for tonight.

She dug around in her purse and found a small bag of change. Quarters mostly. Money she'd stolen from her grandma's nightstand. Then she clutched her bag to her side and headed back out the front door. Two blocks down there was a bar with a pay phone outside. From what she'd heard, a caller couldn't be traced on pay phones. If Dwayne found out about this, he'd kill her. Lexy had no doubt.

Four different cars drifted slowly past her as she walked. The drivers looked ready to kill someone, ready to fight. The guys in each of the cars called out to her as they went by. Rude things. Words that reminded her how many times she'd been forced to do stuff she didn't want to do.

Tears trickled down Lexy's cheeks. She wasn't upset, not really. She was just mad at Dwayne. He should've said he'd kill off more of the EastTown Boyz. Not Marcus Dillinger.

Lexy wiped at her tears, her pace hard and fast. The pay phone was just ahead. She reached it and looked over one shoulder, then the other. No one watching, no WestKnights to rat on her. She picked up the phone and dialed 911.

A woman's voice answered. "Nine-one-one, what's your emergency?"

What was her emergency? Lexy's entire body shook, her mouth so dry she wasn't sure she could talk. She could feel the evil, feel it gaining ground. *Cling to what is good . . . cling to what is good.* She swallowed a few times. "It's . . . it's not an emergency today."

"Ma'am, I need you to be specific." The woman sounded frustrated, like she couldn't be bothered. "What's the emergency?"

"It's . . . Marcus Dillinger." Her heart was pounding so loud she could barely hear herself. Two guys left the bar a few feet from where she was standing.

She hesitated. "Marcus Dillinger, the baseball player?"

"Yes." Lexy looked over her shoulder. What if someone recognized her and told Dwayne? She clutched the phone. *Be brave, Lexy . . . come on.* She squeezed her eyes shut and found her voice. "Someone from the WestKnights is gonna kill Marcus Dillinger tomorrow night at the new youth center."

"Someone's going to kill Marcus Dillinger?"

"Yes." Fear grabbed at Lexy, hissing at her from all sides. She was crazy to do this. They would kill her for it. "Please help him." She slammed the receiver back down and stared at the phone. She could feel it. That scary feeling again. Demons, maybe. Or people behind her, coming up to her. She spun around and there they were. Three EastTown Boyz, red bandanas, eyes blazing with hate.

Coming for her.

Lexy pressed her back against the cold metal phone. She was going to die here. It was only a matter of minutes.

"You dead, WestKnight girl." The older one narrowed his eyes at her. "But we gonna have some fun with you first."

Before Lexy could scream, before she could tell them she wasn't afraid, that they could do what they wanted because she was not a coward, because for once in her life she was clinging to the good, before she could even think about what to do next, a huge police officer stepped out of the shadows. He had big shoulders and longish blond hair.

"Go home, boys." His voice was loud. So loud it rattled through Lexy's soul.

The EastTown Boyz turned toward him and one of them drew a gun. But the cop kept coming, walking right at them. His eyes looked bright, like something weird from a movie. He never blinked. Just kept walking up to them, slow and serious. "I said . . . go home. You don't want to do this."

"Stop, man. I'll shoot!"

The officer looked more like a mountain as he got closer. "Go ahead." He stepped in front of Lexy. He was so big she couldn't see the guys around him. Then the cop pulled a club from the leg of his uniform. "Don't give me a reason."

"Look, man, you're not from around here." One of the EastTown Boyz laughed. "You're the one needs to go."

"In the name of Jesus." His voice was quieter now, calm and different. Like nothing Lexy had ever heard. The man raised his club. "Leave."

A gun versus a club? Lexy figured the EastTown kid would go ahead and shoot. Instead, she could hear their shoes shuffling. Lexy peeked around the cop and saw the three of them backing up fast, their eyes scared. Then they turned around and started to run, and when they did, the kid with the gun stopped, turned, and shot at the cop.

Fired right at him.

But at the same time the officer didn't flinch, and . . .

Lexy gasped. "What . . . Where's the bullet?" *What happened?* Lexy felt a strange sense of something she'd never felt before. Peace, maybe. Or comfort. Who was this guy? What had he said? Speaking in the name of Jesus? Cops didn't talk like that. She moved out from behind him and looked up at him.

The officer wasn't listening. He was still staring at the EastTown Boyz, watching as the reality hit them. The bullet seemed to have gone right through the officer and then ricocheted off the wall. Just a few feet from her.

They began to run as fast as they could down the street until they were out of sight.

Only then did the officer turn to her and put his hand on her shoulder. "You're okay. You need to get home."

The man's eyes had a hundred colors. Green and blue and even a white kind of light. "Who . . . are you?"

"Officer Jag."

She caught the name on his uniform. J-A-G. "How . . . did you know I needed help?"

"Lexy." The cop was calm. "God sees your heart. He has a plan for you." Officer Jag looked down the street and then at the bar a few feet away. When he looked at Lexy again, his eyes were sad. "God's plan for you . . . is so much bigger than this."

Lexy gulped. She didn't know what to say. "How did you know my name?"

"Come on." He looked fierce as he started walking in the direction of her grandma's house. "Stay with me. You need to get home."

Sure enough, the officer didn't leave her side as they walked the few blocks home. Lexy didn't understand anything that had just happened. "I'm serious. How did you know my name?"

"The bigger question is this." He looked down at her, his eyes kind like they had been at first. "Why are you with Dwayne Davis?"

Lexy felt the toughness rise up in her. "Dwayne's my man."

"No." Officer Jag shook his head. "Dwayne's working for the enemy. You stay with him, he'll destroy you."

In all her life, no one had ever spoken to her that way, like there was a plan for her life or like God knew who she was. They reached her grandma's house and the cop walked her to the door. "Think about what I said, Lexy." He looked right through her. "And stay inside."

"Okay."

"Your grandma's Bible is true. Hate evil. Cling to good. Like making that call for Marcus Dillinger." The cop took a few steps back down the stairs. "How you live, it's your choice."

Lexy felt chills on her arms and legs. "How did you . . ." She couldn't finish her sentence. Everything was just too weird. Like maybe she was having a dream. She watched the man turn and walk slowly back down the street. Then in a rush she hurried inside, shut the door, and locked it.

Only then did she realize several things all at once. The officer had no car, not that she had seen. And he had been working alone. Which cops never did in this neighborhood.

And the biggest question. How had a bullet gone straight through his gut without hurting him?

A thought came to Lexy and she felt her mouth hang open for a few seconds. What if Officer Jag was an angel? Come to tell her to hate evil and cling to good? Like her grandma's Bible had told her half an hour ago? She thought about that. An angel named Jag who wore a police uniform and was bulletproof? Not possible. Just like the demons she'd imagined earlier. The whole thing was all in her imagination. Probably because of watching that kid get shot earlier. Like seeing that had made her a little crazy. Yeah, that was it. She was just a little crazy. Maybe she would open her eyes and she'd be in bed.

Lexy blinked a few times and looked around. But she wasn't in bed.

She sat down at the kitchen table and reached again for her grandma's Bible. Slowly she ran her thumb over the soft, crinkly page. The Bible was too old to matter today. Lexy felt the reality of her situation more than ever before. She had done her good deed. She had called and told the police about Marcus Dillinger.

Officer Jag had told her doing good was her choice.

But he was wrong. What was she supposed to do? Find a new family? She was a WestKnights girl. There was no way out, even if she wanted it. She brushed her teeth and fell into bed, but she couldn't sleep.

The man's face, his eyes, stayed with her. Like an Instagram picture in her mind. What kind of regular person could not be hurt by a bullet? Or guess her name? And how had he known exactly what she had read in her grandma's Bible? Maybe he was some kind of magician. And she was about to be on some reality show. There had to be an explanation.

Because angels and demons weren't real and neither was God.

The streets were proof of that.

12

MARCUS HAD A HEAVY heart as he arrived at Chairos Youth Center at just after four o'clock and found the paint buckets in the back closet. A twelve-year-old boy had been killed the previous night, one of the EastTown kids. Police had ruled it a gang killing, probably for points. Gang members ranked themselves by the points they accumulated.

The murder made Marcus sick to his stomach.

He carried the paint to a worktable in the room that needed the most help. As he did he smiled at volunteers working throughout the building. More volunteers than before. The community was behind his efforts. They had opened the place at two that afternoon, and now tutors at several tables were helping kids with homework.

The dream was coming true. Just not fast enough.

Before he could brainstorm ways to keep kids like the twelve-year-old murder victim off the streets, Marcus had to finish the work at hand. In the conversion of the old warehouse to a youth center, several rooms still needed painting to cover up a decade of graffiti and desperation. Tyler, Sami, and Mary Catherine planned to show up around five to help, and by seven o'clock kids would start arriving for pickup basketball and pizza.

Given the gang situation, police and a few volunteer high school basketball coaches would be on hand—to keep the teams fair. The pizza was set to arrive around seven thirty and the activities would wrap up a few hours later. Marcus had been looking forward to this Tuesday for weeks.

Yes, it was a school night. But on the streets kids stayed out till far later regardless of school in the morning. This was one way to give them an alternative. A way to say no to the gangs that were ever willing to accept them.

Marcus made a few trips from the closet to the table getting the cans of paint and brushes and buckets set out. All the while Marcus thought about the murdered boy. What if the center had opened sooner? The kid might've found his way through the doors and never looked back.

He might be alive today.

Marcus was organizing the paint according to room when he heard the sounds of his friends. Mostly Mary Catherine, her voice, her laugh. She hadn't been far from his mind since Saturday night. And while he'd fielded dozens of texts from Shelly in that time, he hadn't heard from Mary Catherine at all.

Another reason why she was special.

They entered the room, dressed in old T-shirts and sweatpants. "A-One Painting Crew at your service!" Tyler had his arm around Sami's shoulders. "Fastest painters in Los Angeles." He grinned at Sami and Mary Catherine.

"That's right. Don't blink." Sami laughed. "The whole place'll be painted."

Mary Catherine looked happy, relaxed. And when her eyes met his, Marcus could feel the same pull, the same attraction from the other night. The chemistry between them made him dizzy. He gave Tyler and Sami a hug as the three approached but when it came to Mary Catherine, he hesitated, slightly awkward.

She sidestepped him. "I get first dibs on the brushes." She grinned. "It's all about the brushes."

"I've heard." He stepped back. Why hadn't he hugged her? Not the other night and not now? He tried not to feel frustrated. Of course he hadn't hugged her. He had a girlfriend and she wasn't interested. Or she wouldn't be if she knew his past.

They got busy, filling trays with paint and dividing the work. Before they started covering the walls, Marcus told them about the boy killed last night.

The news hit them hard. Tyler gritted his teeth. "That's why we gotta get this thing up and running. Kids killing kids. It has to stop."

"They need another way of living." Sami took Tyler's hand. "It's just so sad. Such a waste."

Mary Catherine stayed quiet. She looked at her paint, stirring it slowly. Whatever she was thinking, she didn't say it. Marcus hoped he would have time to ask her later. She cared so much about making a difference. Did the recent violence make her want to do more? Or find somewhere else to serve?

Marcus had a feeling it was the latter.

They started painting, and gradually the mood lightened. Tyler and Sami were amazed by home church at the Waynes' house a few days ago. "I never thought about the family of Jesus like that." Tyler seemed like he was really thinking about the teaching that day. "The cost of being connected to Jesus had to be so great. So emotional. I guess it makes the Bible feel a lot more real."

Marcus agreed. The Sunday service at the Waynes' house had been tremendous. He only wished Mary Catherine had come. But her work with kids at her church was important. She wasn't going to miss that. She cared too much for those kids. And these kids.

Which was the real reason she was here. No matter what attraction Marcus felt between them.

Sometime before seven, Shamika and her little boy, Jalen, showed up to help paint. Jalen wanted to play basketball, but his mom explained that tonight was for the big kids.

"You know what, though, buddy?" Marcus cleaned his hands on a rag and stooped down to the boy's level. "I bet I can find that other hoop for you. We have room right here for a little pickup game."

"Really?" Jalen's eyes lit up. "Can I, Mama?" He turned his bright brown eyes up to Shamika.

She laughed lightly and shook her head. "Marcus, you don't have to do that. We're here to help paint. He knows that."

"Yeah, but a guy has to play hoops." Marcus winked at Jalen. "Right, buddy?"

"Right!" The boy fist-bumped Marcus.

Hope infused Marcus's troubled heart. Playing ball with Jalen later would be fun. He found the junior hoop and set it up in the middle of the room so Jalen could play while his mom painted. Marcus was handing a small basketball to Jalen when he felt someone watching him. He glanced over his shoulder and saw Mary Catherine looking right at him.

Their eyes met and she smiled. Then without a word she returned to her painting. No, the two of them would never date. But Mary Catherine was becoming his friend. And despite the way his heart skipped when she walked into the room, he welcomed her friendship. At least that.

The teens started arriving before seven, hanging around the gym and talking about the teams. A few minutes later the coaches showed up. Without supervision, a pickup basketball game could easily become a reason to fight.

A reason to kill.

But with it . . . well, Marcus could only hope that this might be a place the kids could get their aggression out, a way they could move and compete and connect without bringing the gangs and guns into it.

As Marcus expected, the kids who showed up that night were young. He looked at the teams as the first game started. He'd have been surprised if any of them were older than fifteen.

"Good turnout." Marcus was standing next to Tyler, watching the coaches working with the players. "Thirty-three kids."

Tyler smiled. "Thirty-three boys who won't be hanging with a gang tonight."

A dozen or so girls gathered along the sidelines. Two more played with the guys on the floor. By the time the games were under way, it was almost seven thirty. The pizza would be there any minute.

Marcus watched, and deep satisfaction welled within him. *God, if you would please bless this youth center.* He studied the kids, willing a change for them. *Give these kids a reason to believe in life, in people. A reason to believe in You. And help me know how we can really change things here in the—*

"Marcus!"

His prayer cut short, Marcus turned around. Officer Charlie Kent looked in a hurry as he walked up. His partner hung back, talking to Tyler, Sami, and Mary Catherine.

Marcus felt his heart sink. "More trouble?" He wiped his brow with the back of his hand. There was no relief around here.

"Always." The officer folded his arms and looked squarely at Marcus. His voice was as angry as it was defeated. He was careful to let no one else hear him. "We got a tip yesterday. The WestKnights have a contract on you. They're planning to take you out tonight."

"Me?" A partial laugh came from Marcus, but only out of disbelief. "Why would they wanna kill me?"

"Who knows. The WestKnights lost their leader this past week in a drive-by. Gangs do deadly things when a position is at stake. Sounds like that's what this is."

"The shooting yesterday, the twelve-year-old kid? Was that a part of this?"

"Probably." The officer shook his head. "We're close to making an arrest. A kid named Dwayne Davis. Has a list of robberies and attempted murder charges. We think he's the shooter from last night."

"So . . ." Marcus didn't understand. "Can't you arrest him?"

"It's not that easy. These guys don't have a residence. They're always moving, living on someone's floor. Every door we knock on has a bunch of armed kids."

Marcus nodded. The danger was worse than anything he ever imagined. It made him wonder—just for a moment—if he'd picked the wrong city to build the youth center. He could've built this in the suburbs and at least there wouldn't be bullets flying out front.

Maybe this was a mistake. If someone wanted to kill him for trying to help, then—

No, he told himself. *Don't think like that.*

God had given him this idea. The Lord had provided the broken down warehouse, the funds to renovate it, and the volunteers to help staff it. There was a reason he was supposed to be here. He looked out at the action on the basketball court, even as the officer kept talking, warning him about the dynamics between the rival gangs in the area.

But all Marcus could think about were the kids on the court. That's why he was here. Threats of violence wouldn't make him give up. He'd simply have to be careful. He turned to the officer. "What should I do?"

"The front of the building will be the most dangerous. We have officers patrolling, looking for Davis. But we think maybe you should call it an early night."

Marcus hesitated. He hated breaking up the basketball game. Hated letting the gangs win—even for a night. Any minute the pizza would be here. He clenched his jaw, frustrated. He couldn't put the kids and volunteers at risk. He stared at the officer. "Whatever we need to do."

The officer studied the teens on the court. "Let's dismiss them after this game."

"What about the pizza? It'll be here any minute."

"Maybe they can grab a piece on the way out. Then we can shut down." He pulled his radio from his belt. "I'll call for additional backup until everyone's cleared out."

Marcus studied the kids again. They had no idea their fun tonight was about to come to an abrupt end. Marcus looked across the room at the faces of his friends. The other officer was talking to them and by the look on their faces, they knew about the threat.

A thought occurred to him. Now he wouldn't get to play with little Jalen, either. Everyone would have to go home. He looked over at the junior hoop, but Shamika and Jalen were nowhere to be seen. Marcus had a strange feeling about the mother and son. He hadn't seen them in several minutes. "Hold on." He nodded to the officer. "I have to find someone."

He turned to jog toward the back room where the water bottles were set up, but then something caught his eye. He turned and watched Shamika and Jalen walk toward the entrance of the center. Shamika saw him and waved. "The pizza's here! Me and Jalen are gonna help bring it inside."

"No!" Marcus shouted, but it was too late. Shamika and Jalen were already through the front door.

Marcus ran for the door and tore outside into the night. The pizza guy was out of the car, a stack of boxes in his hands. Cars seemed to be everywhere, cruising down the street, parked across from the center. Marcus could feel the danger, he could sense it to the core of his being.

But where was it coming from?

Suddenly out of the shadows, a woman lunged at him. "Get down!"

Everything happened so fast, the action around Marcus became a blur. He heard gunfire and the sound of squealing tires and felt something burning in his leg. Before he could register any of it, he heard Shamika scream.

"Jalen! No, not my boy! God, please!"

Marcus scrambled to his knees and the pain sliced through his leg. He looked down and saw blood coming from his thigh. *Flesh wound*, he told himself. But Jalen . . . What had happened to the child?

Volunteers were shouting and sirens sounded in the distance. But what about Jalen? Marcus pulled himself to his feet and pushed through the crowd. "Jalen!"

Shamika was still screaming. "Someone help us! No, God, not my boy! Please not my boy!"

Marcus could see him. There was blood everywhere as he knelt next to Shamika. Jalen wasn't moving and now Marcus could see where the blood was coming from. The boy had been hit in the back of his head. He had probably turned when he heard Marcus yell and now . . .

Dear God, no . . . not this child, please! "Has someone called nine-one-one?" he shouted, desperate.

"They're on their way," one of the parent volunteers answered.

Across from him working on the child was the woman who had knocked him to the ground. It was Aspyn. One of the volunteers. She had her hands on Jalen's chest, giving him CPR. Then, as if she could sense Marcus looking at her—despite the screaming and crying happening all around—she looked straight at him. "Pray." She continued her efforts to save Jalen's life. "Pray for the boy. Pray in Jesus' name."

Marcus stared at the boy. Someone had to stop the bleeding. He took off his shirt and put it against the child's head. He didn't know CPR, but Aspyn seemed capable.

Pressing the shirt against the boy's skull, Marcus tuned out the wailing and shouting and took hold of Shamika's hand. "Let's pray."

"I can't lose him!" Her words were a panicked scream. "He's all I have. Please . . . God, please!"

Marcus had never been in a situation like this. He wanted to rewind the clock and have this moment over again. If only he could've stopped Shamika before she walked outside. The bullet intended for him had hit Jalen instead. It was more than he could bear.

But even with all of that, even desperate for Jalen to survive, Marcus knew Aspyn was right. They had to pray. The blood was spreading. He couldn't watch. Marcus closed his eyes and raised his voice, raised it above the crying and shouting and sounds of the approaching sirens. "We need a miracle, Lord. Please, don't let him die. Please . . . save his life. Please, help us! God, I beg you!"

Shamika was sobbing now, but she managed to say, "Amen. Jesus, please, amen."

The ambulance pulled up and paramedics rushed through the crowd. Marcus sat back on the grass and watched as Jalen was whisked onto a stretcher. Shamika stayed with him, running alongside the men as they took her baby to the ambulance.

He should've taken that bullet. Not Jalen.

Behind him he heard Tyler's voice. But at the same time another set of paramedics rushed up and surrounded him. "Marcus, you've been hit. You need to get to the hospital."

His leg? He wanted to tell them he'd be fine. "Go find the shooter. Someone find him!" That's all that mattered now.

Tyler was at his side. "Man, it's a nasty wound. You gotta get in."

"The boy . . ." Marcus stared at the place where the ambulance carrying Jalen had disappeared. "Pray for the boy."

"We will." Tyler squeezed his shoulder. "I'll bring Sami and Mary Catherine. We'll meet you at the hospital."

The paramedics lifted him onto the stretcher. Marcus looked back as they carried him toward a second ambulance and a sudden thought hit him. What about Aspyn? How had the woman known Marcus was about to be hit? She had shoved him to the ground and then just as quickly she was at Jalen's side doing CPR. As if she'd known all this was about to happen. Was she someone connected to the gang? Did she have inside information?

Marcus would tell the police to talk to her. Just in case she knew something. In case she could lead them to the shooter. He scanned the crowd looking for her. Aspyn had volunteered at the center Saturday night. She was a pretty woman, thin with long, straightened hair and green eyes. She must've gone back inside the building.

Because she was nowhere in sight.

The paramedics loaded Marcus into the waiting ambulance and he closed his eyes. How could this have happened? It was supposed to be a fun night for the kids. This was supposed to help the gang problem here on the streets of LA. Everything they'd done, the time and money and prayers for this place. It was supposed to make a difference.

Instead, little Jalen was fighting for his life.

13

JAG WAS FURIOUS.

He knew Angels Walking were required to stay in control emotionally, but he was seriously struggling. He exhaled and replayed the truth in his mind. Angels on earth could feel human emotions. Anger. Fear. Sorrow—all were possible, especially when angels took on human form. By the power of God, an angel walking on earth had to control himself.

That had never been a problem before. Jag had been on many missions over time. The successful mission he and Aspyn had done during World War II, for instance. They had rescued a pilot shot down over Germany. Destruction, hate, violence.

None of it had moved Jag the way this had.

The futility of kids shooting kids. The same gang violence that had killed Terrance Williams.

Jag steadied his breathing. He waited with Aspyn across the street from the youth center. How could this have happened again? The entire mission was in jeopardy. They had known the shooting was possible. He and Aspyn were both on site, ready to intervene, and Jag had done what he could to delay Dwayne. He had disabled the kid's vehicle. But apparently not well enough. Because the shooting had still happened.

Just like ten years ago.

Either way, right now they didn't have time to wonder about what went wrong. Jag had a job to do.

He wanted Dwayne Davis behind bars. Where he belonged, according to man's law. Where he could do no further harm to mankind.

"Aspyn." He looked straight at her. "You did the right thing. You saved Marcus. I'm the one who failed."

"No." Aspyn's eyes were damp with tears. "You did what you could. Police mean nothing to Dwayne."

Anger stirred in Jag's heart again. "If it were up to me . . ."

"Don't." She touched his shoulder. "We need to stay focused." A tear slid down her cheek and she caught it with the back of her hand. "This feeling . . . the sadness. It's the hardest part of being on mission. So much heartache here on earth."

"Exactly." Jag willed the strength of God to settle his being.

Across the street the teens were still milling about; Officer Kent seemed to have things under control. He was dispersing the young people, telling them to go home.

Jag turned back to Aspyn. "We will ask the Father for a miracle where the child is concerned."

Aspyn nodded. "I didn't see this coming. I thought the boy was out of the way. I thought—"

"It's okay. We don't know all things." This was the hardest part of being an angel. Having more knowledge than humans, more power. But not nearly the knowledge or power of the Father. God alone knew when someone would be called home, when a person's time on earth ran out.

But why allow angels to intervene if people were going to die anyway? Again Jag forced himself to relax. *Stay controlled, Jag*, he told himself. *Keep the mission in mind.* One day the answers would be clear, even to angels. For now they were to do their jobs, carry out their assignments.

"I want to be at the hospital." Aspyn straightened.

"You should go." Jag studied her. She looked stronger than before. She would come back and she would work as hard as possible to see the mission accomplished. Jag had no doubt.

Aspyn looked at him, her eyes still filled with sorrow. "The most important thing is prayer. Always."

"You go. I have another matter to tend to."

"Jag." Her voice held the familiar warning. "Be careful. Work in God's strength. Don't let human emotions guide you."

Her words hit their mark. He clenched his fists and relaxed them again. "I won't." He exhaled. "The mission is God's. Not ours."

"Exactly." She nodded to him. "See you soon. Stay low."

With that they were both gone. Jag felt the sense of purpose deep inside him. He needed to stay hidden better. Aspyn was right about that, too. Angels Walking had to stay invisible as much as possible. Sure, they had to materialize. That was part of the mission. And when they took on human form, sons and daughters of Adam might wonder. Christians familiar with God's word knew that sometimes they would entertain angels unaware. But too many displays—like not being harmed by flying bullets—and people wouldn't wonder. They would know. God sent His angels to clandestinely work as messengers and protectors among His people. So that He would get the glory. Otherwise humans might worship angels and miss the One who created them.

Almost as soon as he left the spot in front of the youth center, Jag arrived two blocks away, invisible, just down the street from Dwayne and Lexy, who were standing on the sidewalk outside his car. Angels had keen hearing—so Jag could clearly hear Dwayne cursing Lexy, threatening her.

Anger filled Jag again. He wouldn't let the young man hurt the girl. She was important to the mission. He moved closer to Dwayne. Why so much hatred? How could one created in the very image of God be so full of evil? Jag heard a rush of movement in the air around him. A cold wind came with the sound and in a blur the street was filled with demons. Hissing. Laughing. Taunting him and pushing their way closer to Dwayne.

Then suddenly—as if Dwayne could sense the dark support around him—he raised the gun and pointed it straight at Lexy's head.

JAG HAD TO act quickly. He instantly moved to the pay phone near the bar a block away. He slipped into a tight spot between two houses and materialized as the towering blond officer.

Jag stepped up to the pay phone and dialed 911.

The operator answered on the first ring. "What's your emergency?"

"I'm an officer. I know who tried to kill Marcus Dillinger."

"Identify yourself."

"I'll give you the address. I'm in a hurry." He quickly rattled off the information. "Send several squad cars. You don't have long." He hung up and stepped into the shadows, and instantly he was back on the street with Dwayne and Lexy, invisible. The entire phone call had taken mere seconds.

The demons were closing in on Dwayne and Lexy. A team so murderous and dark. Treacherous and evil. The smell of death hung in the air. One of the demons dug its invisible claws into Dwayne's back.

Jag breathed deep. *I need you, Jesus . . .*

Instantly he was in the midst of the demons. "Go!" He held both hands toward the evil spirits. "Go now!"

One of them hissed and his spiky wings brushed up against Jag. "Fight us, mighty warrior. Our time is short. These two belong to us."

Again Jag felt the rush of anger. This wasn't right. Nothing should stop an angel, not unless . . . What was he thinking? How could he forget?

The name of Jesus.

"In the name of Jesus, be gone!" The humans couldn't hear him, but his voice boomed through another dimension. "Now!"

At the sound of the name of Jesus, the demons withered in size, shrinking back, repulsed, wounded. And instantly the evil band disappeared. They would find someone else to torment tonight.

He stepped out of hiding directly behind Dwayne and Lexy, this time as the police officer again. "Stop." His voice pierced the night air. "Both of you! Police!"

"What the—" Dwayne spun around and pulled his gun.

Jag covered the ground between them in fractions of a second and grabbed the gun from Dwayne.

Jag looked at the pistol in his hand and felt a surge of power. *So this is what it's like?* he thought. He ran his thumb over the handle. He pointed the gun at the teenager. He could kill Dwayne now, but there would be eternal consequences.

It wouldn't take much. The slightest pull on the trigger and Dwayne would no longer be a threat. Jag was breathing harder. He ran his finger along the smooth metal at the center of the gun. *One pull . . . just one.*

Suddenly Lexy cried out, "Jesus, help us!"

Jesus.

At the sound of His name, Jag instantly came to his senses. He felt a heavenly calm wash over him and he moved his finger from the trigger. He would not shoot. Not now. Not ever. The sound of sirens in the distance told him it wouldn't be long. Help was on the way.

"The punishment you're about to receive, you have earned." Jag kept the gun trained on the kid. "But it is nothing to what will come after this life." Jag was within his bounds now. Eternal truths, life-altering messages—these were the job of angels.

Dwayne glared at him. He grabbed Lexy by her hair and held her close.

Before Jag could speak again, three police cars pulled up from different directions and skidded to a stop, their bright lights on Dwayne's car. Six of them jumped out, guns drawn.

Jag was invisible by then, the gun on the ground where he had been standing. He moved, unnoticed, to a place where the shadows were dark and the lights of the police cars could not reach. And like that he was gone.

Immediately he was at the hospital, in the room where surgeons frantically worked on little Jalen. Aspyn stood nearby, praying. Constantly praying. Jag took his place beside her.

He closed his eyes.

That was close back there. He could still feel the gun in his hand, feel the strange and powerful desire to kill. His anger had nearly consumed him. *I'm sorry, Father. I was wrong.* He would need to be more careful. Another moment like that could jeopardize the entire mission.

Jag closed his eyes. Prayer. That's what he needed. More time in prayer. He could not work successfully as an Angel Walking unless he stayed connected to God. His breathing slowed down and a deep peace came over him. He blinked his eyes open and stared at the injured child lying on the operating table. Yes, he would pray. For the child fighting for his life a few feet away and for himself.

That human rage would never consume him again.

14

On THE WAY TO Cedars-Sinai Medical Center, Mary Catherine sat in the back and prayed. Tyler was behind the wheel, Sami in the passenger seat beside him. The car stayed quiet except for the occasional sound of a whispered prayer. Mary Catherine stared out the window. How could this have happened?

Of course the youth center was in a dangerous part of town. But none of them ever really thought the gangs would shoot at them. Why would they? Marcus was only trying to help.

They turned into the parking lot and found a spot near the emergency room entrance. The ambulances were still there, parked close to the doors. Mary Catherine squeezed her eyes shut. *Dear God, be with that child. Please.*

Tyler hurried out of the car and around to Sami's door and then Mary Catherine's.

"Is the bullet still in Marcus's leg?" Mary Catherine hadn't wanted to ask until now. She had seen the blood on his jeans before the paramedics took him.

"I couldn't tell." Tyler looked pale, worried. "I hope not."

Inside they checked in at the front desk and explained they were there for Marcus.

"Come on back. He already has visitors, but we're slow tonight." The nurse opened a set of double doors and met them on the other side. "Can't believe those gangs. Trying to kill Marcus Dillinger? Guy only wanted to do something good for the city."

Mary Catherine trailed after the group. Where was the little boy? Where was Jalen? Was he in one of the rooms with the curtains drawn?

Her heart ached at the thought. Precious little child. He had only wanted to help bring in the pizza. She fought back tears as they walked. They reached Marcus's room and stepped in.

The Wayne family was already there, including Shelly. She was sitting next to Marcus's bed, running her hand along his arm.

"Hey." He seemed to shake off Shelly's touch. He looked at Tyler and Sami and then held Mary Catherine's gaze. The fear in his eyes was tangible. "Any word on Jalen?"

"We came here first." Tyler reached out and clasped Marcus's hand.

"I'm fine." His mouth sounded dry. "I need to know about that boy. The nurse won't tell me."

Shelly slid her chair closer to his bed and ran her hand over his hair. "I'm sure he's okay."

"He's not okay." Marcus shot her a harsh look.

Shelly's sad smile didn't waver. She moved her hand to his shoulder. Meanwhile Coach Wayne and his wife were talking quietly, whispering a few feet away.

Mary Catherine felt out of place. The cold, shrinking feeling deep inside her could only be jealousy. Which she hated. She focused her attention on Marcus's injured leg.

He lay stretched out on the bed, one leg of his jeans cut off. The bandage was halfway up his thigh and, if the wrap was any indication, the wound was serious. He had an IV in his arm, and he looked tired.

Sami looked at Marcus's leg. "Did they get the bullet out?"

"It didn't go in. Just grazed me."

"Poor baby." Shelly was on her feet, hanging over the side of the bed like she wanted to crawl up next to Marcus.

Mary Catherine had seen enough. "I'm going to go find Jalen's mother. I'll let you know what I find out."

She didn't wait for a response. Out in the hall she found the nurses' station and asked how to get to the pediatric ICU. "Take the elevator to the fourth floor." The woman hesitated. "Other than parents, patients are only allowed one visitor at a time."

"Thank you." Mary Catherine was already on her way to the elevator. At the fourth floor she walked quietly to the nurses' station, but before she could ask, she saw Jalen's mother in the hallway outside one of the rooms. She was sitting on a chair, her head in her hands.

Mary Catherine approached and took the seat beside her. "Shamika. It's Mary Catherine. From the youth center." She put her arm around Shamika's shoulders. "How is he?"

The woman lifted her head. Her eyes, which had shone

with hope earlier today, were swollen from crying and dark with fear and defeat. "How did this happen?"

She wasn't looking for answers, so Mary Catherine let the moment pass. "Is he in surgery?"

"Yes." She sniffed and brushed the backs of her hands beneath her eyes. "They have to remove part of his skull. Because his brain was swelling." She shook her head, bewildered. "They have to get the bullet out. It went from his head into his neck."

Mary Catherine didn't want to ask any more questions. Especially when Shamika probably didn't have answers. Like whether the boy would walk again or how much damage had been done to his brain or his spine . . . or if the doctors even expected him to live.

All of it was one minute at a time. Mary Catherine took her arm from Shamika's shoulders and reached for the woman's hands. "Can I pray with you?"

"Would it matter?" She probably wasn't trying to be rude or difficult. Her question didn't sound cynical. "I mean it. God could've protected my boy from that bullet. Why pray now?"

Mary Catherine had spent a great deal of time on this issue. She had done a summer of Bible study on the power of prayer and the reasons bad things happen in the first place. She kept her tone even. "I'm not sure anyone knows exactly why certain things happen, but I know this. Evil doesn't come from God."

Shamika thought about that for several seconds. Gradually she nodded her head. "I suppose." She stared at her hands. "But really . . . why did this happen?" Fresh tears began to fall down her cheeks. "He was just being good."

For a long moment Mary Catherine said nothing.

"I'm serious." Shamika's voice was sharper this time. "If you can tell me, then tell me."

Mary Catherine hadn't planned on saying anything. She had no real answers. She took a deep breath. "The Bible says this place, this earth . . . it's broken and fallen. God gives us a way out through Jesus. Even still, every one of us will die someday." She paused. "This isn't our home, Shamika."

She ran her right thumb over her empty left ring finger. "Jalen's daddy left me when I was six weeks pregnant. I figured if he couldn't love me, no one could. Not even God."

Mary Catherine put her hand alongside Shamika's face. "That's not true. God loves you so much. He has a plan for you and Jalen and whatever that plan is, it's good. Even now."

Confusion lined Shamika's face. "There's nothing good about this."

"No." Mary Catherine felt frustrated with herself. She wasn't helping at all. "Of course not."

"So what does it mean?" Shamika's eyes filled with tears again. "God loves us. He has plans for us. But here we are, sitting in this hospital while Jalen fights for every breath."

There were no simple answers. "I only know that God is great. If we choose Him, then one day we'll have eternity together. No more tears, no sorrow, no pain. No shooting or gang violence. No lonely nights. Never again."

Her tears came harder. "I just want my baby back. I want him to live and laugh and be . . . like he was three hours ago."

Mary Catherine took hold of Shamika's hands once more. "Then let's pray. Let's ask God for that."

"Okay." Shamika looked like a little girl, desperate and

lost. She took tight hold of Mary Catherine's fingers. "Please . . . go ahead."

Mary Catherine nodded. "Dear God . . ." Tears flooded her eyes and fell onto her lap. The little boy had been so happy, so trusting that all of life would stay the way it had been in that moment. Filled with love and joy and fun. She tried to find the words. "Lord, we don't understand evil or why things like this happen. But we need Your help to get through it." She struggled to keep her voice steady. "Father, we ask You for a miracle for Jalen. That he would live and laugh and that he would one day soon be just like he was a few hours ago. We ask this in Jesus' powerful name, amen."

When she finished praying she hugged Shamika. "Let me give you my number. So you can update me on how he's doing."

They exchanged information and Shamika was just starting to explain how Jalen's birthday was coming up in a few weeks when the doctor opened the door at the end of the hallway and walked toward them.

His face was taut, his expression deeply concerned. "We've done what we can. We removed the bullet. He's resting now."

Shamika stood. "Is he . . . breathing on his own?"

"No." The doctor looked troubled. "He's on life support." He paused. "I have to be honest, Mrs. Johnson, Jalen may not make it through the night. He's a fighter, but the damage . . . it's considerable."

Quiet sobs came over Shamika. Mary Catherine stood next to her and turned her eyes to the doctor. "Will you bring him back here?"

"Yes. In a few minutes." He put his hand on Shamika's

arm. "He's unconscious. Once he's back in his room, you can talk to him. He may be able to hear you."

Mary Catherine helped Shamika into the room and again her tears came. The woman covered her face with her hands, stifling her sobs. "Not my boy, God . . . please . . . bring him back to me. I can't do this."

Shamika didn't seem to be able to move at all. Not toward the room or toward Mary Catherine. Not at all. Mary Catherine prayed silently. *God, give her peace and strength. Help her be strong for her little boy. Show us You're here. Please.*

Gradually Mary Catherine felt the woman beside her start to relax. After a while the doctor brought Jalen back to the room. He looked so small, lost in the sheets and bandages, tubes and wires. Mary Catherine stayed by Shamika as she took up her place beside her son.

"I'm scared," Shamika whispered. She lowered her hands from her face. Jalen's head was fully wrapped and he had a breathing tube in his throat and mouth.

Shamika put her hand on Jalen's much smaller one. "Baby, it's Mama." She hung her head and grabbed a few quick breaths, clearly fighting for control. When she lifted her head, she studied her boy and then brushed her knuckles softly against his cheeks. "Mama's here. Jesus too, baby. It's gonna be okay." She wiped her tears with her free hand. "You keep fighting, Jalen. You're gonna be stronger for this." She looked back at Mary Catherine and the smallest flicker of hope flashed in her eyes. Then she turned back to Jalen. "We'll both be stronger."

The door to the room opened and an older nurse poked her head in. "Mary Catherine?"

"Yes?" She turned to the woman.

"Your friends are out here. They want to talk to you."

Mary Catherine hugged Shamika again. "Want me to stay? I will. I can call in to work tomorrow."

"That's okay. I wanna be alone with my baby."

"I understand." Mary Catherine searched Shamika's face. "Call me or text me if you need anything. We'll get everyone to pray for Jalen, all right?"

"Yes." She managed the slightest smile. "Thank you."

"You're not alone."

Shamika nodded and turned to Jalen again. "I'll be here. Until he opens his eyes and talks to me again."

That was all they could ask for. That Shamika might believe enough to expect the impossible. To look for a miracle.

Mary Catherine stepped out of the room. Tyler and Sami were waiting for her. Sami hugged her first. "How is he?"

"Fighting." She blinked back a wave of tears. "The doctor said it doesn't look good." She pulled a tissue from her purse and pressed it to her eyes. "We have to pray for a miracle. We need to believe."

"Poor little guy." Tyler put his arm around Sami.

Sami sighed. "We all prayed in Marcus's room."

Mary Catherine didn't want to think about Marcus. "Is he staying overnight?" Spending time with Shamika had been good for her. She hadn't once pictured Shelly sitting next to Marcus earlier, or the way the scene had jabbed at her heart.

"No." Tyler stepped up. "Shelly and the Waynes are gone. I guess the doctors are finishing up paperwork. We can take him home." Together the four of them had only Tyler's car. "We could come back and get you later."

"I'll be ready in a few minutes. I can meet you downstairs." She took Sami's hand. "Is that okay?"

"Of course." Sami looked beat, too. They all did. She and Tyler hugged Mary Catherine again. Longer this time. Then they left for the elevator.

Mary Catherine had spotted a small chapel just down the hall. She didn't want to interrupt Shamika's time with her son, and she hardly wanted to be with Marcus after seeing him with Shelly earlier. Not tonight. Not when she couldn't get a grip on her emotions.

She waited until Tyler and Sami were gone, then she headed toward the chapel. It was right across from the elevators. She went inside and found it empty.

The room was small and dimly lit. Just eight pews and a wooden cross at the front. Mary Catherine sat in one of the middle pews, dropped to her knees, and brought her hands to her face. She prayed for Jalen and for his mother and for the future of the youth center. She prayed the shooter would be caught and that progress would someday be made on the streets of inner-city Los Angeles.

Not until she had talked to God about all that did she pray for the thing that was weighing most heavily on her heart. Her words came in quiet whispers. "I let myself start to fall for Marcus, Lord . . . and that was a mistake. I'm sorry. That's not the life You want for me. You've made that clear. So protect my fragile heart, God. Please. When I see Marcus let me see him as a brother. Only that. In Jesus' name, amen."

She lifted her head and gasped.

Sitting across the narrow aisle from her was a police officer. Big and blond, his hat in his hands. He looked at her and nodded politely. "Sorry to startle you. I didn't want to interrupt."

"Is something . . . did Jalen . . . ?"

"No. The boy is still with us. Your prayers matter, Mary Catherine. Keep praying."

"I will." She sniffed and squinted at him, trying to make out the name on his badge. "Have I met you? At the center?"

"No." He put his hat back on his head. "I'm Officer Jag. I'm not from around here, but I was there when the shooting happened. I wanted to update you."

Mary Catherine felt her heart beat faster. "Did they catch him? The shooter?"

"They did. Dwayne Davis is behind bars, which is where he'll stay. But the girl . . . she's very young. She still has a chance."

"What girl?" Mary Catherine turned in the pew so she could see the man better. He had the most unusual eyes. Like a hundred colors in one. And a peace seemed to emanate from him. Maybe because of his uniform. She wasn't sure.

"The girl is Lexy Jones. Dwayne's girlfriend. She's been heading down a dark path." The officer clearly had more to say. He glanced at the back door of the chapel as if he were in a hurry. "Anyway, Marcus asked about the Scared Straight program."

That was true. Mary Catherine knew about that. "He was told it didn't work that well."

"We have another program now. It's newer. More involved. It's called Last Time In. Kids get a tour of the jail, the inmates tell them the truth about being incarcerated. Then they get four weeks of counseling—three times a week. It's intense, but it can work."

Mary Catherine nodded. She liked the idea. "Did you tell Marcus?"

"I can't stay. I'm hoping you might tell him."

"Okay." Mary Catherine had just asked God for a break from Marcus. Now this. "Is the program available here?"

"It's in place, but they need a grant to continue. Ten thousand dollars." Officer Jag stood and moved out of the pew into the aisle. He held his hand out to Mary Catherine. "If you could tell Marcus, I'd appreciate it."

"I will." Mary Catherine stood and shook the man's hand. As she did, the connection worked its way instantly to her soul. Like there was power in his touch. Their eyes met and held and Mary Catherine had the strangest feeling. Like she was on holy ground.

"About your prayers. Just remember . . . God knows better than we do. He always does. Even when it doesn't make sense." He looked to the door again. "Keep praying."

His bright eyes held hers and then he left.

Questions pelted Mary Catherine's soul. How had the officer known she was here? And how did he know she was a friend of Marcus's? How did he know her name? She had no answers. The nurse at the desk must've seen her come this way and told him. And maybe the nurses also knew who she had come with and that they were here with Marcus.

What other explanation was there?

Mainly the officer wanted her to tell Marcus about the Last Time In program. The idea sounded amazing. Certainly kids like Lexy Jones weren't going to stay away from gangs and violence just because a youth center opened in their neighbor-hood. They needed something more.

If the program needed money, Mary Catherine could fund it. She had an account her parents had set up. Money they put aside for her every year as a birthday gift. She didn't need it, so she hadn't touched it. When the time came to use it, she could only justify using it to help someone else.

This would be a perfect reason.

Now she had to tell Marcus. She didn't want to talk to him today. In light of Jalen's life-threatening injuries and the terrify-ing shooting, the news could wait. At least until tomorrow.

But who was Marcus supposed to talk to about the pro-gram? Officer Jag said he wasn't from around here, so then who was the contact? Mary Catherine hurried out of the chapel and stared down the hallway. The man had been gone for less than a minute.

So where was he?

She walked as quickly as she could to the nurses' station. The woman sitting behind the desk was the same one who had been there before. "Hi . . . Officer Jag came into the chapel to talk to me. Can you tell me where he went?"

The woman blinked. "Officer Jag?"

"Yes. He's tall, blond hair. Light eyes." She could see the woman wasn't tracking with her. "He must've come by here."

"There hasn't been an officer on this floor. Not for an hour at least."

Frustration rattled Mary Catherine's nerves. "He was just here." She pointed down the hall toward the chapel. "He left from right there."

"I'm sorry, miss." The woman looked indignant. "I told

you. I haven't seen an officer. Certainly no one by that description." She paused. "What did you say his name was?"

"Officer Jag." She realized that she hadn't gotten a full name. "He said he wasn't from around . . ." Mary Catherine felt her shoulders sink. "Never mind."

She jogged down the hallway toward the chapel and kept going to where it dead-ended. There was no way out. The only direction the officer could've left was right past the nurses' station. Mary Catherine headed that way. This time the woman at the nurses' station was buried in paperwork.

That had to be it. The nurse had been too busy to notice the man.

A sigh made its way through Mary Catherine and she walked to the elevator. Her friends would be ready to go. On her way to the emergency room, Mary Catherine remembered Officer Jag's words about prayer. *God knows better than we do. He always does. Even when it doesn't make sense.*

That was what the man had said, right? Clearly, he had to have been talking about Jalen. The little boy needed everyone praying, everyone believing. Good that the officer was a man of faith.

The city needed more like him, wherever he was from.

She reached Marcus's room. He was sitting up now, getting instructions and paperwork from a nurse. Tyler and Sami were waiting near the door.

Marcus looked at her. "How is he?"

"Not good." She stayed by the door with her friends. "He needs a miracle."

The ride home was quiet. Marcus sat in the front with Tyler, and the two of them did most of the talking. "Police came in when you guys were gone." Marcus leaned his head against the seat. He looked exhausted. "They have the shooter in custody. His girlfriend, too."

"Good." Tyler didn't hesitate. "Makes me think they should arrest everyone in both gangs. Run their rap sheets. Figure out what new crimes they're linked to." He glanced at Marcus, his hand tight on the steering wheel. "Maybe then the younger guys wouldn't be so quick to join."

Mary Catherine stayed silent in the backseat. She looked out the window and thought about Shamika, spending the night at her son's side. The conversation in the car faded and Mary Catherine lifted her eyes to the stars overhead.

God could do this, of course. He could give them a miracle for Jalen.

Now she could only pray that He would.

JAG STOOD NEXT to Aspyn on the opposite side of the child's bed, invisible. Aspyn was ready to fight—just like Jag. She wanted to see the mission succeed and she wanted justice.

"Earth is so difficult . . . full of pain." She held her hand over the boy's head. "Jesus, heal him. Let him live."

Jag loved the heart of his teammate. She was a very great example to him, especially after tonight. "My anger . . . I nearly lost it."

She turned and stared at him. "Dwayne Davis?"

"Yes." Jag still felt ashamed. The feel of the trigger beneath his finger would stay with him always. "I could've killed that boy. I wanted to."

No matter what, they had to be honest with each other. Aspyn faced him. "Why didn't you?"

"I'm an angel. I want to do God's will. The name of Jesus reminded me."

Aspyn exhaled, relieved. "Who said it?"

"Lexy. The girl." He straightened himself, empowered, convinced that his perfect God was with him even in his imperfection. "God used her to get my attention. Just in time."

"She needs help." Aspyn's tone was heavy. She looked at Jalen again. "So many pieces of this mission. We can't miss a moment."

That had never been more true. "I spoke to Mary Catherine in the chapel."

"Do you think she has an idea? Who you are?"

"No." He felt another reason for regret. "I wasn't as careful with Dwayne. The guys on the streets think I'm some monster cop. I need to be careful." He looked deep into her eyes. "I'm sorry. I've talked to the Father about it."

"Then you are forgiven." Aspyn took hold of his hand for a moment. "Let this go." She moved closer to the bed and studied the child. "The hardest thing about earth is that love is not enough. It's never enough."

Jag let her words settle in his soul. He shook his head. "Love is always enough, Aspyn. But there are different kinds of love."

"True." She checked the monitors surrounding the boy. "The child is fading. We need to pray."

And so for the rest of the evening they begged God for a

miracle, asking that He intervene in Jalen's body and that He give doctors wisdom beyond their abilities. Most of all they asked that Jalen be surrounded by love. Not the earthly sort of love that could so easily fail.

But heaven's love.

A love that would always be enough.

15

Marcus was in the middle of an upper body workout in his home gym the next morning when he received the text from Mary Catherine. He hadn't known what to say to her last night, how to bring up the fact that he hadn't asked Shelly Wayne to come to the hospital.

None of it mattered compared to the shooting. He'd gotten word from Officer Kent an hour earlier that Jalen had survived the night. He was still on life support. Still critical.

Now Marcus looked at his phone. The text said simply, *Can we meet this morning? If you're feeling up to it? I need to talk to you about something related to the shooting.*

Marcus had no idea what she wanted to talk about. He only knew that he wanted to see her. More than he wanted to do anything else today. He moved his fingers across his phone. *Definitely. I'd like that. How about eleven o'clock at the Silver Lake Whole Foods. They've got great coffee.*

Her response took a few minutes. *Great. See you then.*

The last thing he wanted was to finish his workout. He was out of danger, barring infection, but his leg throbbed. He couldn't run for a week, but otherwise he'd be fine. The bullet had only grazed him. Aspyn, the woman from the neighborhood, had saved his life.

Last night at the hospital Officer Kent had come by and Marcus had brought up the woman's name. "She pushed me out of the way before the guy fired. Almost like she knew what was going to happen."

"I saw the whole thing." The officer shook his head. "Like she had some sort of advance warning."

"Did you check her out? I mean . . . I guess I wondered if she knew something."

"She's not from the area. No record of her in any of the searches. But we don't think she was involved."

Marcus picked up a pair of fifty-pound dumbbells. Good that Aspyn wasn't working for a gang. But how had she known to push him out of the way? And how come she hadn't been hit? The whole night still didn't add up, but none of it mattered. Not compared with Jalen's struggle to live.

He pushed through his routine for another thirty minutes and then showered and shaved. If this were a different situation, he would've been thrilled at the chance to have coffee with Mary Catherine. But today would be different; he could feel it. Different from how things had been the other night when they walked around his neighborhood.

The incident with Shelly last night had changed things.

Mary Catherine's text had more of a businesslike feel. She was keeping her distance. Not that he blamed her. He really needed to call Shelly and let her know things weren't working out. The difficult part was Coach Wayne. His coach was also his friend, and the last thing Marcus wanted was to hurt the man's niece.

The whole situation was complicated.

He got ready faster than he expected and found a booth at Whole Foods a few minutes earlier than eleven. A baseball cap low on his brow would keep people from recognizing him—something that was rarely a problem. He was six-three and built like an athlete. But in a city like Los Angeles, Marcus didn't stand out unless he was in uniform.

Five minutes later he watched Mary Catherine arrive and he felt a little dizzy. The girl had captured his attention and maybe even his heart. No matter how poorly last night had gone, no matter how sad everyone was, he couldn't put into words how great it was to see Mary Catherine now.

She spotted him and as she approached she seemed to do her best to avoid a hug. They walked together to the coffee bar, poured their drinks, and then returned to the booth. "I heard from Shamika on the way in." Mary Catherine took the spot opposite him. "No change for Jalen."

"No." Marcus leaned his forearms on the table and waited. The fact that the child had taken the bullet intended for him was still more than he could bear. He stared at his drink and after a long moment he took a sip.

"Thanks for meeting." She seemed less comfortable than she'd been the other night. The shooting had deeply affected them all. "Last night, after I visited with Shamika, I went to the chapel."

"On the ICU floor?"

Mary Catherine nodded. "It's small. I was the only one

there. At least at first." Her tone was intent, as if whatever was coming was very serious. "When I finished praying, I opened my eyes and there was a police officer there. Sitting across the aisle from me."

"Charlie Kent?"

"No." She put her hands around her cup of coffee. "His name was Jag. Officer Jag, that's what he called himself." She shrugged one shoulder. "I didn't get his full name."

Marcus wished he'd worn a sweatshirt. The morning had been cold for Southern California. Not quite sixty degrees yet. They were inside, but a chill hung over the Whole Foods booth. "Jag. Sounds familiar."

"He said he wasn't from here." She looked out the window and then back at Marcus. "He told me about a new program. It's called Last Time In. He wanted me to tell you about it."

Strange, Marcus thought, *that he'd find Mary Catherine and ask her to bring the message.* "Why didn't he come tell me himself?"

"He was in a hurry."

"Oh." Marcus wasn't sure where this was going or why the officer wanted him to know. "Tell me about the program."

Mary Catherine pulled some paperwork from her purse. "I stopped by the police station on my way here." She spread the documents on the table in front of her. "Charlie Kent gave me this. It looks amazing."

For the next ten minutes Mary Catherine went over the information. The program was created by a couple of police officers, looking for an alternative to the Scared Straight program. "Prison is always scary, of course." Mary Catherine sounded more relaxed than when she first arrived. "But this takes kids beyond the scared part."

The program involved a prison tour with volunteers acting as chaperones. Police guards would introduce a group of young offenders to actual prisoners. "So they get a realistic picture of prison?" Marcus liked that part. There had to be a sense of reality if the program was going to make a difference.

"Definitely." Mary Catherine turned to the last page of the paperwork. "What makes it different is the group meetings after the prison tour."

Apparently the meetings were run by the same people who volunteered as chaperones. "I'm assuming the volunteers have to be cleared by police?" Marcus looked up, straight into Mary Catherine's eyes. She was more beautiful every day. At least it seemed that way.

"Yes, and trained." Mary Catherine took another drink of her coffee. "It's freezing in here."

"I know." He held his cup and let the steam warm his face. "I have an idea." He stood and nodded to the store. "I'll be right back."

Marcus jogged to the clothing section at the front of the store. His leg didn't hurt as bad as it had this morning. In no time he found two navy blue sweatshirts with white writing that said simply, "Live Life." *Perfect*, he told himself. He grabbed a small for her and a large for himself, paid for them, and hurried back to the booth.

"Here." He handed her the small one. "Maybe now we can actually think."

She laughed and the sound was music to his soul. There hadn't been a reason even to smile since last night. "Thank you." She took it from him, removed the tags, and slipped it over her head. "Mmmm. Much better." Her smile remained. "I love impulsive."

"I figured." He put his sweatshirt on and instantly felt better. "Okay. Where were we?" He had to be careful around her. She had a way of making him forget what he was doing, what he was saying.

"The program." She furrowed her brow, like she was trying to find the serious place from a few minutes ago. "So, it's all voluntary. The kids have to sign up, and they have to agree to the weekly meetings. Volunteers can share their faith as long as they're clear about it up front. It's up to the kids and their guardians if that type of counseling will work for them. The group meetings are very loosely structured. More of a time for kids to open up."

Marcus was starting to understand. "So Bible study could be a part of the group meetings?"

"Exactly. It's a private program. Police involvement is voluntary and outside official work hours." She looked at the paperwork on the table and then at him again. "As long as the kids agree to be led by that volunteer, then the group can take whatever direction of encouragement everyone agrees on."

"Wow. Amazing." Marcus hadn't heard of anything like it. "So this officer, he wanted me to know?"

"He did." Mary Catherine took a sip of her drink and then sat back, pensive. "Last Time In costs around ten grand. Without that there's no program. Maybe Officer Jag thought you could help."

"Of course." Marcus leaned forward, his arms on the table. Mary Catherine looked adorable in her sweatshirt.

She could've designed it herself. He forced himself to focus. "I can get the money to Officer Kent today. Is that how it works?"

"Actually"—she smiled—"it's taken care of. Don't worry about it."

Marcus was surprised. But the topic seemed off limits. Maybe one day he would be close enough to Mary Catherine to know where the money had come from and what other secrets she hadn't shared. He guessed there were many. "Great." He nodded. "So how do I help?"

"You chaperone." Mary Catherine looked straight at him. "Charlie Kent says most of the kids from the streets love you. Whatever you tell them to do, they'll do it."

"Not Dwayne Davis." He raised his brow.

"But his girlfriend, Lexy Jones. She's a different story." Mary Catherine began folding up the papers in front of her. "Police think she made the call, the one that tipped off the department about the fact that someone from the WestKnights wanted you dead."

"His girlfriend?" Marcus tried to imagine that life.

Over the next few minutes Mary Catherine explained more of the details. The police wanted to offer Lexy a chance at the Last Time In program. "It's either that or she serves five years. At least. She was in the passenger seat when Dwayne fired." Mary Catherine frowned. "Even if she tried to save your life by tipping off the police."

"Has anyone talked to Lexy about it?" Marcus liked the idea. If someone could reach the girl now, it might change her life. It might save it.

"No. She's in jail for now."

Marcus remembered something he hadn't asked Charlie Kent. "How old were these kids?"

"Dwayne's eighteen. They have evidence he committed at least two other murders. He can be tried as an adult, so he's probably looking at life." Mary Catherine sighed. "Lexy . . . she's just sixteen."

"Man." Marcus shook his head. He looked down at his empty cup. The problem was so much bigger than he ever imagined. *God, whatever You want me to do, I'll do it.* He met Mary Catherine's eyes again. "If you're asking if I'll volunteer, the answer is yes."

"Good." Her smile started in her eyes. "I told them I would, too. I'll talk to Sami and Tyler later. They'd be perfect. The whole program takes about four weeks. It's one Saturday and then eight weeknights."

"Perfect. I leave for spring training February eighth." Marcus felt his hope surge. He checked the calendar on his phone. "The timing couldn't be better."

"So . . . that's why we had to meet today." She looked hesitant. "Training starts tomorrow at noon and again Friday night. Saturday is the prison tour. Not a lot of warning." She paused. "I guess usually the volunteers are family or friends of the kids who go through the program. The police volunteers oversee it, but the others who help out usually have a personal reason why they're involved."

Marcus uttered a sad chuckle. "I guess after last night we're qualified."

"Yes." Mary Catherine slid the folded documents across the table. "Look these over." She checked the time on her phone. "I have to run. If you don't hear from me, I'll see you tomorrow night at the police station a few blocks from the youth center. The one on Fourth."

Apparently their time together was over. Marcus stood and waited while Mary Catherine stepped out of the booth. Again she seemed in too much of a hurry for a hug. She did smile, though. "Thanks for meeting. I think this will help. Really."

"I hope so." Marcus didn't have time to say anything else. She was already distancing herself from him. "Thanks for including me." He raised his hand. "See you tomorrow."

She waved and then turned and headed for the exit. Before he had time to think of what to do next she was gone. He picked up the papers from the table and slipped them into the back pocket of his jeans. There was still so much more he wanted to say. He would've wondered whether the last hour had happened at all if not for two things. His navy sweatshirt with the words "Live Life."

And the faint smell of her perfume.

SHE COULDN'T HAVE stayed another moment. Mary Catherine rushed across the parking lot to her car and left in record time. Another minute with Marcus and she would've cracked. She would've asked him why Shelly had been there last night and what he was doing with a girl he didn't really care about.

Her eyes would've given her away and Marcus would've known for sure what she was feeling. How she had never felt more drawn to a guy in all her life. She had tried to talk herself out of everything she felt for him. Nothing about it made sense, and most certainly nothing would ever come from it.

But until she could figure herself out, she couldn't allow Marcus to know any of this.

Not until she was home did she remember the sweatshirt. She looked down and thought again of the sweet, impulsive moment. Marcus running through the store getting them both warmer clothes. Once she was inside she looked at herself in the mirror.

Marcus had no idea how apropos the message was. "Live Life." Yes, that's exactly what she needed to do. And she needed to do so without thinking about Marcus Dillinger. Especially over the next few days. *Treat him like a brother*, she told herself. Yes, she had to learn to think about Marcus differently, stop herself from reacting every time she was with him.

No matter what her heart had to say about it.

16

TYLER WAS THRILLED WHEN he heard about the Last Time In program. It was the first time since the shooting that he and Sami felt there was something they could do. Something that might help the kids on the streets. The youth center alone wasn't enough. Tyler agreed with Marcus.

Mary Catherine had presented the idea, and now Sami was on board, too. Tonight, though, Tyler didn't want to think about the prison program or the little boy still fighting for his life at Cedars-Sinai. Even if only for a few hours.

Tonight was the double date with Marcus and Shelly.

Marcus had talked about canceling. He didn't seem as into Shelly as he'd been at the beginning. But Tyler had talked Marcus into sticking with the plan. Now Marcus and Shelly would meet Tyler and Sami at the restaurant in just a few minutes. Cherry Lane, it was called. A beautiful place situated in the hills above Los Angeles. Tyler walked with Sami through the dining area to a table by the window.

A balcony just off the back gave people a place to admire the view, so after they had their lemon water, Tyler led her outside. He put his arm around her and they looked at the stars. "Reminds me of that night on your grandparents' roof. All those years ago."

"Feels like yesterday." Sami looked into his eyes. "I sort of wish we were having dinner alone. It's been so crazy."

"I know." He took gentle hold of her face and kissed her. "I think Marcus needs tonight."

"With Shelly?" Sami was clearly trying to be nice. But she couldn't hide the disdain in her tone. "I don't get it with them."

Tyler laughed. "No one does. That's why he needs tonight. I have a feeling being around us . . . you know, it'll help him see."

"See what?"

Certainty filled Tyler. "That she's not the right girl."

"I hope so." Sami looked out over the city. "He never looks at Shelly the way he looks at Mary Catherine."

"I wondered about that." Tyler put his arm around her again. "We haven't had time to talk. Feels like weeks." He thought about the two of them, Marcus and Mary Catherine. "Does she like him?"

Sami hesitated. "Everything is complicated with Mary Catherine. She hasn't said, but I can feel it."

"Time will tell." Tyler put his hands on her shoulders and faced her. "You look beautiful. If I haven't told you lately."

"Not since we pulled into the parking lot." She grinned at him. "What if I hadn't found you?"

"What?" He pulled out his most surprised look. "You

didn't find me, baby. I found you. Remember? On Facebook."

Sami laughed. "You have a point." She swayed in his arms. "So what if you hadn't written to me? Where would we be?"

Times like this Tyler could easily be overcome with the impossibility of all that had led them to this place. His blown out shoulder, his time being homeless, and then his job as a maintenance worker at Merrill Place. But nothing really turned around until Tyler met Virginia Hutcheson. The fact that her daughter knew Marcus Dillinger and would think to contact him on Tyler's behalf? No one could've seen that coming, or the fact that Sami would break up with her boyfriend after her few hours with Tyler in Florida.

A movie script with everything that had happened would have been tossed in the trash. Too impossible.

Yet God had done it all.

"Which reminds me." Tyler had asked Marcus to be a little late tonight. He had his reasons. "I know it hasn't been long, you and me. We only found each other a few months ago."

"That's not true." Sami linked her hands around the back of Tyler's neck. "We found each other when we were kids."

"True." Tyler loved her more every day. He let himself get lost in her eyes. "I mean, we've only been seeing each other a few months this time around." He caught her face in his hands. "But I want you to know something."

"What?" She grinned. The stars overhead had nothing on the sparkle in her eyes.

"I love you, Sami . . ." His words stacked up in his heart and he couldn't stop himself. "I know you want things between us to go slow. I understand. You and Arnie were serious and . . . well, I don't want to rush you. But . . . I love you. I do." Suddenly he stopped and at the same time he started laughing. "Maybe I could let you talk."

Sami's smile took up her whole face. "I was wondering." She laughed and the sound mixed with the music to become the most beautiful thing Tyler had ever heard. "First . . . I love you, too." Her laughter faded, and her eyes held his. "I've always loved you."

Tyler looked down. Just to make sure he wasn't floating. He turned to her again. She loved him? "Really?"

"Always." She brought her lips to his and kissed him. "Every day I wake up and thank God for bringing you back into my life." She searched his eyes. "I don't want to think about what would've happened if you hadn't written to me."

"Me either." Tyler wanted to raise his fists in the air and shout for joy. But he controlled himself. "So . . . I know you said you needed time . . . you just got out of a relationship. But . . . I can't wait to ask you." He searched her eyes. "Would you be my girlfriend, Sami? I mean, I'd like to ask you to be more than that." He grinned at her. "But first things first."

She dipped her head for a moment, laughing again. When she looked up he saw nothing but absolute assurance in her eyes. "Yes, Tyler. I'd love to be your girlfriend." She hugged him and the two of them swayed some more. She whispered close to his face. "I thought you'd never ask. With you I'm myself. I feel like I can breathe."

"You believed in me when no one else did."

"Always." She put her head on his shoulder. "Don't ever leave me."

"I won't." Just then one of their favorite songs came on. James Taylor's "You've Got a Friend." "Dance with me?"

"Forever." They waltzed around the deck, and Tyler could picture where this would go. The wonder of it all filled his heart. But then, wonder was part of the process. Choosing to see and believe, to hold on to faith even when nothing made sense. The way he'd felt a year ago. But all of that might as well have been a lifetime away. Someday soon he would ask her grandfather for her hand in marriage. And one day in the not too distant future they would dance like this at their wedding.

Tyler could hardly wait.

MARCUS AND SHELLY were fifteen minutes late to dinner, just like Tyler had asked them to be. They reached the table just as Tyler and Sami were returning from the deck out back.

"Hey, guys!" Marcus hugged Tyler, then Sami. Shelly did the same. "You two look happy."

"It's official!" Tyler held Sami's hand as they sat down. "We're in love."

Shelly looked confused. "I thought you two were already . . ."

"It's a long story." Tyler laughed. "But it's all good now."

Marcus looked from his friends to Shelly. He figured she might need more of an explanation, but she was checking her phone. No longer interested in Sami and Tyler. Marcus hated the way that made him feel about her.

Shelly looked at him. "Sweetie, order me a glass of chardonnay. Whatever the waiter recommends." She winked at him. "Restroom break." And with that she left the table and headed for the back of the restaurant.

Marcus watched her go. Was she serious? Shelly was only nineteen. He looked at Tyler and put his elbows on the table. "She's not twenty-one."

"I was thinking that." Tyler made a face to show he empathized with him. "Difficult."

Sami seemed to be checking the ice in her water. She smiled at Tyler and then Marcus. "How was your coffee with Mary Catherine?"

"Short." Marcus could feel his heart soften at the mention of her name. "Hey, I'm happy for you two. I know Shelly doesn't get it. But the two of you, it means a lot. Another piece of the most unbelievable story ever."

"Thanks, man." Tyler smiled and slipped his arm around Sami's shoulders. "How are things with you and Shelly?"

Marcus furrowed his brow. "I'm trying to figure it out, but it's not really working. I mean . . . just being around you two, it's kind of obvious. She's very young."

The waitress came, and Marcus ordered a Perrier and lime for Shelly. She returned to the table as the drinks were being delivered. Marcus had no idea how she would react. She looked at the drink and then at him. "Tell me this is a Tanqueray and tonic."

"Perrier and lime." He smiled at her. "Come on, Shelly. You're not old enough. No one else is drinking."

"Are you serious?" Shelly rolled her eyes. She was clearly frustrated. "I've been drinking since I was seventeen. You know that."

This was getting awkward. It was as if Shelly didn't re-member Tyler and Sami sitting right across from them. "Well. Drinking's not my thing. I think *you* know that."

"Fine." She raised one eyebrow at him. "Your loss. I'm a better date after a few glasses of wine."

"I'll have to settle for sober." Marcus wished he could dig a tunnel beneath the table, usher Shelly back to the car, and take her home. He smiled weakly at her and then at his friends. "Are we ready to order?"

The entire night continued that way, in fits and starts. Shelly never found the social rhythm that his dates usually found. He felt himself counting down the minutes, glad that it was only a dinner date and not an all-day hike. Something he couldn't have gotten out of.

Throughout dinner, Shelly hung on his elbow. She would pat his arm and lean up and kiss his cheek. Already people were looking at their table, the way they sometimes did if they recognized him as the pitcher for the Dodgers. But with Shelly acting this way, they drew even more attention. The kind of attention that didn't seem to have anything to do with his being a baseball player.

Before dinner ended, Shelly looked over her shoulder. "You think the paparazzi might be here? You know, waiting for us outside?" She fixed her hair. "I've always wanted to be in the tabloids!"

Marcus folded his napkin on his plate. That was all. He smiled at Tyler and Sami. "Early morning for me tomorrow. Running stairs again."

"No!" Shelly gasped. Her voice was definitely louder than anyone else's around them. "Not with your injured leg!"

"My leg's fine." Marcus could feel the stares they were getting. "Anyway"—he slid four twenties to Tyler—"this is for the bill. I think we'll get going."

Tyler stood and so did Sami. Another round of hugs and Tyler seemed to try to ease the awkwardness. "I have to be in early, too. Fun dinner, though."

Shelly was still sitting down.

"We're not leaving! Please tell me we're not leaving!" Her voice was whiny and high-pitched. She wanted to be noticed. There could be no other explanation. So someone would realize who Marcus was and just maybe take their picture.

Marcus felt anger well up inside him. How could he have thought this would be a good time? He clenched his jaw and reached for Shelly's hand. "Come on. I really do have an early day tomorrow."

Thankfully, she stood and slinked up next to him like they were attached at the hip.

"Well, you two lovebirds." Shelly waved her fingers. "It's been real!" She nuzzled Marcus's neck. "Till next time!"

On the way out, Shelly whispered to him, "No one's home at my house. I planned it that way."

Marcus ignored her. Dating Shelly reminded him of every wrong girl he'd ever been with. He felt sick about it. What had he been thinking?

Once they were inside his Hummer, Marcus turned to her. "Shelly."

"Yes, love?" She leaned forward, so her low cut blouse left nothing to the imagination.

Marcus kept his eyes on hers. "Look. Tonight . . . it wasn't good."

She seemed to come to her senses. "What do you mean?"

"Everything." He took a jagged breath. "You seemed really pushy."

"It's a date." She sat back against the passenger door and crossed her arms. "How was I supposed to act?"

Like Mary Catherine, he wanted to say. Instead he found a dose of compassion. "It's fine. Let's just go."

They drove home in silence, and Marcus turned up the radio. Otherwise the silence would've been deafening. He kept his right hand on the wheel so she wouldn't think about trying to hold it. There was no point explaining how he felt. Maybe it wasn't all Shelly's fault. Ever since his walk with Mary Catherine, since her question that night, he found himself wondering the same thing. Who was pursuing whom? And why couldn't he stop comparing Shelly to Mary Catherine?

Marcus walked her up to her front door, but before she could press up against him, he kissed her cheek. "Goodnight, Shelly."

"Are you breaking up with me?" She batted her eyes. She looked sad, but her eyes were dry.

"We aren't in an official relationship. We're just dating." He slipped his hands into his pockets and walked down the stairs. He didn't wait for Shelly's response as he climbed behind the wheel of his SUV and drove off. Only then did he actually feel like he could take a breath. What in the world was he thinking, dating Shelly Wayne? He needed to talk to Coach and explain that things weren't working with her. And not just because of Shelly's antics.

But because all night long the face that filled his heart and mind wasn't Shelly's.

It was Mary Catherine's.

17

MARY CATHERINE MET MARCUS in the parking lot of the police station around noon the next day. Despite all her determination to see Marcus in a different light, to remember the way he looked with Shelly fawning over him, she couldn't get her heart in line.

From the moment he walked up to her she felt the heat in her cheeks. Felt her heart beating faster than before. The faint smell of his cologne made her breathless. *Come on, Mary Catherine.* She swallowed, desperate for a grip. "I have no idea what to expect." Her voice sounded shaky. She looked up at him as they reached the door of the station. She needed to keep her mind on the matter at hand. Learning how to work with the girls during their prison visit.

"Can I say something? Before we go in." Marcus stopped and smiled at her. "You look beautiful. Just didn't think I should miss the chance to say so."

She held her breath for a few seconds. "Thank you." Her

rebellious heart soared at his compliment. He looked great, too. Dark blue jeans and a white short-sleeve shirt. But Mary Catherine didn't dare say so.

Even being attracted to him was wrong. He had a girl-friend, and she had promised God she wasn't going to date. Not ever. But then why did she feel like this? And why was Marcus making things more difficult by being so kind?

"I heard about your date last night." Mary Catherine started walking again. She shot him a teasing look. "Sounds like a good time."

Sami had spilled all the details back at the apartment last night. About Shelly's request for wine and the way she clung to Marcus throughout the night. Sami had said Marcus couldn't get out of the restaurant fast enough.

Now Marcus rubbed the bridge of his nose and shook his head. "She's a lot of work, for sure."

"Well . . ." Mary Catherine grinned, enjoying the game. As long as she could joke with him, she wouldn't have to worry about why it sometimes seemed he felt attracted to her, too. She tilted her head, as if she were genuinely concerned about Shelly and him. "I'm sure you two will figure things out."

Marcus opened the door for her and they walked inside. At first he looked like he might disagree about figuring things out with Shelly, but before he could speak, Charlie Kent approached them. "Marcus. Mary Catherine." He held out his hand. "Great to see you both!"

"Thanks." Marcus took the lead. "Our friends will be here, too. Sami Dawson and Tyler Ames."

"Great. I'm expecting them." He checked a clipboard on the nearest table. He scanned the page. "It looks like we have six young ladies going through the program and a dozen volunteers. Those are the numbers we like."

"We won't meet the girls tonight, right?" Mary Catherine hadn't been sure about that.

"No." Officer Kent smiled. "They're back at home. Once they agreed to the program, we released them from jail." He frowned. "Jail and prison are very different. These girls haven't seen the inside of a prison. This will be an awakening for sure."

Sami and Tyler arrived and together with the other volunteers they were ushered into a classroom. Officer Kent led the training. "These kids are hard and angry and defeated. The only reason they agreed to this program is it beats serving time. They won't change easily. That's important to know."

Mary Catherine pulled her notebook from her purse and scribbled down everything the officer said. Marcus sat next to her and every once in a while their arms brushed against each other. Mary Catherine discreetly moved her chair a few inches away.

His touch was more than she could take.

Charlie Kent continued, explaining another reality for these girls. "Girls around this age, thirteen, fourteen, fifteen . . . they've most likely been sexually abused; many have been raped. More than once for some of them." He leveled his gaze at them. "You feel good about yourself if you feed a teenager a healthy meal? Parents of these girls feel good if a teenager doesn't get raped under their roof." He paused. "They come from broken homes. There's no supervision much of the time."

He told a story where he was talking to the stepmother of

a girl who had gone through the program a few years ago. "She told me she couldn't understand why her daughter didn't want to be at home. She said, 'She's been raped by her uncles and cousins. But never at my house. You'd think that would matter to a kid.'"

Mary Catherine couldn't decide if she felt angry or just nauseous.

Dear God, what difference can we make with these girls? What's the point? She thought about the faces on her refrigerator, the kids from Africa she sponsored each month. *I'd be better off going to their village. Building them a home and providing them food and love,* she thought. Things were too far gone here.

"You okay?" Marcus whispered to her. He studied her eyes. "This is tough."

"It is." She smiled. Why was he so kind to her? "I didn't know . . . it was so bad."

"Me either." He looked sad. "Glad I'm here."

She nodded.

Charlie Kent explained that another problem was the girls' dishonesty. "They lie about everything. Just to feel like they have power. They don't want to share the truth and you can't force them to. Truth makes them feel vulnerable. Remember that when you get to the group-share part of the program. They have to talk a long time before the walls fall enough for them to be honest."

Great. Mary Catherine wrote the word *liar* in her notebook. The girls had been raped and used and sucked into gang activity. They were hard and callused and they wouldn't tell the truth for a long time, if ever.

So what was the point?

The training went on for another hour. They talked about the EastTown Boyz and the WestKnights, how the gangs formed, what their purposes were, and how easily the younger kids got drawn into joining.

"It's all these kids know." Officer Kent folded his arms. "Mom was a WestKnight, Dad was a WestKnight, brother and sister were WestKnights. A kid turns twelve, there's no question about what his future holds. He'll be a WestKnight. Unless someone shoots him first."

Mary Catherine tried to table her discouragement. The training was important. They learned that the EastTown Boyz mainly dealt heroin. WestKnights dealt cocaine. Heroin wasn't as costly as cocaine but the customers were more desperate.

"For the most part kids in gangs don't do the heavy drugs, they deal them. They smoke pot and they drink. But the hard drugs are business to them. They get them from the Mexican cartels and entrepreneur street dealers. It's how gangs stay afloat financially."

When the training was over, the volunteers each collected a booklet of additional information from Officer Kent. "Read through this. Tomorrow we'll talk about prison life. You need to know what to expect. After a week or so we'll give you materials for your group sessions. How to transition these girls from gangs to getting an education and even a job. Practical ways they can find a life outside of what they've known."

Officer Kent also gave each pair of volunteers the name of the girl they'd be working with and her contact information. "We encourage you to reach out before the prison visit Saturday. You can call or text. Just some way so they know you're there for them. You care. Whether they believe that at first or not."

Back outside in the parking lot, Mary Catherine and Marcus met up with Tyler and Sami. All of them looked drained. "That was a lot." Sami linked arms with Tyler. "I didn't feel ready for this before. But I feel way worse now. How can I help a girl who's gone through all that?"

"Who'd you get?" Tyler looked from Mary Catherine to Marcus.

"Lexy Jones." Marcus looked at the information card on the girl. "I think Officer Jag arranged that."

Mention of the man's name reminded Mary Catherine she hadn't talked to Charlie Kent about Jag. Where exactly did he work, and how was he connected to the local department? She turned to Sami. "What about y'all?"

"I love when you say *y'all*." Tyler smiled at her. "Just for the record."

Mary Catherine returned the smile.

"We know, we know." Sami laughed. "It's that Southern thing."

"Exactly." She grinned. "I can't help it if y'all weren't raised right."

"About our girl." Tyler looked intently at the information card he and Sami had been given. "Her name is Alicia. She's fourteen. Arrested for grand theft auto and truancy."

"Looks like we've got the rougher of the two." Marcus made a face that said how serious things were for Lexy. "Our girl's connected to one of the most brutal killers on the street."

"Again . . . how are we supposed to help?" Sami looked lost, like she wasn't sure she could go through with it.

"I think this is where faith comes in." Tyler sighed. "I mean, none of us is prepared, but we're willing. I guess we ask God to make up the difference."

"He's right." Marcus put his hands in his pockets. "Maybe we could do that now?"

"I like it." Tyler gave Marcus a friendly slap on the arm. "You always have the best ideas, man."

The group huddled up, their arms around each other's shoulders. Mary Catherine was between Sami and Marcus, but all she could feel was the way Marcus's arms felt around her. Strong and warm and secure. She had her arm around his waist. Nothing in all her life had felt so natural and wonderful.

So real.

God, help me . . . I can't stop these feelings. Mary Catherine closed her eyes, tried everything possible not to think about Marcus beside her. *See, God? Nothing works. I can never have this except in random moments. Marcus will never be mine. So please . . . help me keep my distance. Help me keep my wayward heart in line.*

Tyler started the prayer and Mary Catherine did everything she could to focus. Tyler asked God to give them supernatural wisdom and protection, that their efforts might truly change the lives of the girls in the program. Mary Catherine listened and prayed along with Tyler, but she found herself wishing the prayer would go on forever.

When it was finished, and after Tyler and Sami headed for his car, Marcus gave her shoulders a light squeeze. His smile warmed her all the way through. Mary Catherine drew a long breath. "Well . . . I think I'll go visit Lexy. Take her to Elysian

Park for a hike. She doesn't know me, so she might not want to go. But I want to try."

"Good idea." Marcus's eyes lit up at the idea. "I'll go with you. I was sort of thinking the same thing."

"Well . . ." Mary Catherine shook her head. "Maybe not this time." She willed him to understand. "Sometimes girls open up better to a girl. At least at first."

Marcus thought about that. "Okay. I guess." He seemed disappointed. "I really would like to meet her before we see her Saturday morning."

"Maybe tomorrow." Mary Catherine folded her arms in front of her. "Thanks for being so kind. And for doing this. It doesn't seem like it, but I have to believe it'll help."

"It has to." He put his hand on her shoulder, but she was already pulling away.

She waved. "I'll let you know how it goes."

He chuckled. "You're always in a hurry."

"I guess." Mary Catherine gave him her best smile. So he wouldn't know how she was really feeling. "I've always got somewhere to be." She turned for her car. "See you tomorrow!"

"See you."

Mary Catherine watched him in her rearview mirror. He stood there, watching her until she drove away. Only then did the tears sting at her eyes. She blinked them back. It was nothing to cry over. She would never have Marcus Dillinger. "Come on, MC." She wiped her cheeks. "Get over it. You're stronger than that."

She had no choice, really. Her heart would figure it out eventually.

A few blocks down the road, she pulled over and used the number on Lexy's information card to text her. *Hey. It's Mary Catherine. I'm the volunteer who'll be helping you this weekend. I wondered if I could come by and take you for a walk. Maybe get coffee.*

Lexy must've had her phone with her, because she was quick to respond. *No coffee.*

"Okay." Mary Catherine tried to think of what to say next. Her fingers worked their way over the small keyboard. *A milkshake, maybe?*

The response took a little longer this time. *Fine. I can't be out late.*

Lexy's answer made her smile. The girl was clearly guilty of far more than staying out late. But like Officer Kent said, these kids would lie. They didn't trust anyone. Least of all some stranger. Still, Mary Catherine felt a glimmer of hope. Lexy was willing. Before she pulled away she texted Shamika. *How's Jalen? The two of you have been on my mind all day.*

Shamika texted back quickly. *The same. His doctors say the longer he's in a coma, the worse it is. Please pray.*

I am. I will. Just like that Mary Catherine had plans for both day and night. She tapped out another text. *I'll come up and visit after dinner.*

Thank you. Shamika included a praying hands emoji. *Sometimes I like to sit here alone with him, because that's most like usual for us. Just him and me. But other times I feel like I'll go crazy if I don't have someone to talk to. I'll see you tonight.*

Mary Catherine appreciated the joy that filled her heart

and mind as she drove away. She didn't need Marcus to feel happy about what God was doing in her life. Didn't need his arm around her shoulders or his kind eyes looking into hers. Days like today it was enough to simply carry out the message on the sweatshirt he'd given her. *Live life.*

With God's help, that's exactly what she planned to do.

18

MARY CATHERINE WASN'T SURPRISED at the small house Lexy lived in or the fact that it appeared to be in one of the roughest projects, just a few blocks from the youth center. Even so, she didn't worry about her own safety. This was the sort of thing Mary Catherine lived for. She knocked on the door and waited.

A young teenage girl answered. She looked down the street one way and then the other. "Come in. Hurry."

Clearly the girl didn't want to be seen talking to her. "Are you Lexy?"

"Yeah." She cocked her head back. "My grandma wants to meet you."

An older woman shuffled into the room. "My name's Anna." She shook Mary Catherine's hand. "I don't understand . . . Why do you want to take my Lexy out?"

Mary Catherine was actually glad the woman cared enough to ask. She explained her role as a volunteer for the

Last Time In program. "The goal is that this will be their last time behind bars."

"I have my own crimes. Years ago." The old woman nodded. She was still beautiful, and clearly Lexy favored her. But her hands shook and she looked frail, timid. "Too many men. I'm trying to make up for it now." Tears filled her eyes. "The guns and violence, kids killing kids. It gets worse every year. You aren't someone unless you're a WestKnight or an EastTown gang member. It's not good for anyone." Anna looked at her granddaughter. "It's not too late for Lexy. She needs a way out."

Lexy stared at the floor, like she was unwilling to look at her grandmother or acknowledge the truth in the woman's statement.

Mary Catherine was still standing. She took hold of the older woman's hand for a brief few seconds. "I want to help." She looked back at Lexy. "The police agree with you. They think she has a chance. That with help she could find her way out of this life." Mary Catherine paused. "If she wants to."

Anna nodded. "Very good." She looked deep into Mary Catherine's eyes. "Take care of her." She wiped at a tear. "She's all I have."

It was a common theme here in the projects. People were broken and battered, scared and alone. Most of them were lucky to have one person who cared for them or lived with them. For Anna, that was Lexy. Her granddaughter. The only family she had.

"We'll be gone a few hours, if that's okay." Mary Catherine had a plan in mind. But she wanted to clear it with this dear woman first.

"Yes. Please." She was trembling again. "Lexy won't talk to me. Maybe she'll open up with you."

There was so much Mary Catherine wanted to say. Questions she wanted to ask. But she needed to get to know Lexy first. "Yes, ma'am." She nodded to Anna. "I hope so."

They were in Mary Catherine's Hyundai and nearly out of the neighborhood before Lexy said anything. "Do all the volunteers do this? Take their kid out for ice cream?"

Mary Catherine thought for a minute. "Probably not." She glanced at Lexy. "I figured it'd be better if we knew each other at least a little before Saturday."

"You know what I did?" Lexy looked small and uncomfortable in the passenger seat. She stared at Mary Catherine with big eyes. "Cops tell you?"

"Yes." Mary Catherine kept her eyes on the road. "You're Dwayne Davis's girl. You were with him when he robbed a Seven-Eleven and you were with him when he killed a boy from the EastTown gang." The light ahead turned red. Mary Catherine looked straight at Lexy. "You were also with him the other night when he shot that four-year-old."

Lexy exhaled and stared out the window. After several minutes she muttered, "Why you want anything to do with me?"

"Do you want to be in a gang?" Mary Catherine felt funny using the word. But it was all Lexy would understand. "Or is it just because of Dwayne?"

Maybe it was the first time Lexy had thought about it. She took her time answering, and for a long time she stared straight ahead. Finally she looked at Mary Catherine. "I like it. Every girl wanna be Dwayne's shorty." Defiance rang in her voice. "But he picked me."

Mary Catherine thought about correcting her English but then let it go. One step at a time. "We're here." She pointed to a Dairy Queen up ahead. "You want a milkshake or a sundae?"

Lexy seemed stumped by the question. They pulled into the parking lot and the two of them walked inside. At the counter, Mary Catherine pointed to the menu. "Have whatever you want."

"Anything?" The word sounded almost angry, as if Lexy didn't believe this. Like there had to be a catch. "What about a burger?"

"Sure. Get a burger and ice cream, if you want." Mary Catherine wasn't hungry. Besides, there was nothing on the menu she could eat. She had to give her heart a fighting chance.

"Okay." Lexy looked up at the menu, then back at Mary Catherine. "What's the thing where they chop up candy and ice cream in a cup?"

"A Blizzard?"

"Yeah." It was the first time Lexy had smiled since Mary Catherine stepped into her house. "I'll have a cheeseburger and that."

The girl behind the counter looked impatient. "What kind of Blizzard?"

Lexy settled on vanilla ice cream with Oreo cookies and hot fudge sauce. "And whipped cream."

"'Please,'" Mary Catherine reminded her.

The surprise on Lexy's face was as real as the air they were breathing. She turned back to the cashier. "Please."

Good, Mary Catherine thought. *It's a start.*

"Where we goin'?" Lexy focused on her Blizzard. "You said we'd be out for a couple hours."

"I'm taking you to Elysian Park. It's near Dodger Stadium." Mary Catherine used her GPS to lead the way. The park was another fifteen miles from the Dairy Queen.

Lexy looked nervous. "You been there before?"

"No. They have trails. There'll be people all around." Mary Catherine smiled, her eyes on the road. "I thought we could walk for a while, get to know each other. We can leave whenever you want and then I'll take you home."

Lexy didn't say anything. Either she didn't have an opinion or she didn't care. Twenty minutes later they parked in the lot at Academy Road and Elysian Park Drive. Mary Catherine had read that the other side of the park could be shady. This part was supposed to have well-marked trails with beautiful views of the city and the stadium.

It was a park Tyler and Sami had told her about.

They started up the trail and Mary Catherine waited until they found their stride. Lexy was still finishing her Blizzard. "What do you want to tell me, Lexy?"

She peered over the edge of her cup at Mary Catherine and shrugged. "Got nothing to say."

This wasn't going to be easy. But the time was worth it. She could feel the girl's guard dropping, even just a little. "Why do you want to be Dwayne Davis's girl?"

Lexy cocked her head back again, doing her best to look tough, no doubt. "Dwayne gonna be leader of the gang. That makes me famous, too."

Mary Catherine resisted the urge to roll her eyes. In Lexy's world, her reason mattered. Mary Catherine was careful to use a gentle tone: "Lexy . . . Dwayne's behind bars. He's not getting out. Not ever."

The cockiness in Lexy's expression faded. Suddenly she looked like a lost little girl. "That ain't true. Dwayne told me he was getting out."

"He's not." Mary Catherine looked at Lexy. They were walking, but their pace was slow. "They've got Dwayne on at least two counts of murder. Attempted murder. Dealing. Robbery. I talked to the police, Lexy. They don't believe Dwayne will ever get out."

The girl looked at her nearly empty ice cream cup, and at the next trashcan she threw away what was left. Again they walked in silence for a while until Mary Catherine could think of the right next question.

"You'd be locked up, too. That's why you're doing this program. So you don't have to. Because you're so young." Mary Catherine wasn't sure how much the girl understood. "You know that, right?"

"I guess." She crossed her arms tightly in front of herself as they walked.

"What happens when your guy goes to prison? Are you still part of the gang?"

Lexy looked frightened again. "The guys, they take turns. They'll fight it out. Who gets me next."

Her answer wasn't entirely clear but Mary Catherine figured she'd heard enough to know. The guys would take turns with her? That could only mean one thing. Lexy was little more than a child, and yet she took it in stride. Like being treated that way was a rite of passage.

"You know something, Lexy?" Mary Catherine had to start

speaking truth into the girl. "You don't have to let them do that. What's in it for you? Being in the gang and having guys do that?"

"They keep me safe." She jerked her head back again. "Once a WestKnight, always a WestKnight. EastTown Boyz don't mess with you if your man's a WestKnight. You in, then."

"So the EastTown Boyz don't hurt you . . . but the West-Knight boys do. How is that a good thing?" Mary Catherine kept her words slow and even. She didn't want to make Lexy too upset. Officer Kent had warned that when pushed too hard most of these girls would shut down. Sometimes for good.

But Lexy wasn't shutting down. Her expression softened, like maybe she had never thought about that before. How staying in the WestKnights could be a good thing when she was going to be hurt either way.

Lexy looked up at her. "What other choice I got?"

"That's what we're going to try to figure out, me and you." Mary Catherine hesitated. "You know who your other volunteer is?"

The girl looked straight ahead, her steps slow. "I get two?"

"You all do." She smiled. "The other one is a guy. Marcus Dillinger."

Lexy stopped walking. She stared at Mary Catherine and her eyes grew wide. "From the Dodgers? The pitcher?"

"Yes." Mary Catherine let that sink in for a few seconds. "The one Dwayne tried to kill."

"No." She started to shake her head. "He can't come. He can't see me." She looked over her shoulder like she might run. "He'll know it's me."

"Lexy." Mary Catherine put her hand on the girl's back. "Honey, Marcus knows who you are. He wanted to do this *because* of that. He wanted to come today. We both believe you have a chance. A way out of this."

"I don't want to meet him." She looked away and began walking again, faster this time. As if she were in a hurry to finish the hike. "I just wanna go home."

Mary Catherine kept up with her. Lexy was shifty and hesitant and probably—like Officer Kent said—ready to shut down completely. Whatever the girl felt deep inside her heart, it would take much effort to find it.

If they could find it at all.

LEXY HAD NEVER felt like this in all her life. She didn't want to say too much, didn't want to open up. But something about Mary Catherine made her do it. Like the white girl really cared.

"Tell me about your parents." Mary Catherine wouldn't give up. No matter how quiet and rude Lexy was, the girl kept trying.

"What's to tell?" Lexy stared at the ground as they walked. "My dad was killed when I was a baby. My mom's in prison. You met my grandma." She was about to tell Mary Catherine how she'd raised herself, but at that exact minute they rounded a corner and stopped. Two police officers were arresting a skinny white man with a long beard. Right here on the trail.

Lexy stopped and next to her Mary Catherine did the same thing. The guy looked creepy.

"Come on." Mary Catherine put her arm around Lexy's shoulder and eased her past the scene.

One of the officers turned to her. "You girls okay?"

"Yes, sir." Mary Catherine answered first. "Is it safe?"

"This park?" The officer glanced at the guy in handcuffs. "It's never completely safe up here. But yes. You can get back to the parking lot okay. Call nine-one-one if you see anything out of the ordinary."

"We will, sir. Thank you." When they got past the men, Mary Catherine gently released her hold on Lexy and picked up her pace. "Let's get back."

"Yeah. Maybe the park wasn't such a great idea."

They didn't talk much on the way back to the parking lot, but Lexy couldn't let go of the feeling that she wanted to trust Mary Catherine. The older girl seemed really interested in her answers. In her as a person. The reality made her feel a lot of things. Hope, maybe. Happiness—if this was what happiness felt like. But something else, too.

Fear.

Lexy had learned a long time ago that the worst thing on the streets wasn't the thugs or the bullets or the way a brother threw a girl on a bed and had his way with her. It wasn't a break-in or a drug bust or getting arrested.

The worst thing was caring.

JAG AND ASPYN hovered over the house where Lexy lived. They watched the two girls pull up in Mary Catherine's car and walk inside.

"Thank You, God." Jag was exhausted. He and Aspyn had more strategizing ahead. No mission had ever been more taxing. Despite that, Jag was overcome with relief. "The things that man on the path planned to do to Mary Catherine and Lexy . . ."

Aspyn closed her eyes. "Unspeakable. You stepped in at just the right time. Pulling him out of the bushes onto the path was the right thing to do. Instead of running, he was forced into the light."

The bearded man had been waiting in the bushes, ready to attack Mary Catherine and Lexy. Jag had appeared from the shadows and ordered the guy to step onto the path.

When the man pushed further back into the brush, Jag grabbed his arm and pulled him out. In one swift move, Jag had the guy pinned to the ground, his arm bent behind his back. That's when Jag had seen the gun in the man's sock. He grabbed it and the guy's cell phone and called 911. Two officers were already at the park. Just before they turned the bend on the trail and drew their guns, Jag dropped the gun, stepped into the brush, and disappeared.

Jag was grateful for the control he'd learned the last time. He had no desire to kill the man in the bushes. Protecting Mary Catherine and Lexy was all that mattered. Orlon had been right. The mission was very dangerous. Evil lurked around every corner and this much was certain.

The stakes had never been higher.

19

Marcus met Tyler at the hospital that afternoon to give blood. Whether Jalen could use it or not didn't matter. Someone could. They were in the lobby waiting their turn when Charlie Kent came in.

"Brought in another two gunshot victims today. They'll both live but they're in bad shape." The officer looked weary. "I haven't seen this much violence in years."

He took the seat opposite Marcus and Tyler. "We made an arrest an hour ago near Dodger Stadium. Story could've wound up very differently."

Marcus couldn't imagine being a police officer in Los Angeles. "What happened?"

"An officer from another precinct was walking the trail. He found a man in the bushes and recognized him from the wanted list. Called for backup and a couple of our guys made the arrest." Officer Kent shook his head. "The guy's on our most-wanted list, multiple homicides, rape, attacks on kids. Escaped prison in Northern California a year ago."

A sense of satisfaction came over Marcus. "Glad you caught him."

"What was he doing in the bushes?" Tyler also seemed gripped by the story.

"That's the scary part. A couple of girls were walking the trail. A few minutes more and they would've walked right past the guy. We think he was planning an attack. Waiting for the young women to walk by."

The pieces came together, and Marcus felt like he was falling, like he couldn't feel his feet beneath him. "What . . . what park did you say it was?"

"Elysian Park. Near Dodger Stadium." Officer Kent stood. "You two here to see the little boy?"

"Yeah." Marcus stood and shook the officer's hand. Were the girls at the park Mary Catherine and Lexy? He tried to focus. "We're giving blood, too. It's something we can do."

The officer shook Tyler's hand next. "That's how we all feel. Trying to make a difference best we can." He tipped his hat. "See you tomorrow night for training."

"Looking forward to it." Marcus slowly sat back in his seat. His heart pounded so loud he thought it would break through his chest.

Tyler stared at him. "You okay?"

"Elysian Park." Marcus couldn't slow his heartbeat. "That's where Mary Catherine took Lexy."

Tyler let the pieces connect for a moment. "You think maybe the two girls were . . ."

"It's possible." He put his face in his hands for a few seconds and then looked up. "I should've gone with them. Forget that girl-bonding thing. The city isn't safe."

"Text Mary Catherine and ask her."

Marcus didn't want to wait that long. He pulled his phone from his pocket and tapped Mary Catherine's number. She answered after two rings.

"Hello?"

"Where are you?" His words sounded too loud, too intense. He forced himself to calm down. Wherever she was, at least she was okay.

"Leaving Lexy's house." Mary Catherine was clearly taken aback by his tone. "What's wrong?"

Marcus put his head in his free hand and exhaled. *Slow down*, he told himself. "Did you take her to Elysian Park? Like you said?"

"I did. It wasn't perfect, but it was a start. She's tough." Hesitancy still rang in Mary Catherine's words. "You sound upset. What happened?"

"Did you see police there?"

"Actually, yes." Mary Catherine paused. "Two officers arrested a man on the path just ahead of us. Kind of creepy."

Marcus stood and paced the length of the waiting room and back. "He was a very dangerous guy. I just talked to Officer Kent and he said . . . the man might've been lying in wait."

"For us?" It was the first time Mary Catherine sounded fearful.

"Possibly." Marcus couldn't believe it. Mary Catherine and Lexy had been in danger and if something had happened . . . He couldn't finish the thought. "God was with you. Looking out for you."

"The officers didn't tell us." Mary Catherine's voice held a fear Marcus hadn't heard from her before. "If Lexy had been hurt, I never could've forgiven myself. We had no idea."

"It's behind you now. Just . . . please, Mary Catherine, be careful. You should've let me come with you." He sat down and leaned back hard. It felt so good to hear her voice, to know she was okay. His tone lightened some. "Remember that next time."

"You're right." A warmth filled her voice. "Sorry. I was kind of quick to turn you down."

"We're in this together, this volunteer thing." He leaned his elbows on his knees. "Let me help, okay?"

"Okay." For the first time since she answered the phone he could hear her smile across the phone line. "Where are you?"

"At the hospital." He wasn't a fan of needles, but this was important. "Tyler and I are giving blood."

"Nice." Again her tone was softer. "How's Jalen?"

"About the same." Marcus felt the heaviness of the child's situation. "We're going to see him and Shamika next."

"I'll be there in a few hours." She sounded like herself again. The fear from earlier gone. "I'll probably miss you."

"See, there you go again. Trying to avoid me." He chuckled. "Just kidding." He paused. "Be safe, Mary Catherine. Please."

"I will."

The call ended as Marcus and Tyler were called back. They took cots next to each other and in no time they were hooked up and watching bags fill with their blood.

"I hate needles." Marcus looked away from the one in his arm. "I have to believe this is for kids like Jalen."

"Really, though?" Tyler moved his arm and winced. "It'll probably help the two gang guys just brought in."

Marcus hadn't thought about that. The possibility didn't sit well with him. Give blood for guys caught up in gang violence for what? So they could get back out on the streets and shoot each other again? He gritted his teeth and tried not to think about it.

"You and Sami doing anything this weekend?" He put one arm behind his head so he could see Tyler better. "Besides the prison tour, obviously."

Tyler laughed in a way that was more concerned than humorous. "That'll probably leave us pretty worn out."

"True." Between donating blood and the prison tour, Tyler was right.

"Hey, I almost forgot." Tyler faced him. "Tomorrow morning Sami and Mary Catherine are going to the beach. Supposed to be another warm day like last week."

"Sounds fun." He uttered a brief laugh. "Mary Catherine didn't tell me about it."

"Well, Sami did. She asked us both to come."

"Really?" Marcus smiled. "Did she check with Mary Catherine?"

"Come on, Dillinger." Tyler laughed. "You don't really think MC's trying to avoid you. I mean, she agreed to work with you on the prison program, right?"

"She didn't really have a choice." Marcus gave Tyler a wary look. "Remember? A police officer asked her to talk to me about it."

"Well . . . don't forget she could be a little leery, what with Shelly Wayne and all."

Marcus sighed. "Yeah. About Shelly." He looked out the window and thought about the situation. "I need to talk to Coach."

"Why?" Tyler made a face. "He won't be upset if things don't work out with you and Shelly."

"She's his niece." Marcus felt trapped. "I never should've agreed to call her."

Tyler waited, a knowing look on his face. "Whatever you do, you need to figure it out. The other night was awful."

They finished giving blood and Marcus gulped down the orange juice and crackers. He stayed close to the wall until he felt less light-headed. Tyler took it all in stride. "You live with your arm hanging halfway to your knee for a few months and giving blood'll feel like a day at Disneyland."

The two friends laughed as they left the unit. But as they reached the elevator and rode it up to the intensive care unit, they grew quiet. "I keep praying." Tyler drew a tired breath as they walked down the hall toward the nurses' station. "I just wish God would wake the boy up."

Tyler had agreed to wait while Marcus visited the boy. Marcus felt the familiar ache in his heart as he reached the child's room. The door was partly open and Shamika was inside, sitting close to her son, holding his hand and talking softly. She looked up as Marcus stood at the doorway.

"Please. Come in." Shamika stood and hugged him. "Thank you for coming."

"How is he?" Marcus walked up to the bed and put his

hand over the boy's much smaller one. He looked up at the machines, whirring and buzzing and clicking like before.

"He's still in a coma." Shamika's face looked tearstained. "I'm begging God he might wake up today." She paused and her voice fell. "Doctor says it needs to be soon. For Jalen's brain to work right."

The weight of the situation pressed in on Marcus's shoulders and sucked the air from the room. Jalen had been so trusting, so willing to help that night.

"Is there anything I can do? Do you need help?"

"Ask people to pray. Please." Her eyes grew watery. "I want God to know I'm not giving up."

Marcus nodded. "I can do that. I'll tell everyone." He needed to do more of that. Of course he and his friends had been praying. But who else had he asked? More than half a million people followed him on Twitter and he hadn't said a word. He pursed his lips. "I promise you, Shamika. I'll get people to pray for your boy."

AS THEY LEFT the hospital, Marcus and Tyler were quiet. They didn't talk until they were outside in the parking lot. The whole time Marcus thought about Twitter. All of Los Angeles knew he'd been shot at. The *Times* had run the news on the front page. So everyone who followed him on Twitter would've already heard that he'd been a victim of gang violence in his attempt to make the youth center a success.

Why hadn't he asked anyone to pray for Jalen?

"I have an idea." Marcus pulled out his phone. "You still on Twitter?"

"Yeah." Tyler hadn't started the car yet. He found his phone in his front pocket and looked at it. "I haven't used social media since I came here."

"Maybe now's the time to start." He opened his Twitter app. "You got a hundred forty characters to ask everyone listening to pray for Jalen. Let's do this."

Marcus's tweet was simple.

There's a little boy fighting for his life in an LA hospital. He took the bullet intended for me. Ask God for a miracle. #prayforJalen

Marcus reread his words and then looked out the window. *Lord, forgive me for not thinking of asking them sooner. I'm new at this. And please . . . help Jalen. He needs You more than ever, God.*

He sent the tweet and looked at Tyler. "Done."

"Me, too." Tyler slipped his phone back in his pocket. "Let's see what happens."

THEY WENT TO In-N-Out across the street for burgers and talked a little more about Jalen and Shamika and the youth center. And whether they were in over their heads.

Marcus thought maybe they were.

Halfway through the meal Marcus checked his Twitter. "This is crazy!" He couldn't believe it. "Almost a hundred thousand people have retweeted it. And it's only been twenty minutes."

Tyler checked his and found a similarly high number of retweets. Marcus stared at his phone and blinked back tears. The gesture meant more than any of his followers could've known. Reading their comments, Marcus could see some of them were doing more than simply retweeting. They promised to pray. At a time when violence seemed the norm and kids didn't seem to care about each other, clearly there were some who actually did.

It was a surge of hope Marcus needed—especially since he needed to go by the youth center later and see how things were going. He'd hired a full-time director a week ago, and today the guy had reported that things were calm.

Marcus wanted more than calm, of course. But in light of the events this week calm was an improvement.

As they walked to their separate vehicles, Tyler gave him a light punch in the arm. "You're going with me tomorrow morning. To the beach." He slid his phone back in his pocket. "No excuses."

He still lived with Tyler, so it'd be easy to go. But Marcus wasn't sure. "Someone should ask Mary Catherine."

"Sami said she'd be fine." Tyler held up his hands. "Really, man? You're letting the girl intimidate you."

"We'll see." Marcus tossed his keys in his hands. "I'll think about it."

"We're all friends." He pointed at Marcus. "See you at nine tomorrow."

The discussion was over.

Marcus drove to the youth center, and the whole way he debated whether he should go. He thought about Mary Catherine all the time and found himself counting down the hours till the next time they would see each other. But going with Tyler to the beach felt a little intrusive. Mary Catherine hadn't invited him, no matter what she told Sami.

He tried to put the thought from his mind. At the center he checked in with the new director. The report was mostly good. Kids were still coming for help with their homework, still showing up to play basketball every night around seven. Lots of them had asked if there would be pizza again this Tuesday.

"You'd think the shooting would keep them away." Marcus still didn't understand life on the streets.

"It has no effect at all." The director used to be a football coach at an area high school. He was perfect to manage the youth center. "These kids think nothing of a shooting. Very different from the way you and I might see it."

The futility stayed with Marcus as he left. He planned on going home and getting in another workout before turning in for the night. But there were too many thoughts battling for his attention.

Instead he drove to Dodger Stadium.

Spring training was coming fast. A couple of months at Camelback Ranch in Arizona, and then they'd be in full swing for the season. He was on the roster as their top pitcher again, so his time with Mary Catherine would be infrequent at best.

The stadium was empty, the way he expected for a Thursday night in early January. Marcus used his key to get into the back of the facility and then found a spot near the top of the bleachers. The sun was setting, spreading pink and blue across the sky.

Something about being here always helped him think.

Helped him get his priorities right. He'd been reading his Bible now—ever since the walk with Mary Catherine. He'd bought the e-reader version of the Voice Bible—a new translation designed for people like him. People who had no real experience with Scripture. He could read it any time he wanted right on his phone.

This morning he'd read the book of James.

Don't just be hearers of the Word of God. Be doers. The message stayed with him still.

The first chapter was the reason he'd asked Tyler to go with him to give blood today. It wasn't enough to wish people well and offer a quick prayer. God's people needed to act. Matthew West had a song about it. "Do Something."

He rested his forearms on his thighs and stared out at the stadium. His surface wound from the bullet was healing. One day soon the place would be packed, people cheering on his team, screaming his name. But what did they know of Marcus Dillinger? Sure, he was clean-cut. He stayed away from drugs and drinking and he'd given a bunch of money to open a youth center for kids in the inner city.

But what about his faith?

The question had plagued Marcus many nights, even since he'd known for sure that God was working in his life, that God had answered his challenge back in October. Okay, so he believed. So he did a few good things for the community—if they actually were good.

Did that mean he was a Christian?

Marcus breathed in sharply through his nose and sat up straighter. *God, I'm here . . . What do You want from me?*

No answer whispered across his heart. But another Bible

verse came to mind. The one he'd read yesterday in Romans, chapter ten. He pulled out his phone and read it again. *Romans 10:9—So if you believe deep in your heart that God raised Jesus from the pit of death and if you voice your allegiance by confessing the truth that "Jesus is Lord," then you will be saved!*

He had heard people pray for salvation before, but sitting here, the winter breeze cool against his face, Marcus wasn't sure he'd ever actually done that. He'd attended house church at the Waynes' week after week. But even though he appreciated the stories and the teaching, he'd never made the message personal.

Never made that sort of a deal with Jesus.

Marcus lifted his eyes to the sky and like a parade, he could see all the girls. All the careless nights. The reason he could never stand before Mary Catherine as anything but her friend. *Lord, I know I already apologized for those times. For who I was back then. But where do I go from here? What happens now?* He thought about his anger toward the shooter, the futility and impatience that had consumed him most hours since Jalen had been shot. *I guess sin can be more than sleeping around. I'm sorry for my attitude, too.*

Suddenly, there in the quiet of the empty stadium, he could feel the presence of God. Marcus did the most natural thing he could do. He lifted his hands toward heaven and prayed.

The verse from Romans played again in his mind. This time he spoke out loud. "Father, would You get rid of the filth in my heart, please? I believe in You."

The cool breeze picked up speed, sending a low whistling sound through the stadium.

Marcus wasn't finished. "From the depth of my heart, Jesus, I believe You are God and that You died on the cross and were raised to life for me." His words were quiet but powerful. "I want You to be with me. I want to be saved. I am nothing without You. I mean it." Marcus felt tears on his cheeks. "Even if I were the only person on earth You would've died anyway. So here's my confession, Father. Jesus is Lord. Now and forever."

He lowered his hands and dragged them across his cheeks. There was no describing the feeling inside him. He felt whole and clean and full of light. Of course he would mess up again. He could never be perfect. But at least now he had assurance. If the bullet hit him next time, he'd go from life on earth to life in heaven.

Because the Bible said so.

But there was something else. He'd learned last week at the Waynes' that the Book of Acts talked about times when people got baptized. He spent the next half hour searching for the word *baptism* in his Voice Bible app. Every time, it seemed like people made the decision to get baptized after they decided to believe in Jesus for salvation.

Believe *and* be baptized. That's what the Bible said.

He remembered the beach trip in the morning. Could he be baptized then? Would that even be possible? Without hesitating he called Coach Wayne. "Coach. It's Marcus."

"Hey!" The man sounded happy, the way he usually sounded. "I've been meaning to call you. How's the little boy doing?"

"Still hanging in there. No change." Marcus felt a ripple of discouragement. "His mother's asking everyone to pray."

"I saw that on Twitter. Almost a hundred and fifty thousand people have retweeted it. That's incredible."

That many? Gratitude filled his heart. Who knew where the request would go from here? But he'd done what Shamika had asked and now—with so little effort—people were praying. Marcus drew a breath and tried to focus. "I'm calling you for a couple of reasons."

"Go ahead." There was the sound of a closing door. "I just stepped outside. What's on your mind?"

"First . . ." Marcus wasn't even sure how to explain what had just happened. "I'm here at the stadium by myself. I just gave my life to Jesus. Like for the first time. For real."

"Marcus! That's amazing!" Deep emotion came across in Coach Wayne's voice. "Rhonda and I have been praying for that. Actually, I was going to pull you aside this Sunday after church and ask you where you were at in your faith journey."

"Now you know." Marcus laughed. "I've been reading the Voice Bible. I love it. Everything's so clear. Like God's speaking straight to me."

"Incredible, right?"

They talked a few more minutes about Scripture and how it was God's Word. God-breathed. But there was more Marcus needed to talk to the man about. He tried to find the right words. "Coach . . . something else. About Shelly."

"Yes." His voice grew more pensive. "I was going to talk to you about her, too."

Marcus stood and paced down the empty row and back. How was he supposed to say this? "I'm planning to talk to her later tonight. It's just not . . . it's not working out with the two of us." He paused. "I'm sorry, Coach, I really didn't mean to get this involved and now . . . I'm just so sorry."

For a moment there was only silence on the line. Marcus felt a pit in his stomach. Was his coach angry with him? If so, what could he do to make things right? He was about to offer another apology when he heard a light laugh coming from the man.

"I think you read me all wrong." Coach Wayne sounded almost relieved. "I was going to warn you about her. She's always been a little wild. Having her around more lately hasn't been good for our own daughter." He laughed again. "I was going to ask if you and Shelly would do your visiting outside of our home. Seriously."

Relief washed over him. He'd worried about this for nothing. "She looks for trouble, that's for sure."

"She's my niece, and I pray for her. One of these days something will get her attention and she'll need more than her good looks to get by." This time there was no denying the approval in Coach's voice. "Good decision, Marcus. You don't need that sort of distraction."

"Definitely not." Marcus realized he'd been holding his breath. He exhaled and sat back down. "So I guess that's two good choices tonight."

"Yes." His voice became more serious. "I know it won't be easy, talking to Shelly. But she'll understand. She's had lots of boyfriends."

"Thanks, Coach. There's one more thing." Marcus smiled. "If you're not busy tomorrow around nine thirty, could you meet us at Zuma Beach? Me and Tyler and Sami and Mary Catherine?"

"Sounds fun." There was a smile in Coach Wayne's voice. "Just because?"

"Because I want to get baptized. I wondered if you'd do the honors."

Again there was silence for several seconds. Marcus could practically see the man's face when he finally spoke. "It would be one of the greatest honors of my life, Marcus. Rhonda and I will be there. The kids, too."

The call ended and Marcus stared at the sky, soaking in the love and joy and peace that surrounded him. Mary Catherine would want to be there for his baptism. So would the others. There would be no fanfare, no media, no fear of bullets flying.

Just him and his closest friends and the greatest decision Marcus had ever made.

The decision to follow Jesus.

20

THE SUN WAS BRIGHT in the early Friday morning sky by the time Aspyn took her place at the short block wall that separated Zuma Beach from the parking lot. She watched Mary Catherine drive her Hyundai up and park near the wall.

Help me, Father. The timing has to be perfect.

She could picture her angel team in heaven, watching, all of them praying. Aspyn could feel their support.

Mary Catherine and Sami climbed out of the car and grabbed boogie boards, towels, and a few bags. Invisible and silent, Aspyn stayed with them as they headed down the sand toward the water. Her job was very specific. It would be nearly impossible to pull it off without being noticed.

The girls set up ten yards from the water, spreading their towels out on the sand. Aspyn watched closely, never taking her eyes off Mary Catherine. Finally it happened. Mary Catherine took her cell phone from her pocket and checked it.

Aspyn knew why. She was expecting two very important

phone calls. One from her mother—who had called Mary Catherine the night before to tell her the news that her father's health was failing. Even though they were divorced, her parents cared about each other. Today the man was in a hospital in Nashville, where doctors were deciding whether he'd need lifesaving surgery.

The second call set to come in sometime this morning would be from Mary Catherine's own doctor. He had studied the tests she'd had done over a week ago and now he had the results. Aspyn watched Mary Catherine turn the ringer on her phone all the way up. Then she set it near the bottom of her towel.

"What time will the others be here?" Mary Catherine checked the time on her phone. "It's already nine."

"About half an hour." Sami was slipping her wetsuit on.

Good, Aspyn thought. She needed both girls to take to the water before the Wayne family and Marcus and Tyler arrived. Otherwise what she was about to do would be impossible.

Father, get them in the water. Please draw them in . . . I don't have much time. Suddenly in the nearby waves, a pod of dolphins appeared, splashing and chattering among each other. Aspyn looked up to heaven and smiled. God was beyond creative. *Thank You, Lord.*

Mary Catherine noticed the dolphins. "Look!" She tossed her phone on the towel and grabbed her wetsuit from her bag. "Hurry! Maybe we can ride with them again."

The girls hurried to finish getting dressed, grabbed their boards, and jogged to the surf. They jumped over the white water and made it out to the flat sea just before the breakers.

The place where the dolphins were still tossing their heads and jumping through the waves.

Perfect. Aspyn slipped behind the closest lifeguard station and became a jogger. Simple navy shorts and a white tank top. The most discreet jogging outfit she could think to wear. She pulled her hair back with a rubber band from her pocket and studied the scene. The sand felt wonderful on her feet— something angels only experienced on missions. Sand in heaven was different. Softer.

Aspyn scanned the beach. No one else was out here this early. The girls would have to stay distracted if she were going to pull this off. She took a deep breath and began jogging. She eased her way to the shore and started to close the forty-yard gap between her and the place where Mary Catherine's beach towel was set up.

Aspyn loved this feeling and hated it at the same time. The way her heart pounded was something intrinsically human. But the reason was terrifying. So much was at stake in the next few minutes.

Stay distracted. Please.

The dolphins weren't going anywhere. A few more seemed to join in, jumping and splashing not ten feet from where the girls were riding out on their boogie boards. *Hurry*, she told herself. *Get it done!*

Aspyn was closer now. She kept jogging, her face straight ahead as if she were any normal runner, enjoying any other day. As she neared Mary Catherine's towel she kept her eyes on the girls. They were still distracted by the dolphins, still too caught up in the moment to notice a jogger on the beach.

The plan could work. Aspyn reached the towel, stopped,

and grabbed Mary Catherine's cell phone. In a quick move, she turned it off.

She had to hold the button a few seconds to see that the device was completely powered down. Then she dropped it back on the towel and resumed her jogging. Mary Catherine and Sami were facing the beach now, riding a wave into the shore, laughing and looking back at the dolphins.

They never once looked her way.

Aspyn kept jogging and a ways down the beach she met up with another jogger. Blond and tall. "That was textbook." Jag smiled at her. "And what about this sand?"

"I was just thinking that. So different than the sand in heaven." Aspyn could breathe again. "Rougher."

"Like all of earth." He lifted his face toward the sun as they jogged. "No time to waste, you know."

"Theme of this mission." She looked back. The girls were out near the waves again. Her action had gone completely undetected.

They jogged up the beach to the next lifeguard station, slipped behind it, and disappeared.

Jag was right. They couldn't waste a minute. They had a Nashville hospital to visit.

21

THE WATER FELT WONDERFUL, cool and fresh and smooth against Mary Catherine's skin—the part not covered by her wetsuit. All that and a ride with the dolphins. Mary Catherine couldn't stop silently thanking God.

Sometime today she expected two difficult phone calls. One about her father's health. One about her own. But whatever news she received later, at least they'd had this time out here in the ocean. So far the morning couldn't have been more perfect.

And it was about to get better.

She and Sami had found out late last night that the guys were joining them along with the Wayne family for a very special reason. Marcus Dillinger was getting baptized. It was hard to believe that she had ever assumed Marcus to be shallow and predictable.

Nothing could've been further from the truth.

Marcus had a genuine love for people and a new faith vibrant and central to his life.

They rode another wave in and as Mary Catherine stood she saw the Wayne family and Marcus and Tyler walking in from the parking lot. She turned to Sami. "They're here!"

"This will be something." Sami stood and wiped the water from her face. "I'm so proud of Marcus. For wanting to do this."

"Me, too." They each held their boards under their arms and jogged back to their things. They pulled extra towels from their bags and dried off. They planned to go back in the water later, so they peeled their wetsuits only half off.

Mary Catherine had brought her Whole Foods "Live Life" sweatshirt for the occasion. Certainly baptism was a great time to think about living life. She slipped it on and worked her fingers through her hair. She hoped the calls didn't come in during Marcus's moment.

But if they did, she'd have to take them. If her father was sicker, she was ready to get on a plane in a few hours and fly to Nashville. Even if it meant missing the Last Time In program. Marcus could handle it by himself if he had to.

The others walked up and Tyler slung his arm around Marcus's shoulders. "Could there be a better day for a beach baptism?"

Sami led the way to meet them. She hugged Marcus and then Tyler, and stayed there, her arm around his waist. "We're so happy for you, Marcus."

"I don't know what took me so long." He smiled and then turned to Mary Catherine. "God's been talking to me about a lot of things."

The Wayne family joined them—Ollie and Rhonda and their three kids. Shane and Sam wore bathing suits and sweatshirts. Sierra looked distant in jeans and a lightweight jacket.

Coach Wayne spoke first. "Thanks for inviting us. We couldn't miss this." He and Rhonda gave hugs to the others. Ollie patted Marcus on the back. "I remember when our kids were baptized. It's a big day."

Conversations started between Rhonda and Sami and Tyler, and at the same time Ollie stepped back to say a few words to his kids. In the fraction of a moment when no one else was talking to either of them, Marcus walked up to Mary Catherine. He wore a bathing suit and a T-shirt, and he stood so close their arms were touching.

Never mind the sweatshirt she was wearing. Mary Catherine could feel every inch of contact with him.

"Hey." He smiled at her. "Thanks for being here." His eyes held the familiar teasing. "I sort of intruded on your beach morning."

"Not at all." She felt her defenses falling. Every time she was near Marcus Dillinger the attraction was stronger. "I'm glad to be here. Really."

The others were talking and for that moment it was just Marcus and Mary Catherine. He glanced at her. "I ended things with Shelly last night."

Mary Catherine felt suddenly light-headed. Marcus had cut things off with Shelly? Had he really just said that? She shaded her eyes. "You broke up with her?"

"Technically we were never in a relationship." His voice was little more than a whisper. He allowed a sad chuckle. "But she thought we were."

He was trusting her with his heart. Whatever that meant, Mary Catherine loved the feeling. She kept her voice quiet. "How did she handle it?"

"Not well at first." The breeze off the ocean wrapped itself around their private conversation. "I think she understood eventually. I told her she was too young and . . . well, truthfully I didn't see her the same way she saw me."

Mary Catherine winced. "Yeah, that would've been tough."

"She didn't hang around. Her friends were waiting for her back at her house." His smile melted her. "She'll be fine."

The feel of the ocean air, the sun on her shoulders, Marcus standing so close his words felt like velvet against her skin. All of it made Mary Catherine feel a little dizzy. She wasn't sure what to say.

"Anyway, I wanted you to know. That whole scene at the hospital the other night. The way she was at dinner with Sami and Tyler. I didn't want any of it. I needed to act on how I was feeling."

Mary Catherine reminded herself to breathe. "You seem happier."

"I am." He nodded toward the water. "And I'm about to make another great decision."

"Definitely." Mary Catherine wanted the moment to keep going. Even when standing here with him could never lead to anything. Feeling good wouldn't buy her a long life. "Thanks for telling me."

"I should've done it sooner." The sunlight caught his eyes. "Shelly wasn't real." He didn't blink, didn't take his eyes off hers. "Next time I won't settle for anything less."

Real. That was her word. Mary Catherine didn't want their alone time to end but the others were done visiting. They circled around, looking to Marcus. Ollie Wayne wore a bathing suit and a T-shirt. "Let's do this!"

"I'm ready!" Marcus whipped off his T-shirt and threw it on Mary Catherine's towel. The group walked close to the water, Mary Catherine near the back.

Her head was spinning. She must've told Sami a hundred times before she got the news about her heart, about her years being cut short. Real was all she wanted in a guy. Back when she thought she had forever.

He would have to be real in his beliefs, real in his character. Real in the way he treated her and everyone else.

And now Marcus wanted *that* in a girl. She wanted to pull Sami aside and ask if she had somehow told Marcus. How else could he have known how that one word would speak straight to her soul? But that was impossible. Sami didn't have heart-to-heart conversations with Marcus.

She felt her feet sink into the wet sand a few inches, but she didn't care. The feeling was a reminder that she was really here, this was really happening. That Marcus had just stood next to her and told her he was done with Shelly because he wanted someone real.

The wind settled down—as if all of heaven wanted to hear clearly what was about to happen. Mary Catherine stood with Sami and Tyler. Rhonda Wayne and her kids stood nearby in another cluster, as all of them directed their attention to Ollie and Marcus. The two men walked out until they were waist deep.

Mary Catherine looked around, amazed. Not only was the

beach quiet, it was empty. This divine moment was for them alone. She turned her eyes back to Marcus.

Ollie put his hand on Marcus's shoulder. "I've talked to Marcus Dillinger about Jesus for a long time." He hesitated, and after a few seconds it became obvious that the coach was struggling. Fighting to get the words past his emotions. Finally he coughed a little. "Anyway. This is a big day."

Marcus nodded. His smile was so big Mary Catherine could feel it all the way to the place where she stood.

"So you all know how this works." He looked at the rest of them on the beach. "Marcus asked Jesus to be his Savior. Now he wants to give a public demonstration of that faith. The symbol of dying to self and being raised to new life in Christ." Ollie looked at Marcus again. "You ready, man?"

"So ready!"

"What he means is, it's freezing out here without a wetsuit." Coach Ollie laughed. Then he turned his attention fully to the matter at hand. "Marcus, because you've placed your faith in Christ, and because you want to publicly declare your allegiance to Him, I now baptize you in the name of the Father, the Son, and the Holy Spirit."

Marcus put his hand over his face, plugging his nose, and Ollie dipped him beneath the surface of the water.

As Marcus went under, Ollie continued. "Buried with Him in baptism." Ollie helped Marcus back to his feet. "Raised with Him to new life in the power of the Holy Spirit." He pulled Marcus into a big hug. "Congratulations, my friend."

Mary Catherine led the applause on the beach, and the others quickly joined in. The moment was perfect. Flawless.

Only as the two men headed back to the shore did Mary Catherine realize she was crying. She wiped the tears from her cheeks. Marcus Dillinger was exactly the sort of guy she had always dreamed about.

But she could never let him know, never give him any sign that she was interested. In fact, she would be better off leaving Los Angeles altogether. Depending on what the doctor said, she might take a year and go to Africa. The way she'd always dreamed.

Anything would be better than feeling this way about a guy she could never have. The Wayne family rushed up to Marcus, congratulating him and hugging him. Mary Catherine and Sami and Tyler waited until he made his way to them.

"Man, that was beautiful." Tyler gave him a hearty hug. "I remember when I was baptized. Had a lot of years without God, but now look at us! Ready to change the world!"

"You got it!" Marcus looked exhilarated. The water beaded on his light chocolate skin and his green eyes flashed with joy. He hugged Sami next and then stepped up to Mary Catherine.

Every other time they'd been together, she had avoided hugging him, avoided being in his arms. Especially when it would only make it that much harder to admit the truth. That they could never be more than friends.

But this was not a moment to resist.

She put her arms around his cold, wet, bare waist and he pulled her into a gentle embrace that took her breath. Once, Mary Catherine had read about feeling born for a certain moment. If that was true, then this was that moment. Not jumping from a plane or swimming with the dolphins. But this.

The way she felt in Marcus Dillinger's arms.

He held on to her longer than the others and when he drew back he put his hand alongside her face. "Thank you. For being here."

There seemed to be so much more going on between them than their words could begin to acknowledge. Mary Catherine couldn't look away from him, couldn't remember that there was anyone else on the beach. She hesitated long enough to hold on to the feeling. "Congratulations. I'm so happy for you."

Marcus released her and turned to the others. The group talked for a few minutes, relishing the happy occasion. Sami shared about the dolphins, though now there wasn't one in sight.

"You girls and your imaginations." Tyler pulled Sami close, grinning at her. "What's next? You climbed on the back of a dolphin and took a ride up the shore?"

"Hey!" Sami gave him a playful shove. "It's true." She looked to Mary Catherine. "Right? Tell him!"

"I believe you." Marcus was toweling off, shivering from the cold water. He winked at Mary Catherine. "I'll bet it was amazing."

"It really was." She laughed in Marcus's direction and then looked at the others. "There had to be a dozen of them. For like twenty minutes."

The conversation turned to the volunteer program and their training that night. "Let us know how it goes." Ollie Wayne looked at his daughter. "One of Sierra's friends is going through the program."

Coach Wayne didn't elaborate, but clearly the matter

made Sierra uncomfortable. Mary Catherine remembered that Rhonda Wayne had said the family was struggling with their only daughter. She would have to ask Rhonda about it later.

After the Wayne family headed back to the parking lot, Tyler pulled a wetsuit out of his bag. "I promised my girl I'd ride boogie boards with her."

"Finally." Sami laughed and pulled hers back over her shoulders.

"You can use my board." Mary Catherine was still warming up from her time in the water earlier. Besides, she would rather stay on the beach with Marcus than get back in the ocean. She peeled off her sweatshirt and stretched out her legs. "I'll get some sun."

"Is that possible?" Marcus grinned at her. "You don't look much like the tanning type."

"I know." She rolled her eyes. "I have British skin. I can actually spend an hour on the beach and look more pale."

Marcus laughed. "I'll stay here with you. The water's freezing."

He sat next to her. Again their arms touched and Marcus smiled at her. "You're warm."

"The sun feels great." She lifted her face to the sky and closed her eyes. Could he tell how hard her heart was beating? Mary Catherine tried to still her nerves. What was she doing? And what was the point? This—whatever this was—couldn't go anywhere. Sitting this close to Marcus was like a form of torture.

But it felt too wonderful to even think about stopping.

For a while they sat that way, their arms touching,

watching Tyler and Sami riding the waves. Tyler wasn't very good on the boogie board. No matter how hard he tried he kept falling off. The scene made for great entertainment, and after a few minutes Mary Catherine and Marcus were both laughing.

"That's my buddy! Mr. Surfer." Marcus laughed again. Then he leaned his head close to hers. "Good thing I don't have a wetsuit. Honestly, I'd be worse than him."

"I'd like to see you try. Someday."

"We'll see." Marcus sighed. "I should probably stick to pitching."

"Yeah, maybe." She shot him a teasing look. "If Tyler's any indication, pitchers might not be that great at riding waves."

Marcus drew one knee up to his chest and chuckled. He turned so he could see her better, but the move broke the physical connection between them. "So . . . what do you know about pitchers?"

"Hmm." She laughed. "Well, for starters they might be better on dry land." Her smile came easily. "Oh . . . and the fact that you're the best."

He tilted his head, searching her face, clearly trying to read her. "Have you ever seen me pitch?"

"Yes." Mary Catherine remembered it well. She had watched on TV as Marcus pitched the winning game of the last World Series. "You're very good." She felt the teasing in her eyes. "I'm actually a baseball fan."

"You are?"

"Yeah. But . . . not really the Dodgers. I grew up loving the Braves."

"The Braves?" He stood and walked a few steps toward

the water before returning. "Are you serious? That lousy team?"

"Yes!" She laughed out loud. "Definitely the Braves. We used to drive down to Atlanta for a couple of games each year." She loved this, the easy way they had together. It was more fun every time they talked. "Nashville has the minor league Sounds. But if you wanted the real thing, Atlanta was the place to be."

"Okay, then." He grinned. "I guess I can sit by you. Since you grew up not knowing better." He settled back on the towel and this time they sat closer than before.

"Very kind of you." The feel of his arm against hers was intoxicating. Mary Catherine had to work to feel the sand beneath her. Otherwise she would've thought she was floating.

"You know. Southern gentleman and all."

"Yes, sir." She milked her accent for all it was worth. "Kind gentleman like you doesn't come around every day."

He tipped his head back and laughed. "I love that! I should've been born in the South." He gave her a mock stern look. "That part about not coming around every day, don't forget it, young lady."

"Deal." She thought about finding her sunglasses in her bag, but the sun was still at their backs. Their faces still had enough shade to talk without the glare of the sun being a problem.

He stretched out his legs again. They were several inches from hers, but with every movement, his arm brushed against hers again. They fell quiet, watching Tyler and Sami. Finally she felt Marcus inhale. He looked at her. "I keep thinking about the other day, you at Elysian Park with Lexy." He shook his head and stared at the ocean for a beat before looking back at her. "I don't know what I would've done if . . . if something had happened to you."

"I'm glad the police were there." She was touched by his concern.

"The world can never lose a girl like you, Mary Catherine. You're the rarest kind of real."

Her head was spinning again, her heart leaping like the dolphins in the waves earlier. "Thank you." She had the strongest desire to rest her head on his shoulder. But she couldn't. This was all pretend. She wasn't being fair to him or to herself. If they were going to get close like this, she would need to tell him the truth about her heart.

Truth she was going to learn more about any minute, when her phone rang.

"Tell me . . ." His voice was softer now. He looked at her eyes, straight to her aching heart. "Why do you run? When I'm around?"

"I don't run." She broke eye contact and turned to look at Tyler and Sami again. "I'm busy, that's all."

"No." His fingertips touched the side of her face. He waited until she looked at him. "You're not that busy. Only around me."

She wanted to beg him to stop this part of the conversation, stop it before she had no choice but to be honest. She shrugged and smiled. "Of course, you had Shelly, remember?"

"She wasn't the problem. You know that." He wasn't giving up. "I just want to know. Like . . . is there someone else? I know you said you hadn't found *that* guy, but maybe there's someone. Someone you didn't tell me about?"

A single sad laugh came from her. "No. That's not it." She wasn't sure how much longer she could look at him without giving in to her feelings, without forgetting every true thing about her health and her future and letting her heart win.

Just this once.

"So what is it?" He lowered his hand and allowed the slightest space between them. "You don't like ballplayers?"

"You're the first one I've been friends with." She let her smile ease up some, enough that she hoped he could see she was being honest. "Relationships . . . they just aren't for me. It's complicated." She didn't wait for him to protest. "Maybe I'll explain it someday." She stood and stretched out her hand to him. "For now let's not think about it. Life's too short to worry."

He reached out his arm and their fingers touched and held. The feeling was as familiar as it was consuming. Like they'd held hands a thousand times before. He hesitated and then stood, still holding her hand. He looked down into her eyes and she could only allow the feeling between them. A heady wonderful feeling she was sure they were both experiencing.

When he spoke, his words were barely louder than the sound of the surf. "It feels right . . . being with you."

His words hit their mark. She hesitated and then grinned. "Come on!" She gently pulled him toward the shore.

"Don't tell me you're taking me back out into that water." His easy expression said he wasn't going to push the issue, wasn't going to insist on understanding everything about her right now.

But he also wasn't going to give up.

"Yes!" She led the way to the surf. "It'll be warmer now." They ran to the water. If she had wondered how he felt about her, now she knew. The pull she felt toward him, the way he could look straight through her, Mary Catherine could feel it long after they were waist deep in the water. She knew it because of one thing.

Marcus still had hold of her hand.

22

Marcus waited until he and Tyler were halfway home before he laughed out loud. "Okay, so what's with that girl? Just when I think I have her figured out, she throws me off again."

"I thought you might be thinking about her." Tyler laughed, too. He leaned against the passenger door and looked at Marcus. "Man, you got it bad for her. The whole beach could see."

"Just a couple of friends celebrating a great day at Zuma." He shook his head and kept his eyes on the road. "That's how she sees it."

"What about that holding hands thing?" Tyler was definitely enjoying the banter. "She didn't seem to fight that very much."

"True." He felt baffled. "She said she's not into relationships. Something like that."

"Well . . . maybe you'll actually have to chase her." Tyler

grinned. "She might be the only single girl in the world who wouldn't jump at the chance to date you."

"She's definitely on the list." He replayed the moments with her again in his mind. "I know this. There's no other girl like her. It's like nothing could take her down. Like she'll be celebrating life until she's a hundred years old."

Tyler laughed again. "I just hope it doesn't take you that long to get her to change her mind."

Marcus rolled down the window and let the warm January air drift through his SUV. "I might just wait that long." He leaned back and smiled. "If she doesn't drive me crazy first."

NOT UNTIL AFTER Marcus and Tyler left did Mary Catherine realize she hadn't heard from either her mom or the doctor. *Strange*, she thought. She dug around on her towel and found her phone.

It was turned off.

That's weird, she thought. *Maybe the battery died.* She held the button at the top of the phone and the screen came to life. After a few seconds she could see for herself. The battery was still full.

So when had she turned it off?

Before she could figure out an answer she watched several messages come through. Two of them were voice mails, one from her mother, one from her cardiologist. Sami was gathering her things, but Mary Catherine needed to check the messages first.

She noted the time of the calls. Her mother's came in

right as Marcus was being baptized. The doctor's happened fifteen minutes later, when Marcus had just taken the spot beside her on the towel. She would've missed all of that if her phone had been on.

She had no time to worry about it. She played the message from her mom first. Her mother's voice came on the line and Mary Catherine put her hand over her other ear. She needed to focus, needed to hear every word.

"Honey, call me. Good news." That was it. All her mother said. The message was the last thing Mary Catherine had expected. She dialed her mother's number and waited.

"Hello, honey!" Her mom sounded happier than she had in months. "Your father's doing so much better!"

"What happened?" Mary Catherine felt the sting of tears. Her father wasn't healthy. She would need to get out to Nashville again soon. Before she could think about a trip to Africa. But for now he was at least out of danger. *Thank You, God . . . thank You.*

Her mom was explaining what had happened, how they'd gotten much closer since his illness. And how she'd been spending more time at the hospital with him. "He looked like he'd need heart surgery, and you know your father. With his weight . . . he's just not a candidate right now."

"I know." Mary Catherine felt the burden of her father's health again. "One day, maybe."

"Anyway." Her mother paused only long enough to catch a quick breath. "This new doctor visited us today. A pretty woman. She found a better medication for the IV. It only took an hour and his numbers were so much better." She sounded deeply relieved. "Makes me wonder if the woman was an angel. Anyway, just wanted you to know he's good for now. Your dad asked me to tell you that he misses you. We both do."

"Miss you, too. Tell Daddy I love him."

"I will. Love you, too."

The conversation ended and Mary Catherine stared out at the water, to the place where Marcus had been baptized little more than an hour ago. God was with them. No matter how terribly the week had gone or what evil existed in the world, the Lord was still at work.

He had allowed her divorced parents to find friendship again. And He had sent a doctor to heal her father.

Which meant now she could still do the Last Time In program with Marcus. Mary Catherine stared at her phone. The other message was from her cardiologist. But suddenly she didn't want to hear it. The news could wait. She only wanted to live in the moment and remember every amazing thing about the morning and her time with Marcus.

She stood and walked to the edge of the water, her eyes trained on the horizon. The time with Marcus today had been a dream. Better than a dream. He was funny and sensitive and he wanted to take their friendship deeper. To a place where there were no secrets.

Mary Catherine thought about the message waiting for her, the one from the doctor. Her failing health was her greatest secret, the one thing she never wanted to share with Marcus. She didn't want him feeling sorry for her or trying to convince her she was wrong about her decision to stay single.

Sami came up alongside her. "How's your dad?"

"He's great." She turned and smiled. "Some new doctor

came on the scene today and gave him a different medicine." She still couldn't believe the news. "He won't need surgery after all."

"So you can stay with the prison program."

"Yes." She grew quiet, looking back at the ocean again. "Was it obvious?"

"You and Marcus?" Sami laughed quietly. "Very." She faced Mary Catherine. "Did you tell him? About your heart?"

"No." Mary Catherine wanted to run down the beach, far from the reality of her health. "I can't tell him. I shouldn't have told you."

"Why?" Sami sounded hurt. "Don't say that. I won't tell anyone. Not even Tyler." She didn't say anything for a few seconds. "It's just . . . with Marcus . . . you told me you didn't want to date. You might only have ten years. Remember?"

"I still feel that way." She exhaled and felt the weight of the entire beach on her shoulders. "I tried to tell him."

"What'd you say?" Sami wasn't pushing. She was only being a friend.

"I told him relationships weren't for me. I said it was complicated."

Sami looked surprised. "He didn't ask for more of an explanation?"

"He would've." She ignored the hurt inside. "I made him go to the water with me instead."

"The hand-holding?" A sparkle started in Sami's eyes and turned into a smile. "It's okay, Mary Catherine. Why do you have to be so hard on yourself? You don't know what's going to happen. You might end up in a rocking chair next to me when you're eighty." She hesitated. "Only God knows the number of your days."

"True." She longed for the scenario Sami described, longed for a reason to believe it was possible. "But my heart condition . . . it's a real thing, Sami. I can't put that on someone else."

"Maybe you don't have to. Just wait it out. Have fun." She breathed in deep and did a little spin on the sand. Then she angled her face, empathy marking her expression. "Isn't that what you taught me?"

"Yes." Mary Catherine smiled. If only it were that easy. "In everything but love."

"Maybe especially in love." Sami wasn't giving up. There was a pleading in her voice. Like she was desperate for Mary Catherine to relax her way of thinking. "You told me to visit my old boyfriend when I was in Florida. And look at Tyler and me now."

"Sami." Mary Catherine needed her friend to understand. "I can't do that to Marcus. Don't you see? He deserves the sort of love that can live on and on." She felt tears choking her, making it impossible to speak. She turned to the ocean again and waited.

Sami came up beside her again. "I'm sorry. I didn't mean to make you sad. But you're just friends. You can at least give that much a chance."

"It's just . . ." She sniffed, still struggling. "I feel more. And I can't."

"Maybe you can." Sami hesitated. "No one knows the number of their days. I could fall over right here on the sand."

Her words were gentle this time. "I would never regret loving Tyler. Even if we only had today."

Mary Catherine nodded. She understood what Sami meant. She really did. It just wasn't fair to either of them—her or Marcus—to let him think there was a chance. A chance at love and a normal life together. Why let something begin when the ending was already written?

They'd spent enough time talking about it. Mary Catherine smiled at her friend. "Come on. Let's get back." She walked slowly to her things and packed them into her bag. "Besides, I'm not sure he even likes me."

"MC, that's the most ridiculous thing I ever—"

"Okay, okay." Mary Catherine laughed and it felt wonderful for the moment to be light again. "Maybe he likes me just a little."

Sami made an exasperated sound. "You'll make plans to get your pilot's license, but you won't let yourself fall in love." Sami gathered her board and her bags. "Maybe just think awhile on your priorities. Okay?"

"I have." She grinned. "Conversation closed. But speaking of priorities, is it your turn to vacuum? Because I think it is."

They both started giggling and then walked in comfortable silence back to the car. Mary Catherine was grateful for Sami, for a friend who cared and could laugh with her.

The ride home didn't include a single mention of Marcus. Mary Catherine was relieved. There really was nothing to say, nowhere the topic could go.

Not until they were back at the apartment and Mary Catherine was in her room did she close the door and listen to the message from her cardiologist. The man's secretary had simply advised her to return the call. Her test results were in. Mary Catherine waited, her hands trembling. If only she could put off the news, put it aside and forget about it. *Father, I need You . . . I can't do this without You.* She closed her eyes and waited. After a minute or so a feeling of peace came over her. Peace enough to make the call.

She opened her eyes and tapped the call button.

A receptionist answered. "Dr. Cohen's office."

"This is Mary Catherine Clark." She couldn't shake the feeling that the news would be bad. "I missed a call from your office earlier."

"Yes, hold on." The woman sounded efficient. There was no reading her tone. "The doctor would like to speak to you."

"That's fine." Mary Catherine dropped on the edge of her bed and waited. The seconds felt like days.

"Hello? Mary Catherine?" It was Dr. Cohen. He was in his forties. One of the top cardiologists in Los Angeles.

"Hi. I missed your call earlier." She paused. "Is it about my test results?"

"Yes." He sighed. Not a quick sigh. But the kind that doctors tended to do when the information ahead might be difficult.

She closed her eyes again. *Whatever it is, God, You're in charge. You know the number of my days. I believe that.*

"Mary Catherine, I'm afraid the results were worse than we expected. Your valve has deteriorated greatly. But more than that, your heart is further enlarged." He paused. "I shared your results with a few respected cardiologist friends of mine. One in New York. One in Boston."

Mary Catherine slid off the edge of her bed to the floor. She brought her legs to her chest and let her forehead rest on her knees. "Okay. Yes?"

"We all came to the same conclusion. Mary Catherine, I'm afraid we'd like to put you on the heart transplant list. The sooner the better."

A black hole seemed to open up in the spot where she was sitting. Darker and darker, blacker and blacker. She could feel herself falling into it and the whole time she was certain of one awful reality. There was no bottom. She would keep falling for the rest of her days.

Because this was the worst possible news he could've told her.

"Mary Catherine? Do you understand, dear?"

"Yes, sir." Her voice was soft and shaky. "So . . . what's next? What should I do?"

"We have to have you into the office in the next week or so for a complete checkup. You'll need more tests and blood work. Then there'll be a screening exam and some paperwork. All of that before we can get you on the donor list."

In the black hole where she was falling, Mary Catherine couldn't catch her breath, couldn't exhale fully. Like she was drowning in her own bedroom. "You mean . . . you want the surgery soon?"

"It's never that easy." He sounded discouraged by the fact. "Your heart and valve can go on for probably another nine months or a year. Even after your appointment it could be months before we get you on the transplant list. It's a process. Many people never get a donor, Mary Catherine. I need to be honest."

She still couldn't believe what he was saying. The transplant she'd expected in the years to come was supposed to be a valve replacement. Not a heart transplant. What about Africa? What about helping with the youth center? How was she supposed to get her pilot's license if she was waiting for a heart transplant?

"Did you hear me?" The doctor's words were kind. "I'm so sorry, Mary Catherine. I know this must be a shock to you. Frankly, it was a shock to me. That's why I sought the other opinions." He waited a beat. "I'm very, very sorry."

"It's okay." She was still falling, still trying to get a full breath. What about mornings on the beach and swimming with the dolphins?

"I'll transfer you back to the receptionist. I'd like you to book the appointment as soon as possible."

"Yes, sir." Mary Catherine couldn't lift her head, couldn't do anything but feel herself falling. What about her brand-new job as a graphic designer at Front Line Studios in Santa Monica? She was supposed to be there next year when their first movie hit theaters.

A heart transplant?

Sometime before the end of the year?

Falling . . . falling. Mary Catherine stood and steadied herself on the edge of her bed. Then with her remaining energy she walked to the window and looked at the blue sky. The beautiful Southern California sky. How could this happen?

She thought about her friends. Now she would have to tell Marcus. Not right away, but sometime soon. She'd have to tell all of them. If only she could stop falling, stop the blackness of the dark hole she'd stepped into. Before the call she'd thought she had till she was thirty. Another seven years at least.

Suddenly thirty felt like an impossible number. Like a gift.

Maybe there was some mistake. She felt fine, right? She wasn't short of breath or struggling with chest pains. People waiting for a heart transplant were very sick. Too weak to get out of bed. Mary Catherine clung to the window frame and thought about her morning, about the feel of Marcus's arm against hers. *What about moments like that, God?* There would be no time to make a difference, no time for learning the guitar or taking voice lessons.

She wouldn't live long enough for any of it. Mary Catherine closed her eyes, but the tears came anyway. The blackness was swallowing up the moment, and still she was falling. Everything was different now. Everything would change. And of course there was something else she would have to give up. The thing she only joked about every now and then and once in a while prayed about. The thing that would absolutely never be possible now.

Her hundred years.

23

Lexy couldn't stop shaking.

It was the morning of her prison tour. Mary Catherine and Marcus were going to pick her up and take her to the prison, an hour away. She stared at her full cereal bowl. She was too scared to eat. Too unsure about what was ahead.

Why had she agreed to the program? They wouldn't have given her very long at Eastlake juvie, right? Less than a year, then she'd have been back on the streets. But going to prison? Even a day there would be terrible.

Prison was the sort of place that took a person in and swallowed them up and never let them see the light of day again. The way prison had done to her mother. Lexy looked at the photo on the wall across from her. She and her mama before the arrest. Lexy stood and walked to the picture. She touched it, running her thumb over their faces. In the photo her mama's arm was around her shoulders and their smiles were the same. Their eyes, too. The arrest came the next day, an afternoon Lexy thought about all the time. The day her mama was locked up and sent away.

The last day the two of them had seen each other.

Lexy might've been maybe six in the picture. Her mama, maybe twenty-two. Her mom was beautiful and intelligent. She could remember sitting with her mom on the couch that week and watching TV. *America's Funniest Home Videos*, Lexy could still remember. Her mom was laughing and so Lexy had laughed, too.

When she was little . . . Lexy could remember laughing a lot with her mama. Why had her mom gotten into drugs? She could've done something different with her life. So why didn't she? Lexy stared at the photo and blinked. The reason was obvious. No matter how long she looked at the photograph, no matter how the two of them seemed there on the wall.

Her mother didn't love her.

Lexy was alone after her mama went away. Her grandma tried, but she never knew what was going on in the house. The summer Lexy turned eight was the first time she remembered the neighbor boy locking her in his bedroom and taking advantage of her. He was fourteen. At least she thought so. It had happened too many times since then. The bad all blended together. And none of it would have happened if her mama had been around.

Mamas are supposed to keep their babies safe.

Supposed to keep their babies in school and out of gangs.

Lexy felt her anger rising, taking over her heart and soul. If she had a soul. One day when she had babies, she wasn't going to leave them. She would move out of the slums to some nice place like Reseda. Lexy's grandma was from Reseda. Nice town in the San Fernando Valley.

Gradually a resolve built in her.

She had prayed to God for help and he'd given her the chance at this program. It was a little late to start wishing she'd served time instead. If she was going to make a change for her own kids one day, then this was the only way.

The Last Time In program. Whatever happened today, she could deal with it.

Her grandma's Bible was open again on the other side of the table. The way it was always open. *Hate evil . . . cling to good.* That's what the blond police officer had told her. And then he'd showed up again, right when Dwayne was going to kill her.

A sick feeling slammed into Lexy's stomach. Yes, Dwayne was definitely going to kill her. He had wanted to hide out at her grandma's house that day, but all of a sudden he looked at her like he was the devil himself and he ordered her back outside to the car.

"I can't have witnesses, baby. You gotta understand." That's what he told her. He said it again and again until they were almost to the car and then out of nowhere there was the blond police officer. Again. Towering and looking like he could take down a whole gang by himself.

Then the craziest thing Lexy had ever seen in all her life. The cop had appeared out of nowhere and grabbed the gun. That wasn't even possible. Anyone knew people couldn't just appear out of thin air.

But that's what the officer did.

Even that didn't scare Dwayne. Lexy thought the cop

would shoot her boyfriend right there on the street. That's when she had shouted out for help from Jesus.

Lexy didn't understand it, even still. Didn't know why she had called out the name Jesus, but something about that moment seemed to change things for the cop. Like he blinked a few times and he took his finger off the trigger. After that Lexy knew he wasn't going to shoot.

He was too good for that.

Hate evil . . . cling to good.

She was reminding herself when a text came through on her phone. It was from one of the WestKnights. *You in or not, baby? You're mine tonight. Dwayne's gone. I got next dibs.*

She stared at the text. Just stared at it as the words cut their way through her. Then she texted back without thinking. *I'm in.*

She looked at it and her heart felt hard and dead again.

He sent one last text. *Be ready.*

Tears slid down her cheeks. Who was she kidding? She would never have kids if she could help it. But if she did, she'd be just like her mama. How could she not? She was too far into the WestKnights to back out now.

There would be no babies, no family, no little house in Reseda. No life different from the one her mama gave her. No way to hate evil when it was a part of the air she breathed.

The time in prison today would not be her last time in.

It would be a preview.

24

Mary Catherine could've won an Oscar for how she pulled herself together and pretended to be fine. The acting had begun Friday night at the last training session and continued on to this morning when Marcus picked her up for the prison tour.

She was still in the dark hole, still falling. But she could see the light of day. If she didn't have a year left, she was going to live her days like never before. Starting today with the Last Time In program. This day wasn't about her.

It was about Lexy.

In the driver's seat beside her, Marcus seemed somehow aware that she was different. "You sure you're okay?" He'd asked her twice already. "Sorry. It's just . . . something in your eyes."

A smile lifted the corners of her lips. "I'm fine. Just tired. I was up late reading."

"Your pilot's manual?" He grinned at her.

"No, a novel." She told him the name. "My favorite author just had a book come out. I can't put it down." At least that much was true.

"I didn't know you were into reading." It sounded forced. Like he was trying to believe her. "Me, too. I love fiction."

"You do not." She laughed and she could feel the doubt in her eyes.

He raised his brow and pointed to himself. "Are you saying athletes don't read?"

"Not many of them." Even in light of her news, something about being with him made her forget everything but the moment.

"I take exception to that statement." He tipped his baseball cap to her. "This Southern gentleman loves to read. For real." His eyes stayed on the road. "When you finish this book that kept you up so late, I wanna read it." He glanced at her. "Deal?"

She was still laughing. "Deal."

The mood stayed light as they drove to Lexy's, but after they picked her up it changed. Lexy seemed completely shut down. More than she'd been the other day. Mary Catherine sat in the front seat next to Marcus and tried. "How were the last few days?"

Silence.

"Lexy." She kept her tone kind. "I know this isn't easy. But please answer me."

Silence.

"Okay, then tell me about your grandma. How does she feel about you going for the prison tour today?"

Again nothing.

Marcus reached over and gently touched Mary Catherine's leg. Then he shook his head briefly, as if to say it wasn't worth it. He mouthed the word *later*. Then he turned the radio to the local Christian station. Francesca Battistelli came on. The song was a new one Mary Catherine loved called "If We're Honest." She hoped Lexy was listening to the words.

Mary Catherine sang along. "'Truth is harder than a lie, the dark seems safer than the light . . .'" As the song played out a thought occurred to her.

The words applied to her own life as much as they applied to Lexy's.

Mary Catherine leaned back and let the lyrics wash over her. She loved every song by Francesca. This one and the one that had first given her hope that God might have more time for her than the doctors believed. The song was called "Hundred More Years." Mary Catherine looked out the window while the song played. Despite her best efforts at ignoring her own situation and trying to make today about Lexy, she felt the tears.

Life wasn't fair for her or for Lexy. Neither of them would likely ever have the lives they'd dreamed about. Mary Catherine's teardrops spilled down her cheeks before she could do anything to stop them. She wiped them with the back of her hand, careful not to catch Marcus's attention.

But he must've seen, because he reached out and took hold of her hand. He let the song play on, right to the last line . . . *If we're honest.*

Mary Catherine loved how her hand felt in Marcus's, loved that he would reach out and comfort her when he saw her tears. She smiled at him, no longer embarrassed by her watery eyes. Life was not all laughter and mornings at the beach.

It was okay to cry.

The music switched and it was Matthew West's "Strong Enough." Mary Catherine sniffed and settled into her seat. Crying might have been allowed, but it wasn't possible during Matthew's song. She sang along, quietly at first. "'You must, you must think I'm strong, to give me what I'm going through.'"

Then, to her surprise, Marcus began to sing, too. Louder and more off-key than her. "We'd make quite a duo for *America's Got Talent*." He was still holding her hand and now he winked at her.

It was impossible to stay sad around him. Plus the words to the song were too powerful. Okay, so she needed a heart transplant. And sure, not everyone on the list received one. Maybe she did only have a year left.

But she absolutely refused to use her days trying to stop falling, trying to see past the blackness. There would be time to cry, yes. But she had to believe in the message of the song. Especially with Marcus singing it at the top of his lungs beside her. That God was strong enough for her. Strong enough for Lexy.

After a minute, he released her hand and pretended to sing into a microphone. "I'm ready for *Fifteen Minutes*."

From the backseat Lexy said her first words of the morning. "Maybe not yet."

"Hey now." He looked at her in the rearview mirror. "You barely know me."

"Still." Lexy sounded disgusted. But it was a start. A way to connect. A bridge they could maybe cross again later today.

The rest of the drive was upbeat, and Mary Catherine didn't have to pretend to be okay. She actually felt it. Not until they reached the prison and started across the parking lot did Lexy hesitate. "I feel sick. Maybe we should turn back."

Mary Catherine stopped with her and so did Marcus. The prison loomed in the near distance, a monolithic structure made of block walls and razor wire. Everything about it looked intimidating.

No wonder Lexy felt sick. She was probably terrified, something they'd gone over in training. Mary Catherine put her hand softly on Lexy's shoulder. "Lexy, we'll be with you." The girl didn't jerk away. Mary Catherine smiled. "You'll be fine. I promise."

"Yeah." Marcus's voice was light and easy. Another tool they'd picked up in training. "Besides, I can't sing in there." Marcus had removed his baseball cap and left it in his Hummer. He peered at Lexy, clearly trying to see past her walls. "It's just a tour."

Lexy gave him a rude look. "I know." Whatever spurred her forward, she started walking again. "Come on." She looked back at Mary Catherine. "We can't be late. That's one of the rules."

They made their way past four security checkpoints, and then they were ushered into a large cement room with no windows and just one door. Tyler and Sami and the girl they were helping were already there. Sami had tried to meet the girl before today, but she hadn't been willing to meet.

Which was too bad because, as it turned out, Sami and

Tyler had Sierra Wayne's friend. Alicia Grange. The girl was tiny with pale blond hair. She looked barely old enough to be in middle school, let alone fourteen. Grand theft and truancy? Mary Catherine hoped the program worked for the girl.

For all the girls.

Over the next ten minutes the room filled up until all six girls were present along with their chaperone volunteers. At exactly ten o'clock the door opened and six prison guards pushed their way in. All of them seemed angry and put out, upset they had to be there.

This was part of the plan. Mary Catherine knew it. So did all the volunteers. But it was another thing to see the angry guards coming at them. Mary Catherine had to remind herself that these were volunteers. That no matter how it looked in this moment, these men and women cared very much for the girls in the program.

As for the volunteers, they would be advocates for the teens, people the teens could turn to when the reality of the prison visit became too much. That was one of the differences between Last Time In and Scared Straight. The point was to build connections between the teens and the volunteers. That way the volunteers would have a better chance of helping the teens stay off the streets in the days and weeks, even years, to come. At least that was the hope.

Mary Catherine tried not to think about the years she might not have to influence Lexy.

The guards moved toward them. They had their clubs out, and two of them were slapping them against their hands. *Here we go*, Mary Catherine thought. She stood close to Marcus, with Lexy standing in front of them. Already she was shaking.

"Got a buncha girls wanna spend their lives in here, that right?" The biggest prison guard lunged forward so his face was inches from the first girl. "You wanna be here? You gonna be a career criminal, missy?"

"No."

"That's 'No, sir'!" he screamed at her face. "Say it."

"No, sir!" The girl's voice could barely be heard.

"Louder!" He couldn't have been more than an inch from her. "Say it louder!"

"No, sir! I don't wanna be a career criminal, sir!"

The guard stepped back, his face an angry twist of knots. "That's better."

Mary Catherine had to remember to breathe. She could feel Lexy backing up, getting closer to her. Even in the first few minutes, Mary Catherine felt like the program was starting to work. Lexy was feeling a trust connection with her.

And the tour hadn't even started.

The other prison guards stepped into the action. Each of them went to a different girl. A muscled guard moved up to Lexy.

"Your guy's leader of the gang, right?"

Lexy didn't answer. She cocked her head back, the way she'd done when Mary Catherine first met her.

"We got a smart one here, do we!" He moved closer to her. "You dating the leader of the gang? Talk to me, gang girl. You've got no rights in here."

"He ain't the leader yet." Her words were soft, her eyes directed at the blank wall at the other end of the room.

"'He's *not* the leader yet. Sir'!" He enunciated each word for her.

Lexy put her hands over her ears. "He's not the leader yet, sir." She still didn't sound very loud.

The officer towered over her, his physical presence intimidating to everyone in the room. "Next time you forget you'll do pushups."

For a brief moment, Lexy looked back at Mary Catherine. Terror flashed in her eyes. Mary Catherine nodded. Lexy had to obey. That was part of the program.

"Don't look at your volunteer, gang girl." He twisted his head so his face was almost up against hers. "I changed my mind. Next time is now."

Lexy moved reluctantly to her hands and knees.

"You're going to do pushups, gang girl. Hurry up!"

Mary Catherine knew this would be the hardest part. Watching the guards treat the kids like they were prisoners. It was part of the program. After all, if they kept on the way they were headed, they would wind up here. And this would be a part of their everyday life. Having a prison guard in their faces, ordering them to obey.

This treatment was important. But it was almost impossible to watch.

Lexy began doing pushups. She was stronger than she looked. Mary Catherine would've guessed the girl wasn't quite ninety pounds. But her arms were strong.

Meanwhile, down the line the other guards questioned the teens. Some were being forced to do jumping jacks. Others looked terrified. One girl had to march to the opposite wall and back. Four of the six were crying by the time the guards stepped back and folded their arms. Lexy was one of those.

"Time for your fellow inmates. You make it back here, and

these women will become your family. Your best friends." It was the first guard. He was still bellowing, still lunging toward the girls with every other word. "You don't wanna know everything they'll become to you." He looked at his fellow guards. "Right?"

"You don't want to know." One of the guards shook her head.

"We'll let *them* tell you." The shortest officer walked to the door. "Follow me."

Marcus put his hand on the small of Mary Catherine's back as they walked with Lexy into the hallway and down a corridor. On the way they passed a row of cells and every one they passed was teeming with angry women.

The inmates pressed up against the bars, shouting obscenities and gesturing to the girls. Mary Catherine wanted to turn back. She could only imagine how Lexy and the other girls must feel. *Please, God . . . let this work. It's so hard. Please speak to Lexy at the depths of her soul.*

At the end of the corridor there was another room—this one much larger. At least it appeared that way through the window. The short guard turned and faced the group. "This is where you meet your new friends." She unlocked the door.

All around the room, the guards unlocked the doors of the smaller cells and the inmates joined the group in the open space. The area had four cement tables, built into the floor, each of them with attached cement benches.

Otherwise the room was empty.

Sixteen prisoners came out and started walking toward them. The collective anger from them was like a physical force. Something Mary Catherine had never experienced before. She was tempted to put her hand on Lexy's shoulder but that wasn't allowed. The volunteers were supposed to be a presence of shelter, safety. Hope, even.

But they weren't supposed to interfere.

Suddenly Lexy crumpled to the ground. "No!" She turned around and glared at Mary Catherine. "You didn't tell me!" she shouted at the closest guard. "How come no one told me?"

Marcus took Mary Catherine's hand again. "Pray," he whispered to her.

"I am." She had no idea what was happening. But the meltdown seemed to be caused by an inmate walking straight for Lexy.

A woman who looked almost exactly like her.

"No, Mama, no! You can't do this!" Lexy started to turn around and run for the door.

But the guard caught her by the arm and turned her back around. "What's the matter, gang girl? Didn't you think you'd see your mama here? You wanna be just like her, right?"

Mary Catherine felt the blood leave her face. Lexy had said that her mother was in prison. But Mary Catherine had no idea the woman was in this prison. Mary Catherine felt sick. This was turning out to be the worst idea ever.

"No!" Lexy was still trying to run.

This time the prison guard lowered his voice, as threatening as he could sound. "You keep throwing a fit and I'll lock your mama back up. Then you won't see her at all."

Lexy grew calmer. Tears streamed down her face as her mother approached. For a brief few seconds, Mary Catherine wondered if the woman was going to start crying, too. She looked upset. But then, just like the other inmates, she came to Lexy and started yelling.

"Don't cry, little girl. This ain't a place for tears," Lexy's mother snarled at her. "Last time I saw you, you was all sweet and pretty." She jabbed a finger close to Lexy's face. "Now look at ya! You a gang girl now, Lexy. That it? All cool, hanging with the boys." The woman couldn't have been very old. She looked like Lexy's older sister.

"Stop it, Mama." Lexy turned her head, her body convulsing with sobs. "I hate you! Leave me alone!"

Mary Catherine felt tears in her own eyes. The scene was too disturbing. Lexy clearly didn't know she'd see her mother here. Let alone have her mama turn on her this way.

"No, little girl!" Her mom shouted louder. "I will not leave you alone!" Her mom moved so she could get her face up close to her daughter's. "You wanna be here with me, I'll show you what it's like."

Her mom rattled off a list: the danger of showers, the way young inmates could get owned by older inmates. The way inmates could sell the young ones to other inmates for a pack of cigarettes.

"You hear that, daughter!" Lexy's mother yelled. "A pack of cigarettes!" She practically spat in Lexy's face. "You want this. Don't forget it!"

Lexy looked ready to faint. She was sobbing and only every so often did she manage to say anything. "Please, Mama. Stop it!"

Mary Catherine could feel her heart breaking. There was a reason for all this. But watching Lexy's mom shout at her, yelling at her mercilessly, was more than Mary Catherine had planned for. Only one thing could be worse than this sort of prison tour.

Coming here forever.

ASPYN AND JAG had hovered over the prison tour from the beginning. It was the ugliest hour they'd spent on earth.

"I'm going to see the girl's mother." Aspyn nodded at Jag. "She's back in her cell already. You all right by yourself?"

"Go ahead." Jag looked like he understood. His job was to keep Marcus and Mary Catherine safe.

Instantly, Aspyn was an orderly ready to clean up after the prisoners. Her uniform was light blue and she had a mop bucket. She walked out of a janitor's closet and past a few cells to the one where Lexy's mother was. The woman was alone, her back to the others.

She was crying.

Aspyn slipped into the cell and shut the door behind her. "What's wrong, Camila?"

The woman spun around. Everything angry and hateful about the way she'd looked earlier was gone. She took a step back. "Who are you?"

"I'm new." Aspyn had one hand on her mop. "Gotta clean up. But I heard you crying."

It took a minute for Camila Hernandez to believe she wasn't in danger, that Aspyn didn't want anything from her. Aspyn started moving the mop slowly over the floor. So she wouldn't raise Camila's suspicions. This moment was for Camila alone.

"You didn't answer me." Aspyn moved her mop slowly in a circle between them. "What's wrong? Why are you crying?"

Camila melted against the back wall of her cell. "My girl . . . she was in there. I haven't . . . seen her in so many years."

Aspyn slowed the mop. "You wanted to be with her, right?"

"I did." She covered her face with her hands. "I love her so much. I never stopped loving her. This is the last place I wanna see her."

Aspyn and Jag had figured this was going to happen. They knew Lexy's mother was an inmate here. And now Aspyn felt herself hurting for Camila. "You're doing the right thing. Don't give up." Aspyn set the mop aside and went to Camila. She took hold of the woman's hands. "Write your daughter a letter. Do it now. Do you have paper and a pen?"

The woman sniffed. "I do." She pulled a small plastic box from beneath her bunk. "In here."

"You write it. I'll make sure she gets it." Aspyn took a step back. "Your daughter will know you love her."

"I miss her so much." Camila allowed another wave of tears. "I wanted to run up and hug her. I missed . . . everything. All her growing up years. I'm the worst mama ever."

"No." Aspyn wanted Camila to hear her. "You're doing everything you can to keep her out of this place. That makes you a loving mother."

Camila shook her head. "She'll hate me forever."

"Write the letter." Aspyn needed to go. Lunch would be over soon and she couldn't be caught.

For a long time Camila only stared at the paper and pen. Then she sniffed and nodded. "I will." She lifted hesitant eyes to Aspyn. "Can you help me?" She looked embarrassed. "I'm not . . . that good a writer."

Aspyn felt her heart melt. "Yes." She took the paper and pen from Camila. "Tell me what you want to say."

"Okay. I'll try." The woman struggled to find the right words, but in the end the message was all hers. Camila seemed calmer. "You'll make sure she gets it?"

"I promise." Aspyn hesitated. "You ever pray, Camila?"

"I want to learn."

"There's a Bible study once a week in your cell block. Did you know that? Monday nights."

"I never go."

"Start." Aspyn smiled at her. "God has plans for you, Camila. Even now. Even here."

The woman looked dazed. Like the news was hard to believe. Aspyn couldn't wait another minute. She nodded. "I'll get the letter to Lexy."

With that Aspyn stepped out of the cell and back into the closet, and disappeared.

25

MARY CATHERINE WANTED NOTHING more
than to take Lexy in her arms and comfort her. The poor girl.
The day was dragging on, but Lexy never recovered from seeing her mother as one of the inmates. After lunch it was more
of the same, and by the time the prison tour was finished, Lexy
looked like she might pass out.

Tyler and Sami's girl also spent most of the day crying. If
Mary Catherine had to guess, she doubted the girl would ever
steal again. School probably looked like a dream vacation
compared with this.

Marcus stayed by Mary Catherine's side as they ushered
Lexy through the main space and into the corridor. They were
halfway to the holding room where they'd started when a
woman mopping the floors stopped Mary Catherine. "I got
something for you."

"What?" She stopped. The woman looked familiar, but
she couldn't place her.

"Here." The orderly kept her eyes averted. She handed Mary Catherine a folded piece of notepaper. "This is for Lexy." Then the woman put her head down and kept mopping.

The group was still moving, so Mary Catherine had no choice but to keep walking. "Did you see that?" she whispered to Marcus.

"What?" He looked behind them and back at her.

"That woman. She was mopping the floor." Mary Catherine held up the letter. "She handed me this. Said it was for Lexy."

Marcus looked back again. "There's no one there."

"She was just—" Mary Catherine turned around and stopped for a second. "Where is she? She handed me the note like five seconds ago."

"Maybe she stepped into a closet. You know, to put the mop away."

Mary Catherine started walking again, backward, and then turned around. Lexy was a ways ahead of them. "That's so weird." She gave Marcus a puzzled look. "She looked familiar, too."

They reached the first checkpoint. None of them had been allowed to bring in phones or purses or anything else. Now they were checked again and Mary Catherine produced the letter. "This is a letter for our participant. From her mother."

The prison guard took the letter, opened it, and read it. He shrugged. "Fine." He nodded to Mary Catherine as he handed it back. "Put it in your pocket. Anyone asks you tell them Sikes said it was okay."

"Thank you, sir."

Mary Catherine could only imagine what Lexy's mother

might've written to her. How she had gotten the letter to the orderly and how the orderly had known to get it to Mary Catherine made no sense at all.

When they reached Marcus's Hummer back in the parking lot, Mary Catherine did what she'd wanted to do all day. She hugged Lexy for a long time. "I'm sorry. About all that."

Lexy resisted the hug. "I didn't know . . . my mama was gonna be there. Someone shoulda told me."

"We didn't know either." Marcus stood on her other side. "I'm sorry, too. Today was brutal."

"Yeah." Lexy slid past them and climbed into the backseat of the SUV.

They were on the freeway before the girl spoke again. "What happened to the boy?" Her tone was softer than before. "The one Dwayne shot?"

"He's still in the hospital." Marcus looked in the rearview mirror. "He's in bad shape. Everyone's praying for him."

Lexy started crying again. Mary Catherine could hear her. Even through her tears, she managed to speak. "Can . . . we pray for him? Right now? Please."

"We can." Mary Catherine turned around best she could in her seat.

"Father, we've asked You before, but now we come to You again with Lexy. Lord, please give Jalen a miracle. Please wake him up and by Your divine touch, would You please heal his brain? Let him talk to his mama again and let him live the way he did before. We know it's a lot, God, but You can walk on water. You can calm the seas with a whisper." Her voice was raw with emotion. "We believe You can do this. In Jesus' name, amen."

Through her tears, Lexy managed two simple words. "Thank you."

In the front seat, Mary Catherine doubted the girl was used to saying *thank you*. The Last Time In program was working, like the training promised. But Mary Catherine had wondered if anything would pierce the darkness that surrounded Lexy Jones.

Until now.

Mary Catherine waited until they were fifteen minutes from home before she pulled out the letter. "Your mama wrote you something. She had someone give it to me before we left."

At first Lexy didn't seem like she was going to let them know she cared. She didn't respond for five minutes. Then she muttered, "What's the letter say?"

"You can read it."

"No." Lexy hesitated. "How 'bout you read it? I'm not that good at letters."

It occurred to Mary Catherine at the same time it must've occurred to Marcus. Lexy couldn't read. At least not very many words. Otherwise she never would've wanted two people she still didn't know well to read the letter from her mother.

Before Mary Catherine opened it, she looked back at Lexy. "Has your mother written you before?"

"Never." She raised her chin. "I hafta hear it to believe it."

"Okay." Mary Catherine unfolded the piece of paper and started at the beginning. "Here it is. 'Dear Lexy, this janitor lady is helping me write this to you.'" Mary Catherine felt her heart react. The cycle of drugs and violence and illiteracy felt almost hopeless. "'I'm so sorry for today. That wasn't me in there. It was me acting. All I wanted to do when I saw you was run up and take you in my arms.'" Mary Catherine blinked back tears. "'The way I used to do when you were little.'"

Marcus put his hand on Mary Catherine's shoulder, silently lending his support.

"Keep reading." Lexy didn't sound as hard as before. "Please."

Mary Catherine worked to find her voice. "'I made so many mistakes, Lexy. I never should've gotten involved with that man. I wouldn't be here if I could've said no. Instead I've spent every day since they locked me up sitting here and missing you. I think about what you must look like and how big you must be getting. I think about you in school making better choices than me.'"

Tears ran down Mary Catherine's cheeks. She wiped them before they could fall on the letter. "'You're with your grandma and I know she's a God-fearing woman. So I believe you can find the right way, Lexy. The way I missed out on. The right way is with God, baby.'" Mary Catherine blinked so she could see. "'I said I'd do the program today on one condition. If I could work with you. Because you see, baby, in those minutes even though I was yelling at you, I was near you. I could see your eyes and your face. The face I've missed so much.'"

Mary Catherine lowered the letter. She looked at Marcus and shook her head. "I can't," she whispered. "It's too sad."

Lexy leaned up as far as the seat belt would allow. "Is that all?"

Marcus gave her shoulder the slightest squeeze. He mouthed the words *You can do it*, neither of them wanting

Lexy to know how difficult the moment was for Mary Catherine.

"No. There's more." She sniffed and lifted the letter again. "'So please forgive me. I never wanted to yell at you. I wish I could see you every day, baby, but not in here. Not like this.'" Mary Catherine wiped her eyes again. "'I keep a picture in my mind, Lexy. You and me when you were six years old. Kindergarten graduation. Grandma took our picture. All I want to do every day is go back to that time and do life over again. I'd learn how to be a better reader and writer, and I'd be there for you at nighttime, to read to you and teach you how to sound out words. I'd make sure you and I were safe, away from the gangs and shootings. And I'd spend every day showing you how much I love you.'"

From the backseat, Mary Catherine could hear Lexy sniffling.

She had to finish. She wiped her tears once more. "'But, Lexy, baby, I can't go back. We don't get to do life over again. So, baby, please just know that everything today was an act. It wasn't me. It was my way of keeping you out of here. And that's the only way I have left to love you. My precious daughter. I just wish I could've hugged you before you left. I love you always. Every day. Even from here. Love, your mama.'"

If Mary Catherine hadn't felt drained after the prison tour, she definitely felt it now. She folded the letter and handed it to Lexy. "I'm sorry. I wish you and your mama could've had this moment together. Away from everyone else."

Lexy took the letter. "Thank you. For reading it." She pressed the letter to her chest and looked out the window.

Like she was seeing all the way back to the time when she was six years old. Her kindergarten graduation.

There was no room in the car for music or conversation. Not after that. Mary Catherine sank low in her seat and again Marcus reached out and took her hand. He'd been wonderful all day, attentive to her and Lexy, and always aware whenever the situation felt too intense. He had taken her hand or put his arm around her a number of times today.

She appreciated all of it. Especially now. He ran his thumb along her hand and kept driving. Mary Catherine thought about the woman's letter, and the miracle it was that the janitor woman had found them before they left. Especially considering it was the only letter her mother had ever written to her.

All her life Mary Catherine had been aware of people less fortunate than her. While her parents dined at the country club, she would go with her youth group friends to serve dinner at the Nashville Rescue Mission. Her parents would vacation at Atlantis in the Bahamas, but when they started taking two or three trips there each year, Mary Catherine opted for mission trips to Africa and Guatemala instead.

Still, never in that time had she thought about this segment of life. The people behind bars. How desperate and defeating to wake up every day in those small cells. And then to know that the extent of your freedom involved the common space on the other side of the cold metal bars.

More than that, Mary Catherine had never thought about the families those prisoners had left behind. Yes, they all had done something to deserve punishment. Crimes against people and society. There was a reason they were in prison.

But what about Lexy? What had she done wrong? Her daddy was dead before her third birthday, and her mom was serving time before she stepped foot in first grade. No wonder the pattern of crime and punishment continued in the inner city. Kids had no one else to follow. Mary Catherine closed her eyes. *Lord, please let this program work for Lexy. I'll do everything I can—as long as I can. But we can't do this without Your help.*

They dropped Lexy off ten minutes later, and again Mary Catherine hugged her. "We'll be back to pick you up on Tuesday at six." She searched Lexy's eyes. "Okay?"

"Okay." For the first time since Mary Catherine had met the girl, she didn't look defiant. She looked lost and broken. The letter from her mother was still clutched tight in her hand. "Maybe someday . . . you can read me the letter again."

"I'd like that."

Lexy walked inside without looking back.

"What a day." Marcus held the car door open for Mary Catherine.

"So hard." On the way back to her apartment, they didn't say much. But once more Marcus held her hand. As if there was no way to get through a day like this without physical support. As she showered that night and turned in early, she thought about her heart. Something she hadn't thought about all day. So what if she didn't have much time left to make a difference? Her life mattered today. It had mattered for Lexy.

Right now that was enough.

JAG SAT NEAR Jalen's hospital bed. It was Tuesday afternoon and they'd been keeping watch over the child for nearly three days straight. He was off his breathing tube, but he still hadn't woken up. Today, though, something was different. Jag could sense a breakthrough.

Something about the aroma of prayer that had made its way to heaven. That had to be it. Orlon had told him and Aspyn before the mission began. Keep praying. Make sure everyone is praying.

There were times Jag wondered what people thought about prayer. Most humans didn't understand it. They thought God was a genie, someone to beg favors off . . . or a Father to turn to when things went wrong.

But that wasn't prayer at all.

Praying was simply talking to God. Of course, the Lord loved hearing from His people. Whether they were believers or not. When Marcus Dillinger asked his Twitter followers to pray, it started a tidal wave of sweet requests directed straight to heaven.

It wasn't that a child like Jalen needed so many voices praying on his behalf. God heard the desperate prayer of a single voice in a dark room. But sometimes something happened that caused the world to sit up and take notice. A time when miracles could sway a generation to believe in God.

Miracles amidst tragedies.

And in that way, God would be glorified. Which wasn't always easy for people on earth to see or understand.

"Do you feel it?" Jag looked at Aspyn. This mission had kept them busier than either of them had ever imagined. "Something's happening with the boy."

"Yes." Aspyn held out her hands. "It's God's energy. It's all around us."

"It'll be any moment now." Jag hovered closer to the boy. "Come on, Jalen . . . Jesus, breathe life into him. Please, Jesus. We need You now. Here. Please."

Aspyn was praying too, and there in the chair beside the bed, Shamika had never stopped praying. Even when she doubted, she kept seeking God's help. Never stopped believing.

Suddenly the boy made the slightest coughing sound.

Jag could hear the celebration starting in heaven. The other angels cheering as they watched. "Come on. Wake up, boy." Jag held his hands over the child's heart. "We feel You working, God. Be glorified through Jalen."

And with that the boy began to sputter. His mother was on her feet instantly. "Jalen! Jalen, it's Mama. I'm here, baby. Wake up, Jalen." She began to cry, her voice desperate to see another sign of life from her son.

Again Jalen coughed and his eyes began to blink. They didn't open. It would take a few minutes. But he was coming to. That much was certain. "Nurse!" Shamika ran to the door and yelled into the hallway. "Please! Someone come here! My baby is waking up."

The miracle was unfolding. Jag felt the sense of deep wonder and awe, the feeling that never grew old. When death was denied the last word.

If Jesus were standing here, He'd be crying. Jag was sure. This was the reason He'd died on the cross. So that what was dead might live again.

"Jalen! Baby, I'm here." Shamika hurried back to her son's bed and put her hand alongside his face. Her hands trembled, and her voice was unsteady with the weight of her emotion. She kissed her son's cheek and took hold of his hand. "I've missed you so much, Jalen. Please . . . open your eyes, baby." She whispered low near his cheek. "Come back to me, sweet boy. I want to see you smile again. God, please bring him back to me." She brought his hand to her lips and kissed it. "Jalen . . . Mama's here!"

Again the boy tried to blink his eyes open, and this time his eyelids opened just a hint. Slowly his lips parted. He peered at Shamika. "Mama? I'm hungry!"

"Okay, baby. We'll get you something to eat." Then without hesitating, Shamika did what most humans forgot to do in a moment like this.

She fell to her knees. "Jesus, You did this! You gave me my boy back. Thank You, Lord. Thank You." With words and tears she continued to give praise to Jesus, the One who had brought her son back to life, the One from whom all good things flowed.

Including this.

26

MARCUS WASN'T SURE WHAT he had expected from the first group meeting with the girls, but he had never imagined this. They met at six o'clock that Tuesday in a classroom at the police station—one of the requirements. Tyler and Sami sat with Alicia, the small blond girl, and Marcus and Mary Catherine sat with Lexy.

Just the six of them.

But the topics that had come up made Marcus glad for the training. On the surface the girls looked very young. Too young to be in trouble. But they were sadly wise beyond their years. Today's focus was on the difference between love and abuse.

Since they were allowed to discuss God in the group meeting—as long as the participants were willing, and they were—Marcus started the meeting with God's definition of love. He read it straight from 1 Corinthians 13 in his Bible.

"'Love is patient; love is kind.'" Marcus looked up at the

two girls. They seemed despondent. Like they weren't listening at all. He kept reading. "'Love isn't envious, doesn't boast, brag, or strut about. There's no arrogance in love; it's never rude, crude, or indecent—it's not self-absorbed. Love isn't easily upset.'"

Lexy was the first to roll her eyes. Marcus stopped reading and waited for her to speak. Finally she tossed her hands up. "Okay." Hurt filled her tone. "You want to talk about 'love isn't rude'? Dwayne's rude all the time." She looked at Alicia at the other side of the table. "That's how guys are, right?"

"Definitely." The girl fidgeted, twisting her fingers together. Clearly uncomfortable. "Love always means someone's angry."

For the next half hour they talked about how for these girls love felt the exact opposite of how it was described in the Bible. Lexy announced that last week Dwayne had threatened to kill her.

"See, Lexy?" Mary Catherine's voice was kind. "That's what we're talking about today. Dwayne has harmed you emotionally and physically. That's not love."

Marcus loved watching Mary Catherine in this setting. It was like she was made for this role. She looked past Lexy's exterior hardness and spoke to the girl's heart. Now that their time together was winding down, both girls had opened up a little.

Lexy talked about the guys she'd had before Dwayne, and Alicia talked about her current boyfriend. Though Alicia's crimes involved theft, her relationships had apparently been equally bad for her. Marcus's heart hurt for the young girls. It would take more than ninety minutes to teach them that abuse was not the same as love.

But they had made more progress than Marcus dreamed.

It was like Officer Kent had told them at the first day of training. These kids were starving for someone to invest in them, to care enough to listen and give guidance. Sure, they'd throw up ten-foot walls at the beginning. They might do that at every meeting. But eventually they'd talk, and then there were only two rules for the volunteers.

Listen. And don't act shocked.

Which was hard, Marcus had to admit. Where were the people who were supposed to care for these girls and cherish them? Because of neglect or lack of supervision or bad patterns, their lives had been destined for violence and abuse, crime and even prison.

Today's meeting, though, proved there was hope. The girls were talking and they were listening. That was a better start than he had expected for their first gathering.

When the meeting was over, they took the girls to Dairy Queen. Part of the program was introducing normal moments, where the girls could be kids. Marcus couldn't believe how easily the girls laughed and enjoyed themselves. A different environment changed everything.

They were about to leave when Mary Catherine's phone rang. She stepped away to answer it and almost at the same time her eyes lit up. "He is! That's amazing!" She put her hand to her mouth and shook her head. "Shamika, I can't believe that. Yes, I'll tell them." Her eyes shone with unshed tears, her smile filling her face. "It's a miracle for sure."

The call ended and she motioned the others close. Lexy and her new friend came closer, clearly interested. "What happened?" Lexy was the first to ask.

"Jalen's awake! He's talking to his mama."

"That's amazing." Marcus came to Mary Catherine first, and then Sami and Tyler did the same. They formed a circle, their arms around each other.

"I can't believe it." Sami's eyes welled with tears. "This is the best news."

Marcus felt his knees shaking. "He wasn't supposed to live."

"I know." Mary Catherine's eyes shone with joy. "Now they think his brain will be fine!"

"Wow . . . thank God!" Marcus whispered the words. He loved that they were all together when the news came in. His Twitter followers were still spreading the word, still getting people all over the world to pray for the boy.

"Should we go there?" Sami sounded hopeful. "I'd love to see him."

"Maybe tomorrow. Shamika said the doctors are doing tests." Mary Catherine opened up the circle, her eyes on Lexy and Alicia, who were standing awkwardly a few feet away.

"We can all go together." Tyler sounded thrilled. "I've seen God do a lot of things, but this is at the top of the list."

Marcus put his arm around Mary Catherine's shoulders. Their friendship was more comfortable now. So much of what they'd been through together had been intense. He wanted to be there for her, to be available in the highs and lows.

And this was one of the highest highs of all.

Only then did Marcus notice Lexy. The girl had her hands over her face, her back turned to them. He watched her walk slowly outside, like she was in a trance, and sit at one of the tables. Again she buried her face in her hands, her shoulders shaking.

"What's up?" Marcus looked at Mary Catherine.

A knowing look came into her pretty green eyes. "I think I know." She motioned for him to follow her. "Come on. Let's go talk."

Tyler and Sami stayed inside with Alicia. Marcus led the way, opening the door for Mary Catherine as they joined Lexy at the table. Mary Catherine sat next to her and put her hand on the girl's back. "Sweetie, what's wrong?"

Lexy was sobbing. Marcus realized the great changes happening in the girl. She had been so hard when Mary Catherine first met her. But at the prison tour and again today, her heart was plain for all of them to see. She still had miles to go if the journey was to make a difference. But these moments of opening up with her emotions were another beautiful answer to their prayers.

After a minute, Lexy lifted her head. Her eyes were red, her face wet. "Nothing."

Marcus was confused. "Nothing's wrong?"

"No." She sniffed, and another few sobs came over her. "I told God if He was real, then He needed to save that . . . that little boy." She shook her head. "I didn't believe He could do it." She covered her face with one hand this time. "So He must be real." She looked at them again. "God must be real."

There was a stinging in Marcus's eyes as he watched the scene. Mary Catherine slid closer to the girl and put her arm around her back. "That's right. He is real. And He loves you, Lexy. More than you could understand."

"I thought I'd pick something really hard." She wiped her

cheeks with the backs of her hands. "Something only God could do. If there was a God." The sobs were still coming. "But . . . but if there's a God, then why would He love me after . . . after all the things I've done?"

They had so far to go. Marcus drew a deep breath. "Lexy, we all have things we shouldn't have done. God wants us to be sorry for that and tell Him. Then, well, we can have a fresh start. A new life."

"For me?" The hardness flashed in her eyes again. "In my neighborhood? It'll take more than that where I come from."

"Maybe there's another way." Marcus refused to feel defeated. "There's always another way with God."

Lexy thought about that and slowly she nodded. A smile lifted the corners of her lips and she turned to Mary Catherine. "When you go see the boy tomorrow . . . can I go?"

Mary Catherine shared a quick look with Marcus. There might be legal reasons why Lexy shouldn't go to the hospital. After all, she'd been in the car with Dwayne when the shot was fired. Mary Catherine moved closer to Lexy and looked intently into her eyes. "I'll see what I can do."

"I know . . . you probably think the mama wouldn't want me." She sniffed. "All I wanna do is tell 'em I'm sorry."

"Okay." Mary Catherine was beyond kind. "I'll talk to them. I'm sure they'll be so glad you're sorry. And that you were praying."

Lexy nodded again. "I need to get home. I told my grandma I wouldn't be late."

Tyler and Sami and Alicia came out then and said their goodbyes. "I have to work early tomorrow." Sami made a face. "I'm thinking about quitting. Finding a job that really matters." She and Tyler shared a smile. "We'll see! Mary Catherine is rubbing off on me."

Marcus and Mary Catherine took Lexy home, too, and the minute they were back in the car alone, Marcus felt his heart soar. "You have time for dinner? We could pick something up and take it to my house?"

It looked like Mary Catherine might say no, find some reason why they couldn't spend another few hours together. But then she found her best teasing smile. "I could cook."

"Organic, no sugar, no bread." Marcus laughed. "Or . . . we could get pizza?"

Mary Catherine pressed her shoulder into the seat. "Seriously. I'll make you almond chicken. It'll be better than pizza. Promise!"

"Actually, that sounds pretty amazing."

They went to Whole Foods near his house and picked up the ingredients. Then they worked together in the kitchen. "You be my sous chef. How's that sound?"

"It sounds like a girl's name." He washed his hands. "But if you have to call me Sue to pull off this meal, go ahead." His computer was on a desk at the edge of the kitchen. He turned on Pandora and found a piano station.

Mary Catherine was trying to explain that the word *sous* meant he was her assistant for the night. "Just think." She grinned as she handed him an onion and a bell pepper. "You might fall in love with organic cooking. The way I did. This night could change your life."

She turned to the sink and Marcus stood there, just watching her.

He had never met anyone like her, the way she didn't care

what people thought of her, the way she grabbed onto life like every day might be her last. He smiled. Yes, he might fall in love, and no question this night could change his life. But if that happened it would have nothing to do with the cooking.

The chicken was in a colander and Mary Catherine was separating the pieces. She looked over her shoulder. "Hey. You're supposed to be mincing those."

"Mincing." He found a knife and a cutting board. "I know cutting and slicing. I believe you were going to give me a demonstration on mincing. Wasn't that it?"

She moved to the adjacent sink, washed her hands, and dried them on a clean towel. "Okay." She came to him, her eyes sparkling. Night had fallen and it was just the two of them in the house. "Step aside."

He did, but not too far. The smell of her perfume filled his senses and made him wish they were more than a couple of friends making dinner together. She took the teaching seriously. "Mincing is smaller, neater." She cut a slice of the onion and then, using small movements, she turned the slice into tiny squares no bigger than the head of an eraser.

"Looks like a lot of work." Marcus laughed. "You sure we can't just slice them?"

"It's not hard. Here." She handed him the knife. "You try it."

He was utterly aware of her presence, the way their arms touched, the movement of her hands. He took the knife and gave it a try. The work was tedious, but he managed it.

"Perfect!" She leaned closer, moving the pile of minced onions to the side. "You got it?"

He wanted to take her in his arms and dance across the kitchen, forget about the onions and everything. Everything but her. Instead he did a slight bow. "Glad it meets your approval, Miss."

She giggled at him. "You sure you weren't raised in the South?"

"I wish." He held her eyes. "Maybe I would've met you sooner."

His words seemed to touch her deeply. Her laughter softened and she smiled at him. "I would've liked that."

"Me, too." He looked at the onions. "Better get cooking."

When it came time to prepare the chicken, Mary Catherine made a mixture with almond flour and spices. She dipped each small boneless chicken piece into a bowl of almond milk and then coated it with the almond flour. In the pan, she melted coconut oil and fried the chicken in that.

"Uh, can I just say . . ." Marcus hadn't smelled something so good in months. "You can cook dinner at my house anytime."

"Told you it would change your life." She kept the teasing tone. Probably because it was safe and fun, given her determination that she didn't want more than a friendship.

Marcus didn't care. He only wanted to be with her. The teasing was fun for him, too. He sautéed the minced vegetables along with sliced zucchini and they ate out on his deck. The night was unseasonably warm. Still seventy-five when they sat down to eat.

"It's beautiful here." Mary Catherine looked out over Silver Lake. "Sami told me about the view."

"You need to come over more often." The meal was perfect. But it was nothing to how wonderful it felt sitting here with her, outside of training or prisons or anything to do with the youth center. It reminded him of that first walk. Before the shooting.

"So the Wayne family lives around the corner?" Mary Catherine grinned at him. "No wonder you're so close with them."

"Rhonda loved you. She really wants to get to know you better."

"I'd like that."

"By the way." Marcus held up a bite of the almond chicken. "You've sold me. Organic cooking definitely just changed my life." He chuckled. "Seriously, I had no idea it would be this good."

"Food the way God made it actually tastes better. That was one of the things I had to learn."

"So you really don't eat sugar or bread? Like ever?"

Mary Catherine laughed. "You make it sound like a punishment."

"I guess I can't imagine." He took another bite. "Tell me you didn't want ice cream earlier."

"Sure, it tastes good. But I didn't want it." She raised her brow. "Sugar causes disease. Diabetes. Dementia." She gave him a silly look. "And yes. I do eat pizza once in a while. I'm not perfect."

He stared at her, studying her. Memorizing her high cheekbones and the shine in her eyes. "Awfully close."

She smiled. "You're too kind."

"Just honest."

They finished their meal, and the whole time their conversation was easy and fun. Marcus could feel himself falling into her gravity, but he didn't care. The sensation was mesmerizing. Together they carried the dishes in and Mary Catherine looked back at him. "When will Tyler be home?"

"I think he and Sami went to the movies." He pulled his phone from his pocket and checked the time. "Probably not for another hour."

Mary Catherine nodded. They worked rinsing their plates and scrubbing pans. The whole time Marcus tried to think of a reason to make her stay. It was just after nine o'clock. "You don't work tomorrow, right?" He gave her a hopeful look.

"I don't. The studio's closed every other Wednesday." She dried her hands on the towel.

"Can you stay? For a little while?"

"Well . . ." She seemed to struggle with the idea. But then she smiled and slipped her hands in the back pockets of her jeans. "I noticed your pool table."

She was constantly surprising him. "You play?"

"Play?" She cocked her chin. "I thought about going pro. Decided it would take too much time."

The air between them was electric. Marcus was grateful for the distraction of a pool game. "Well, then . . . rack 'em up."

Halfway through the first game, Marcus started to laugh. "I thought you were kidding. About going pro."

"Never." She feigned an innocent look. "I never tease, Marcus. Not ever."

"Not about pool. That much is for sure." She was three balls ahead of him. "You could win a fortune at this. How'd you learn?"

"Played with my dad." Mary Catherine held her cue stick at her side and smiled. "It was the way we connected."

Marcus shook his head. "The man taught you well."

They played two games, and she won them both. "I could suggest best of five. But I'm afraid that would become best of seven at this rate."

Her laughter mixed with the piano music drifting through the house. "Maybe something less competitive."

"I have backgammon." He nodded toward a shelf in the family room. "Nobody touches me at backgammon."

"Next time." She smiled. "I should go."

"It's early." He didn't break eye contact with her. "Let's step out back again. The stars are probably just perfect." He reached for her hand and hesitated, drawn to her in a way he could barely fight. But she had made herself clear at the beach. He couldn't push for more. "Come on." He walked with her outside and they took up their spots at the railing, staring at the lake.

"You were right." She lifted her face to the sky. "The stars are gorgeous."

"I don't come out here often enough. You can feel God on nights like this."

"Mmmm. I like how you said that." She put her head on his shoulder. "You're right. I can feel Him, too."

Marcus was losing the fight. Why would she put her head on his shoulder if she only wanted to be friends? He slipped his arm around her waist and they stayed that way, the music falling all around them.

A buzzing came from Mary Catherine's phone. "Sorry." She pulled it from her pocket. "I'll turn it off."

But before she did, she looked at the message. "It's from Shamika." Mary Catherine adjusted the brightness so she could read it. "She says Jalen is doing even better." A soft gasp came from her. "The doctors think he'll make a full recovery!" She texted back as quickly as her fingers could move. "Amazing!" She turned her phone off and slid it back into her pocket.

Then, as if it were the most natural thing, she hugged him, impulsively linking her arms easily around the back of his neck. "I can't believe it. So much has happened. So many highs and lows. I mean, only God." Her laugh was part surprise, part relief.

Marcus slipped his arms around her waist. "I wondered how I'd go on. At the youth center." He spoke near her face. "If the boy never woke up."

The hug was meant as a celebration. One of those extreme highs they'd shared over the last week. Except after a few seconds, neither of them seemed to want to let go. She rested her head on his shoulder again. The song was something instrumental by Chicago.

He leaned back, searching her eyes. "Wanna dance?"

"I'm not very good at it." Her voice fell to a whisper as they started to sway.

"I doubt that." He held her close and led her slowly across the deck. Never mind that they were outside. The magic of the moment made him feel drunk with joy. Was this really happening? They were dancing under the stars and Mary Catherine wasn't fighting him?

"You, on the other hand . . ." She tilted her face to his. "You're quite the dancer."

"Took it for a year in college." He laughed. "Coach thought it would give the pitchers better balance."

"Did it?"

He looked at the sky and then back at her. "It gave me this."

"Well then." She didn't look away. "I guess it was worth it."

The song was ending, and Marcus could barely breathe. They were back at the railing and he slowed their movement, stopped their swaying. "Mary Catherine." He swallowed. He didn't know what to say. He only wanted this feeling to last forever.

She put her head on his chest again. "I'm sorry."

"No." He gently lifted her chin so she would look at him. "Don't be sorry."

Her eyes told him whatever was happening between them, she was feeling it, too. "I can't . . . I'm not . . ."

"Shhh." He took her face in his hands. It was too late to stop, too late to do anything but kiss her. The way he had wanted to kiss her since their walk that night. Slowly he brought his face to hers. Their lips touched and the feeling was light and passion and desperation, all at the same time.

She didn't fight him, didn't try to pull away. Instead she returned his kiss, working her hand up his neck to the back of his head. Marcus was consumed by her, taken by her in a way that affected his entire being. She moved him, body and soul. He drew back, checking her eyes. "You okay?"

"I need to go." Her lips were still parted, her breathing faster than before. "Marcus . . . I want this." She hung her head and when she looked up the sadness in her eyes was greater than the heat a few seconds ago. "I can't. I'm sorry." She leaned up and kissed him again, slowly, deliberately. But it was a goodbye kiss.

Marcus could feel the difference.

She stepped back. "Take me home. Please."

He shouldn't have kissed her. Marcus reached for her hand. "I'm sorry. I should've waited."

"No." She shook her head. "It's not you. It's me. I can't . . . explain it." She allowed him to hold her hand as they walked in and got her things.

On the drive, disappointment greater than the breadth of the sky washed over him. What was wrong with her? When they reached her apartment, Marcus killed the engine and turned to her. "Is it me? You're not attracted to me?"

A single laugh escaped her and she let her head fall back. "Are you serious?" She looked at him, her cheeks slightly redder than before. "I can't even think around you." She took his hand and looked deep into his eyes. "You make me feel . . . like I've never felt."

"So . . ." Hope shot through Marcus. "Maybe we need to take things slower. Stay with Tyler and Sami so"—he laughed—"you know, we don't wind up dancing under the stars."

The laughter left her and she looked at her hands for a long few seconds. "It's not that." She angled her face and turned her eyes to him once more. "Please, Marcus. Trust me."

He wanted to argue, but there wasn't room. She had left him no choice. He climbed out, helped her from her side of the car, and walked with her up to the door. When he hugged her, she let herself linger. But she eased back before either of them might think about another kiss. "Thank you." She smiled, her eyes as sincere as summer. "I had the best night ever."

"Me, too." He wanted to stop time and make her explain things. How could she slip into her apartment without helping him understand? If they both felt this, then how come . . . ?

Her smile was marked with longing. "Bye."

"Bye."

He waited until she shut the door before turning around and heading back to his car. In all his life he'd never felt like this. The way she made him feel. And since she was as drawn to him as he was to her, he had no idea what the problem was or why she wouldn't tell him. He knew only one thing.

He wouldn't give up until she did.

27

Except for their group meetings at the police station on Thursday and a hangout with Tyler and Sami Saturday night, Mary Catherine did a good job of avoiding Marcus the rest of the week.

She had no choice.

Her doctor appointment was that Monday morning and as she signed in at the office, she knew her hurting heart had nothing to do with her health. The night at Marcus's house had been the best. Mary Catherine had told him the truth.

The pull Marcus Dillinger had on her was beyond anything she had ever experienced. She had replayed that night a thousand times and always she was sure. There was nothing she would've done differently. He made her laugh and feel, and in his presence all of life was good and right and whole.

By the time they stepped out on the deck after the pool games, Mary Catherine didn't care about her damaged heart or the time she didn't have. She had that night. It was all she could think about.

The nurse stepped out and called her name. "The doctor will see you first. We'll do paperwork and blood tests later. Before you leave."

"Yes, ma'am." She followed the woman to a familiar room, changed into a hospital gown, and waited.

A few minutes later Dr. Cohen stepped inside.

"Mary Catherine." He shook her hand. His face was masked in shadows. "I'm sorry about all this." He raised his brow and gave a single shake of his head. "It took me by surprise." He pulled up a chair and sat down, facing her. "A heart transplant is always a possibility for anyone with your condition. But I really thought you'd only need a valve."

The Internet had given Mary Catherine ample time to research. "I wrote down a few questions." She pulled her phone from her purse. "Is that okay?"

"Of course." He crossed his arms, waiting.

She opened her notes app and started at the top. "'Why not a valve transplant first? It wouldn't be as invasive, and it could buy us more time.'" She looked at Dr. Cohen. "Right?"

"Well . . ." He angled his head one way and then the other, as if he were weighing the possibility. "I had a patient last year. Tried to replace his aortic valve and his ascending aorta—exactly the surgery you would need in that scenario." He gave a sad shake of his head. "Young guy. Just twenty years old. Suffered a heart attack during the procedure, which created more damage. He had to be resuscitated nine times before we finished operating."

The doctor explained that the surgery did such damage to

the young man's heart, he was suddenly rushed to the top of the transplant list. "Thankfully, he got his heart. He's doing well."

Mary Catherine hung onto those last few words. "A person with a heart transplant can do well?"

"Yes." Caution sounded in his tone. "There are nearly two hundred thousand patients waiting for a heart. Conditions have to be just right."

"But if . . ."

"It's a long road, but yes. We know of heart transplant patients who are still alive twenty, twenty-five years after surgery. It's rare but possible."

Possible.

For the first time since the call from the doctor's office a week ago, Mary Catherine didn't feel like she was falling. The blackness that sucked her hope and light and energy cracked and she could see blue sky again. "I . . . guess I didn't know that."

"It doesn't always work that way. If a patient gets a heart . . ." His brow raised again. "*If* . . . well, then, sometimes the patient is sickly for the next few years and then we lose them. Their bodies can reject the organ or vice versa. Lots can go wrong."

"Dr. Cohen." Mary Catherine smiled. "You should know me better than that. I'm not a lots-can-go-wrong kind of girl. I believe in the most rare possibilities." They'd been over this before. "Remember?"

"Yes." The doctor smiled, patient. "Because that's where God works best."

"Exactly." She tried not to think about Marcus. "I had

made a plan not to fall in love. Given the situation." Her smile took some effort. "But from what you just told me, there's still hope."

"For love?" The doctor had a fond way of looking at her. As if she were his daughter.

"For life. To really live."

"Your situation is complicated, Mary Catherine. I don't want to give you false hope."

"Hope can never be false. It's the product of faith, the substance of things not seen." She exhaled and tried to settle down. "I didn't know heart transplant people could live that long. That's all."

"I'm afraid I have more, Mary Catherine."

She blinked and sank a little into the examination table. "Okay."

Dr. Cohen opened a notebook and went over her tests in detail. Her situation was much worse than he had expected. Worse than Mary Catherine had known.

"You'll start feeling symptoms soon. Tiredness, shortness of breath." He peered at her, sterner than before. "You need to curb the things that give you an adrenaline rush. I know that'll be hard."

Mary Catherine stared at the man and then let her gaze fall to a spot on the floor. "Adrenaline rush?" She muttered the words and then looked at him again. Her whole life was an adrenaline rush. "Like . . . skydiving?"

"That, obviously. But boogie boarding . . . sprinting . . . competitive games. Anything that makes your heart work too hard."

The darkness was back. "You're asking me to quit living?"

"No." He sighed and closed the notebook. "Mary Catherine, I'm asking you to take it easy. Be serious about this. Until we can find you a heart."

She nodded, but inside she was falling . . . falling the same as before. "And you think it'll be at least six months before I'll be on the list?"

"Yes." He frowned. "I'm so sorry. You'll need to talk once a week with a counselor about what's too much activity now and what's appropriate health and wellness care as you near your time on the list. We have a myriad of blood tests for you today and . . ."

Mary Catherine couldn't hear him. He was still talking, still telling her all that was required of her and how her life would change while she waited to be placed on the list. Something about the time being sped up if her next series of heart tests in a few months were significantly worse than they were now. All Mary Catherine could think about was adrenaline, and the fact that it had been hurting her heart.

The very thing that made her feel alive was taking years off her life.

Dr. Cohen was explaining something else, something about how though she wasn't quite sick enough to be on the list, she was getting there quickly. But Mary Catherine was picturing the children on her refrigerator, the ones she sponsored. What if she didn't get a transplant? Or what if she got one and it didn't take? She would never have another time like now to go to Africa, to live there and move among the people and love them the way she had always dreamed.

She couldn't have Marcus, that much was certain.

At least she could have this. "Dr. Cohen." She must've interrupted him because he looked like he was caught midsentence. "I'm sorry. I have to tell you something."

"I understand this is difficult." His patience remained. "What is it?"

"I'm moving to Africa. In a month." She couldn't pose the idea as a question. He'd never let her go. "I'll be living in Uganda for six months." She was aware she sounded a bit intense. She softened her tone some. "I . . . thought you should know."

"Mary Catherine, you can't move to Uganda. Not when we're trying to get you on the transplant list."

"You're doing the tests today, right? Any additional tests can be done there. They have a hospital. We can have the results sent to you."

Dr. Cohen looked caught off guard. "That would be . . . well, it would be highly unconventional. You'd have to return at a moment's notice. The minute we could get you officially on the transplant list."

"I understand." A surge of elation rushed through her. Her damaged heart had cost her so much, but it wouldn't cost her this. She would leave California as soon as possible. Spend a week with each of her parents and then fly to Uganda. She was connected with a ministry there, and they were always looking for volunteers. If she had it her way, she would spend the next six months building a new orphanage. Something that would serve the people for decades.

Even if she couldn't.

"I have to tell you, Mary Catherine, I completely recommend against a move to Uganda. With your heart this way."

"I have no symptoms. I feel wonderful." She thought

about dancing with Marcus the other night. "Better than wonderful. If I'm going to move to Uganda I should do it now. Before I start to feel . . . whatever you said."

Again he looked stumped. "How quickly can a person get home from Uganda? That's what I want you to find out. You'd need a couple days' travel at least." He removed his glasses and massaged his brow. "I'm not sure that would get you here quickly enough ."

"I won't wait that long. If I start to feel sick, I'll come home."

"You understand that this goes against the advice on adrenaline?" Dr. Cohen set his notebook on the counter beside him. "I ask you to keep things calm, and you tell me you're moving to Uganda."

"It's a calm place, Dr. Cohen. Really." She grinned. "No amusement parks, no skydiving. Very simple."

"Let's get through your blood tests and paperwork." He stood and pulled his stethoscope to his ears. "Let me take a listen." He moved around behind her and pressed the base to her back. "Breathe."

Mary Catherine filled her lungs.

"Again."

She did as he asked. He spent several minutes listening to her heart through her back, and then through her chest. When he was finished he exhaled, like someone not willing to keep fighting. "No more than six months. You got that?"

"Yes, sir." Mary Catherine felt the exhilaration surging in her veins. It wasn't the kind of joy she'd known the other night in Marcus's arms. But it was something better, given the circumstances.

It was a plan.

She could check one more thing off her dream list and maybe while she was busy working with kids and babies in Africa she would get better. Stranger things had happened, right? Look at little Jalen.

The doctor left her to get dressed. She could hardly believe it was going to happen. Sure, her doctor was reluctant. But still he had cleared her to go to Africa. Her favorite nurse drew her blood that day. Sally Hudson. Sally was small and pretty with blue eyes and a warm smile. She was quick with a kind word or a Bible verse.

Usually when Mary Catherine needed it most.

"Hey, honey." Sally sounded subdued as she led Mary Catherine to a chair in the lab. "I heard about your tests."

"I still don't believe it." She held out her arm so Sally could reach her vein. "I keep thinking there has to be a mistake."

"Well, don't you go believing everything a doctor says." Sally put a stretchy band around Mary Catherine's upper arm as she felt around for the vein. "In 2001 I was diagnosed with leukemia. No one in my family was a match."

She inserted the needle in such a way that Mary Catherine didn't feel a thing. Sally smiled at her. "Doctors told me I didn't stand a chance without a bone marrow transplant. So I did the only thing I could do. I cried out to Jesus." The nurse focused on the blood draw. "Changed my whole life."

Mary Catherine appreciated the story. "You look super healthy."

"A few years later they found a donor. Perfect stranger. Perfect match." She finished filling three vials with Mary Catherine's blood. "Only God has the number of your days."

"I believe that."

"You have one chance to write the story of your life. Make it a bestseller." Sally put a piece of cotton and a bandage over Mary Catherine's arm on the place where the needle had been. "Look at this." She took a framed photo from the desk behind her. "This is my family. My daughter Angie had us all meet in Ohio for a family reunion. That's me and my husband. Our four kids and ten grandkids. That was the day we had our annual candy-making." Sally had never looked happier. "If I listened to every awful thing a doctor told me, I would never have prayed for a miracle."

Mary Catherine held onto Sally Hudson's words long after she left the office. But as she drove home through heavy traffic she let her mind drift. She was no longer stuck on an LA freeway. In her mind, she was on Marcus's back deck, dancing beneath the stars, feeling the amazing attraction and lost in his arms. *Stop*, she told herself. There was no point thinking like that.

She would go to Africa and she would believe the trip might even be good for her. She would watch for symptoms and head back if her blood work or tests or pain level changed. She had to go. The trip would give her the one thing she desperately needed, the one thing she had to figure out before she changed her mind.

How to say goodbye to Marcus Dillinger.

JAG WAITED AT the door of the examination office, Aspyn at his side. They were both stunned. "I didn't see this coming."

"How could we have?" Aspyn looked ready to fight, ready to take action. Only this time there was nothing to act against. They could do nothing about this problem.

Because it was inside Mary Catherine's chest.

"The enemy will stop at nothing." Anger filled Jag's heart. Illness was part of a fallen world, the handiwork of the darkest forces on earth. "There has to be something we can do."

They had known Mary Catherine had a heart condition. That she would need a valve transplant in a few years. Not a big deal, they figured.

But this . . .

"We have to find a reason for her to stay." Aspyn's eyes blazed. "We need to ask Orlon."

"And pray for wisdom." Jag was in his element here in LA. But a heart condition? One that threatened to take Mary Catherine's life in less than a year? "It will take all of heaven pulling together."

They watched as Dr. Cohen typed his notes, filling out a report on his visit with Mary Catherine. The man sat alone in his office. He looked deeply defeated. A call came in and he answered it.

Jag and Aspyn listened intently.

"I told her I consulted with you and that we all agree." The doctor stared out the window. "No . . . I didn't tell her that." He paused. "It's such an unusual case. She isn't sick enough for a transplant today. But six months from now . . . you're right. It might be too late." He released a tired sigh. "She's in serious trouble." He waited. "Yes, I know. I tried to tell her."

"It's worse than we think." Jag's voice was distant.

"There's nothing more we can do." Aspyn's tone was broken. "It will have to be another Angels Walking team. Months from now."

"In Africa?" Jag's frustration nearly overwhelmed him. "We have to think of a way to keep her here, in Los Angeles. With Marcus."

It was a dilemma they'd battled for the past week. Finding ways to keep Mary Catherine and Marcus together. Jag's mind raced, still every time an idea came to him the impossibility was greater. Especially now that Mary Catherine was determined to leave.

Aspyn was right. They seemed out of options.

They moved to the waiting room, where Mary Catherine was filling out a stack of paperwork. Jag felt the heaviness in the room, the deep discouragement coming from Mary Catherine. *It's okay, dear girl*, he wanted to tell her. *Jesus isn't finished with you*. This Angels Walking mission might be nearly over.

But they hadn't lost yet. The greater battle was still at stake. Jag forced himself to hold on to that truth.

Even if the next stage of the war took them to the opposite ends of the earth.

28

Marcus could feel her slipping away. He picked Mary Catherine up each Tuesday and Thursday for the meetings with Lexy at the police station, but no matter what he suggested, she wouldn't spend time with him. Not alone.

Tyler and Sami were talking with Alicia, while Marcus, Mary Catherine, and Lexy listened. The program had been incredibly beneficial for both girls. At least it seemed that way. They hadn't had a run-in with the law, and every week they opened up a little more.

Lexy planned to be homeschooled by her grandmother for the next few years and get a job. She didn't know what the future held, but she was finished with the WestKnights. She had made that decision two weeks ago. Even sent texts to everyone in the gang. She got some pushback, but nothing like what she expected.

Sadly, there were plenty of girls ready to ride shotgun with guys from a gang.

The conversation now was about future plans, what Alicia would do in the coming months while the school year played out. Marcus tried to listen, but he struggled to focus. Mary Catherine was sitting beside him. He could feel the way she moved, sense the way she loved these lost girls.

She consumed him. There was nothing he could do to change the fact.

He let his mind drift. The two of them never talked about what had happened between them that night at his house, and he didn't push for answers. When they said goodbye he could see the pain in her eyes, the same pain that stayed with him whenever they were apart. It was insane to think that he hadn't figured out what a treasure she was until the beginning of January.

Now it was the first Thursday in February, the last meeting at the police station with the girls. Tomorrow morning Marcus and Tyler would leave for Glendale, Arizona. Spring training would begin Saturday. And then he wouldn't see her for two months.

For some reason, Marcus had the sense he didn't have long with Mary Catherine. Maybe because he was leaving tomorrow. But it was more than that. He couldn't quite get his mind around the feeling. Yet still it was there. No matter how hard he tried or how much he prayed, he couldn't find his way back to that moment with her in his arms, under the stars on his deck.

Marcus had thought of a hundred scenarios. Reasons she wasn't willing to think about dating him. Plausible possibilities for why she wouldn't talk to him about it. Some days he figured there must be something going on back in Nashville, something she had to make right before she could move on. Maybe it was someone her parents wanted her to marry.

Or maybe that was it. Her parents. Maybe they wouldn't approve of her dating a biracial guy. Whenever that thought crossed his mind, Marcus always dismissed it. If race had been an issue, she would've said something by now.

There were times when he thought maybe she had something physically wrong with her. Like she couldn't have kids or she was allergic to baseball diamonds. Maybe she'd suffered some traumatic event as a child and she wasn't able to form lasting connections with people. That was a legit disorder, right?

Marcus shifted in his seat, his eyes on Alicia, who was still talking.

Whatever the reason, there was no denying it. The feeling was there each time they were together. And lately she had kept her distance again, the way she had when they first started hanging out.

A few days ago after the meeting with the girls, Marcus and Mary Catherine took Lexy to the youth center. The new director was doing a great job. His work meant that Marcus could stop by when he wanted to, pay for pizza each week, and still get on with baseball. For now that was a more realistic setup.

That night they had played a pickup game of basketball with some of the teens who were there. When it was over he and Mary Catherine had high-fived. But when he tried to hold her hand, she eased away from him. "Gotta get water!" she had told him.

Sure, she had been out of breath. But that wasn't why she left so quickly.

Marcus tried to stay in the moment. Alicia was done talking. She smiled at Tyler and then at Sami. "Is it okay if . . . I still meet with you? Like once a month or something?" She looked uncomfortable for the first time that afternoon. "I think I might really need that."

Involvement in the program after the first four weeks was optional. But all of them were willing to help. At least they'd agreed on that at the beginning.

Tyler stroked his chin, clearly trying to find an answer for the girl. "Marcus and I leave in the morning for a few months." He looked at Sami.

"I'll be here." Sami reached over and patted Alicia's hand. "We can definitely meet."

"Me, too?" Lexy looked from Sami to Mary Catherine. "Could we maybe all meet?"

"I want to." Mary Catherine was quick with her answer. "But I'm not sure about my schedule."

Sami smiled. "I can promise you girls this. I'll be available for both of you. Once or twice a month at least. But let's talk and text more than that."

Marcus sat back in his seat and looked at Mary Catherine. Something had just happened, but he couldn't figure out what. Why wasn't Mary Catherine saying anything? How come she didn't offer to meet with the girls? He met her eyes, but she looked away. A sick feeling started in his stomach and quickly moved to his heart.

Just like he thought, she was pulling away. Not just from him, but from all of them. Whatever else happened, he had to get to the bottom of this. Figure out what was wrong and why she was distancing herself. By tomorrow it would be too late to sort out what was happening, to hear what was going on in her heart. So that left just one option.

He would have to find out tonight.

MARY CATHERINE COULDN'T look Marcus in the eyes. They were all four going out to dinner after the final meeting with the girls. She had already told Sami her plans to move to Africa. She would tell the guys tonight. At the same time.

The session ended, and Officer Charlie Kent joined them along with a few new volunteers. Mary Catherine recognized one of the women as Aspyn, the neighbor who had pushed Marcus out of the way the night of the shooting at the youth center. Mary Catherine and the woman exchanged a smile.

Officer Kent asked the four of them to talk about how they thought the program had gone, and then finally he turned to the girls. "Would either of you like to tell our new volunteers about the difference this time has made?"

Mary Catherine didn't expect either of them to say anything. They'd come miles since a month ago. But that didn't mean they would share here. But even as she was telling herself the reasons Lexy wouldn't talk, the girl raised her hand. "I'd like to say something."

Lexy sat up straighter. Something else she wouldn't have done at the beginning of the program. "Before, I just always assumed I'd be in prison one day." Her eyes looked tender. "Like my mama." She turned to Marcus and then Mary Catherine. "I didn't know I had a choice. But now I know I got someone who cares about me. I don't need to hang with the guys, risking prison and getting killed. I belong somewhere else now."

Moments like this Mary Catherine wondered if she was making the right decision. Maybe she was supposed to stay in Los Angeles and help Lexy. She could stay out of Marcus Dillinger's way and keep from falling in love with him. And never—no matter what—have a night like the one at his house. If she could do that, she could stay.

But she would miss her one chance at Africa.

When Officer Kent was finished, the group dispersed. Aspyn walked up to Mary Catherine. "Remember me? From the youth center that night."

"Of course." Mary Catherine would never forget. Marcus was alive today because of this woman.

"I wondered if you heard about the latest situation. The kids on the street are talking about the program." Aspyn smiled. She put her hand on Mary Catherine's. "You've done a wonderful job."

"Thank you." Looking into the woman's eyes was like looking into the ocean. They were that light, that complex.

"Anyway"—Aspyn glanced at the door—"there's another dozen girls ready to go through what Lexy did. But we only have a handful of volunteers." Aspyn gave Mary Catherine a single sheet of paper. "This describes the need." She smiled. "I told Officer Kent I'd ask you to stay on. You and Sami. The city really needs you."

Mary Catherine looked at Marcus across the room. He was talking to Tyler, his long legs and filled-out shoulders reminding her of what it felt like to be in his embrace. She looked back at Aspyn. "I'm afraid I may not be staying in Los

Angeles." She took the piece of paper. "I'll keep it in mind, though."

"Okay." Aspyn didn't move. She looked deep into Mary Catherine's eyes. "Just remember . . . you don't have to go halfway around the world to find a place to help out. The need is very great right here." She smiled again and then slipped her purse onto her shoulder and headed for the door.

For a few seconds Mary Catherine wondered how Aspyn knew. How was that possible? Had she somehow talked to Sami? Or was she just guessing, assuming Mary Catherine might be leaving for some sort of mission work?

The woman had to still be just outside. Mary Catherine hurried to the door to call after her, but the parking lot was mostly empty. Just a few cars, nothing and no one else. She took a few steps out the door and looked to the left and then to the right. The woman had already driven away.

But her message remained.

It was a message Mary Catherine would keep with her. So that she would know there was a place for her here. If she was ever healthy enough to come back and take on work like this again. For now, she didn't dare dream of a time like that. She looked at Marcus again and felt the now-familiar hurt. No, she would stay in Uganda until she was sick enough to need a heart. Then she'd come back.

Not a day sooner.

MARCUS MADE RESERVATIONS at Gladstones in Malibu. A bit of a drive, but not bad considering the beautiful winter night. The moon was full, so he requested a table by the window. They arrived a few minutes early and found the place nearly empty.

Exactly as Marcus hoped it would be.

With his and Tyler's flight to Arizona set for the morning, anything that needed to be said had to be said now. Tonight. They took their table and chatted about the Last Time In program while they ordered and waited for their food. Only then did Sami look at Tyler and Marcus and finally Mary Catherine.

"I have an announcement." She folded her hands and smiled. "I can't believe I did this, but I quit my job!"

"What?" Mary Catherine lived with her, and she apparently hadn't heard anything about this. She laughed softly. "And you say I'm impulsive."

"I know. You changed me." Sami laughed, too. "I didn't make up my mind till today at work. I decided my time had to be worth more than handling public relations for businesses and movie stars." She grinned at Marcus. "So I took the marketing and community affairs job at the youth center. I'll mostly work from home, but I'll be there a few days a week."

Tyler looked hesitant about her decision. "I told her it was too dangerous. It's one thing to meet with the girls at the police station. But the youth center . . ." He took Sami's hand and paused for a moment. His smile started in his eyes as he looked at her. "I'm happy for you, Sami. And I'm proud of you." He turned to the others. "She told me it was something Mary Catherine would do."

Marcus sat next to Mary Catherine across from the other

two. Mary Catherine was about to say something, he could sense that much. But he had the worst feeling that whatever it was, he didn't want to hear it.

Then just when he wasn't sure he could take another moment of her pulling away from him, beneath the table Marcus felt Mary Catherine reach for his hand. She didn't let go. "Sami, you'll be perfect. The community is ready for change. I really believe that."

"After working with the Last Time In program, I figured I had to make a change." Sami smiled at Mary Catherine. "Because you have to live your life, right?"

"Right." Mary Catherine gave Marcus's hand a slight squeeze. "Speaking of which . . ." Her smile looked weak. "I have an announcement, too."

Only Sami didn't seem surprised. She simply turned approving eyes toward her friend and waited.

Mary Catherine looked at Sami and then Tyler. "I'm moving to Africa. I'll leave here in the middle of the month to spend a few weeks with my parents in Nashville. Then I'm off to Uganda."

Marcus released her hand. He turned to her, but she wouldn't look at him, wouldn't face him. He worked to keep his tone even. "What . . . brought this on?"

"I've been planning it." Finally she turned to him. Her eyes begged him to understand. "It's something I've always dreamed of doing. I just got clearance a few days ago."

Clearance? Marcus felt like he was going to be sick. He wanted to take Mary Catherine down to the beach and hear the real story, the reasons she would've chosen to leave. Especially now, when she was making such an impact with Lexy.

When she had admitted feelings for him. He struggled to keep his tone even. "What do you mean, clearance?"

"I've been in contact with a ministry in Uganda. They need someone to coordinate the building of a new orphanage." Again her smile didn't reach her eyes. "We figured it out this week." She tried to sound upbeat, but she was definitely failing. "I'm their girl."

There was nothing Marcus could say. Any conversation about the issue would have to happen later, when they were alone. If they were alone. Tyler and Sami made small talk about Africa and how Tyler had always wanted to take a mission trip there. Maybe one day they would all go.

The banter did nothing to ease the devastation Marcus was feeling. Halfway through dinner he thought of another question. "How long will you live there?"

"That's the good news." She hadn't tried to take his hand again. "Only six months. I should be able to make sure the orphanage is built and established in that time."

Marcus did the math. Six months meant she'd be back sometime in August or September. Just when baseball season would be wrapping up. Was this why she hadn't wanted a relationship? Because she knew that behind the scenes she was working to move to Uganda?

In some ways the idea was better than the other scenarios Marcus had imagined. He'd be busy pitching and traveling. He was frustrated she hadn't told him sooner, but six months away didn't have to be the end of things between them. They could talk and Skype, right?

He felt bad for pulling his hand away. He reached for hers and she willingly let him. This time he slid his fingers between hers. The way they'd never held hands before. She smiled at him, a sad sort of smile, and again her eyes said more than her words could. At least here.

"Everything will be so different tomorrow." Tyler put his arm around Sami's shoulders. "Sami told me she might make a trip to Arizona halfway through spring training." He smiled at Mary Catherine. "She hoped maybe you'd come with her."

"Yeah." Mary Catherine frowned. "She told me that earlier today. I would have. If the move to Uganda hadn't come through."

Marcus wished she'd quit calling it a move. She was taking a trip. Nothing more. He wasn't going to let her go, not until she told him she didn't care about him.

A somberness hung over the table as they finished eating. Tyler was right. Come tomorrow everything would be different. But Marcus wasn't finished with tonight. He would drive her home and they would finish this conversation later. She didn't have to be afraid of being gone for six months. He would've waited much longer than that.

He could hardly wait to tell her.

29

Mary Catherine was quiet on the drive back
to her apartment. Halfway there, Marcus asked if she could
come back to his house. So they could talk about her trip.

"I really can't." They weren't holding hands this time. "I
have to work tomorrow."

Marcus didn't respond.

She hated this, hated the look in his eyes. He didn't understand, and she couldn't blame him. The trip to Uganda
worked in her favor. Her leaving meant she had one reason
why it wasn't an option to give in to their feelings. Their lives
were going in different directions.

They were both quiet until they reached the apartment.
She wanted to talk to him. This was the last time they'd see
each other for a long time. Maybe forever—depending on how
things went with her heart. She couldn't let him leave here
upset with her.

"Walk me up?"

"That's all? Just walk you up and say goodnight and that's it?" He wasn't angry, just confused. She could see that much in his eyes. She understood. The chemistry between them, the attraction and pull—it was undeniable. They had so much in common. She prayed God would give her the words to help them both understand.

"Sami's out with Tyler." Mary Catherine smiled at him as they reached her apartment door. "Come in. Please."

He looked relieved. The truth was, neither of them were willing to say goodbye yet. Once they were inside they sat together on the sofa. The lights in the room were dim—perfect for the farewell ahead.

The space between them felt like an ocean. Marcus pulled one leg up so he could face her. "Why didn't you tell me?"

"I wasn't sure." Mary Catherine didn't want to hurt him. She had never meant to get involved so quickly. "I mean, I always talked about Africa."

"Not moving there." His tone wasn't antagonistic. He only wanted to make sense of what was happening.

"It . . . came together quickly."

Marcus exhaled and for a minute he looked away, looked at the apartment and the photos on the walls. "You've never asked me inside before."

"I wanted to." He was dissolving her defenses again. "I just . . . I didn't want either of us to get hurt."

"That's what this is about?" He reached for her hand and again she let him take it. "I'm not worried about getting hurt. What I feel when I'm with you . . . it goes all the way to my soul."

Mary Catherine nodded. "I know." She eased her fingers between his. "It's that way for me, too. With you."

"So what's six months? You miss baseball season, big deal."

"I don't want to miss it. I want to be at every game." She paused. "I watched you pitch that World Series win from right here."

He looked in her eyes, to the places only he had ever seen. "I wish I'd known you then."

"Me, too." She ran her thumb over his hand. "I've thought about this. How we've gotten so close so fast." She tried to smile, but it didn't touch the sadness in the air between them. "I think it was all the tragedy. The shooting. Jalen. Lexy. Even the program."

"And our faith." He looked like he wanted to slide closer to her. But he kept his distance. "Your most beautiful crazy amazing faith made me take a harder look at God. The Bible. One day after we were together I drove out to Dodger Stadium and gave my life to the Lord. It was the day before I was baptized."

"Mmm. I didn't know." It was another reason why the connection between them was so strong. What they shared was more than physical and emotional attraction. It was spiritual. If only she had more time.

Marcus didn't look away. "What did Aspyn tell you today?"

"She said the program needs more volunteers. She was hoping I'd stay on for another round."

"See . . . that's what I don't get." He leaned his shoulder into the sofa and looked at her. As if maybe the answers were in her eyes.

She loved the way his pale blue sweater made his eyes look even lighter. The connection between them was so strong it breathed life into her. At least it felt that way.

"I wish . . ." His voice was thick with emotion. "I wish you would let me love you, Mary Catherine."

Tears clouded her view. She had known tonight would be difficult, but she hadn't expected this. All she wanted was to be in his arms again, kissing him under the stars as if she had ten thousand more nights like this.

She didn't want him to see her cry. Without saying a word, she stood and walked to the window. She leaned on the frame and looked at the dark sky. Through the glare of the streetlight she couldn't see a single star.

There was no need to turn around. She could feel him coming to her, the way she always felt his presence when he was near. He slid his arms around her shoulders and pulled her to him. "That makes you sad? That I want to love you?"

With all her being she wanted to stay facing the window, to keep from turning into his embrace. But she could no more stop herself than she could tell herself not to breathe. Or her heart not to beat.

"Marcus." She turned and faced him and nothing else in all the world mattered. "It makes me sad because you can't."

He didn't want to fight with her. That much was evident in his eyes. They were deep and afraid and full of the most incredible love. All at the same time. He nodded. "Okay." For a moment it looked like they might kiss. Because neither of them was strong enough to resist this kind of pull. He ran his thumb softly over her cheekbone. "I'll wait then. Till we're both back here. When the season's over and you've had your time in Africa."

A quiet terror ran through her veins. She wasn't getting through to him. If he waited for her, things would only be worse. He would be devastated when he learned the truth. And that wasn't fair. Her health was her problem. "That's just it." She searched for the next words. "I might not come back, Marcus. I might stay in Nashville."

A new sort of fear filled his expression. "You can't do that." He worked his fingers back into her hair. "Please. Tell me you'll come back here."

"Sometimes . . . it just can't work." She thought about telling him the whole truth . . . or lying to him, convincing him she wasn't interested. But he would never believe her. Not when she was seconds away from changing her mind about Africa. That was the effect he had on her. She put her hand on his chest. If only her heart were as strong as his. Her eyes searched to the deepest places in his soul. "Can you understand that?"

"No." He held her closer, and for a few seconds he brushed the side of his face against hers. "I won't understand that. I'll wait for you. And if you don't come back here, Mary Catherine"—he looked into her eyes again—"I'll find you."

There was no fighting her feelings. Love fell like autumn leaves around her, filling her heart and soul and senses. She lifted her face to his as easily as if they'd loved each other all their lives. The kiss started slowly, desperately. But the passion came quickly and made Mary Catherine feel things she'd never felt. She understood how easily two people could fall.

Even the air around her felt like something from a dream. Like all her life had led to this one single moment. She kissed him again. "I'm sorry."

"Don't be." He kissed her jaw and her cheekbone. "What if God made us for such a time as this? To be together?"

"I can't." She was drowning. If she didn't step back from him now, she might say things she'd regret, make promises she could never keep. She was breathing hard. They both were. She put her hands on his shoulders to steady herself. "Could you . . . could you be my friend? While I'm gone?"

The muscles in his jaw tensed. For a long time he thought about her question. Mary Catherine knew why. Marcus didn't want to be just her friend. She didn't want that either. But it was all she could offer him.

Finally he nodded. "Yes." His wanting her was still in his eyes, the way she was sure it was still in hers. "If it means staying in touch with you. Sharing my heart with you. Then, yes." He pulled her close again, and this time they shared a hug. Nothing more. He ran his hand over the back of her head. "I'll be your friend, Mary Catherine. If that's what you want."

The moment was ending—Mary Catherine could sense it. She took a half step back and looked at him one last time, memorizing his face. "If . . ." Tears filled her eyes and she had to blink to see him clearly. "If I was going to love someone . . . it would be you."

She put her hands on either side of his face and one last time she kissed him. The feeling was different than just a moment ago. Because this time—once again—the kiss meant goodbye. "I always said I could only love a guy who was real." She smiled. "Remember? When you said you wanted real?"

He nodded, never breaking eye contact with her. "I meant you. I told you you're the most rare kind of real."

"You, too. I mean it, Marcus." She pressed her fingers beneath her eyes. "I've never met a man like you. And for what it's worth . . . it nearly kills me . . . to say goodbye."

He didn't understand. She could see that in his expression, in the depth of his heart. But she'd said all she could say. He mustn't know about her heart. She wouldn't tell him. This night would not turn into an hour of pity, of worrying about her and convincing her not to leave. She had to go to Africa. The move was the one right thing she could do in the little time she had left.

She walked with him to the door and stepped outside with him. He hugged her one last time. "I'll email you. I'll text and call. Whatever way I can get to you." He smiled, but tears glistened in his eyes, too. "I'll be the best friend you ever had."

The sound that came from her was more cry than laugh. "I believe it." She allowed herself to get lost in his eyes one last time. This was what she had prayed for, what she had hoped for. That he wouldn't leave here upset or angry. She placed her hand against his cheek. "Thank you."

There was no need to explain. Marcus was clearly willing himself to understand.

He kissed her forehead, and then he stepped back and held up his hand. "Bye, Mary Catherine."

"Bye."

The distance between them hurt more with every step he took. She wondered what could possibly be worse. A love that might only last a year . . . or feeling the pain of watching him go?

She stood there until he drove off and then she didn't try to stop the tears. Her empty arms ached from missing him. And he hadn't been gone five minutes. She lifted her face to the sky. "I don't like to ask why, God." She hugged herself, the tears still streaming down her face. "There's a reason you gave me this heart. I know."

A wave of exhaustion came over her. She leaned against the apartment door and the sobs began to come. Quiet, full-body sobs. She was going to be okay. This was the life God had given her. Soon she would begin to feel symptoms of her failing heart. She would feel tired and short of breath and she would know the end was near.

Whether they found a heart for her or not.

When that happened she would let herself relive this night again and again, replaying it from her place in a cold hospital room. And she would feel once more what it felt like for just an hour to be loved. Really loved. And when the time came to leave this place for heaven, she would do so with a full and healed heart. Because she would know at least this much.

She had spared Marcus Dillinger the pain of loving her.

MARCUS COULDN'T STOP the tears.

He brushed at them, angry and unsure of everything. Why couldn't she believe him? He would wait for her. Six months . . . six years. Whatever it took. He didn't want to love anyone but her.

But if she wanted his friendship, he would give her that. It was his only hope, and probably more than she'd planned on offering him. Whatever the reason.

Instead of going home that night he went by Coach's house. He needed to talk in the worst way. He pulled up in front of the Waynes' and texted him. *You home?*

The response came quickly. *Sure. What's up?*

I'm out front. Can you come here?

The porch light was on in less than a minute, and Coach Wayne stepped out in shorts and a sweatshirt. He walked to the SUV and slid into the passenger seat. "Marcus."

"Coach."

He looked concerned. "You okay?"

Marcus couldn't remember anyone seeing him cry. He kept his composure. "I'm in love with Mary Catherine."

Coach Wayne visibly relaxed. He smiled. "That's a good thing, right?"

"No." Marcus wasn't sure how to explain the situation. He was still trying to understand it himself. "I mean, she doesn't want me. Or she doesn't want love." He looked straight ahead, but all he could see was her face, her green eyes. "She told me she only wants to be friends."

"Hmmm." His smile faded. "I didn't know."

"She's moving to Uganda." Marcus looked at his coach again. "For six months."

"I knew that. She talked to Rhonda about it."

Marcus wished he could've heard that conversation. Hopefully Rhonda Wayne tried to talk Mary Catherine into staying. Not that it mattered now. She was leaving. Her mind was made up.

"She said I could keep in touch with her . . . while she's gone."

"But you want more than friendship."

"Yes." Marcus kept a rope around his emotions. He needed answers, not pity. "What do you think? Can I be her friend and still . . . pursue her?"

"I think so. Ultimately the One who knows best is God." Coach Wayne gave him a pat on his knee. "If she's part of the plans He has for you, then yes. Chase that girl, Marcus. You'll know when it's time to let her go. If that time comes."

Marcus nodded. He liked how Coach said that. There was only one other thing he wanted to do. "Would you pray with me?"

"Of course." Coach Wayne kept his hand on Marcus's knee. "Father, You know how we men need to chase. Give Marcus the ability to do both—love and chase—even in the form of a friendship. At least until You make Your plans for his life clear. Keep Mary Catherine safe and grow the connection between her and Marcus according to Your will. Thank You, God, ahead of time. We trust You in all this. In Jesus' name, amen."

"Amen." Marcus felt a little better. "Thanks."

"You got it. We can talk more on the plane if you want." He opened the car door. "See you in the morning."

Marcus drove home, his heart still heavy. He had no idea when he'd see Mary Catherine again. He was back to baseball for now.

Back to chasing sunsets.

He thought about Shelly and how he hadn't known whether he had pursued her or she had pursued him. The idea sounded ridiculous now. But then, he had never known what it meant to want to pursue a girl until Mary Catherine.

If God would allow him to chase after her, he would do so every day, with all his heart. He would pray for her and check in on her often. She wanted his friendship, so there would be good days ahead. Times when they would text and laugh and tease. Times when they would share their hearts and fears and hopes and dreams. Even from different continents. And not for one day would he think about giving up on her.

Not unless God Himself made that clear.

TYLER AMES MADE the drive to Sami's grandparents' house early the next morning. Two hours before the flight to Arizona. There was something he had to ask them, something that couldn't wait.

Her grandfather opened the door. It was only seven thirty, but already the older man was dressed in a stylish dark gray suit, ready for the next power meeting. "Tyler." He opened the door and Tyler stepped inside. The man looked slightly bothered. "How've you been?"

"Well, thank you." He shook the man's hand. "You?"

"We'd like to see our granddaughter more often." He softened a bit. "Of course, we've been at our San Francisco home." He chuckled, but he made no attempt to invite Tyler into the house. "We've only been back a week."

"She told me she's planning to come by. Maybe tonight."

"Perfect." Mr. Dawson studied him. "You look good, Tyler. Coaching now, isn't that right?"

"Yes, sir. It's going better than I hoped." Tyler needed to get the question out. If he didn't get back on the road soon he'd miss his ten o'clock flight. "Anyway, I came because Sami and I have gotten very close."

The man remained unmoving. As if he had no idea what was coming.

"We share the same faith, same dreams and goals." Tyler could feel sweat on his palms. He would probably be one of the few guys in history turned down at this phase of "the ask." He put the thought out of his head. "Anyway, before I leave for Arizona this morning, I wanted to ask you."

Mr. Dawson blinked. "Ask me what, young man?"

"For Sami's hand in marriage. I want to marry her, sir." Regardless of what happened next, Tyler felt a rush of joy. Just saying the words left his heart practically bursting.

Tyler really wasn't sure what Sami's grandfather was going to do next. For several seconds he only stood there, like he was either in shock or thinking of a way to tell Tyler no.

But then his expression changed and his eyes grew damp. "Tyler." He hesitated. "I believe I owe you an apology."

"Sir?"

"You see . . ." His chin quivered and he shook his head, clearly trying to find the words. "When you left Samantha . . . she was never the same." He put his hand on Tyler's shoulder. "I vowed you would never break her heart again." He allowed the hint of a smile. "Can you promise me that, Tyler? That you'll never break her heart again?"

Tyler gave the man a hug, the kind a father and son might share at a reunion. "Yes, sir. With everything I am, I promise you."

Mr. Dawson stepped back and this time his smile stretched across his face. "Well, then. My answer is yes. You have my blessing."

Sami's grandmother joined them. "What's this?" She was wiping her hands on a dish towel. When she saw Tyler she stopped short. "Hello, Tyler. Is everything okay?"

"Yes, ma'am." He was one step closer to marrying Sami. The whole world was okay. "I asked your husband's permission to marry Sami." He hesitated. "Samantha."

"And I said yes." Mr. Dawson put his arm around his wife. "Looks like we'll be hosting a wedding!"

Sami's grandma hugged him. "We're very proud of you, Tyler. Of the man you've become. I'm sure Samantha will be very happy."

"Any idea when you'll ask her?" Mr. Dawson crossed his arms.

"Soon. If I can pull my ideas together." Tyler grinned. He'd never felt so sure of anything. "I have spring training first. But sometime after that."

He wrapped up the conversation, got back in his car, and headed to the airport. They wouldn't have much money, not at first, anyway. His salary with the Dodgers was still entry level. And now she'd taken the job at the youth center. The pay was half what she'd made at the PR firm. But none of that mattered.

There was nothing but sunshine and happy days ahead.

He was about to ask Sami Dawson to marry him.

Epilogue

Angel Town Meeting—Heaven

ORLON FELT THE SAME concern as everyone on his team. The mission had taken a very difficult turn. The baby who was supposed to be born in time might never be born. Their greatest goal was definitely in jeopardy. Like everything else good and true and right on earth.

The angels entered the room, their faces somber, serious. Usually at the end of an Angels Walking mission there would be cause to celebrate, reason to know they had succeeded.

Not this time.

When every angel was accounted for, Orlon moved to the front of the room. "I'd like Jag and Aspyn to join me."

The Angels Walking team moved to their places beside him. "I want to make one thing clear." Orlon's voice was strong, resolute. "You did not fail this mission."

Jag set his jaw, his face slightly raised. If any angel needed this talk, he did.

Orlon continued. "Jag . . . you and Aspyn were the perfect angels for this mission. Just as we all agreed before you left. You were given several tasks, and you succeeded in each one of them." He ran through the list. "Most of all, you kept Marcus Dillinger alive and saw that his would-be killer was placed behind bars."

Jag put his arm around Aspyn. The two of them looked down for a few seconds, as if they were remembering the intensity of their time on earth.

"I can't remember a recent Angels Walking mission with so much danger, where so many lives were at stake." Orlon looked at the other angels. "We watched and we prayed. And now we will give thanks to God for His miraculous intervention and for the success of the work done by Jag and Aspyn."

This was one of Orlon's favorite parts of being an angel. Listening to the applause break out through the room, the soft utterances of Jesus' name and the praise meant to glorify God alone.

When the noise settled down, Orlon took a deep breath. "Any questions?"

An angel in the front row raised his hand. "Did you ever see Ryan Williams? The little boy you saved the last time you went on an Angels Walking mission?"

Orlon could tell by the look on Jag's face that the meeting hadn't occurred. He put his hand on Jag's shoulder. "The boy is a police officer. Just out of the academy."

Deep concern filled Jag's eyes. "I . . . I didn't know."

"Yes." Orlon looked to the angel who had asked the question. "Ryan may be a part of another mission. We'll have to see."

"I'd . . . like to watch when that happens." Jag's tone was proof that the long ago failed mission still stayed with him. "If that's okay."

"Definitely."

Other questions came. Concerns about how Jag was able to control his anger. Orlon was curious about that, too.

"Very simply, I didn't control it. I felt everything a human feels and in light of the little boy being shot, I wanted to kill. The desire ran through my veins." Jag looked at Orlon. "I'm being honest."

"We know." Orlon was grateful for the way things had turned out. "The question was, how did you find control?"

"The name of Jesus. Lexy shouted Jesus' name, and the anger left me. All in a rush. I belong to Him. I couldn't think about acting on my own after that."

Orlon felt a sense of pride over Jag's actions. Many angels in the room would've struggled with the same challenge. It was another reason why it was so important to choose the right angels for each mission.

Angels Walking always came with risks.

This one more than most.

Jag and Aspyn were dismissed back to their places among the others.

The unknown ahead was their greatest problem now. Orlon faced the angels and straightened to his full height. "We must talk about what's next." He hesitated. "The main concern now is Mary Catherine."

He let that sink in. "She will go to Africa, and she will get sick. The next stage of our mission will be nearly impossible. There will be very great heartache." Michael had confirmed that much. Orlon looked at their faces. "You are heaven's most prepared angels. Experts in matters of the heart. But we will need two very experienced angels next time around."

The meeting was dismissed and Orlon spoke to Jag as he left the room. "I'm proud of you. I know how hard this mission was. There wasn't an hour of rest."

"Thank you, sir." Jag ran his hand through his blond hair. "I just wish we could've done something for Mary Catherine."

Orlon smiled. "You did."

"Sir?" Jag clearly didn't understand.

"You kept Marcus Dillinger alive."

With that Jag smiled and headed after the other angels. When the room was empty, Orlon got down on the golden floor and lay his face to the cool stones. For the next hour he talked to the Father, begging for wisdom and direction.

If they failed the next mission, there would be no going forward.

All of heaven and earth would pay the price.

Dear Reader Friend,

I promised you this time around I'd share my own angel encounter. Like all interactions with angels, I can't be sure I was really in the presence of a heavenly being. But I know this.

There's no other way for me to explain what happened.

It was 2007 and I was headed to Atlanta, Georgia, for the International Christian Retail Show. That year my book *Even Now* was up for book of the year—the first time a novel had been nominated. Before I left, my mom and dad drove to my house—just to say goodbye.

My dad, Ted Kingsbury, was especially emotional. "I wish I could be there," he told me. "I know you're going to win."

It was the same way with my dad ever since I was a little girl. He would read what I'd written and rave over it. From the time I was twelve he would tell me, "Someone has to be the next bestselling novelist, Karen . . . it might as well be you!"

All my life my dad believed in me, and that night before I left for Atlanta with my kids Kelsey and Tyler, my dad was convinced the big award would be mine.

The award show happened two nights later, and my dad's prediction came true. *Even Now* was named book of the year. Back home my dad was so excited. He spent the next day talking to my mom and calling my husband, Don. "We need to throw Karen a party," he told them. "Let's think of something."

But the party was not to be.

That afternoon my dad suffered a massive heart attack. One minute he was talking with my mom, and the next he was out. Laid back in his recliner like he'd fallen into a deep sleep.

My nephew Andrew was thirteen at the time. He was the first to think something was wrong. He called 911 and an operator talked him through giving my father CPR for the next fourteen minutes. Keep in mind my dad was very heavy and he wasn't on a flat surface. He was in a recliner.

By the time paramedics arrived, my dad was blue and unresponsive. Andrew ran into the next room and started sobbing. He thought he'd done something wrong. He believed his grandpa's death would be on his shoulders.

The house was chaotic, the paramedics working feverishly on my dad. Ten minutes became fifteen and there was talk of calling in the time of death.

Suddenly a police officer rushed into the house. He found my mother and pulled her aside in the next room. "Do you believe in Jesus?" he asked her.

"Yes!" she cried out. "Yes, we're believers."

With a peace-filled intensity, the man looked straight into my mom's eyes. "We're going to pray that God gives your husband life again." He pointed back to where young Andrew was still crying. "We're going to pray because otherwise that boy out there will spend the rest of his life thinking this was his fault."

And so the officer took hold of my mom's hands and he prayed. "Dear God, we ask that the power that raised Lazarus from the dead would breathe life into Ted Kingsbury this very minute. In Jesus' powerful name, amen."

The very second the officer said, "Amen," from the other room the head paramedic yelled, "We have a heartbeat!"

They were able to keep my dad alive all the way to the hospital, where he lived another six weeks in ICU. We had time to tell him everything we ever wanted to say. We laughed and remembered every wonderful memory and we prayed every possible prayer.

When he died, our family was at peace and so was my dad.

Later my mom tried to find the officer who randomly came into the house to pray with her that day. She called the police station and asked the paramedics. No one had ever heard of the man.

We came to believe that the officer was an angel, sent in response to so many prayers being cried out on behalf of my dad. An angel, maybe, on an Angels Walking mission.

Now you know why I allowed Jag to be a police officer.

Keep a lookout this fall for book three in the *Angels Walking* series. Mary Catherine, Marcus, Tyler, and Sami have so much ahead. The Wayne family, too.

Until next time, keep your eyes open. God is working all around us. Sometimes it's just a matter of looking.

In His light and love,
Karen Kingsbury

P.S. Connect with me on Facebook or Twitter, @KarenKingsbury. If you found yourself changed while reading *Chasing Sunsets*, if you became closer to God or if you gave your life to Jesus for the first time, then drop me an email at Karen@KarenKingsbury.com. Write "Life Changed" in the subject line. If you do, I'd love to send you a Scripture letter I put together. Also, if you are unable to afford a Bible, and if you are unable to borrow one from your church or a family member, I will send you one. Simply write "Bible" in the subject line of your email.

Forever in Fiction

A SPECIAL THANKS TO ANGIE RHYNE, who won the Forever in Fiction item at my One Chance Foundation auction in 2012. Angie chose to name her mother, Sally Hudson, as a character in this book. Sally is small with beautiful blue eyes that long ago gave her the nickname "Blue-Eyed Sally." She loves her family, including her husband, four children, and ten grandchildren. Her favorite vacations are the ones that take her back to Ohio to visit extended family. Sally loves reading and cooking—especially her annual "candy-making day" with her daughters and granddaughters. Beyond that, Sally found a faith in Jesus when she was first diagnosed with leukemia in 2001. She needed a bone marrow transplant, but no one in the family was a match, so Sally and her family prayed. A match was found and Sally received a lifesaving transplant. Years later she had the opportunity to meet her donor in what was an emotional reunion.

In *Chasing Sunsets*, Sally is a nurse at the doctor's office where Mary Catherine is a patient. In the book, Sally's story serves as an encouragement and allows Mary Catherine to believe that God is not finished with her just yet.

The One Chance Foundation is an organization that grants money to people at the end stage of adopting. For more information, please check my website—KarenKingsbury.com.

Reading Group Guide
Chasing Sunsets

KAREN KINGSBURY

Use these questions to go deeper into the story or to encourage discussion with your small groups.

1. Read Ephesians 6:12. According to this verse, what are our struggles against? Are they from this world? Explain.

2. Where did you most see the spiritual battle being waged while reading *Chasing Sunsets*?

3. Why was Jag concerned he was the wrong angel for this Angels Walking mission? What did you think about his past?

4. How can failing make us better equipped for today? Give an example from your life.

5. The term *chasing sunsets* is brought up early in the book by Marcus. What was that in reference to? Have you ever flown west and thought that you were chasing the sunset? What else could that term mean? Discuss it.

6. Have you ever considered the possibility that angels might fail? Discuss what happened to Jag in his Angels Walking

mission a decade ago. Do you think the Bible supports such an idea? Why or why not?

7. Read Genesis 19:11. According to this Bible verse, is it possible one duty of an angel is to fight men? How did this play out in *Chasing Sunsets*? Is it comforting to imagine angels fighting on your behalf? Explain.

8. In your opinion, what was the most intense part of this Angels Walking mission? Can you think of an intense time in your life when things took a miraculous turn? Talk about it.

9. What do you think of the idea that not all people can see angels when they're on earth? Talk about an angelic encounter you or someone you know may have had.

10. Hosea 12:2–4 tells a story of man overcoming an angel. How do you think that could happen? Was Jag at risk of being defeated by Dwayne? Explain your thoughts.

11. Lexy had a very difficult life. Why do you think girls like Lexy are drawn to guys like Dwayne? Explain.

12. Do you know much about gang warfare? Are gangs a problem in your area? Talk about that. What is your city doing to stop gang violence?

13. Talk about Marcus Dillinger. How did he feel after a shooting erupted outside his new youth center? Where was he finally able to find real meaning? Give examples.

14. Marcus was baptized at the beach. If you were baptized, talk about the experience. If not, talk about a special time at the beach. Why do you think we are drawn to the water?

15. The Wayne family has an open-door type of home, always welcoming people into their lives. Do you know anyone like that? What do families like that teach you? Why?

16. The Waynes also had a home church service every Sunday. Have you heard of house churches? What is your experience with church?

17. Early in the book, Mary Catherine learned that her heart was in trouble. At that point, she took a new position on ever falling in love. Explain how she felt. Do you agree with her? Why or why not?

18. Have you ever watched a documentary on the Scared Straight program? What are your thoughts about that type of tactic with at-risk kids? Talk about the Last Time In program. How was it different from a traditional Scared Straight program?

19. Do you agree with the idea of volunteers acting as advocates for at-risk kids? Share personal examples.

20. Mary Catherine talked often about moving to Africa. Have you ever dreamed of doing something like that? Share your stories.

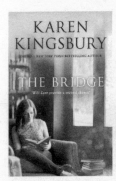
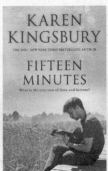
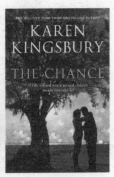

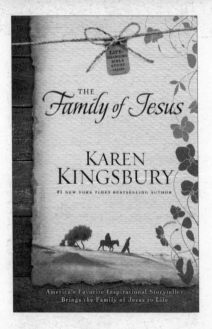

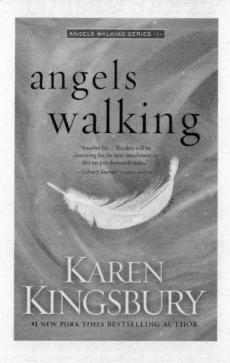

Karen's Newsletter, Blog, & FREE Chapters!

Sign up to receive upcoming news, inspirational blogs, and life-changing moments from Karen. It's easy. And once a month receive a new, FREE Chapter on the Baxter Family!

Sign up at
KarenKingsbury.com

CONFESSIONS OF A
RUGBY
MERCENARY

JOHN DANIELL

EBURY
PRESS

3 5 7 9 10 8 6 4

First Published in New Zealand by Awa Press in 2007
This edition published in 2009
by Ebury Press, an imprint of Ebury Publishing
A Random House Group Company

The Random House Group Limited Reg. No. 954009

Addresses for companies within the Random House Group
can be found at www.randomhouse.co.uk

A CIP catalogue record for this book is available from the British Library

The Random House Group Limited supports The Forest Stewardship
Council (FSC), the leading international forest certification organisation.
All our titles that are printed on Greenpeace approved FSC certified paper
carry the FSC logo. Our paper procurement policy can be found at
www.rbooks.co.uk/environment

Printed in the UK by CPI Cox & Wyman, Reading, RG1 8EX

ISBN 9780091930684

To buy books by your favourite authors and register for offers visit
www.rbooks.co.uk

First edition published in 2007 by Awa Press
16 Walter Street, Wellington, New Zealand.

Contents

Agen	Sporting Union Agen Lot et Garonne
Bayonne	Aviron Bayonnais
Biarritz	Biarritz Olympique
Bourgoin-Jallieu	Club Sportif Bourgoin-Jallieu
Brive-la-Gaillarde	Club Athlétique Brive Corrèze Limousin
Clermont-Ferrand . . .	Association Sportive Montferrandaise Clermont Auvergne (Montferrand)
Castres	Castres Olympique
Montpellier	Montpellier Hérault Rugby Club
Narbonne	Racing Club Narbonne Méditerranée
Paris	Stade Français
Pau	Section Paloise
Perpignan	Union Sportive Arlequins Perpignan
Toulon	Rugby Club Toulonnais
Toulouse	Stade Toulousain

Introduction

Mercenary is not a pretty word. It sounds like a cold-eyed thug ready to change his loyalty for money. I am a mercenary, and so are most of my friends. If, as George Orwell said, serious sport is war minus the shooting, we are its soldiers, playing out make-believe conflicts in front of partisan crowds. We do this for money and for the love of the game, but mainly for the money.

As a rule we are known as professional rugby players. This is a bit like calling a spade a shovel: you could be forgiven for thinking they are the same thing, but if you have to actually work with one you soon see the difference. To understand what makes them different (professionals and mercenaries, not shovels and spades), you need to know about rugby.

These days rugby may look like an organised career move, but I fell into it for want of anything else to do. My degree in English literature hadn't proved to be the instant passport to a high-flying career in journalism I had hoped. I had done some work for a regional television station, but the station had quickly gone bust. After finishing a temporary job as assistant producer for Radio New Zealand's Morning Report, I was looking for something to turn my hand to.

Foreign shores looked attractive. Friends from university were fetched up in far-flung, exotic places such as Paris, Moscow and New York. I applied to the Australian High Commission for a job organising a forum in Nauru, a remote island with a population of 11,000 people and a landscape scarred by a century of phosphate mining. The job hadn't previously featured on my ideal career path, but I was gutted to miss out. Various other possibilities turned out to be deadends. I was stuck in the young person's Catch-22 where all jobs require experience and there is no way to acquire experience because you can't get a job.

And then rugby went professional. It felt like winning Lotto without even buying a ticket. At 24, I already had fifteen years' experience of the game, and given the limited time span of a rugby career I could even be said to be approaching my peak. Rather than struggling to get on to the bottom of the ladder in some other rat race, I could slot in somewhere in the middle of the newly created, and apparently relatively lucrative, rugby market.

Of course, no one starts out playing rugby because of money. Like any sport, you get into it because it looks like fun, or you are press-ganged by an overbearing father. As is often the case in New Zealand, I started playing at school. Wherever you start, part of rugby's attraction is the reassuring sense of belonging to something bigger than you. You make friends with team-mates, and have a role to play in a group that needs you to perform well. Representing your school or your club or your town against all comers, you share the joy of victory and the bitter taste of defeat, discover the benefits of hard work, learn how to complain about the referee and the unfairness of it all, and generally grow up.

So far, this is much like any other team sport. The magic of rugby, though, lies in its peculiar emphasis on two basic pillars—inclusiveness and interdependence. Compared to a relatively simple game such as soccer, rugby's rules are complex enough to need a variety of different body types and skills. In a rugby team there is a place for everyone: fat kids (or 'big-boned children', if their parents prefer) prop the scrum; the tall and ungainly like me are predestined to play lock; rangy, athletic types become loose forwards; the more dexterous, intelligent players run the game from the halfback positions; nimble runners find themselves in the outside backs. If you are scrawny, slow, dull-witted and uncoordi-nated, you may find your participation limited to bringing on the oranges at half-time; the writing is on the wall. You could always become a referee.

Put simply, the aim of a rugby team is to get hold of the ball, and to organise so that one player places the ball behind the goal-line to score a try. Equally important, of course, is preventing the opposition doing the same thing. All this re-quires teamwork, certain special skills and physical courage. I am not going to get involved in rules or tactics because that would take up a book in itself. Yes, you can kick the ball between the posts as well, but that isn't really the heart of the game. History buffs will tell you the reason a try is called a 'try' is that when the game was first played it was worth nothing: putting the ball behind the line merely gave you the chance to *try* for a shot at goal. But the game has moved on since then.

The nature of rugby as a contact sport—'collision sport' is perhaps more appropriate—means physical courage is important. In terms of injuries, rugby is right up there at the top of the table. Throwing yourself at someone running at full speed is, under normal circumstances, verging on the insane, and not something that comes naturally. For young men this is, of course, part of the attraction: the danger raises the stakes, and by facing up to it you get to prove to your peers that you are reliable and brave. Your mates have to prove themselves as well—each player must provide his own particular skills if the team is to be successful, and strong bonds of mutual respect soon form. The performance of the team becomes a source of pride, reinforcing the sense of belonging to the community. Rugby players—including women—are often seen as macho, and there is a pleasingly primal element to the game that appeals to unsophisticated but deeply rooted parts of our nature.

Rugby associates itself with old-fashioned values: virility, self-sacrifice and pride. One of the great rugby clichés is about having 'pride in the jersey'. I groan inwardly whenever I hear this, but it is a kind of shorthand for the bedrock on which the game is built. This is where mercenaries part company with professional rugby players. The idea behind having pride in the jersey is that when you pull on your team colours you are representing not only yourself, or you and your mates having a muddy-kneed run-around, but a whole community. You are supposed to feel a debt of honour to all those who have gone before you, and to the people who will be supporting you because you represent them. The French refer to this as *l'esprit de clocher*, which my dictionary bluntly defines as parochialism, but the sense is more romantic. Literally, a *clocher* is a church's clock tower. Symbolically, it stands for everything a good Frenchman holds close to his heart—his family, his friends, his town—the roots of an existence.

You can only really have pride in the jersey if the jersey, and what it stands for, mean something to you, otherwise it's just another jersey, black, white, red, blue, multicoloured or whatever. I spent three years at my secondary school in New Zealand thinking of the First XV as heroes, and then I became one of them. There was a purity and intensity to the thrill of playing for that team I have seldom felt since.

The biggest kick for a New Zealander, of course, is pulling on the black jersey. In 1992, I played for the New Zealand Under 21s against Australia. The night before the game my team-mate Mark Mayerhofler said we should be ready to die for the jersey. I can remember thinking this was a bit strong—but then he went on to be an All Black and I didn't. The next day, with 20 minutes to go, I comprehensively buggered my shoulder in a tackle. The other lock had already gone off so there were no more replacements, but I was really feeling it. The team physiotherapist had a look at my shoulder and said, 'The coach wants you to tough it out.'

This is the sort of thing young men dream of: twenty minutes to go, a hard-fought victory beckoning against the hated Australians in front of thousands of people, and New Zealand needs you to tough it out. But when you are actually on the field, unable to lift your arm because you feel as though you have been shot with an elephant gun, your thoughts run more along the lines of, 'Fuck this for a game of soldiers.' No one's paying you. There's every chance that if you keep playing the injury is going to get worse; at the very least it will hurt like hell at every moment of contact. But of course you stay on. It's New Zealand against Australia. Pride in the jersey. You love it, really.

If you think this sounds as though I am trying to present myself as a hero, you're probably right, although anyone else in the team would have done the same thing—in just the same way as we had all spent the long hours training and playing to get ourselves to a level of performance where we were good enough to be chosen for the national team. This was 1992, four years before rugby went professional. None of us imagined we might make money out of it. When I started playing for Wellington in 1994 it was the same thing—long hours of training, games eating up the weekends, and all for what?

In reality, there was a raft of different reasons for participation. Playing for a top team conferred social status. You had the opportunity to prove yourself, and enjoy the fun and the camaraderie of team spirit. And there was the sheer pleasure of doing something well. But at bottom there was one thing that justified all the necessary energy and drive and ambition and—although the wholesome idealism of it pains my cynical soul—it was pride in the jersey.

Finally, in 1996, we started getting paid: we became professional rugby players. At first this didn't seem to change anything. We were still playing for the same team. The training hours were the same (we didn't make enough to give up our jobs). We just got a cheque at the end of the month.

But then things did change. That season I had what I can best describe as a 'complicated' relationship with the Wellington coach, Frank Walker. At the beginning of the season he asked me to captain the side. I felt this was a bad idea—I was inexperienced, and there were plenty of players better qualified for the job. However, being a sucker for flattery, I allowed myself to be persuaded to take the less glamorous, but equally less onerous, role of vice-captain. Then, after a good series of wins, we lost one game, and as we were going into the changing-room for the next game Frank sent the team manager to tell me that it wasn't worth my while getting changed: I was being dumped.

My chances of a Super 12 contract—a full-time professional salary—for the coming season instantly went west. But if I looked hard enough there was an upside: although I no longer had any hope of fulfilling my ambition of playing for Wellington in the Super 12, I was also free of the emotional and contractual ties that had bound me to my home town.

Before the advent of professional rugby, a player played for the team in the town where he lived. You lived in that town because you worked or studied there, or simply because you were brought up there and it never occurred to you to move.

In any case, you made it your home for reasons other than rugby. However, the arrival of professionalism meant you could choose a team (providing they would have you) and that team's hometown would become your home: all you had to do was play rugby for them.

Of course, this meant 'pride in the jersey' went out the window. You could find yourself wearing colours that meant nothing at all, alongside team-mates you didn't know and who didn't speak the same language as you, in a town you previously didn't even know existed. You would be doing this because the team's management had agreed to pay you a sum of money large enough to make you want to move there and run around doing all the things that you used to do for love and not for money. You would have become a mercenary, like me.

Having decided I was fresh out of rugby-playing luck at home, I went to England and had an interview with Dick Best, director of rugby at Harlequins. He said some nice things and offered me £20,000 a year, plus a £1000-a-game win-bonus for all championship games, including the Anglo-Welsh league. All up, it amounted to around £30,000 a year. As this was about NZ$90,000, and considerably more than a Super 12 contract, it looked pretty sweet, although I later found out that I could have hoped for more. Some crazy figures were flying around in the early days of professionalism in England.

I had a similar interview at the London Wasps Rugby Club with Nigel Melville, who said much the same things and came up with much the same offer, contingent on my getting a work permit. This quickly became the sticking point. In order to play in England, you had to have a British passport or have played for your country in the last 18 months, in which case you were considered expert enough to be able to pass on useful pointers to your team-mates—although, as there was no distinction made between playing for New Zealand or Croatia at international level, this was a bit of a loophole.

Meeting neither of these criteria, I left for France, where clubs were then allowed two foreign players, and found myself in contract negotiations in a smoky room just outside Paris with Christophe Mombet, the coach of Racing Club. Racing, Mombet said, usually paid players between 5000 and 10,000 francs a month. It was a pittance compared to what the English clubs were offering, but they would throw in accommodation as well. I said I wouldn't come for less than 10,000, there were smiles all round (damn, I obviously went too low), a handshake and the deal was done.

If this sounds like a bleak story of a wayward young man selling his soul for a few dollars, of the corrupting power of market forces, and of the road to disillusion with a once pure and noble sport, well yes, there is an element of that. As singer Cyndi Lauper pointed out, 'Money changes everything.' But there are plenty of upsides. Rugby's global marketplace gives players the opportunity to see different cultures from the inside and make new friends, while being well paid to do what we love.

There is something of a French Foreign Legion flavour to a team made up of individuals from so many disparate backgrounds: Montpellier, the club for which I was playing when the events described in this book took place, has, as well as New Zealanders, Georgians, South Africans, Samoans, a Muslim and a Jew, an Englishman and an Argentinian, all united for a common cause. And while the relationship between a player and his new club seems more of an arranged marriage than a love match, over time the right amount of goodwill on both sides can lead to it becoming highly beneficial for all concerned. For all the martial metaphors, poorly controlled aggression and bloodthirsty crowds, serious sport, if it is warlike, is, crucially, *minus* the shooting.

The truth is that the lot of the rugby mercenary is hard to beat, and the rich rugby culture of France is as good a place as any to get your knees muddy and your hands dirty. My grandfather spent a few years on the fields of France wearing the drab khaki of our country's colours in World War I, and God knows we have it sweet compared to his generation.

When I signed up to play rugby in France, the flow of players from New Zealand was just a trickle. Today it is more like a flood, as top All Blacks such as Tana Umaga and Byron Kelleher take advantage of the spoils to be had from donning French club jerseys. This is one of the great sea changes of rugby in our time, with revolutionary implications for the game not only in the southern hemisphere but around the world. Unless you are a power-broker at the IRB or a big wheel in a national union, whether or not it is good for rugby is a moot point: it's happening, and we had better get used to it.

1

Montpellier, Chez Moi

This is my third season playing for Montpellier, a medium-sized town—about 200,000 people, swelling to 400,000 if you count the outlying agglomeration—in the south of France, a few miles inland from the Mediterranean, in the middle of the bulge of the gulf of Lyon. Just a few weeks before I arrived in July 2003, Montpellier Rugby Club was crowned champion of the second division, winning entry to the first division, or Top 16 as it was then.

A club's accession to the first division, once the hangover wears off, is typically followed by a mad scramble for more money to sign up players and boost squad depth and experience for the following season. The Ligue Nationale de Rugby lays down the dates for the official transfer season, which runs for about a month through June into July, during which time contracts are officially ratified. Most clubs will have started looking for players in January or February, and will have signed pre-contracts with most of their new recruits by May. So by the time the little club from the second division arrives, delighted to have earned the right to sit at the same table as the big boys, they realise that the big boys have already chomped through the best parts of what was on offer, and all that is left are scraps.

As chance would have it, I was one of those scraps. I had come to the end of my second contract with Perpignan, a town 100 miles further down the Mediterranean coast, just north of the Spanish border. Although a smaller town than Montpellier, Perpignan had a bigger club. This club had just made it into the final of the European Cup, and its ambition was to become part of the small circle of genuine heavy-weights—Stade Français in Paris, Stade Toulousain in Toulouse, and, more recently, Biarritz Olympique in the Basque country on the Atlantic Coast—who have been con-sistently at the top of the pile in the French professional game. As a result, there had been an end-of-season clear-out of those players not considered up to scratch and, along with fourteen others of the 30-man squad, I had found myself out of a job.

This wasn't entirely unexpected, and through various agents I had been tarting myself around since late December —with decidedly mixed results. I had had one solid offer from Montferrand, but hoping for something better I had put them off and they had found someone else. I had really wanted to play for Stade Français in Paris, but a barrage of wheedling phone calls had met with nothing but silence. As far as the ten or so other clubs in the first division went, I felt like Goldilocks. The big ones were too big; after my experience with Stade Français I didn't bother trying Toulouse, who were in even less need of an aging journeyman. But the small ones, who were at least decent enough to appear interested, were too small.

Things were getting desperate—in fact they had been desperate for a while—when Montpellier, who looked as though they might be neither too big nor too small but just right, appeared on the scene. As far as the rugby went, I was well aware that Montpellier would struggle, but there are other things that you look for in a club. *Midi Olympique*, the French rugby weekly, had conducted a survey of players' preferred clubs, taking into account several quality-of-life factors as well as rugby. Montpellier had figured in a highly respectable fifth place, behind Toulouse, Biarritz, Paris and Perpignan, but in front of bigger names such as Castres, Clermont-Ferrand (Montferrand) and Bourgoin.

The day I was to sign in Montpellier, Biarritz, having just realised they were a lock short for the coming season, called to see if I were interested. After a few hours of indecision I decided I would be better off playing a relatively important role in Montpellier than sitting on the bench—or worse, as an afterthought—in the star-studded Biarritz team, and there was more chance of my girlfriend finding work in the economically dynamic town of Montpellier than the beach resort of Biarritz. On top of this, Montpellier were obviously keen to have me, and as already mentioned I am a sucker for flattery, although I have to admit I was disappointed that the ferocious bidding war for my services, for which I had been hoping, did not materialise.

The agent who would have signed me to Biarritz told me that I had made a mistake, and that we were going to spend a difficult year being steamrolled up front and torn apart out wide. It was with these comforting words ringing in my ears that on a sweltering July morning I rolled up to a ground borrowed from the local army barracks for the first day of training.

At Perpignan the first few weeks of pre-season training had taken place out of town on a borrowed ground, but the rest of the time we had trained at the stadium itself, or at the annexe next door. The stadium complex had also included the weights room, and, brilliantly, all our laundry had been done on site. Montpellier, I discovered, had more of a gypsy flavour. On any given day we might be at the stadium, or the military barracks, or just out of town at another borrowed field, or doing weights at any one of three different places. And if it rained all bets were off: you could be anywhere, or training might simply be cancelled. The strip worn for the game and the coloured bibs that we wore to distinguish ourselves at training were washed once a week, but after that we were on our own as far as laundry was concerned.

To be fair, Montpellier is a very young club, and by the time you read this a brand new state-of-the-art stadium with annexe grounds and wet-weather training pitches should be up and running. In any case, running around like blue-arsed flies trying to find the right ground does wonders in inducing humility, particularly in those of us who suffer from a hope-less sense of direction, as does dealing with the pile of reeking gear that has fermented in the kitbag you forgot to empty into the washing-machine.

Arriving in a new club is always difficult. For a start, there are all the obvious, non-rugby-related difficulties that revolve around moving to a new home. And then, as with any new job, you have to prove yourself to your new colleagues, while treading carefully through the potential bitchiness caused by your taking the place of someone who was part of the tight-knit community, and the widely held (and not entirely unfounded) suspicion that you are being paid more than the guys who got the team to where it is now.

French rugby is, of course, a small world, and if you're lucky you will already know some of the team, having played with them in another club. At Montpellier, there was at least one friendly face with whom I had played in Paris several years earlier. Unfortunately, there was also a senior player with whom I had an ongoing vendetta, having spent a winter afternoon a couple of seasons earlier trading cheap shots with him while we were wearing different jerseys.

As I tried to fit in, I spent some time worrying about the coming season. It was clear there was some genuine talent at Montpellier, but not nearly as much as there had been in Perpignan. This was logical, given Montpellier's late arrival and small budget: while it is not an absolute guarantee of success, money buys talent, pace and physical presence, so the smaller a club's cheque-book, the less it gets. To their credit, Montpellier had signed on for another two years nearly all the players who had played the season before, so that, having played their way into the first division, they would have the opportunity to show what they were worth. The club had then added a handful of experienced players who, like me, were coming to the end of their careers.

When I say 'to their credit', the club had acted honourably but not necessarily wisely: they could easily have jettisoned half a dozen players of limited potential, and signed the others for only one year, which would have been long enough to head-hunt replacements for those who hadn't adapted. Coming from a club like Perpignan, I was used to a culture of ambition that—in the spirit of the age of the mercenary— had little time for honourable gestures. While ruthless ambition can be short-sighted, there is something to be said for it when you are staring down the barrel of relegation.

The positive side of keeping on the same players is that the group clearly having the confidence of the club president is good for morale, and the social fabric is less likely to tear than if individuals were to try and pull in different directions, as often happens when things get difficult. Every club likes to think of itself as a family with tightly knit bonds, but in Montpellier this had been closer to reality than at most clubs. Players who had retired often stayed involved in some way, through coaching or in a less official role, and this made for a good atmosphere. You got the feeling the club looked after its own, and you were not simply a piece of meat to be junked when you passed your sell-by date. Understandably, this is increasingly rare in the professional world.

Obviously, though, a good atmosphere is no substitute for results. Two teams would go down to second division at the end of the year, and in the eyes of most pundits Montpellier was odds-on favourite to be one of them. To bridge the talent gap that existed between a good second-division side and the kind of team that could expect to be still in the first division at the end of the year, the coach decided to try bringing everyone up to scratch through drawn-out training sessions that in the summer heatwave seemed never-ending and often counterproductive: more quantity than quality. The team made progress, but I wasn't sure it would be enough.

The first few games of the year were friendlies, and not very encouraging. Luckily for us, 2003 was a World Cup year, so while the big teams' stars were battling for world supremacy in Australia, the rest of us played out an unimportant French cup competition, which allowed us to get to grips with the harsh realities of life in the first division without actually having the knife at our throats. The results were not promising—one win from six games—but not as bad as I had feared. The team took great pride in throwing everything into *le combat*, a good starting point but not really enough. It is possible to grind out a win simply through dogged defence and a good kicking game, but you have to be extremely good at both to pull it off on a regular basis. Top-level rugby is not really a choice between the rapier and the cudgel: *everyone* has a cudgel, so you better have one too, and the bigger the better. But you would be well-advised to have a rapier as well, and to know how to handle it.

We were happy enough smashing things up, but our swordsmanship wasn't what it might have been, so when we came to play our first championship game against the swashbuckling European Cup champions Toulouse it looked like we were on a hiding to nothing. They had several players unavailable on World Cup duty, but were still, on paper, vastly superior to us. Two minutes into the game they scored an effortless try from broken play and it looked as if all our worst fears were to be realised. Then something extraordinary happened. Stung by the prospect of being slaughtered in front of a home crowd, we clawed our way into the game, first getting an edge and then dominating outrageously. Toulouse scored a couple of catch-up tries at the end, but the final score had everyone—especially me—scratching our heads and rubbing our eyes: Montpellier 50, Toulouse 31.

Rugby is not the sort of game where upsets often occur, so this result was a big deal and gave us all a badly needed confidence boost. As it turned out it wasn't, though, the fore-taste of a glorious run in the championship. After we scraped a win in the next home game, reality kicked in and we lost eight on the trot, slipping inexorably down the table towards the relegation zone, before getting our act together in the spring and finishing a quite satisfactory tenth in our first season in the Top 16. The next season was much the same. Widely seen as promising candidates for the drop, we had a good start with an extraordinary win early on against Stade Français, a big team, 49–26, but a worrying dip in the winter brought us dangerously close to going down, only to finish strongly in eleventh place.

The season we are facing will again be a difficult one for Montpellier: the Top 16 has been squeezed down to the Top 14, but two teams will still be relegated, so eleventh, which looked comfortable enough last year, will be stressful. The club has upped its budget to €6.6 million, from €5.5 million last year, and there is a little more talent around. As a result, as pre-season training starts everyone is feeling upbeat. At the training camp we agree that we should be aiming to finish the season between sixth and eighth in the championship.

From the outside this may sound unambitious. Surely, you may think, as professional sportsmen we should be aiming to win every game and thus the competition? A few years ago I would have agreed, but experience tells me that even banking on finishing in the top eight sounds like hubris. Montpellier is growing as a club, no doubt about it, but so are the other teams, and if you want to move up the ladder it means pushing someone off from higher up. Of the teams that finished in front of us last year there are perhaps two we could overtake—Brive and Narbonne—with the possibility of a third, Agen, should they have a bad year. That would have us in eighth place. To place higher than that would mean that one of the big clubs—the clubs qualified for the Heineken Cup, Europe's premier competition—would have to have a season way below par, or that we would have to have a blinder. Which isn't impossible, I suppose.

Equally, it's not impossible that we will have a shocker, be overtaken by the clubs behind us, and go down. But in all probability we will scrap our way through the season feeling threatened by the drop without it actually coming to that. In any case, that is as much as I dare hope for. In my last year in Paris when I was playing for Racing, the club went down and it makes for a hell of a season. Internal bickering, the threat of financial meltdown linked to the lack of results, and a general feeling of guilt at poor performance and your own inability to change the course of destiny are all things I would rather avoid, particularly as I think this will be my last year of rugby.

We start back on July 8, a week before we are supposed to according to the *convention collective* signed between the players' union and the clubs, but since we went on holiday at the start of June, a couple of weeks before everyone else, no one makes a fuss. Professional rugby in France runs on an eleven-month cycle (twelve if you are an international called up to play on the summer tours to the southern hemisphere), with competition finishing in June and starting again at the end of August after six weeks of pre-season over July and August.

Rugby is supposed to be a winter sport, but with 28 French Championship fixtures, nine European Cup fixtures, about a dozen international games, and a handful of friendlies at the start of the season, hardly a weekend goes by without a major game of some sort, and top players can play up-wards of 40 games in a year. By comparison, players in other countries play a maximum of 30 or so games, international and domestic competitions combined. The jury is still out on the effect the French schedule has on the players' health, but in the meantime money is the motor: more competition equals more revenue from television and sponsors, and nothing looks like getting in the way of this equation. The players who play the most are generally the ones who get paid the most, so they tend not to argue.

Pre-season traditionally starts with a battery of physical tests and this year is no exception. Fat tests, speed tests, weight tests and fitness tests are all performed and statistics compiled with scientific rigour, and there is much discussion and excitement about various individual performances: the wingers are all over themselves to be the fastest man in the team, while the props do battle on the bench press. As I am consistently among the slowest, weakest and fattest it is not a moment I relish, although I am reassured by the knowledge that everyone forgets about the statistics as soon as we actually start playing rugby.

The year gets off to a particularly unimpressive start, even by my low standards, when I pull up lame halfway through the 12-minute test (running as far as possible round a track in 12 minutes—something I can normally do reasonably well). A bad knee that I have been carrying since last year's pre-season blows up, promising to hinder my preparation. If I were to be cynical about it I would call it a blessing in disguise, because the coach steadfastly refuses to see that we are overtraining, and at my advanced age I could well do without the first month of endless running and full-contact, mortal combat-style training sessions. At 33, I am the oldest player in the team.

The bad knee means that I have to do my fitness work on a winch, a sort of bicycle contraption for the upper body where you 'pedal' with your hands. As an engine of physical torture, it is right up there with a rowing ergometer, and it is with little regret that I rule myself out of doing even this with a spec-tacular, some might say virtuoso, display of incompetence, that has me slicing my hand open on the winch's revolving disc wheel when my sweaty palms slip off the handle. I narrowly miss cutting a tendon and am rewarded with total rest for two weeks, while everyone else slogs through the summer heat.

By the time I come back we are into the friendly games, just a couple of weeks out from the start of the championship. My injured knee is still playing up, so I tend to put most of my weight on my other knee, particularly when coming down to earth from line-out jumps. This is not a great idea—lifting in line-outs means you get up to heights that nature never intended, particularly when, like me, you weigh 110 kilograms and are not predisposed to feats of athleticism, so when you hit the ground you need both legs to properly brake your fall. Just before half-time against second-division Lyon, the inevitable happens when my supposedly good knee gives out, and although it doesn't hurt or even swell up there is an ominous clicking and scraping every time I use it.

This is a worry. If I was not unhappy about missing the grind of pre-season, I am less zen about missing the start of the season. I also have the unpleasant feeling that my body is starting to betray me. For years I have suspected that my mind was writing cheques that my body couldn't cash, and it may be that the metaphorical debt collector is now taking, if not a pound of flesh, at least a good handful of cartilage, and perhaps some other important tissue. Most of my generation have stopped playing, and I fear I may have signed up for one season too many and my body will let me down. This is compounded by the fact that, while I have considered myself an essential part of the starting line-up for the last two years, the club has had the foresight to bring in a new lock, an Englishman called Alex Codling, to beef up their options in the second row, and he will now have the chance to establish himself as number one while I am out of the running. I am all for healthy competition for starting jerseys within the team as long as I get mine.

There is even another young lock waiting in the wings, which makes six of us for three places (two on the field, one on the bench). This is too many for my liking, particularly as the others all look distressingly competent. Worse still, the young lock doesn't look as though he will be happy to bide his time waiting for his chance. He is Georgian, and although I say young this doesn't mean baby-faced. At 22 he is a great bear of a man, and seems to spend all his spare time in the weights room. His name is Mamuka Gorgodze and he is dubbed, inevitably, 'Gorgodzilla'—although if you value your life you don't say this to his face. During the pre-season mortal-combat sessions he ran around smashing people into the ground, both with ball in hand and with the kind of sledgehammer tackles that cave in ribcages.

One of his victims, our South African centre Rickus Lubbe —no lightweight himself at a respectable 102 kilograms— swore under his breath as he was picking himself up after being stomped by Gorgodzilla, and the beast quickly turned on him: 'What you say? You say I fuck my mother?' (His English isn't great, but he seems to have the basics under control.) It took the intervention of four of us to reassure him it was just an expression, the Gorgodze family honour was in

23

no way being questioned, and no blood sacrifices would be necessary.

Luckily our other Georgian, Mamuka Magrikividledze, was on hand to help in the calming down. Although Mamuka is a good guy with a sense of humour, he is another 127-kilogram ogre who looks as if he eats babies for breakfast. God only knows what Georgian team runs look like. I imagine a horde of monsters tearing lumps of flesh out of each other, with the unforgiving Tbilisi winter as a backdrop.

My usual plan for dealing with enthusiastic, well-muscled youngsters who are looking hungrily at my jersey and show-ing off their physical prowess is to adopt a kind of Obi Wan Kenobi (Alec Guinness, not Ewan McGregor) aging-sage-who's-been-around-a-bit style of patter—something like, 'It's all very well standing there looking shiny and strong, there is much you have to learn before you can be ready.' In Gorgodzilla's case this is true: he so revels in his physical strength that he tends to disregard the rules of the game, and looks highly put out when referees have the cheek to penalise him for ripping people's arms off and beating them to death with the bloody limb, or whatever his circus trick of the moment happens to be.

Unfortunately we seem to have a communication problem —I'm talking but he's not listening. One day at scrum training we have too many locks and not enough loose forwards, and I take it upon myself to suggest it would be a good idea if he were to perhaps play in a different position. 'Mamuka, you play number eight.' He doesn't look happy about it, but complies for a few scrums before coming back to me, 'I have idea. *I* play lock, *you* play number eight.' The old Jedi mind trick, it seems, doesn't work on everyone.

From a layman's point of view, this talk of 127-kilogram behemoths sounds impressive. The terrifying thing for a spindly, six-foot-six, 110-kilogrammer like me is that these men are only just above average size. One of our props, a Samoan New Zealander called Philemon Toleafoa, tips the scales at 140 kilograms. This would be all very well if, as you would imagine, he lumbered around the park from scrum to line-out at the pace of an asthmatic snail, but instead he reaches alarmingly high speeds in a very short time, and takes great pleasure using his shoulder as a wrecking ball on anyone brave enough to be in his way. Our seven props average around 125 kilograms each, although there are a couple of lightweights of my weight. Before professional rugby came along and allowed players to spend more time in the gym, rugby players tended to be larger than average but only a few were genuinely outsize. These days you may get the impression from watching a game on television, or even from seeing one live, that players are still of more or less ordinary size. This is misleading. Standing next to one another they look relatively normal, but alongside them average-sized people— about five-foot-eight and 70 kilograms—look like under-nourished leprechauns.

2

Home and Away

Our first championship game of the season is against Castres at home. Castres have always been a good side on paper, but for one reason or another they rarely make it into the semifinals. They are blessed with a sponsor, Pierre Fabre, who runs an eponymous pharmaceutical company that is big enough for him to write out large cheques to keep the club of this small town in the top half of the table.

This year they have brought in Laurent Seigne, formerly of Bourgoin and Brive, as coach. Seigne's methods are well-known in rugby circles for being a little old-fashioned. Gregor Townsend, the Scotland and British Lions first five-eighth, told me that, before one game at Brive, Seigne had made the forwards—boots and all—run over him and his fellow centre in the changing-room because he didn't consider them sufficiently enthusiastic about *le combat*. He also broke one player's nose with a head butt during a pre-match talk. So it will be no surprise if Castres are more physical this year than they have been in the past. Some of them may be scarred for life, but then no one said it would be a cakewalk.

We have two locks out injured, so although I am not really ready to be playing I sit on the bench with both knees heavily strapped, praying that, if I get on, they will hold up. As we are running through warm-up exercises, Alex Codling, the English lock, vomits. He had warned me that this might happen because he suffers from some sort of lung disease, but the other boys don't know this and most of them don't look pleased, particularly because he throws up in the middle of a grid in which we are about to start doing forward rolls. To top off the performance he then moves slightly to his right so someone else has to roll forward into what is left of his lunch. Most of us shuffle a couple of feet away from the ugly little pile while trying to stay focussed, and someone who hasn't seen what's happened arrives to take his place.

Castres have a powerful forward pack based around Kees Meeuws, the former All Black tighthead prop. We hold up all right up front, but start to get pinged by the referee for things that are more the result of inexperience than being over-powered. There are plenty of errors on both sides; it's still early in the season, summer really, and crushingly hot, so the ball is slippery with sweat and neither team manages much continuity. We seem to grind away without much reward, while they get easy penalties from scrums, which their full-back, the robotic Romain Teulet, kicks with dispiriting regularity. We manage a couple of three-pointers ourselves, and when the half-time whistle blows at 12–6 to them I have a feeling that we are in with a chance if we can just get some forward momentum.

The first quarter of an hour of the second half shows up my misplaced optimism for the wishful thinking it is. Their forwards are the ones who get the forward momentum going. Two quick tries, and with 25 minutes to go the game is more or less over at 24–6. I am sent on to take Alex Codling's place just after the second try, and after we kick a penalty I allow myself to think that perhaps the cavalry has arrived in the nick of time. (Reserves love believing this kind of crap.) But really I do absolutely nothing to stem the tide. I get side-stepped by their centre, and by the time my wobbly knees react and get me back to where I need to be to make the tackle he is already five yards past me. A few minutes later I am one of three people holding up Meeuws when he scores. In fact, my only satisfaction comes from landing a good punch on their replacement hooker after the little bastard bites me in a maul. With about ten minutes to go we score a consolation try. It makes the score look a little less ugly, but 34–16 is still a kick in the teeth, and a very bad start to the season.

At the after-match we see television replays showing that Meeuws didn't actually ground the ball, but by then it's too late: the use of the television referee is only for games that are televised live, and Canal+ rarely screens our games. So the post-mortem clutching at straws starts. Our new fly-half, former French international David Aucagne, although he had played well and kicked goals as required, had managed to butcher the easiest of chances after chipping through a kick that was missed by their cover defence, knocking the ball on when all he had to do was pick it up and fall over the line under the posts.

To try and cheer ourselves up, we play the game of re-calculating the scores according to what might have been. Subtract Meeuws' try and the conversion from their total, add on Aucagne's 'try' and the imaginary conversion to ours, and abracadabra, it was a close-run thing at 27–23. From here it is only a short step to questioning a couple of refereeing decisions that gave them kickable penalties and—*voila!*—23–21 to us would have been the final score had the game been played in a truly just universe. This is the kind of wilful self-delusion that did for Madame Bovary.

From a completely objective viewpoint, 34–16 is probably a fair reflection of the gap between the two teams, and therefore not much of a drama. Castres look like a good side and should beat plenty of other teams. The problem is that we are playing in France, and when you play at home in France there is no room for objectivity. Here, rugby is more of an art than a science. Despite all the video analysis and number-crunching of the modern game, part of its charm is that it remains bloody-mindedly irrational. I have already mentioned the French idea of *l'esprit de clocher*—the credo of collective duty to the town, the team and the jersey. The peculiarity of the French version of 'pride in the jersey' is that it manifests itself much more strongly when you play at home. At home, the team is like the local militia, entrusted with the sacred duty of repelling the invaders and upholding the honour of the town—and everyone is watching. It doesn't matter that, intellectually, the players are capable of seeing the absurdity of playing differently at home and away. Everyone recognises that the pitch is the same size, the number of players the same for both sides, the ball the same shape, the referee (arguably, but we'll come back to that) neutral. *You win home games*. Away games you try to win, but at the back of your mind there is always the thought that if you lose, well, there's always next week, and next week is at home.

This highly developed sense of geographical awareness is linked to another very French idea, that of *terroir*, the notion that a product draws its identity from the soil in which it is produced and its character from the culture that surrounds it. I can't help but find this romantic sense of rootedness appealing. Rugby thrives in the hothouse environment of small French towns. Apart from the fully fledged cities of Paris and Toulouse, and to a lesser extent Montpellier and Montferrand, all the clubs in the Top 14 are based in towns that have populations of a 100,000 or less. The team's performance is a measure of the town's virility and skill, and gives its citizens an opportunity for civic pride when they compare their status with that of their big city cousins. Living in this kind of emotional climate, the players feel obliged to respond to expectations, because as their town's champions their honour is on the line more than anyone's.

In spite of the arrival of the professional era and the widespread use of mercenaries like me, to whom it had never previously occurred that you might play differently on one rugby ground as opposed to another, expectations remain the same. Yet even the French players are from somewhere else originally—most clubs have no more than a handful of genuine home-grown players—and it seems odd that, say, a Catalan playing for Biarritz or a Basque playing for Bourgoin should feel any greater surge of emotional power playing 'at home' than would an Australian, but it is still the case.

The home club does have a few very slight advantages. The home changing-room is normally slightly bigger and better equipped; the players know the ground better and can read swirling wind conditions; the home club always provides the match ball, and some clubs have different makes of ball that kickers find fly differently. Here in Montpellier (and I suspect everyone else is the same), the ball boys are told to swiftly gather balls that we kick into touch, so the opposition can't take quick throw-ins.

Most importantly there is the crowd, which likes to think of itself as the sixteenth man, capable of influencing a match with its voice. At Perpignan we used to let the other team run out first, leave them out there soaking up the whistles and the jeers for a minute or so, and then arrive to a roar that made the hairs stand up on the back of my neck. These days the teams have to come out of the tunnel at the same time, and the ground announcer is obliged to read out a little speech exhorting the fans to encourage their team in a spirit of fair play—for what that's worth. The opposition kicker, their fullback under a high ball, a referee or touch judge making a questionable decision (and generally speaking, any decision that goes against the home team is considered question-able)—everyone gets a raspberry.

And it is quite possible that the actors on the field, both players and officials, are influenced by this, consciously or not. More than once I have seen passes that were not forward whistled by referees, simply because the crowd called for it. But even this hardly accounts for the difference—usually about 20 points, depending on the exact circumstances—between a team's performance at home and away.

It had never used to make much difference to me where I played, whether there was a big crowd and, if there was, whether they were for me or against me. I suppose that, like anyone, my ego is puffed up by the presence of a lot of spectators. And even if the crowd were screaming insults, at least it meant they were paying attention. But this didn't affect the way I played. As with most New Zealanders, my motivation was internal, or at most revolved around what my teammates might think of me if I performed badly.

But I am conscious of having undergone a change in the way I feel during my time in France. Where I was once calm and phlegmatic (which the French see as typically Anglo-Saxon), I now get wound up just watching a game I think is important, and can blow up for the mildest of reasons. It is impossible to live in a vacuum, and the culture in which I operate has rubbed off on me. When I play a home game there is urgency to my preparation, but when playing away I am quite relaxed. I don't think this affects my performance, but I may be kidding myself. In any case, the stress of losing a game that you know you need to win is so great that, given Montpellier's away record, I would give myself an ulcer if I worried equally about every game. Over the last two seasons combined we have won only two championship games away from home.

Perhaps the best known example of the home-and-away mindset is the 1999 World Cup semifinal between France and New Zealand. As part of their preparation, the French team had visited New Zealand a few months before the competition, and been annihilated by 50 points. They had been particularly depressed by this result because they hadn't thought they had played badly: they had simply been beaten by a vastly superior team.

The semifinal was to be played at Twickenham, in front of a crowd of largely English spectators, with a smattering from New Zealand and France. The English spectators were supposedly neutral, although the French always assume that English-speakers invariably stick together: '*Vous êtes tous des Breteesh.*' But the French arrived in the role of underdog, and an All Black victory seemed so inevitable that the *Breteesh* decided to cheer for their European neighbours. It would be simplistic to say that this alone led to the extraordinary upset that followed. The All Blacks, it seemed, had peaked too early in their preparation and appeared tactically naïve, while the French, after a dismal start, grew progressively stronger, helped by the serendipitous arrival, through injury, of certain key players originally omitted from selection. But the psychological impact that hearing '*Allez les Bleus!*' ring around fortress Twickenham had on the French players was immense, and played an important role in their famous victory.

So this loss to Castres is discouraging for several reasons. Losing this heavily at home means we are clearly not competitive with the big boys, which is bad news because our next three games are all against teams who are qualified for Europe, and our next home game is against Toulouse, who, unfortunately for us, don't seem to suffer from the French version of travel sickness. Their supporters' chant on away trips is '*On vient, on gagne, et on s'en va,*' an irritating Gallic version of '*Veni, vidi, vici*'. It is quite possible that, after four rounds of the competition, we will resemble one of the more disappointing entrants in the Eurovision Song Contest: *Montpellier, nul points*.

This, in turn, will mark us out as a potentially winnable away game in the eyes of all the other teams, so they will approach the match in a different way than they might otherwise have done. Vultures. The first ten games of the Top 14 are to be played back-to-back this year, so if we start off on a losing streak we won't have the opportunity to gather our breath for some time. From a personal viewpoint, I had been hopeful that with a bit of adrenalin my knees would miraculously rise to the occasion, even though I was having trouble running in a straight line, but they remain resolutely uncooperative. I will need to stop playing for at least two weeks and hope they come right with physiotherapy.

The good news is that most of the teams that we are counting on being between us and the bottom of the table have suffered the same fate we have. Toulon, who have just arrived from the second division, went down to Biarritz, while Pau and Bayonne lost to Montferrand and Toulouse respectively. No one scores a bonus point (achieved by scoring four tries, or being defeated by seven points or less).

Narbonne, who I hoped would get off to an equally bad start, have somehow managed to beat Stade Français, and Brive have beaten Bourgoin. These last two games at least hold to home-and-away form: neither Narbonne nor Brive would have a hope of winning in Paris or Bourgoin. The fact that four teams have lost at home is ominous for the future of the championship. It looks as though we will quickly be divided into 'haves' and 'have-nots'.

From a mercenary point of view, winning and losing is a more complex equation than it may look at face value. If you are in the starting line-up, then obviously you want to win. Being in a winning team is always more fun, whether you are amateur or professional. There may also be win bonuses, though they are rare in French rugby and I believe rightly so: if you have got this far it is because you are a natural competitor and love playing the game, so while you will choose a club largely according to the size of the monthly cheque, when you are actually on the field you have a one-track mind, and promises of more cash are unnecessary.

Things get complicated when you remember that a team is made up from a squad of more than 30 players, of whom only 15 can be on the field at any one time. It's one thing if you are injured, or a young player with a future who needs to develop his skills in the second team and have occasional run-outs in less important games. But once you have arrived at a certain age, and you are not injured or being rested, the fact you are watching a game rather than playing it is hard to swallow.

Some players resolutely accept the coach's decision to put them on the bench or drop them completely, but I am not one of them, and I am sure I am not the only player to have sat in the stands watching someone else play in what I consider to be my jersey, and to hope that the team loses and the coach realises the error of his ways and reinstates me the following week.

Unfortunately, this is something of a luxury. If you are locked in a life-or-death relegation battle, as seems to be the case with Montpellier all the time, you know that losing a must-win game can lead to trouble. Relegation can lead to unemployment at worst, and at best a drop in your market value as a player and a subsequent scramble to find a new club. So the ideal solution is that the team wins but that the guy playing in my position has a nightmare of a game, bringing me back into the frame without the team having to suffer for my egotism. Like many players I am slightly superstitious, so I don't stoop to hoping for an expedient injury as I suspect that would be bad karma. And filling in for someone because they're injured feels a little like keeping the seat warm.

The Saturday after the Castres game, we travel away to Clermont-Ferrand. My knees rule me out of playing, so what I know of the game is from the subsequent video analysis and different reports. Montferrand are a strange club in that they always have a pile of money. Their budget, at €10.6 million, is second only to Toulouse, and is largely provided by the Michelin family, who run the world-famous tyre company out of this industrial city in the heart of the Massif Centrale. This means the team have a pleiad of French and international stars and are consistently thought of as potential

French champions, and yet, despite participating at élite level since 1925 and making it to the final on seven separate occasions, they have never won a championship.

Last year they had a disastrous start to the season, which saw them at the bottom of the table halfway through, before they sacked their coach and brought in Olivier Saïsset, my old coach from Perpignan. They went on to win a remarkable series of games and just qualify for the European Cup. They are not a team that inspires fear, but they are full of potential and could run riot at any moment if you give them the sniff of a chance. The previous weekend they beat Pau at Pau quite comfortably so are on the crest of a wave, while we know our chances of a win are slim to nothing. Still, we have to improve on the outing against Castres, so we throw everything into it.

The game is a tit-for-tat affair, with each team having their moments. Our line-out causes them trouble, robbing them of munitions with which they might overrun us, and we give them quite a run for their money, even leading 15–17 at one point in the second half, before cracking defensively in the last half-hour. Coco Aucagne kicks a penalty just before the end, which brings us up to a respectable 29–23. So we end up with the bonus point for defence, which has everyone reasonably happy as we open our account to get us off the floor of the championship table.

3

Fear and Loathing

oulouse are again the reigning European champions, and by anyone's standards they are a good side. They arrive in Montpellier missing Fabien Pelous, the French lock and captain, and Isitolo Maka, the ex-All Black number eight, but their line-up remains mouth-watering for the aficionado and cold-sweat-inducing for the opposition. Individuals such as Welsh captain Gareth Thomas, Yannick Jauzion and Fred Michalak ooze class, and most of the players on the bench would walk into any other side

Like Montferrand, the team is full of highly paid stars, but that is where the two clubs part company. These men mesh together in a side that understands the culture of winning. Under coach Guy Novès, who has been in place for ten years, Toulouse have been so successful that, by their own high standards, any year they are not European or French champion is a bad year. It helps that they have the biggest budget in the championship—€17.15 million—and that the city of Toulouse is the acknowledged capital of French rugby so they have a rich pool of talent on which to draw. The mercurial genius of Michalak, for example, was discovered more or less by accident, when he was thrown into the first team at the tender age of 18 after a string of injuries to the Toulouse halfbacks.

We are up against it and we know it.

Once again, my knees have me watching from the sideline, and within ten minutes I am trying to avert my eyes and think happy thoughts as what is happening on the field looks like turning into a massacre. Toulouse are already 10–0 up. However, we dig in and batter away at their forwards. The Toulouse pack are no pushover, but they are not as likely to leave you floundering in their wake as are their backs, so you are better off trying to take them on up front, rather than sending the ball wide, or kicking deep, and exposing yourself to counterattacks.

Gaining ground by centimetres, we start putting them under pressure and go to the break 6–13, although with our big Samoan centre, Ali Koko, getting a yellow card for a high tackle just before half-time, we can look forward to an uphill grind. We kick another penalty shortly after the break, and at 9–13 are still in the game with ten minutes to go. However, we have been harshly penalised a couple of times in the line-out by the referee, Monsieur Mené, and the platform for our driving mauls is weakened when we need it most. (Mené whistles us for fake jumps, but two weeks later will let exactly the same thing go when refereeing a 'big' team.) In the last ten minutes we crack, and when Toulouse score two penalties and a try to Thomas, we can muster only a penalty at the death: 12–24. No bonus point, *nada*.

The following week, we are up against Bourgoin. Bourgoin are a solid team, based around an excellent forward pack with French internationals Pascal Papé, Olivier Milloud and Julien Bonnaire, and an efficient kicking game from Benjamin Boyet at fly-half and Alexander Peclier at fullback. They haven't lost at home in the championship for something like three years, and let's face it, Montpellier are unlikely to break that run.

Club Sportif Bourgoin-Jallieu, to give it its full name, resides in an agglomeration of two small towns just outside Lyon, in the shadow of the alps, remarkable for nothing much other than the consistent success of their rugby club. Trivia fans may be intrigued to know that their colours, sky-blue and claret, are copied from the Birmingham football club Aston Villa: apparently the club was founded by an English expatriate. Its money comes mainly from its president, Pierre Martinet, a catering tycoon.

Although Bourgoin have been European-qualified for some time, their small squad of only 28 professionals means they are never really competitive in the Heineken Cup. In 2005 they suffered a 90-point thrashing in Dublin against Leinster, and are unlikely to ever threaten the big three. Their depressed local economy and rickety stadium hint at an uncertain future. Their home-grown players, their strength for so long, are being slowly picked up by the bigger clubs with bigger salaries.

For the moment, though, they are a damn sight bigger than we are, so it is with some satisfaction that we give them a fright, leading 3–0 for half an hour, before they score a converted try. At half-time it is 7–3 and unfortunately our young centre, Seb Mercier, thrown in at the deep end because of injury, misjudges a pass a couple of metres out when he could have just slid into the line. A try would have made the second half more interesting; instead they canter out to a comfortable 17–3 win.

A month later Bourgoin host Agen, and the aging Stade Pierre Rajon is the scene of one of French rugby's famous *bagarres générales*, or all-in brawls. After the half-time whistle blows, Luc Lafforgue, the Agen captain, goes over to the Bourgoin halfback Michael Forrest, says something, then clocks him. Predictably, all hell breaks loose. Most of the players were on their way to the changing-room but they turn around and start laying into their opposite numbers—or, failing that, anyone within reach. Spectators lean over the railings to get in their tuppence worth, the referee blows his whistle to no effect, and the rain of kicks and punches continues to fall on all sides for the best part of a minute, as scores, real or imagined, are settled.

Eventually things calm down and, as is often the case in a whirlwind of enthusiastically thrown but poorly aimed punches, no one is seriously hurt. The referee hands out red cards to the two captains, Lafforgue and Bonnaire, and everyone goes off to the changing shed for ten minutes to rediscover their *sang-froid*. Bourgoin have their stadium suspended for a game and so have to play a match away from home, and the two captains are suspended for two months but let off with less for good behaviour. As the match was televised, the punch-up is quickly taken up by various television channels and re-broadcast, occasionally with hand-wringingly pious commentary about how scandalous and shocking we should find the violence. However, the action is gleefully devoured by most of the viewing public, particularly rugby fans, who have never minded a few uppercuts to go with their up-and-unders.

Rugby players are often referred to as modern gladiators. Ice hockey, American Football and Australian Rules are the only other team sports that can be said to approach the same physical intensity, and in all of them the occasional dust-up is considered part and parcel of the game. If we're honest, it is also part of the attraction, because people love watching a scrap. From schoolyard to bar-room, the one thing certain to draw a good crowd is the shout of 'Fight! Fight!'

Even if you stay within the rules, with the move toward the high-impact game the physical confrontation is still spectacularly dangerous. People used to love watching Jonah Lomu running with the ball, not just because he had exceptional grace and agility but also because there was a genuine whiff of danger if anyone tried to stop him. This may not have registered with the casual observer, but as a rugby player who is pleased never to have been in a position to have had to try to tackle Lomu myself, I feel nothing but admiration for the players (most of them much smaller than me) who were in front of him, and at least made an effort. They must have felt they were taking their life in their hands, and were probably only a slightly misjudged tackle away from that being the case. Such action may look balletic and aesthetically pleasing to the people clapping politely in the stands, or watching slow-motion replays from the comfort of their sofas. On the field, though, it is nature red in tooth and claw. Rugby is a respectable version of blood sport.

Because there is always an element of danger, there is, naturally, fear. In order to overcome this, players often use anger, supposedly channelling the adrenalin into a useful and more controllable energy. This is what getting 'fired up' is all about, although most players would be hard-pressed to admit it because physical fear is seen as cowardice, and no one wants to be thought of as suffering from that. And many players are not conscious of fear as such. I didn't feel it until I was relatively old, and had seen players suffer serious injuries.

Using anger, and even hate, as tools is, however, emotionally lazy and, particularly for hot-blooded Latin types, adds to the danger. (Anglo-Saxons tend to keep their motivation inside a disciplined framework.) The game demands a certain amount of precision and constant decision-making, and over 80 minutes anger, although useful in short, intense bursts, is counterproductive. I have seen players crying with emotion before going on to the pitch because they were so wound up, and this is not helpful. If, for example, you're a hooker, you have to throw the ball into a line-out at exactly the right height and speed to make sure your side win it— wanting to rip out the opposition's throats is no use at all. Still, anger is commonly employed in France, where it is often confused with courage, particularly by smaller teams who know they are going to struggle on talent alone and are looking for something to compensate.

French rugby has more frequent boil-overs than rugby elsewhere. The stories I have heard about the sport in 'the old days'—only about 20 or 30 years ago—are enough to make your hair curl, even when taken with the obligatory grain of salt. Various individuals have regaled me with tales of what can only be described as psychopathic behaviour: taking 10-metre run-ups to boot people in the head, crippling players by wrenching joints into unnatural angles, and so on. One club allegedly turned out the lights in the corridor just as the two teams were lining up together to go on to the field, thereby offering their boys the chance of a surprise attack on the opposition under the cover of darkness and out of the referee's line of sight. The opportunity, I was told, was not wasted.

Toulon, only slightly more subtle, used to deliberately send the kick-off directly into touch at the start of their home games, so they could start with a scrum on the halfway line, followed by an inevitable flurry of fists that allowed them to remind the opposition of the importance of following the script—that is, we are playing at home so we are going to win, and if you want to get in the way of that you will see hell unleashed, and this is just a taste. Such tales are told with misty eyes and big grins. These days, thankfully, the use of the yellow card system, or 'sin-bin', has made a big difference. Referees hesitate to send a player off for the whole game for a single measly punch, particularly when it could be justified retaliation for an unseen misdemeanour, but they have fewer qualms about sending guys off for ten minutes. Everyone knows that being a man down for ten minutes can turn a close game, so players are not as quick on the draw as they used to be.

To outsiders the violence is shocking. I remember walking behind two officials from the Irish province Connacht after an unimportant European Shield game last season. We had lost by 50 points the week before in Ireland, and then scraped out a slim victory in the home game, more by foul means than fair, and there had been a number of unpleasant incidents. One of the Irishmen was saying to the other how disgusted their boys were, and the other replied, 'It's just not rugby.' Feeling slightly shamefaced, I mentioned this to my fellow lock Michel Macurdy, who, unabashed, replied, 'They shouldn't have put 50 points on us.'

In France, I'm afraid it *is* rugby. But it is so engrained in the culture that the French don't think of it as unusual. During a game against Australia in 2005, Fabien Pelous, the French captain, elbowed Brendan Cannon in the face, causing an injury that obliged the Australian hooker to leave the field and have several stitches put in so he could continue. Pelous did this in open play, out in the middle of the field, but so far away from the ball that the referee and touch judges didn't notice.

After the game, when the Australians were understandably upset, he said they needed to wait and see what the video replay looked like, obviously hoping the incident had not been picked up by the cameras. Unfortunately for him it had been, and the images were appalling. When asked to justify his action, he couldn't even say it was retaliation for some unseen skulduggery on Cannon's part, just that Cannon had been in the way and deliberately blocking him.

I have a lot of respect for Pelous as a player, and I have done some dumb things in the heat of action on the rugby field so I'm not going to throw stones. What was shocking, though, was that Bernard Laporte, the French coach, berated the French media, saying they shouldn't have shown the images and be making such a fuss. He went on to say this would never have happened in New Zealand. That is simply not true, as witness the 'spear tackle' by the All Black captain, Tana Umaga, on Brian O'Driscoll during the 2005 Lions tour: although judged an over-vigorous clearing-out by the disciplinary board, it led news stories for the best part of a week.

Having said that, there is much hypocrisy about the use of violence on the rugby field. In his book *A Year in the Centre*, O'Driscoll complained about being eye-gouged while playing against Argentina. 'Don't ask me why they do it. It has no place in rugby. The best way to put a cheat in his place is by consistently beating him.' This sounds fair enough, until you read the Welsh centre Gavin Henson complaining in his book *My Grand Slam Year* that he had been eye-gouged by O'Driscoll, who apparently rubbed it in by asking, 'How do you like that, you cocky little fucker?'

When I arrived in France in 1997 I was shocked by the violence. At 25 I wasn't old, but I wasn't exactly wet behind the ears either. However, the first game I played—a run-out with the Bs in Dijon while I waited for my licence to come

47

through—so opened my eyes that my initial reaction was to close them again as quickly as possible, before someone stuck their fingers in them. I should have realised there was something unusual going on when I saw some of my new teammates putting on what looked like cricket boxes. Why the hell would anyone need to protect their balls in a rugby game?

Mercifully, no one assaulted my unsuspecting genitalia, but my nose was broken by a punch at the first line-out, and the game resembled a street fight. At one point a line-out degenerated into a brawl on one side of the field, but the ball made its way out to the opposite wing where the backs had their own little disagreement to sort out. On both sides of the field, players and spectators were getting stuck in with boots and fists, and even umbrellas and gumboots, while Dijon's resident New Zealander and I were left standing in the middle of the pitch, not knowing whether to laugh, cry or start punching each other.

A bit of niggle is an occupational hazard for rugby players, especially forwards, all over the world. The contact area, particularly in rucks and mauls, is a pile-up of bodies, every one of whom is intent on extracting maximum advantage to his side from the effort he puts in—whether getting the ball back for his team, pinching it from the opposition, or simply getting in the way of the other lot. The law has a number of grey areas that can be exploited, and even the best referees have trouble keeping track of what all 30 players are doing at any one time.

Everyone has their own way of dealing with this, but people who are bending the rules should not be surprised to receive a little discouragement from the opposition who see the hand reaching into the ruck or feel the pull on the jersey from behind. Rugby players pride themselves on being hard men, but the difference between what it means to be 'hard'—respected for your ruthless, uncompromising attitude that inspires respect, if not fear, in the opposition—and 'dirty'—over the top—is a knife edge. Violence is only indiscipline if you get caught. Otherwise, physical intimidation is seen as a useful weapon.

My club coach at Marist St Pats in Wellington, Kevin Horan, a hard man from whom I learned a lot, used to tell us, 'Take the smack in the mouth, put your hands in your pockets and take the three points.' This epitomised what I think of as the right attitude to violence: shit happens, but always keep in mind the greater good of the team. It's about self-sacrifice, putting your body on the line, and not getting involved in vendettas that will distract you from the job. It is high-minded and I used to live by it. The problem is that it has one huge blind spot: it assumes the referee will spot the bastard who's had a go at you and take appropriate action.

One of the great specialties of French rugby is *la fourchette*, the eye-gouge. This is particularly effective because it is discreet. In the kind of car-crash situation that is the ruck or maul, with bodies arriving from all directions, it is very difficult for an observer to see a finger slipping unobtrusively into someone's eye. But you, the owner of the eye, know all about it, and quickly forget about whatever you are doing. The only thing that matters is getting that bloody finger out of there. You try to hold on to the finger so that you can see who the owner is, but invariably it slips back into the grunting morass that surrounds you.

It is a particularly unpleasant feeling having a dirty finger-nail scraping along the back wall of your eye socket. It's even worse if, like me, you wear contact lenses and then have to fiddle around trying to get the lens back in place, or grope around on the ground looking for the tiny transparent object, without which the rest of the game is going to be hard to follow. In fifteen years of rugby in New Zealand I was eye-gouged twice, and I remember feeling physically sick after-wards that anyone would stoop so low. Within the first month of being in France I lost count of the number of times it happened.

I should now own up to having been in the wrong in a couple of eye-gouging incidents myself. In a court of law, the defence would plead extenuating circumstances: in both cases we were playing 'must win' matches at home in Montpellier that really were 'must win': defeat would mean we had one foot—or more—in the second division. These games are referred to as 'life or death', which with hindsight sounds overblown, but it is easy to lose perspective. And in both cases my victims were serial offenders. After a three-match losing streak we were just ahead of Biarritz, but couldn't score from our usually successful five-metre line-out drives. There were probably any number of reasons for this, including our own incompetence, but at the time the most glaring seemed to be the Biarritz hooker, Jean-Michel Gonzalez, bush-pigging his way into the middle of our maul and then somehow pulling it down cleverly enough to avoid being penalised.

After he had done this for the third time, I decided some-one needed to discourage him. I opted for my first foray into one of the great French traditions and stuck my finger in his eye. Since it was my first time I was a bit nervous, and not wanting to do any serious damage, and a bit worried about the icky feeling of shoving a digit into another man's skull cavity, I didn't push hard enough. But I had another crack and it went in, and he looked gratifyingly unhappy. We were both face-to-face on the floor, so he knew very well who had done it. At the after-match we had a beer and I apologised. He replied with a smile, '*C'est le jeu, c'est le jeu*'—'That's the way the game is played.' He is of the old, old school, and having played in the first division for nearly twenty years and been capped for France thirty-four times it wasn't anything he hadn't seen at least a hundred times before.

We lost that game, but it is worth pointing out that the following year we played Biarritz in similar circumstances and towards the end of the game had a chance for a line-out drive from a penalty about 15 metres out—and again Gonzo came around on the wrong side of the maul, but this time with his head up, more for form's sake than with any real determination, which meant the referee could see him; he was even laughing as he did it. We duly got another penalty, pushed over from five yards out and won. I would probably be flattering myself to say that his treatment the previous year had changed his attitude, but you never know.

The second time around we were playing neighbouring Béziers in a derby match, and a three-match losing streak had blown out to a very worrying seven-match losing streak.

Bézier's hooker, Sebastian Bruno, had been mentioned in our team talk as having been particularly effective at slowing down our ball in the rucks in the away game that we had narrowly lost, and it was imperative he not do it again.

In my experience, no one actually singles out a member of the opposition and says, 'We have to get so-and-so off the park.' This would be considered ethically dodgy. However, there is an open-ended nature to certain instructions that allows for plausible deniability, while indicating that our best interests would be met were so-and-so less intimately involved with proceedings than he might have been planning. Of course, these instructions can be interpreted in any number of ways.

Anyway, Bruno was up to his old tricks again almost immediately, and I found myself with my finger in his eye suggesting that he would spend a more pleasant evening were he to remain out of our rucks. I don't know whether it made any difference, but we squeaked home and stayed up.

The other trick, just as effective as the eye-gouge but without the uncomfortable guilty feeling that (in my case at least) goes with it, is simply putting your hand near the eyes of the guy who has his hands on the ball or on the wrong side of the ruck. Everyone knows that this is the prelude to the dirty finger going in, so there is a rising feeling of panic in the victim, who immediately takes evasive action.

Obviously, eye-gouging is illegal and I am in no way condoning it. More than one player has partially lost their sight because of it, and being responsible for depriving anyone of their sight is not something anyone in their right mind would want to have on their conscience. I'm telling you about it simply because it happens. And one of the reasons it happens is because it seems to be widely accepted. The French Fédération has a recommended six-month suspension period for anyone caught eye-gouging, but it is almost impossible to catch the perpetrators.

In my first year in France I played for Racing against Montauban in Montauban, and ended up on the wrong side of a ruck trying to pilfer a ball. One of the opposition eye-gouged me, right in front of the referee, who duly blew his whistle and awarded a penalty against the owner of the offending digit. A penalty—the same punishment that is meted out to players who are offside, or backs who creep up inside the ten-yard zone before a line-out is deemed to be over. Not a red card followed by a six-month suspension. Only one player has been suspended for eye-gouging since I have been playing in France, Richard Nones from Colomiers, and he was suspended not by the French but by the European disciplinary board in 1998. He appealed on the grounds that he was innocent and that the touch judge who cited him was mistaken. There was a lot of French huffiness, largely because it was considered ludicrous to suspend anyone from their job for two years for such a banal crime.

The attitude of French referees tends to be more *laissez-faire* than that of their British and Commonwealth counterparts. This is not necessarily the fault of the ruling body, which has laid down reasonably strict guidelines in an effort to discourage violence. Rather, the men in the middle who have to enforce the laws often don't have the heart to do so.

The French attitude is perhaps best summed up in the language. A player who goes round smacking the opposition because they've been cheating is known as *le justicier*, the bringer of justice who casts himself in the role of judge, jury and executioner. There doesn't seem to be any irony involved. (Tellingly, the 'Anglo-Saxon' style of abiding by the law in the spirit of good sportsmanship is known as *le fairplay*—a word that has had to be imported because there isn't a French equivalent.)

One year it was announced that there was to be a crackdown on retaliation. The man who started a fracas was to be issued a yellow card, but the *justicier* who tried to finish it was to see red. Shortly after this we played a home game in which one of our players was kicked by one of the opposition's. As I was standing next to the man with the frisky boots, I felt honour-bound to have a slap at him. The referee saw the whole thing and called us both over. Both teams had been reminded of the new ruling and I was getting ready to be first into the showers as he went for his pocket. Out came a yellow for the other guy. The referee turned to me. 'You shouldn't have punched him,' he said. Then he sighed and shrugged, 'But it was a reflex action, and I understand. But you must not do it again!' I can't help sympathising with the referee in this kind of situation: the thinking behind the law is fine in theory, but in practice you couldn't really apply it without encouraging mayhem. If it had been enforced, coaches up and down the land would have been encouraging their troops along the lines of, 'Get your retaliation in first then, lads.'

4

History, Culture and Cash

It's the fifth game of the season and already we have the knife at our throat. With a grand total of one point from the four previous outings, we are equal second to last with Toulon, one point ahead of Pau. Bayonne have seven points, comfortably ahead of us, after a home win against Pau and an away draw at Brive. If we lose today we are in all sorts of trouble, because Bayonne, unlike Castres and Toulouse, are a little team, and if we can't beat the little teams when we play at home then we simply aren't up to it.

Bayonne resemble us in many ways, with a forward-oriented game that they seem to have trouble exporting from their home ground. They arrived in the first division last year and did well to stay up, and now they are looking to consolidate and move away from the danger zone at the bottom of the table. They are a much older club, formed by a group of rowers (officially they are part of an omnisport club known as *l'Aviron Bayonnais*—Bayonne Rowing) who were looking for an energetic winter sport a hundred years ago and who won their first French championship in 1913. Montpellier Rugby Club, a youngster by comparison, is celebrating its twentieth birthday in 2006. Bayonne are direct rivals with us for relegation.

Once again I am on the bench, and I go on after only quarter of an hour when Michel Macurdy breaks his hand. My knees are still heavily strapped—this is my first game back—but, mercifully, they seem to be doing more or less as they are told. We are already 7–0 up and quickly pull out to 10–0. With ten minutes to go to half-time their back-rower Yannick Lamour gets a yellow card, but even with one man up we can't capitalise when we should and are in danger of getting the shakes. All it would need is a quick try to put Bayonne back in the game and we could all start snarling at each other in typically French fashion over whose fault it is and the whole thing could fall apart.

I don't recall ever playing in an non-French team that did anything other than encourage each other on the field, though my memory may be selectively glossing over the darker moments. But, under pressure, French rugby players have the nasty habit of stating the obvious. There is nothing more irritating on a rugby field than having your team-mates tell you that you are screwing up, especially when you are well aware of this. While playing for Perpignan I missed a tackle that led to a try, and my captain said to me, 'You had to tackle him. Why didn't you tackle him? They scored a try because of your missed tackle.'

Different people deal with this in different ways. Some

blow it up into a full-scale argument, while others stalk off in a sulk. It's difficult to take it on the chin. You're thinking, 'I know they scored a try because I missed a tackle. Do you think I did it on purpose? What sort of idiot do you take me for? What gives you the right to tell me that I'm crap? So you've never missed a tackle in your life?' Not the most positive line of thinking.

Montpellier, for all the flannel about being a tightly bound group of friends, are quite capable of this sort of back-biting. During one unimportant European Shield game, after a missed tackle had led to a try, our captain, Jérôme Vallée, let fly at the backs while standing under the posts, accusing them of not trying hard enough, while the forwards were working their arses off. Unsurprisingly, this led to a shouting match with Coco, who felt he was the target, and the whole episode did nothing for our much-vaunted team spirit.

Luckily it doesn't come to that as we grind them down up front; the Bayonne pack, difficult to get an edge over in front of their home crowd, seem strangely apathetic, and are obviously suffering from away-game syndrome. A couple more penalties from Coco and another yellow card, this time for Cédric Bergez, Bayonne's lock and captain, yet still we can't score the try that would finish the game. Finally, with ten minutes to go, Lamour gets another yellow card, making his sending-off permanent, and the floodgates open. A number of times I find myself in the unfamiliar role of halfback, slinging the ball wide to our backs, who are carving massive holes in the defence. Two converted tries and a penalty make for an easy-looking 33–0 score-line, and our one regret is that we didn't get the fourth try for an attacking bonus point.

Pau, our next destination, is known as *la ville anglaise*. It became a recreational centre for wealthy English holiday-makers in the nineteenth century, before the nearby resort of Biarritz became more fashionable. Today, its proximity to the Pyrenees makes it a popular centre for winter sports. It is another medium-sized town in the south-west where rugby has a long history: *La Section Paloise*, our opponents today, first played a competition game 100 years ago. The club qualified for the Heineken Cup as recently as 2001 but they have been on the slide ever since, with frequent turnovers of staff and players, and last year had to play off to avoid relegation. (There are no play-offs this year.) At €6.54 million their budget is slightly smaller than ours, and having failed to win a game they are currently placed thirteenth. The game at Stade du Hameau is our first real opportunity for an away victory.

One of the knock-on effects of regularly losing games is that individual confidence often evaporates. Instead of taking the kind of risks that lead to scoring opportunities, players limit their potential for being involved in cock-ups: if you don't take risks you don't make mistakes. Not only does this make for boring games, it is also counterproductive. We are shocking at Pau but so are they—it's not a question of home-and-away. The only charitable conclusion to be drawn is that both teams are paralysed by the high stakes; having finally managed to win a game the previous weekend, we can give ourselves a bit of breathing space with a win, while a loss will have Pau breathing down our necks again.

With the honourable exception of our rugged flanker Cédric Mathieu, the one guy on the field to have a standout performance is Pau's young fly-half, Lionel Beauxis, who plays for the French Under 21s. His siege-gun boot keeps us away from their line, and our inability to string together more than a couple of phases of play does the rest. Pau's driving mauls allow Beauxis to get in range for a couple of drop goals in the first half, and they both fly over from 40 metres. Coco Aucagne, on the other hand, is having a bit of a nightmare. He played most of his rugby for Pau, including during his international career in the late 1990s, and in front of his old home crowd he is feeling the pressure. Still, our incompetence is equally matched by their jitters and it's only 9–6 to them at half-time and then 9–9 shortly after the break, when Coco puts a penalty over, but then they slowly pull away.

I watch the whole *débâcle* unfold from the stands and find it hard to believe that the replacement bench is not being used. Even when, ten minutes into the second half, one of our locks, Sam Nouchi, gets a yellow card for pulling down a *cocotte* (literally a casserole, but in French rugby parlance a maul), I don't get on. More surprisingly, Régis Lespinas, our young fly-half who has also played for the French Under 21s, doesn't get on either. Despite everything, we were still in the game up until the last 20 minutes, and a change of rhythm injected by Régis might have let us sneak a win.

When I quiz our coach Nourault about this afterwards he says he didn't want to destroy Coco's confidence: pulling him off in front of the old home crowd would be potentially shattering for him, and he seems a bit fragile as it is. In my view, Coco's confidence is in a parlous state exactly *because* Nourault spends his time ordering him what to do, and not trusting him enough to make his own decisions. Not taking him off when he's playing badly isn't fooling anyone, least of all Coco, who is experienced enough to understand the situation. At first glance it might look like loyalty, which sounds honourable if a little misguided, but really it's just weakness; because Nourault wants to look like the good guy, he avoids taking the hard decisions. We come away without even a bonus point at 21–12, with all the points for both sides coming from kicks.

Perhaps I am being unfair to Nourault. After all, he has relegated me to the bench and this may be colouring my judgement. Alex Codling, the Englishman who arrived to play lock at the start of the season, has done his back in, and looks like being out of the picture for some time, and Michel Macurdy has broken his hand, so there are only three locks left. If Nourault is not using me now he must have really lost faith in me, even though I thought I did well enough against Bayonne. He has a fetish for line-outs, which doesn't go in my favour: although I am tall enough, I don't have the explosive power you need to jump well in the middle, so I find myself more often in a lifting role. Sam Nouchi is about the same size as me and a better line-out forward, so this probably gets him the nod. He is technically a good player— when I was at Perpignan, Saïsset gave me a list, made up by the French selectors, which ranked the locks in the first division. The division was then made up of 20 teams, so about 80 locks were in competition. Sam was placed fifth, just behind the locks of the national side. (I was thirteenth, which is probably as high as I ever got.) But he often doesn't seem very interested, and in my mind I'm a better player because I want it more.

This is the fifth year I have played under Nourault. I was coached by him in Paris for my last two years, and was captain under him and Jacques Fouroux at Racing. Although it was a difficult time for both of us—results were bad and the club was relegated—we respected each other, and formed something of a bond when we both played significant roles in ousting Fouroux, who was a brilliant ideas man and a highly successful coach (and ex-captain) of the French side, but in club rugby had trouble turning his theories into practice. After I later moved to Perpignan, Norault recruited me for Montpellier, and as I was a senior player he consulted me regularly and listened to what I had to say, even if he rarely implemented my ideas. My 'special relationship' with Nourault, therefore, means that my non-selection, difficult to take at any time, has a sting of betrayal about it.

Sitting on the bench, I have time to make a rough calculation about the game. Montpellier and Pau each have budgets of around €6.5 million, a total of €13 million between them. Both teams play 26 championship games in a year, plus six European Shield games. (The latter are often used as run-outs by teams like us, who know we won't win the competition and are in severe need of a breather from the rigours of the French championship. However, for argument's sake we'll give them equal weight.) There are friendly games and so on, but they are for preparation: the *raison d'être* of the professional team is to perform in the competition. So while hotels and gear and transport costs are included in a club's budget along with salaries, what happens on the field in competition is the end-product: all the time and effort and money poured into a team can be judged only by this.

So dividing €13 million by the number of competition games—32—gives you the value of the money invested by the two clubs in a particular performance: €406,250 or about €200,000 apiece. That is the amount of money being spent on the sorry spectacle we are producing on this particular Saturday afternoon. (True, I don't get the exact figure while sitting on the bench—I have to use a calculator afterwards. But you don't have to be a genius to see that €13 million divided by 32 is quite a lot of cash.)

Money is, of course, the dark heart of the game at professional level. Shamateurism, *l'amateurisme marron*, had been around for years in France, and in most of the rest of the world, before 1995, when the IRB finally squared up to reality after the Rugby World Cup in South Africa. It had become clear that the temptation of big dollars from rugby league and Kerry Packer's World Rugby Corporation was threatening to lure top players away from rugby union's traditional structures, leaving a gaping hole at the top level of the game. The IRB gave its blessing to pay-for-play, and suddenly it was all on as clubs in the northern hemisphere and national unions in the south rushed to make sure they had a legal hold on their talent: contracts.

My first-ever contract was signed with the New Zealand Rugby Football Union in January 1996. Because the NZRFU was still a bit iffy about professionalism, and the legal documents had been drawn up in the scramble of late 1995, it was a contract with All Black Promotions Limited: I wasn't being paid to play, I was being paid to be available for promotional work. This was just window-dressing of course: the sum total of my promotional work was an hour spent in a McDonald's restaurant in central Wellington wearing a Wellington polo shirt and signing (not very many) autographs. No one seemed to know quite what they were doing in the brave new world of professionalism, and at times the whole thing seemed a shambles. Marty Leslie, who later went on to play for Scotland, jokingly pencilled in another three zeros to his match fee for Wellington in the National Provincial Championship. The contract was duly signed and, in theory anyway, he should have been paid a million bucks a game.

Looking back, one of the things I particularly like about that first contract, apart from the feeling that we were getting what seemed like free money, was that there was no differentiation between players. Everyone's Super 12 contract was worth the same, NZ$65,000—$50,000 for the Super 12 itself and $15,000 for the National Provincial Championship. All Blacks were, understandably, a big step up on $250,000.

During my first year with Racing, while playing against Aurillac I had my ear half ripped off at the bottom of a ruck. There was no mistaking that it had been a deliberate act: the ball had already made it out to the backs when the boot went in. As I sat fuming, having the ear painfully sewn back together—repeated attempts to anaesthetise it had not worked as the lobe was so thin the needle kept going right through it—Gerald Martinez, the club president, came in to see how I was. I told him I wasn't being paid enough money for this kind of crap. He asked how much more I wanted. I told him another 2000 francs a month. He agreed immediately. I should have been chuffed about getting a 20 percent pay rise on the spot, but instead I again kicked myself that I hadn't asked for more in the first place.

The point of the story is that it is hard for a player to know how much he is worth. Money is difficult: as Philippe Guillard writes in *Petits Bruits de Couloir*, his excellent book on the vagaries of French rugby: 'If you ask for nothing, you get nothing. And if you ask for too much, you get nothing.'

According to the economics I learnt in the fifth form, the 'market' is supposed to sort out appropriate levels of remuneration. But as I recall (it was a long time ago), to come to the correct conclusion it relies on perfect competition and perfect knowledge, and in rugby this is far from the case. Within the French club scene, teams play each other so often that it is relatively straightforward for a club to assess a player's ability, and decide how much they want to pay him. As a rule of thumb, they find out what he is being paid and offer him a bit more, although this can get a bit complicated if several clubs are interested in the same player.

Young players who look as though they will have a promising career may see big jumps in their salaries. And, of course, playing for France guarantees you good wedge: anyone who has played more than a couple of games for the national side is likely to be on at least €15,000 net a month. On top of this come match fees and win bonuses, as well as sponsorship deals. Certain positions are highly prized because of their rarity—tighthead props, fly-halves and hard-running number eights all fall into this category, along with goal-kickers.

Where it gets really complicated is when players who arrive from overseas are more or less unknown quantities. Star players from big-name international sides are well-known and sought after, even though they are often past their best, take time to adapt to the different style of play in France, and so underperform in the eyes of the uninitiated. A club will calculate not only the added value to the team of having this kind of star player on the field, but also the added revenue in attracting corporate sponsorship and more spectators.

Players like me, journeymen of a reasonable standard but not internationals, and certainly not stars, are hardest to evaluate. Often a prospect will have some Super 14 experience, so the clubs will look at his video footage, but even then it's not easy to tell how a prop, for example, will adapt to French scrummaging, where the laws are supposedly the same as in the southern hemisphere but the referee's interpretation very different. And for a player, the salary he negotiates when he arrives on the French scene will be crucial: barring brilliant performances (or catastrophic ones) it will be the base figure for his time in France.

It could be anywhere between €3000 and €15,000 a month. The current average is around €7000, which is exactly what I'm on. Throughout my nine-year career in France my pay-packet has closely mirrored the average, going from roughly €2000 in 1997 to €3000 in 1998 and 1999, €4000 in 2000, €5000 in 2001 and 2002, €6000 in 2003 and 2004, to €7000 this season. There have been times when I've felt outrageously underpaid, and others when I have felt guilty about getting too much, so the levels have probably been about right.

Ironically, I played my best rugby on about €4000: my performance has decreased as my wage has increased. Partly this is because I was underpaid early on, and partly because budgets have increased exponentially over the last ten years. Partly, though, I have just become better at negotiating.

While these figures are a long way from the multiple-zero-laden cheques that professional footballers tuck into their banks every month, French rugby pays well—nearly four times the country's average wage. From time to time players are unwelcomingly reminded of our privileged position. When I was at Racing, the president, Éric Blanc, informed us that his mother had performed superhuman feats as a nurse working long hours for less than half what we earned. At a training camp at the start of 2007, Alain Egea, the president of the Association—effectively the club's amateur side, comprising youth teams, women's rugby and *l'école de rugby* — told us we were lucky compared to workers in the 'real world', and must always be on time. Montferrand coach Alain Hyardet went to the length of taking his players to the Michelin factory to show them what life was like in this 'real world'.

It is true: we are lucky to be well-paid to play a sport we love, and it doesn't hurt to be reminded of this from time to time. But the implicit criticism that we are spoilt overgrown children puts everyone on the defensive. And there are several counter arguments. For a start, if it's such a doddle, why isn't everyone doing it? And while we are on the rugby field, we are missing out on crucial first steps in the 'real world'; it is not easy to pick up a new career in your thirties, when you quit. The money *is* good. But when we hang up our boots only two or three high-profile players such as Jonny Wilkinson will be able to retire; the rest of us will take up starting positions in the rat race. The lucky ones will have paid off a bit of their mortgage, and the very lucky ones will have made some investments as well.

And then there is the fact that players risk having major injury worries for the rest of their lives. The average office worker may work longer hours for less pay, but he is unlikely to get eye-gouged, or to have to throw himself in the path of rampaging behemoths who want to smash him into the ground and dance on his fallen body.

As a rule, the best way for a player to bump up his salary is to sign a one-year contract, play well, and hawk himself around for the following season. 'What you're on, plus a bit more' every year, as opposed to every two or three years, means the coin starts piling up nicely. Loyalty to a club is not always rewarded by good contracts, and can even be a handicap if, for some reason, you are particularly tied to a region. At Perpignan, for example, one of our players was paid roughly four times as much as another in the same position, even though there was nothing to choose between them on the field. One player had a farm that tied him to living and playing rugby in Perpignan, whereas the other was free to move to the club with the biggest chequebook. No prizes for guessing who got screwed.

The downside to hawking yourself from club to club is the stress. You need to be playing, so other clubs can see what you have to offer. If you are injured, have a run of poor form, or are not playing for some other reason, you will be less in demand and can spend a nervous few months waiting for the phone to ring, watching time tick away to the end of your contract, and wondering where you will be in a few weeks. Every year, there are players who are unemployed at the start of the season. Some never get picked up, while others have to drop a division or two, and find themselves on significantly less cash. Even if you do manage to find a club, there is the scramble over the summer break to find a new place to live, uprooting yourself and your family, and, once there, getting to know a new town and a whole new set of people.

I have often found myself in the role of interpreter in discussions between clubs and prospective new players, and I have seen some interesting decision-making. In my last year at Racing, Éric Blanc took over as president, and just before the season started he got me in to translate in a discussion he was having with two rugby league players from England, John Scales and Jamie Bloem, who had been recommended, in a roundabout way, by Dave Ellis. Ellis is now the defence specialist for the French national side, but in those days he was doing this job for Racing.

There was much small talk, but no light was shed on the men's playing ability, compatibility with the team, or even their passport eligibility. Eventually Blanc said to them in broken English, 'Are you strong? And fast?' 'I can bench-press 130 kilos,' Scales said. 'I can do the 100 metres in about eleven seconds,' Bloem said.

On the strength of this, they were signed up for just over 20,000 francs (€3000) a month plus apartment—1000 francs more than I was getting as an established player. Blanc had assumed that Bloem was English because he spoke English, but it turned out he had a South African passport. This oversight meant three months' delay getting his paperwork sorted out before he could play.

Racing's organisation was borderline comic throughout that whole year (it was no surprise that we were relegated) but this kind of thing goes on everywhere. In 2005, after a friendly game against the Italian side Viadana, I was having a few beers with Viadana's New Zealand players when one of them, Harley Crane, said that he would be keen to come to Montpellier the following year. We grabbed the president, Thierry Pérez, and asked him if he was interested. Harley, a specialist halfback, had been playing centre that night, so his real game hadn't been on show. I explained this and it didn't faze Thierry in the least. He shook Crane's hand and said, 'Très bien.' It was the classic 'what you're on, plus a bit more' and within a couple of minutes the deal was done. Later, I asked Pérez, an independently wealthy real-estate developer, how he had come to such a rapid decision. It had, he said, been simply a gut feeling.

The people who are supposed to ensure the smooth running of the player-transfer market are the agents. The advent of professional rugby led inevitably to the creation of this particular job, and in the first few years, when the rugby landscape resembled the wild west, there was more than one cowboy getting ten percent of players' salaries for what looked like not much effort at all.

Even today, when things have calmed down, players are inclined to think the price is too high. But a good agent can make a big difference to a player's career, and if he gives his client good advice and finds him the best deal, will more than earn his fee. Agents are better placed than players to know the going rate, and theoretically have the player's best interests at heart since the bigger the player's wage, the bigger their own take.

The problem with agents, though, is finding a good one. I have had dealings with five, and not one has ever been sitting beside me holding my hot little hand when I signed a contract. One got paid but that was a scandal, because his only effort was to give Perpignan my phone number after a former coach of mine, Yves Ajac, had given the Perpignan coach Olivier Saïsset the nod on my behalf. Admittedly, there is an element of self-inflicted injury in my unsuccessful dealings with agents; by juggling various possibilities, and generally trying to be too clever, I have got myself into trouble on at least one occasion.

In 2001, in an effort to rid themselves of the kind of reputation that would make used-car salesmen look like paragons of probity, the more legitimate agents formed a union and reached agreement with the Ligue Nationale de Rugby and the Fédération Française de Rugby. This included an obligation for clubs to use only agents with licences. These licences last three years, and since 2003 agents have had to pass an exam to obtain one.

French law now prohibits players from using more than one agent, but it is well known that some agents have better connections to certain clubs than others, and so the law is sometimes flouted. In 2003, for example, I wanted to play for Stade Français. At the time, and maybe still today, Stade Français recruited most of its players through an agent called Pascal Forni. Another agent, Bruno Xamma, had already approached me with the possibility of going to Montferrand. I preferred Stade Français but I wasn't about to throw out Montferrand in case this didn't work, so I agreed with Xamma that if I went to Montferrand it would be through him, but otherwise I was with Forni.

Forni knew this as well, but he also knew (quite quickly, I think) that Stade Français didn't want me. Instead of passing on this information, he rang Hyardet and told him I wasn't interested in Montferrand, and was only using it to try and gain some leverage on Stade Français. As a result of this Machiavellian move Hyardet and Montferrand went sour.

I should have been stuck back with Forni, who could now get commission on me by selling me to someone else, while he placed another one of his players at Montferrand. But I was unhappy about Forni's dirty tricks—he obviously hadn't banked on Hyardet telling me what had happened—so I made my own way to Montpellier. In the meantime, Biarritz called and made an offer through another agent, Laurent Quaglia, while coming to an agreement with Montpellier not to get an auction going for my services.

If you think this sounds confusing, it certainly made my head hurt. Forni, to give him his due, had a stable of around 200 players, and I suspect my incessant calling got to him. Rugby players waiting for news from their agents are like hopeful young lovers staring at the phone, willing it to ring, and fretting about why their sweetheart hasn't got in touch: coltish and panicky. 'Has he lost the number?' we ask ourselves. 'Has something terrible happened? It can't do any harm if I give him a quick ring, just to see how things are going.' And this, in my case, was three or four times a week over a period of a couple of months.

The year before this I had had uncomfortable dealings with Pau. The club wanted to buy me from Perpignan, who were keen to sell me on. Although I had a year left on my contract, Perpignan had bought two new locks and were happy enough to get rid of me if they could turn a profit. Pau were to pay €25,000 to Perpignan and were supposed to up my salary as well, so I went over to have a look around, meet the president and the coach, and talk about their plans.

David Escloupier, a part-time agent from Perpignan, was handling the negotiations, but he didn't come over with me. No expenses were paid. I drove from Perpignan for four hours, put myself up in a hotel, and although I was to meet with them at nine the next morning, didn't get to see the president, André Lestorte, until after five in the afternoon. By then I was decidedly tetchy, having wasted a day and being about €400 out of pocket.

Lestorte seemed to think the whole thing was a done deal and I would be delighted to come and play for his club. Or perhaps the matter had already been stitched up between him, my agent and Marcel Dagrenat, the Perpignan president, and he was convinced I had no other options. Unhappy about being treated like a piece of meat, I was starting to think just the opposite. The coach was unconvincing, and the clincher came the following day when Lestorte faxed through a written copy of the terms we had discussed. Although we had verbally agreed on €6000 a month, the figure in the document was more like €5000; he had clearly decided to skimp on my pay because he thought I had nowhere else to run.

At this point I no longer had any financial interest in going to Pau, and was sceptical about how the club was going to fare. Meanwhile, though, my agent was encouraging me to go: if I didn't, he wouldn't get paid. Despite threats and cajoling from both Dagrenat and the agent, I opted to stay in Perpignan. Biarritz made me an offer but weren't prepared to pay the transfer fee, and Dagrenat refused to let me go without someone coughing up.

Herein lies a problem with agents. They are supposed to be acting for players, but they are usually paid by clubs. Players don't like the idea of ten percent coming out of their salary—it feels too painful to have to hand a chunk of money you feel is rightfully yours to someone else—so the usual arrangement is that clubs pay the fee directly to the agent, although this is, of course, money they would otherwise give to the player. This means the agents are, effectively, employed by the clubs as head-hunters, and in situations where conflict arises between a player and a club, they will often advise the player according to what the club wants, not according to what is best for the player. In their eagerness to stay onside with clubs, they are, if you like, double agents. While there are hundreds of players, and the pool of talent is constantly being renewed, there are only a small number of clubs, and it is not unknown for presidents to bully agents with the threat of refusing to work with them again if they don't get players to do what they, the club, want.

5

Brawn and Brains

Brive is a small town of about 50,000 souls in the department of Corrèze in the Limousin region. The town is picturesque, the countryside beautiful (Brive is just à few kilometres to the east of the Dordogne), and the food excellent, but there is not a lot going on—apart from rugby: the stadium seats 15,000 and is often full. The Club Athlétique Briviste Corrèze Limousin, to give it its full name, has been around since 1912 but has never won the French championship, despite making it to the final on four occasions, most recently in 1996 when it lost to Toulouse 20–13. Its big claim to fame is winning the European Cup in 1997, with a comprehensive 28–9 victory over Leicester Tigers.

The following year, having made the final again, they narrowly lost to Bath, 19–18. Internal political strife and a slump in performance led to their being relegated in 2001, but they came back in 2003 with a new president, Jean-Claude

Penauille, who didn't seem to be afraid of putting his hand in his (deep) pocket, and they now have a respectable budget of nearly €7 million, and a team to match. They play in black and white striped shirts, and are currently placed tenth on 12 points, while we are still in twelfth on just five points. The previous week, while we were playing appallingly in Pau, they nearly pulled off a huge upset in Paris, leading against Stade Français throughout the game until crumbling in the last ten minutes.

I finally get to start a game: if I hadn't got a look-in after the débâcle at Pau, the toys would really have gone out of the pram. Playing against Brive suits me perfectly. It's an away game, so we won't be suffering from performance anxiety, and although they play a relatively open style there is a bit of drizzle before the game and the ground is soft, so my aging bones aren't going to have to cart themselves to all four corners of the field trying to keep up with a really quick game.

Their forward pack are not bad but they're not man-eaters either, and I think we can put the squeeze on them up front. We start badly and are trapped in our own territory almost immediately, getting out only after conceding a penalty to their young fly-half, Maxime Petitjean. David Bortolussi does the same for us a few minutes later, and then Petitjean replies: 6–3 after about ten minutes. We are putting pressure on them now. I pick up a ball from the base of a ruck, wrong-foot the defence and get the ball out to Régis, who chips through for Alex Stoica, who duly picks it up and falls over the line. After only quarter of an hour it is 8–6 to us. Petitjean puts another one over, but then their captain, Jérôme Bonvoisin, collects a yellow card. During our ten minutes of fifteen players against fourteen we manage a penalty from Bortolussi, and we go to the break ahead by 11–9. However, we should have cashed in more. To win an away game you can't afford to let slip moments where you have an edge.

As you would expect, Brive come out much more purposefully in the second half, while we seem strangely lethargic. Slowly, they start to impose a stranglehold on the game. Under pressure we give away penalties, Mika Bert sees yellow, and the points start piling up. It is now 18–11 to them. We seem to have blown a wonderful opportunity. With ten minutes to go we kick another penalty, and perhaps the game's not over yet as the pendulum swings back in our favour.

Meanwhile, though, I am in trouble. A few years ago at Perpignan I suffered a stress fracture in my foot. Now, as I try to hold up one of our scrums that has gone into reverse, the injury bites again, and after limping around for five minutes I ask for a substitution. I go off, and Gorgodzilla comes on. He might be just the man for the job as we are bashing away at the line without success; it would be nice to see him fling a couple of black and white jerseys out of the way and go crashing in under the posts. But Brive lost at the death last week and they're not about to let it happen again. Their desperate defence holds up, and we have to be happy with the bonus point. It would be easy to be happy with the bonus—it is, after all, better than nothing—but I am gutted we didn't win. During the long bus ride back to Montpellier we have time to think of the 20 odd minutes in the second half where we unaccountably went to sleep.

If I'm unhappy about the loss, from a personal point of view I'm pleased with the way I played. The good-game gods smiled on me for my return in the number five jersey, and I should start again next week. I had a bit of a run-in with Lionel Mallier, the former French international flanker with whom I used to play in Perpignan; he was a bit dark about my pulling down a maul, but there was nothing in it. It was a scrappy game, neither side managing to hold on to the ball long enough to build up any real momentum, but I was in my element. I would like to be able to tell you that my natural game is haring upfield with the ball in hand, throwing off would-be tacklers with sledgehammer fends, and bamboozling the defence with my crazy-legged running style, but that just isn't the case. I do my thing in the darkness of close quarters, hitting rucks, trying to speed up the recycling of our possession, or slow down theirs, and perhaps snaffle a ball or two, grunt-work in scrums, taking a few line-outs or kick-offs, setting up mauls and making tackles close in, and occasionally out wide, in cover defence. If I get to run with the ball three or four times in a game I'm happy, and it isn't normally for more than a few yards.

From the club's point of view there was also the big positive of successfully blooding a newcomer from the *Espoirs*: Fulgence Ouedraogo, our 20-year-old flanker, was thrown in the deep end and swam like a fish. He is blessed with a remarkable natural athleticism, all lean, rippling muscles, and seems to have discovered the secret of perpetual motion. Lifting him in line-outs is a joy because he leaps like a salmon heading upstream. And, crucially, he has a good head on his shoulders—he's well disciplined, learns fast and runs good lines in support, adapting quickly to rugby at élite level. We should be seeing much more of him in the first team, and there's no reason he shouldn't play for France in the next few years. Of course, all these gifts alone would be worth nothing to him if he didn't work hard at it, and he does.

It is not enough in rugby simply to have physical attributes, although this gives you a head start. Three elements make up a player: physique—basically explosive speed, stamina and strength, although flexibility and balance are also important; technical skills—all-round skills such as catching, passing and tackling, and position-specific skills such as line-out throwing for hookers; and psychological skills—discipline, decision-making and mental toughness.

It is not a question of 'nature versus nurture'. Nature sets the parameters for your abilities—it's no use wanting to be a winger if you run as though you're towing a caravan, or hoping to be a lock if you have to stand on tiptoe to reach the kitchen cupboards. But in truth the physical entry barriers to rugby—at least at club level, if not for international sides—are relatively low, provided you are prepared to train hard. If you start young and are pigheadedly determined to succeed, have access to good facilities and are well-advised, you have a shot. The pigheaded bit is important, because mental strength is at least as important as physical strength.

Professionalism in rugby has led to enormous advances in physical performance as each team and each individual looks to get an edge on the competition. Coaches tend to love fitness sessions and weights tests: the latter are easy to measure, so they can line up a list of figures next to everyone's name and see who is stronger than whom, who is progressing, and so on.

I am not a fan of the weights room—perhaps I would be if I were better at it. In the good old amateur days when this kind of training was optional, I would usually take the easy option. This was a mistake; if there is one thing I regret about my career, it is that I didn't do enough work on basic explosive strength in my late teens and early twenties. When I was eventually forced into a serious weight-training regime, because it was part of my job description, the results were not spectacular (I am known to some French players as '*épaules de serpent*'—'snake shoulders'), but I did gain extra confidence in the contact area, which has become a battleground. When I started playing for Wellington in 1994, offensive tackles were still relatively rare; today a tackle that is not offensive is considered a wasted opportunity.

Obviously, though, strength is useless unless you know how to channel it well. My team-mate, our prop Antony Vigna, for example, is almost as hopeless as I am at pumping iron, but in a scrum I would back him against any of the guys in the team who rack up great rows of 20-kilogram weights, squatting or bench-pressing until the bar sags. Often players —particularly props—who are phenomenally strong in the weights room try to bully their opponents with muscle, ignoring technique, and get themselves in trouble. For these kinds of practical skills there is no substitute for being well coached and then endlessly repeating the same movement, both in training situations and in games, in order to assimilate all the subtle variations you may need to call upon when you're under pressure and the guy opposite is trying to get an edge on you. This is why experience is so highly valued, particularly in the forwards. You can train all you like to do things right—passing, catching, kicking, and pushing are all relatively straightforward to master—but on the field it's what you do in the very short space of time you have before someone stops you doing it that shows whether you're really up to it.

This is where the brain comes into play. What is referred to in New Zealand as 'the top two inches' is without any doubt the most important part of a player's rugby armoury. It's no use having silky skills and a rippling torso if you don't take the right options. Rugby is a relatively complex game, and much of its richness comes from this complexity.

Let's say a halfback has a ball in front of him at the base of a ruck, the sort of thing that happens maybe a hundred times or more in a game. He has to decide what to do from a multitude of possibilities. He can pass it to his fly-half. Or, if he has a big enough blind side, he can decide to change the direction of play by passing it to a winger or fullback. He can pop it up to a forward coming in on the charge, or he can run with it himself. He can try to organise his forwards into a driving maul, or tell one of them to pick and go; or he can choose to kick high into the box for his winger to chase, or hoof it further down the ground for position. He has a split second to decide which of all these options is the best, given the field position of his team, the speed at which the ball is delivered, and the defensive positions of the opposition.

If he has only one defender on him and a hole outside, he may back himself to have the speed to get around him, particularly if the defender is a tight forward. So let's say he goes himself, and makes a half break before being caught from behind. Does he try to stay on his feet to offload a pass to his support, who will run into the breach he has created? If he can do this he will have gained some ground and created forward momentum, which will make it easier to continue the attack. But there is the possibility of a second tackler arriving and trying to rip the ball off him before he can get it away, so perhaps he should choose the relative security of going to ground and setting up a ruck.

You get the picture. Over the space of a couple of seconds he has had to calculate all the various possibilities, decide which is best for the team, and act. Top sides now programme play through several phases after the original set piece, so players are in prearranged positions with their roles mapped out for them. Even so, you still need to be able to adapt your choices to the situation, and the complicating factor of the opposition means things don't always go as planned.

The number of choices are greater for the guy with the ball in his hand, but every player has to be constantly assessing his own actions and maximising his value to the team. In defence, for example, you find yourself on the inside shoulder of a guy who's made a tackle. As a ruck forms, you have to decide: should you go in to try and win the ball and take the advantage for your team? The problem is that, while doing this, you are leaving the other defenders a man short if you don't succeed—a potentially disastrous situation if the ball comes out quickly and your lot have not had time to reorganise.

Even in a maul, which looks like a lot of uncomplicated shoving and sweating, you need to think about the angle on which you are pushing, both vertically and horizontally. If, while defending, you go from down to up, taking an opposition player with you, you are reducing the efficiency of the opposition's driving platform—it is difficult to push effectively when standing up—but you are also less efficient. If you try to force them down you run the risk of being penalised, but if you can make it look as though they fell over themselves you have stopped them in their tracks, and may even recover the ball. You can push them towards the touchline, limiting their options so they are obliged to get the ball out before taking it into touch, or you can wheel the maul towards the open side, forcing the ball-carrier into the open, and a position where he can be tackled. Or, if you like vanilla, you can just try to push straight.

Clearly, no one spends time consciously calculating any of these things. Everything happens so fast you run purely on instincts you have honed over the years, and hopefully some useful advice from your team-mates, who may be able to see things that you can't. (Good teams communicate constantly: players help each other choose the right options by letting others know what is going on around them.)

To be really good you have to consistently make the right decisions, and have the physical ability and technical knowhow to execute them. Deciding to attempt a drop goal from halfway is a good option if you kick it over. But if, like me, you have two left feet and the ball goes spinning off into the arms of the opposing winger, who then scores under your posts, it is a bad option.

During breaks in play there is time for a breather, and a chat with team-mates, where you can reassess your options in relation to your strengths and weaknesses and those of the opposition with a little more lucidity. This analysis is a particularly important task for leaders, and should also have been mapped out to a large extent in the game plan you will have discussed with the coach after watching video analysis.

The other great thing about the human brain is that it can keep driving you forward when your body is starting to flag. Your legs may be full of lactic acid and your head in oxygen debt, but you will continue to perform. This is often described as courage or 'guts', but it is more than that. For a player, courage is simply a prerequisite: if you are playing rugby year-round you can't shirk, because the opposition will quickly start exploiting your weakness. If you turn up to a game thinking you will get by on courage alone, you may get lucky if the other lot are feeling cowardly, but this is unlikely.

So courage has to be supplemented by mental toughness and intelligence. Mental toughness means you are always looking to get more from yourself and your team-mates, setting targets such as holding on to the ball for a given number of phases, disciplining yourself to get a lower penalty count, or staying an extra half-hour at training once the coach has called it a day, because you want to get the preparation absolutely right, not just get home in time for dinner. When you get knocked back by a loss, or being beaten in a one-on-one situation, rather than bleating about the referee or the ball being slippery or generally feeling sorry for yourself, you need to be able to analyse why it happened, and how you can avoid it happening again.

Intelligence, too, is essential. In martial terms, a full frontal assault on the enemy can be described as 'courageous' but it may be stupid as well, particularly if you end up getting slaughtered in front of the guns when a simple flanking manoeuvre would have been successful.

There are any number of great players in world rugby, but while we have some quality players in Montpellier, I would struggle to say, hand on heart, that any are 'great'. One I particularly respect though, because of his hard-nosed attitude, is Olivier Diomandé. I wasn't pleased to see Olivier when I arrived at Montpellier: we had spent an afternoon trading cheap shots in Paris while I was playing for Racing and he was at Nîmes. In those days he was an average prop playing for a below-average side, and his game seemed to revolve around head-butting and eye-gouging. He went on to have a couple of seasons at Bordeaux, then came to Montpellier, which was then in the second division.

Here he started to convert himself into a hooker. He still played most of his rugby at prop, but he wasn't guaranteed a first-team place as a prop. He wasn't guaranteed a first-team place as a hooker either because the captain, Didier Bes, was hooker, but Bes, at 36, was coming to the end of his career, and Dio felt he could establish himself as first choice after Bes left. He was in his late twenties, which is pretty long in the tooth to be looking at positional changes, and he could easily have refused to move, but he threw himself into it, slimming down to become more mobile, practising his line-out throwing relentlessly, and weight-training like a man possessed. He was open-minded and humble about learning from other people, and grew into a key role, playing nearly every game in the last two years.

This year Olivier has been faced with a new challenge: Nico Grelon, an excellent player, has arrived from Perpignan to compete with him for the hooking berth. The two have different strengths: while both are good at bread-and-butter scrummaging and line-outs, Dio does a lot of work in the tight and Nico is more of a ball player. They complement each other perfectly as options, but both want to wear the starting jersey.

Hookers tend to have forceful characters and are often entrusted with leadership roles. These two are no exception, so there has been a good deal of alpha-male rivalry about who gets to be the top dog. There was an illustration of this recently when we were having live scrummaging training— two packs against each other. It is difficult to overemphasise the psychological importance of the scrum in French rugby, and as the keystone the hooker is responsible for the scrum. The two packs were evenly matched, so any slight advantage counted.

As we got ready to pack down for the first scrum, Nico's eight (which I was in) was bound and in position first, giving us an edge in preparation for the initial impact—which is 60 percent of the scrum. Seeing this, Dio started undoing his binding, saying that it didn't feel right, broke up the scrum behind him, and started the whole process again about 30 centimetres off the mark. This is an old trick, seldom spotted by referees; it means the opposition have to either shuffle over on to the new mark, or break up again and reform. Either way, the team that was initially late is now ready first, and so have the slight edge.

As you would expect, there was much moaning about this level of cynicism at training, and I wasn't happy about it myself since we were the ones being disadvantaged. However, Dio stood his ground, grinning, and Nico broke us up and we moved. What I grudgingly admired was that Dio wasn't prepared to cede the slightest advantage to his competitor, even in the relatively unimportant context of training. That is his mindset. It isn't necessarily pretty and he may not be making any friends, but it is effective.

One of the most talented people I've played with is New Zealander Manny Edmonds, who plays fly-half for Perpignan. Manny, whose family moved to Australia when he was six, played for New South Wales in the Super 12 and two tests for Australia before coming to France at the relatively young age of 25. He had more or less blown his chances in Australia by banging down the door of the coach, Bob Dwyer, at five in the morning, after an evening out, to have a chat about why he hadn't been selected for a couple of games in South Africa. Apparently Dwyer was not convinced by his arguments.

Manny, too, is a fierce competitor, although with him it's less obvious because of the sheer joy he exudes when playing. While the rest of us are pounding around the track, running into people and generally slogging our guts out, he is throwing long cut-out passes, dinking little chips through for himself, dummying, then turning on the gas: he seems to be having a great time.

Even the serious nature of professional rugby, and rugby is taken *very* seriously in Perpignan, doesn't seem to curb his enthusiasm. When he first arrived, he would throw the occasional pass behind his back out of the back of his hand at training. Olivier Saïsset, the coach, was unimpressed, and Manny was told we didn't need any of that flashy Super 12 rubbish so he stopped doing it at training. He just did it in games, more out of instinct when he saw a hole opening up as he ran diagonally across field than from outright insubordination, although there was always a hint of this as well. The problem was that often the player receiving the pass was so surprised he dropped it, even though all he had to do was catch it and trundle 20 yards upfield into the space that had been created. (I have a particularly vivid memory of this because I was one of the offenders.) But what was good was that Manny was trying to drag the rest of the team up to his level, rather than reining in his own talent so we could keep up.

Throwing passes out of the back of the hand is pretty banal these days, but what clinched Manny's genius for me was the Heineken Cup final against Toulouse in Dublin in 2003. I was coming to the end of my time with Perpignan. We were rooming together, and on the day of the game we watched the build-up to the Super 12 final between the Auckland Blues and the Canterbury Crusaders on Sky Sports. Stuart Barnes was talking about Carlos Spencer's innovative tactic 'the banana kick'. Spencer would receive the ball from the right and shape to kick left behind the defence, luring the blind-side wing and the fullback across in cover. But the ball would come off the side of his foot—looking as though he had mistimed it appallingly—and bend out on a curve towards the now vacant right wing, where the right winger would stroll through and pick it up.

It was only an hour or so before we were to leave for the ground, so there was no time to practice the move, but as we went down to the team meeting Manny asked our right wing, Pascal Bomati, if he'd seen it. Pascal was enthusiastic and the two of them decided to try it if the opportunity arose. We had a nightmare first half against the wind, for which Manny was partly to blame, falling off a tackle on Jauzion, who went on to feed Clerc for Toulouse's try. At half-time the score was 19–0.

We ground our way back, and with a quarter of an hour to go it was 22–12. We hadn't been able to pierce their defensive wall by orthodox means. Manny got a ball from the right, and shaped to kick left, looking as though he'd mistimed his kick. Everyone was wondering what the hell was going on, except Pascal, who scooted in, picked up the ball and scored. It was a brilliant example of intelligent risk-taking and perfect execution. (Unfortunately it wasn't enough and we lost 22–17.)

6

Muscles and
Magic Pills

N arbonne is another small southern French town with a long history of rugby. Le Racing Club Narbonne Méditerranée has represented its 50,000 people since 1907, and has twice been crowned national champion, in 1936 and 1979. The town itself, situated on the Mediterranean coast, was established in 118 B.C. as the first Roman colony outside Italy. For more than a thousand years it flourished. The Via Domitia and Via Aquitania met here, and this, together with the town's accessible port, made Narbonne an important crossroads. The cathedral and archbishop's palace testify to a thriving past as a trading post and cultural centre, but from the fourteenth century diminished port access for ships due to silting in the Aude River led to a decline in the town's fortunes, and these days the local economy relies on tourism and the surrounding wine country.

Although Narbonne has the smallest budget in the Top 14—only €5.8 million—it continues to hang on, punching above its weight, despite the suspicion it is simply putting off an inevitable drop. Last year the club finished just ahead of us in tenth place, having beaten us in both home and away games.

The first-round game is to be played at Stade Sabathé, Montpellier's home ground. It is important for a number of reasons. First, there is a vital need for us to win and gain four points. Alarm bells are starting to ring, as the championship table currently makes very ugly reading for anyone associated with Montpellier. We have played seven games now for a measly total of six points. And while we were losing in Brive, Toulon beat Bayonne, putting them equal with us, while Pau are only one point behind.

There are also a couple of more emotional reasons. Narbonne is only about 80 kilometres from Montpellier, making this a derby game; they beat us here at Sabathé last year and we haven't forgotten. And five of our players, along with the backs coach, Pat Arlettaz, wore the orange and black of Narbonne before arriving in Montpellier, and games against your old team always have a bit of spice.

From the start, we dominate physically. Narbonne like to play a very open game, so we take them on up front. To try and counter our edge in possession, they live offside. I can't blame them: we do much the same thing when we are being dominated. Dwayne Haare, a big Maori lock who has just arrived from Sydney, is into everything, and we have words on a couple of occasions. There is a bit of pushing and shoving— more handbags at 20 paces than Marquess of Queensberry —but the rest of the Narbonne pack seem more interested in damage limitation. As a result there is little continuity: they either get away with it and stifle our momentum, or are penalised and we kick the points.

Coco is on form, and after 20 minutes we have cruised to a 12–0 lead. Narbonne pull one back to make it 12–3 before Franck Tournaire, the former French prop, gets yellow-carded for taking a scrum down, and the set piece, already going in our favour, becomes a massacre. We kick a penalty to touch, they pull down the maul from the line-out, and we choose to take the scrum. Their pack implodes and the referee goes straight under the posts to award a penalty try.

One of rugby's more esoteric pleasures is being part of a scrum that is destroying the opposition, and nowhere is this truer than in France. You know that every time the referee whistles for a scrum they are dreading the contest, while your confidence is soaring. You still have to work hard for every inch, but they are feeling the pain more than you are: while the pack advancing keeps its shape, the pack in retreat twists and ruptures, as bindings pop under the strain and body positions are contorted. For ten minutes we win every scrum, ours and theirs, and although it might not be much fun to watch, up front we are enjoying ourselves. Nineteen to three at half-time, and it's difficult not to feel that we have broken them.

We exchange penalties in the first few minutes of the second half: 22–6. What was never a great game deteriorates as night falls (all games in the French championship are played in the evening, except for occasional televised matches on Canal+) and the dew makes for difficult handling conditions.

Both teams opt to kick for position and then try to muscle the ball up through the forwards. Narbonne suffer another setback when their captain, Jean-Marie Bisaro, is yellow-carded, and again we exploit our numerical superiority in the forwards when Cédric Mathieu goes over in the middle of a driving maul. A few minutes later, Mika Bert scores after yet another line-out take and drive: 34–6.

Now we can concentrate on scoring a fourth try and pocketing the bonus point. But we are playing in fits and starts, and have lost the edge we had in the scrum. In trying to free up our style of play we get sloppy. Narbonne take advantage of this and score a good counterattacking try. Worse, we are starting to get overanxious as the minutes tick away. I am pinged from the kick-off for tackling a man in the air before he is grounded, and then marched ten yards for holding on to the ball, a stupid error.

As the siren for the end of the game blows we are hot on attack, with a succession of rucks on their line. Time and again it seems inevitable that we will make it over, only to be repulsed by their desperate defence. Harley has come on at centre but finds himself with the ball in his hands at the base of one of these rucks. Our backs change direction and now have a big overlap, but as he goes to swing it wide he sees their defence rush up, so he checks his pass, dummying and scooting inside his marker to go under the posts. But as he dives, a defender comes across in cover and boots the ball from his outstretched hands. It slides away and our bonus point goes with it.

Still, it's a great relief to win, and reassuring that we did it so comfortably. Sam was subbed on for Mika after about 70 minutes, so I played the full 80 minutes, which is something of a personal triumph after the problems I've had with my knee. Over the course of my career I have had plenty of injuries. I've been knocked out several times; dislocated a collar bone; ruptured an eardrum; smashed bones in my hands and feet; broken my nose at least a dozen times; slipped discs in my back; ripped a tendon in my arm; subluxed my shoulder; twisted knees and ankles; had numerous wounds that needed stitching—mainly on my head—and countless bumps and bruises, cauliflower ears and other disfigurements.

Of all of these injuries, my right knee's have been the most troublesome. In 1995 a reconstruction of the anterior cruciate ligament put me out of action for a year. Last year, at training camp, the knee got infected through a tiny cut and I was so run down I couldn't get rid of the infection. After emergency surgery I spent two weeks in hospital, and it was three months before I could play again. And even then the knee wasn't right: the patella tendon, already weakened by the earlier reconstruction, had been partially eaten away, and continually blew up with tendonitis. Only recently, 18 months after the operation, has the knee settled down enough for me to take stairs two at a time; it will probably annoy me for the rest of my life.

This list of war wounds may sound long, but in fact I have been relatively lucky: over 25 years of rugby I have needed only three full-blooded operations (that is, ones performed under general anaesthetic). Scott Robertson, the former All Black back-rower who now plays for Perpignan, told me two years ago that he had had surgery seventeen times, and he may have increased his score since then. And I am still playing. Many players have to stop because of injuries, and every year spinal trauma leaves some in wheelchairs. Unfortunately, smashing up your body is part of the risk you take when you play rugby, although we all prefer not to think about it.

Injuries are the bane of the professional sportsperson's life—up to a point. Career-threatening injuries are obviously a disaster, as is anything that keeps you off the field for more than a few weeks, but as long as your place in the team is secure and you're not missing any really important games, from time to time—say once or twice a season—a little breather with a twisted ankle or a swollen knee can be a welcome respite from the drudgery of training. And while you have time off all the other niggling injuries that have cropped up but been too minor to stop you playing can be worked on by the physiotherapist, or simply allowed to heal.

Perhaps the greatest advantage of this enforced rest is that your mind can wind down. Within a week or two, your appetite for rugby, which has been blunted over the months of intense preparation and competition, returns and you can get back into it with enthusiasm.

If you're really lucky, you have a niggling injury that is considered serious enough to need rest for a day or two more than everyone else between games. Hence, you miss out on the heavier training schedule on Monday and Tuesday, arrive on Wednesday evening for the team run, and by Saturday are raring to go because you feel so fresh. Our centre Rickus Lubbe manages to carry an injury like that for much of the year and, while he is an excellent player in his own right, I suspect this extra recovery time is a major factor in his outstanding season.

Your body is the principal tool of your trade, so the training regime is designed to make sure it is operating at optimum level. There is a delicate balance between doing enough to be at peak form for the Saturday game, and not doing so much that you are knackered. Montpellier's weekly regime varies slightly depending on the circumstances, but typically starts the day after the game with a recovery session at the local pool, and massages from the physiotherapists to work out the aches and pains of the match. (We have three physiotherapists, who rotate shifts so there are always two with the team for training and games.)

Monday morning is the same, with the physiotherapists and the team doctor being available for consultation. Normally we eat together, watch the video of the game, and discuss what happened. The afternoon is taken up with upper-body weight-training and perhaps some running. Tuesday morning it is leg weights and speed-work, while in the afternoon the group splits into forwards and backs so that we can practise position-specific skills such as line-outs and mauls—and occasionally live scrummaging. (Whenever I look over at the backs they seem to be playing touch rugby, but they assure us—the forwards—that they are working hard.)

Wednesday morning is dedicated to an opposition session, and in the afternoon we watch video analysis of the team we are going to play next, run through the game plan, look again at line-outs and kick-offs, and spend the last half-hour on the scrum machine. Thursday is free, although some of the team like to do more weights then, or perhaps on Friday morning.

If we are playing away, we leave by bus on Friday morning, and do some training after we arrive. If we are playing at home, we are free on Friday morning, and then have a light run-through and a few line-outs and kick-offs. On the day of the game we meet for a stretching session seven hours before kick-off (and generally squeeze in a few more line-outs) and then go to our hotel, eat and rest up, before going to the ground an hour and a half before the game.

Different clubs have different variations on this routine, but it is fairly standard around France. Within it there is the question of dosage. How long and how intense should each session be? How much can you ask of the team and different individuals, both in terms of training and games? This is where the coach has to judge the varying needs of the team over the short, medium and long term, consult the physical trainer and, to a lesser extent, the medical staff, and try to come up with the best solution for the group.

There can be tension on several fronts. When it comes to deeming a player fit for service after an injury, for example, the medical staff will err on the side of caution, but if the coach needs this particular player he may try to circumvent them and ask him directly how he feels. Generally players want to play, although this depends whom the game is against—there's no point joining the rush to the front if you're going to get slaughtered. Away games against Paris, Toulouse or Biarritz are not the best way to ease back after an injury. If a player does want to play, he may ask for a jab:

injections of anti-inflammatories and painkillers are rare, but not unheard of. Or he may just hope the injury warms up and he'll forget about it on the field.

When it comes to training, the physical trainer may feel the players are too tired and the volume of work should be reduced, but the coach may think the team needs the extra training and overrule him. And, although it's unusual, you can get tension between the physical trainer and the medical staff, and this is what happens this year.

The first game of the year, against Castres, left a lasting impression on our physical trainer, Nicolas Foulquier. In essence we got bullied by a bigger forward pack, who wore us down up front. Individually, each player seemed to have the advantage of a few kilograms of muscle, and we felt it every time we were in contact. Given that rugby is a contact sport, this is a problem. There are two solutions—either you can buy bigger players, or you can enlarge the existing ones.

Since it was the first game of the season, there was really only one solution. Making players bigger—increasing their muscle mass—isn't easy during a season because there is not much time for heavy weight-training. The weights you do will be more about maintaining strength than progressing. So Nico, in consultation with the team dietician, decided to find the best possible dietary supplement, in the hope we would put on a couple of kilos of muscle and thus become more competitive.

The hitch was that the product he chose, Maximuscle, was English and contained creatine. Creatine is not available in France because the French authorities are not yet satisfied that it has no detrimental side-effects. It is not a question of doping: most of the professional rugby world now takes creatine, and English rugby players appear in some of the advertising. But one of our two team doctors, Bernard Dusfour, was unhappy about players using a substance that had not been given the thumbs-up in France. His argument was that it is easy to lose perspective in the search for short-term results, and his role was to make sure that the players were in good health not only during the course of their rugby career, but after it as well. He put this to the coaching staff, and when they judged that he was being overcautious he resigned. (There may have been more to it than this, but this was what filtered out.)

The players now had access to Maximuscle but we had to pay half the cost, with the club paying the other half. I had taken creatine for a few weeks when I played for Wellington and been sceptical about the results, so being tight-fisted I didn't bother again.

Inevitably, Bernard Dusfour is asked by someone why he resigned. He replies that he didn't agree with some of the nutritional supplements we were taking. A few rounds of Chinese whispers later we are taking steroids. (In French the word is *dopage*, a non-specific, catch-all term for illicit substances.) Rumours of steroid-taking in rugby have been rife for years, and Pierre Berbizier, the former French captain and coach, poured oil on the flames after resigning from the coach's job at Narbonne in 2000. The infernal rhythm of the French championship, he declared, was pushing players to use products that were stronger than creatine: '*dopage*'.

Cue a great wailing and gnashing of teeth by everyone involved in French rugby. If Berbizier had proof of this, why hadn't he spoken up earlier? Who were the guilty parties? Berbizier promptly back-pedalled and said he had just wanted to alert everyone to a *potential* problem. There was no organised doping, but people might be tempted into a 'dangerous spiral'. Everyone calms down, agrees he's quite right to bring such a serious issue to the attention of the rugby world, steps will be taken, case closed.

It would be naïve to think that no one involved in rugby has ever taken steroids. Players looking for a competitive edge are aware of the extra strength and power you can get from illegal drugs, and I don't imagine such drugs are hard to find. A long time ago someone I respected recommended steroids to me. When I looked at him as though he had a forked tail and cloven hooves, he tried to mollify me with a specious distinction: 'Good steroids I mean, not the bad ones.' I was young and idealistic at the time and didn't give it another thought.

Knowing what I know now about the exigencies of professional rugby, and that magic pills and potions may just make the difference between an ordinary career and a good one, would I take them? It's a moot question because at my age it wouldn't make a blind bit of difference. I might look better at the beach (which wouldn't be such a disaster) but it's too late for drugs to have any real impact on my musculature: the body's ability to grow muscle tissue reduces significantly after the age of thirty.

Still, it's worth thinking about the situation that professional sportspeople find themselves in. Apart from the obvious long-term health implications of drug-taking, the danger for a rugby player is that drugs provide a short cut. A game of rugby is more complicated than a 100-metre sprint, or a cycling race where you perform the same action over and over again: pure physical performance is only a part of it. Even if you become stronger physically, cutting corners is liable to make you a weaker person mentally. And just how useful will that extra muscle be? A good weight-training programme, allied to intelligent nutrition, should be preparation enough.

The chances of getting caught should make drug-taking a risky business, but over ten years I haven't been tested once. In France, the rugby authorities take blood samples from all professional players three times a year, but these are to check on the player's health, not to test directly for steroids or other illicit substances. A doctor taking our samples at Montpellier told me that any significant anomalies would be followed up, but it would not be possible to say for sure that you were guilty of drug-taking on the basis of the tests.

Obviously random tests do occur from time to time after a game, although they are not nearly as widespread in rugby as they are in, say, cycling. And these random tests do occasionally find evidence of steroid abuse. Yogane Correa, a lock with the second-division club Albi, was suspended for two years after being tested and found guilty, while Nicolas Couttet, who plays for Brive, was suspended for three months when he was found to have taken an ephedrine-type substance before a game. But for the moment I am sure that rugby does not harbour the kind of widespread organised substance abuse that seems to exist in other sports—cycling, athletics, weightlifting, baseball, American football and soccer, to name a few.

Still, suspicion lingers. Looking at other teams and players who are bigger than you and deciding they are all up to the eyeballs in steroids is a longstanding tradition. When Perpignan went to play Leicester in the 2002 Heineken Cup, I was standing next to fellow lock Jérôme Thion as he flicked through the program notes looking at our locking opponents' measurements. He was shaking his head: 'Look at these guys—two metres tall, 120 kilos, they all run around like rabbits, and they expect us to believe that they don't take something stronger than milk on their cereal?' Jérôme Thion measures 1.99 metres, weighs about 118 kilograms, and has a remarkable natural athleticism that is probably closer to a hare than a rabbit, but you get the picture.

Knowing how hard they have worked to bulk up, players often find it difficult to accept that the competition still seems to be just a little bit bigger. Often this boils down to perception—you get used to your own team-mates and they don't seem as big to you as they do to outsiders, while it is often a bit of a shock to see the other team once they've donned shoulder-pads, boots and headgear.

Even without steroids there is no doubt that, thanks to the extra training that professionalism allows, rugby players are getting bigger and stronger. This has had an unexpected impact on injury statistics. At any given time, of the 600 or so professional rugby players in France about 100 are out with injuries. On the surface, this is no worse than under the old amateur regime, but what has changed is the severity of the injuries. While the full-time medical staff and physical trainers employed by the clubs have managed to greatly reduce the number of pulled muscles and other relatively minor injuries, players are now suffering from more serious problems. As speed and strength increase, the amount of energy released in collisions between players also increases, and although muscle helps stabilise the shock to some extent, the rest of the body—particularly the knee and shoulder joints—is no better equipped than before. Consequently, there is a rise in the number of serious injuries involving ruptured ligaments. It's like an arms race, where the improvement in performance thanks to new technology means you feel stronger and safer—but so does the other guy, and the end result is that you do more damage to each other. There doesn't seem to be any easy solution: no one is about to sign peace agreements.

7

Stadium Gods

They love their rugby in Toulon. Le Rugby Club Toulonnais goes back nearly 100 years and has won the Bouclier de Brennus, or Brennus Shield, the trophy for the domestic champion, three times, in 1931, 1987 and most recently in 1992.

The town itself, with 160,000 inhabitants—or, if you count the surrounding metropolitan sprawl, more like half a million —is centred around the port. Napoleon Bonaparte first made a name for himself here as a young naval officer by playing a decisive role in lifting the siege laid by the Royal Navy in 1793, and today the French Mediterranean Fleet is head-quartered on the *rade*. The stadium is right in the heart of the town, on a site that was a disused velodrome until 1920, when the popular French singer Félix Mayol bought it and donated the ground to the club. The RCT returned the com-pliment by naming the stadium after their benefactor and adopting his lucky charm *le muguet*, the lily of the valley, as their emblem. Although other clubs have more trophies in their cabinets, bigger budgets (Toulon has the second smallest budget of the Top 14 at €5.86 million) and more stars on their team, there is a popular enthusiasm for the game here that is rivalled only by the Catalans of Perpignan.

The massive spectator support means that playing at Mayol is something of a test of character for any visiting team. Toulon are not having a great year and will probably go down, but if you want to win here you had better be prepared to fight for it—and that's not just a figure of speech. Toulon's first game of the year was against the reigning champions, Biarritz, and they gave the Basques a hell of a fright (and a few bloody noses) before going down 10–20. They are an old-fashioned outfit, playing more with their heart than their brains (home-and-away culture is particularly evident—they tend to get hammered in away games) and have been too cautious with their recruitment, but they have a few good players and their forwards are always ready to mix it in front of the home crowd.

The day of our game it is teeming with rain, although this clears just before kick-off. We are in for a shit-fight and we know it. Once again the stakes are high as we go into the game still in twelfth place, just three points ahead of Toulon. If we lose and don't collect a bonus point, we are in the hot seat.

As we arrive at the ground we can see that the way to the normal dropping-off point has been blocked by a crane that is obviously not going to move. Bungle or conspiracy? It's not easy to tell in this part of the world, but I wouldn't be surprised if the locals had decided that a little taste of the Toulon atmosphere in the form of a march through a sea of thousands of red-and-black-wearing supporters would put us in the right mood for the game. The bus driver tries to go around another way but is thwarted again, and at the insistence of our officials he turns into a roundabout the wrong way and ploughs into oncoming traffic, before mounting a traffic island and eventually coming to a halt at the side entrance to the changing-rooms. They'll have to try harder than that to put one over on us.

Still, when we go out to warm up we bear the full brunt of the 14,000-strong crowd—from all the jeering they seem disappointed that we have actually turned up—but at least now we are on the other side of the three-metre-high cage that rings the playing-field. We have talked about not being put off by this, but almost immediately our Georgian prop Mamuka Magrakvelidze starts egging them on, blowing kisses to the stands and laughing. With a few games under my belt I am feeling more confident and slipping back into a leadership role and I bark at him to stop, but the damage is already done—the little bubble we try to put ourselves in to prepare the game is broken. Mamuka likes to show that he is not intimidated by anything—and he isn't—but his provocative gesture is an indication of his individualism, and during the game this individualism is shown up for the costly, ego-puffing exercise it is.

Mamuka used to be a wrestler and started playing rugby relatively late. Because of this, his technique isn't as good as someone who learned the basics much earlier, but his strength and skill in manoeuvring his opposite number in the scrum can be very useful. The problem is that most of his energy goes into this physical battle, and he just doesn't get the importance of teamwork and the interdependent nature of the game. He occasionally forgets line-out calls because they don't seem to be important—he'd rather be proving himself by smashing someone than worrying about the complicated variations we use to win line-outs. But if we lose the line-out because he's not in the right place at the right time, everyone suffers.

Predictably, the match is a mess. We dominate the first 20 minutes, which is surprising because normally Toulon come out spitting fire. They have apparently been given a lecture on discipline, and curbing their natural aggression makes them lose some of their venom. But we can't convert the pressure into points—until the twenty-fifth minute, when Coco puts us into the lead with a penalty, having missed one a couple of minutes earlier.

This seems to kick Toulon into life. Greg Tutard, their centre, busts through our midfield and runs 40 metres before we pull him down. We scramble clear, but they are still on attack. They work a line-out drive from a few metres out, and surprise us by going to the short side. Their South African number eight, Shawn van Rensburg, scores in the corner. The conversion is missed and it's still 5–3 when the half-time whistle blows.

We have the wind in the second half, and start by camping in their 22, but we still can't score. Both sides are tense, the ball is greasy, and the one thing that looks like breaking the deadlock is the scrum, where we are starting to get the upper hand. After nearly 20 minutes, there is still no change to the score. I go in to clear out a ruck—the sort of thing I do twenty or thirty times a game—and as I am trying to shift one of their players off the ball with my right shoulder I feel something like an electric shock ping through the top of my left arm. Straightaway I know this is not good. It's funny how the worst injuries often occur in the most banal situations. There are many times on a rugby field where players crash into each other with such force that you wonder whether they are going to be able to get up, but they just dust themselves off and head off to the next phase. But then, out of the blue, something like this happens.

I lie on the ground, flapping about like a freshly landed fish and feeling sorry for myself. The doctor arrives—at this point Bernard Dusfour is still with us—and I try to tell him what I am feeling. The pain, which was acute for about 30 seconds, has now dropped off. As he tests my arm it seems it may be all right, so I decide to carry on. At the first line-out I detect that this is a mistake: when I try to lift Cédric Mathieu my arm refuses to function.

I cut my losses and head for the shower. In the changing-room I find our president, Thierry Pérez; he is so nervous about the game he can't bring himself to watch. Now that I'm starting to cool down I can feel that the injury is serious, and with my arm hanging uselessly by my side I have trouble taking my gear off. Thierry helps me out in a tender, fatherly way that I find touching—not every club president would be doing this. I give him a cigarette, and as we are both sitting smoking a roar goes up from the crowd. Toulon have kicked a penalty to make it 8–3.

We go out to follow the rest of the game and it's clear that all hope is not yet lost. We are starting to give them real trouble in the scrum, and the referee may be forced into yellow-carding one of their props for repeated offences.

The Toulon pack can feel this, and ten minutes from the end they decide to react. After being shunted a couple of metres, their front-rower Noël Curnier stands up and pops Mamuka, right in front of the referee. It is all they have left, and really it is a gift—the ref is already reaching for his pocket—but Mamuka won't let it rest: he has to go and punch Curnier to even the score. So what might have been a game-breaking yellow card—with only seven men left in their scrum against our eight we would really have them under the cosh, and two penalty kicks in ten minutes would have been perfectly possible—is nullified as they each get one.

To make matters worse, a couple of minutes later Dio cracks and throws a silly punch. Now we are a man down and struggling. The game finishes with us under pressure, and we are lucky to have got away with the bonus point for defence. We are now both tied on eleven points in twelfth equal place, with Pau just a couple of points behind.

The bus trip home is gloomy. My mood is not improved by overhearing a conversation among the coaching staff. If the doctor is right about my injury—he thinks I have ruptured my bicep—I will be out for three months and may need an operation. Alex Codling, the Englishman who arrived at the start of the season to play lock, is out as well—probably for good, as he has chronic back pain and it doesn't look like getting better. Michel has a broken hand and should come back in a month or so. That means three locks out, and if one more goes down we are in serious trouble, so the management are going to buy in a new player. Just when I had made my way back into the team, and with *panache*—Nourault told me after the game he thought I had been playing some of my best rugby—more competition arrives. In the meantime I have to hope the diagnosis is wrong, and that I can recover sooner than expected.

The big game of the weekend is Stade Français v. Toulouse at Stade de France in Paris, and as we make our way back to Montpellier we listen to it on the radio. It sounds a slightly one-sided affair—26–0 for the Parisian side at half-time, before they finish 29–15—but what is incredible is that 80,000 spectators have gone along to watch it. This is a very big deal for rugby in France and, to an extent, rugby in the world. For years rugby has had relatively limited appeal. Its laws make it difficult to follow, and the public, outside the diehard supporters, have found it difficult to get excited about events other than international games and championship finals. But if this many people are going to see a normal club game in the middle of the season, rugby must have a turned a corner, particularly given that France's great sporting rivals, the football teams Olympique de Marseille and Paris Saint-Germain, are also playing this weekend, albeit in Marseille. All week the papers have been full of rugby, and Canal+ has decided to headline its

Saturday night sport with the rugby rather than the football.

Much of the success of this event comes down to the work of one man: Max Guazzini, the president of Stade Français. In the rugby world, Guazzini is an original. For a start he is openly homosexual and you don't see much of that, and although he has never played rugby himself he has a passion for the game and a vision of its potential that has allowed him to build Stade Français from a struggling third-division side to one of Europe's great clubs. Along the way he has turned received rugby wisdom on its head and changed people's perception of the game in France forever.

In 1992, after having amassed a reasonable fortune at the head of French media group NRJ, Guazzini decided to get involved with rugby. Taking over Stade Français in Paris, he immediately democratised the game by offering free entry, first to everyone, then to women and under 18-year-olds, thus building an interest in the sport outside its usual base.

Under his presidency, Stade Français have brought the glamour of show business to the game. Pom-pom girls have become a fixture. So have *Dieux du Stade*—Gods of the Stadium—calendars, featuring glossy black and white photographs of naked, oiled players, together with CDs of songs recorded by players. Such moves show a marketing flair that initially raised a few eyebrows in the conservative rugby world. The knowing flirtation with the homoerotic in the images of well-muscled young men in close physical contact is reminiscent of a Steve Reeves movie, and makes some people uncomfortable. And this year the club unveiled a new pink jersey—another rugby first.

All of this could make Stade Français look a bit silly if they were no good on the field, but they are: they got back into the first division in 1998, won the French championship that year, and have won it three times since.

Guazzini's spectacular success has, inevitably, led to some backbiting. Ticket prices for the game against Toulouse were as low as €5, prompting the president of Paris Saint-Germain to say he could do the same thing several times over if he wanted to. But by filling Stade de France Guazzini proved there is a real market for rugby. Certainly, the razzamatazz of fireworks and a giant karaoke sing-along made for a festival atmosphere, but television viewers also came to the party, with a very respectable 1.4 million watching the game at home.

With this success has come a concern voiced by many of rugby's staunchest supporters, that the game must *garder son âme*—hold on to its soul. It is difficult not to make comparisons with football. Most rugby supporters see the round-ball game as having become decadent and ugly, with widespread corruption, exorbitant pay for players who act like prima donnas, and a general atmosphere of sophisticated cynicism that contrasts with rugby's homespun, down-to-earth values.

Rugby became professional because of a confluence of two factors. The first was a desire for excellence on the part of players and teams; this led to such long hours of training that players felt they should be paid for their time and effort. The second was growing public interest in watching the competition between teams. The motor for change was television: television coverage meant that players could be paid enough money to make rugby a genuine career option.

The success of professional sport is, necessarily, measured by the number of spectators it attracts: more spectators equals more money. Television coverage can enlarge the potential number of spectators exponentially, and so is critical to professional sport. Sponsors know that their names will be seen, not just by the few thousand at the ground, but by people all over the country (and often, through satellite television, all over the world), and television channels pay handsomely for the rights to broadcast matches.

Rugby is an excellent product for sponsors and television companies in the sense that, on a good day, it is both a great spectacle and a vehicle for positive values such as discipline, courage, teamwork and skill. Rugby has been good to television, and television, by and large, has been good to rugby. To accommodate television's needs and make the game more spectator-friendly, rugby authorities have changed numerous rules. At the same time, the presence of cameras has led to a decrease in violent incidents (during televised games, anyway) because players are aware that, even if they avoid getting pinched by the referee or the touch judge, there is a good chance their crime will be played out in slow-motion replays at a disciplinary board hearing, and the camera doesn't lie.

Since the advent of professionalism, rugby has been broadcast more widely in France, leading to an increase in the numbers of people participating in the game, as well as the number of spectators. So everyone is happy: sponsors, clubs, players and television channels are each getting a piece of the cake, and every year the cake keeps getting bigger.

Although this sounds like a wonderful success story—and to all intents and purposes it is—rugby needs to be careful. The desire to appeal to a wider public can result in a game moving away from its roots. Do we really want rugby to be the new football? The problem is that this supposedly independent sport is now, like so many others, dependent on television, not only for reaching a wider audience but also for its revenue. Television is a business, and so all about maximising profit, but the various marketing strategies it employs aren't necessarily good for rugby, or for the individuals who play it.

The most obvious example is the desire to consecrate certain players as stars. In rugby, as in any sport, there are charismatic individuals who stand out. Rugby's interdependent nature, though, means that, no matter how good an individual may be, he can't perform without his team-mates. When, at the end of a game, the 'man of the match' says, 'I couldn't have done it without the lads', he is not just being modest: he is telling the truth. Picking out one player and elevating him above the rest therefore runs contrary to rugby's musketeer-style 'all for one, and one for all' spirit. You may have a great game one week and a disaster the next, but whatever happens you stick with your mates. They stand by you, and you stand by them. That is one of the great pleasures and the great strengths of rugby.

Take the example of Fred Michalak, the young fly-half who was quickly dubbed a genius by the media, and hailed as the French rugby team's version of soccer's Zinedine Zidane. Michalak is a good-looking man (my girlfriend Marion, who is obviously an authority on good-looking guys and a woman of impeccable taste, thinks he looks like a young Marlon Brando) and he was quickly set up as a bright young thing, advertising high-end cosmetics, modelling for Christian Lacroix, and giving countless interviews to the media. He became a highly visible celebrity.

Michalak wasn't complaining, and with people throwing money at him and hanging on his every word you wouldn't expect him to. Unfortunately, though, all this extra attention meant people expected him to perform consistently head and shoulders above everyone else, and like so many 'stars' he was set up only to be pulled down when he showed signs of not living up to his status. During the Six Nations game against Ireland in February 2006 (which France won, despite a 20-minute lapse in concentration that allowed the Irish back in), Michalak was whistled and booed by the public, who were not prepared to forgive an 'off' day from the man they felt owed them a performance in line with his reputation. This prompted Bernard Laporte to defend his player by describing the public as *'bourgeois de merde'*— 'bloody bourgeois'—but other commentators made the more reasoned analysis that rugby had become so successful it had acquired a new public, one that wanted a spectacle in line with their expectations, and would tolerate nothing less.

It's difficult to be completely sure who was doing the whistling; perhaps it was the old school giving Michalak the raspberry because they didn't like the idea of a rugby player strutting around on catwalks. In any case, this 'new public' is, of course, exactly the people rugby has been hoping to attract. They are different from rugby's traditional fan base in that they are more spectators than supporters. They come to a game not to show their support for a team, but to be entertained. For them a rugby game is a product like any other, and if they're not satisfied they are unlikely to spend money on it again, whereas the diehard supporters are capable of re-mortgaging their houses to ensure they get season tickets, and are delighted to see their team grind out a 3–0 win if that's what it takes to avoid relegation, or qualify for the semis. I know of supporters who are so nervous they have trouble eating before important games. Like most players I think this is a bit much, but I can remember when I was fifteen sulking for a whole day because Wellington had lost a Ranfurly Shield game to Auckland.

Professional rugby has already made dents in some of the values that the old school, in particular, appreciates. The importing of foreign players has led to complaints from some supporters that they are no longer able to identify with their team, although you don't usually hear much about this when the team is winning.

The relatively new idea of putting names on the backs of jerseys, along with numbers, is an obvious sop to the marketing people. In the old days, either you knew the team well enough to know who the players were, or you didn't care because the only important thing was the colour of the jersey they were wearing.

One of the things that makes competitive sport special is the atmosphere created by the fans. Even if it doesn't change the way you play, it is nice to know that people are intensely involved in what you are doing. In a sense, the difference between the new package and the old is like that between a small French farmers' market and a supermarket: one is all about the values of *terroir*—flavoursome, small-scale and a bit eccentric—while the other is slick and bland but, because of its greater financial muscle, a wiser economic choice.

Customarily, rugby players say little of interest when dealing with the media. Partly this is modesty, but mostly it's wariness: if we let slip something slip in an unguarded moment it may come back to haunt us. The former French centre Richard Dourthe had a moment of honesty in 2000, confiding in a journalist from *Midi Olympique* who had asked him why he had just signed for Béziers. He replied that, while he realised he should say something about being excited about the club's project, working with a great coach or being able to play alongside some great players, the real reason he had signed was because they offered him a truckload of cash and he would have been a fool to turn it down. A few people applauded his honesty, but only a few.

My own initiation to the merits of keeping your mouth shut and your nose clean came in 1996, when I was with the Wellington Lions and we were about to play Canterbury. I was asked on television whether I might be worried about their pack, which was spearheaded by experienced All Black hard man Richard Loe.

'No way,' piped my cocky 24-year-old self, not at all experienced in media interviews, but determined to say something interesting. 'We're not going to be intimidated by Richard Loe or any of the Canterbury team. They'd better watch out for us.'

The Lions' captain, Jason O'Halloran, was with me, and as we left the studio he turned to me and said, 'Jesus, JD, I'm bloody glad I'm not you. I hope Loey wasn't watching.'

What? Holy shit, it hadn't even occurred to me. This is why we are well-advised to limit pre-match press chat to platitudes: don't give the other lot any ammunition. For the record, I didn't sleep well but we did have a good win. Eat that, Ricky. (If you are Richard Loe and reading this book, please bear in mind that this last bit is a joke.)

8

Merchandise

Perpignan is a few kilometres inland from the Mediterranean, on the French side of the border with Spain that is marked by the Pyrenees. Just over 100,000 people live there. So much for the geography. Historically, the town was part of Catalonia until it was ceded to France under the 1659 Treaty of the Pyrenees that ended the French-Spanish war. Ties to the Catalan identity remain strong. Everyone speaks French, but about a quarter of the population also speaks Catalan, and nearly half understand it. At Stade Aimé Giral the signs are bilingual, although this is more of a marketing ploy to target would-be investors from wealthy Barcelona and its region than because anyone might get lost without them.

Perhaps the most obvious cultural link for any visitor is the Catalan flag, which can be seen waving everywhere in the region, but particularly at rugby games. To the uninitiated these flags look red and yellow; in fact the colours are blood and gold. Legend has it that Wilfred the Hairy, Count of Barcelona, was lying wounded after fighting against the Saracens in the siege of Barcelona. King Louis the Pious came to visit him, fresh from the hard-fought victory. Seeing Wilfred's golden shield next to the bed, Louis dipped his hand in the valiant soldier's blood and drew it down the shield as a mark of honour that would be remembered by future generations. This romantic story is almost certainly apocryphal, but it remains a powerful part of the Catalan identity: the symbol of the rugby club is a diamond with four blood-coloured stripes on a field of gold.

The club is known as USAP, Union Sportive Arlequins Perpignan. Originally there were two clubs in the town: Union Sportive Arlequins and Union Sportive Perpignan. The two merged in 1933, bringing an end to a bitter rivalry. In 1923 they had fought each other to a standstill in a 0–0 draw. There was blood on the grass and ten players were sent off.

The Bouclier de Brennus has been to Perpignan six times since 1914, but the last time was 1955, half a century ago. In 2004, USAP made it to the final, following the European final of 2003. They are undeniably in the heavyweight category, even if there is still a notable absence of silverware in the clubhouse.

For me, Perpignan represents the emotional roller-coaster that makes French rugby such a rich experience. I was picked up by the club from the relative obscurity of Racing and had a great season in 2000–2001, the first year of the Catalan rugby renaissance. In 1998 Perpignan had made it to the

French championship final, where they had lost to Stade Français. They had had a difficult couple of years after that, despite making it to the quarter-finals in 1999 after a remarkable last-gasp victory against Agen in the eliminatory round. In 2000–2001 many pundits thought we would go down, but instead we qualified for the Heineken Cup and gave the eventual champions, Toulouse, a hell of a fright, before losing by just a few points in the quarter-final.

Perpignan signed me up again for two years, and both president and coach couldn't say enough good things about me. By the end of the following year my form had dipped and the president, Marcel Dagrenat, wanted to get rid of me, so he warned me that if I stayed I would spend my last season under contract training with the *Espoirs*, the club's second team, made up of Under 23 players, and in all probability wouldn't be on the list of players submitted to play in the European competition.

I stayed on anyway, and nearly a year later, with five minutes to go in the semifinal of the European Cup at Lansdowne Road, I found myself with the ball at my feet, five yards from the Leinster goal-line. I picked it up, ran into the wall of Irish defence, and slipped the ball behind me to Marc dal Maso, who skirted the Leinster pack that was focussed on smashing me, and threw himself over the line to score the winning try. We were in the final. It was probably the highlight of my career. A month later, struggling with an ankle injury that would still have allowed me to play, I travelled to Dublin for the game, only to be told the night before that my services would not be required.

Dagrenet's ruthless attitude did not surprise me. I had arrived at the club in 2000, a few months after him. At that stage, the club was being run by men who were passionate about rugby but had difficulties adapting to the new professional age, and finances were shaky. Knowing of Dagrenat's expertise in this area, a group of ex-presidents and USAP officials had approached him to take over the presidency.

Dagrenat decided to implement what he knew from his experience in the business world. He had made a decent amount of money running supermarkets, and his strength lay in efficiency—extracting maximum value for the least expenditure—and planning ahead to make sure you were carrying the right amount of stock. Obviously this was a good general rule for business, and 'pile it high and sell it cheap' had made more than one man rich. But would it be enough to run a professional rugby club?

At first the answer seemed to be yes. Almost immediately things began to turn around for the good. Dagrenat pulled in new sponsors, increased profits through merchandising deals and opening bodegas at the ground, and generally transformed the club into a money-making machine. But maximising a team's potential requires some understanding of the subtleties of human nature. Over the course of a season each player will have times when he plays less well than at other times. However, given the right conditions he will bounce back. Too often, though, at Perpignan the conditions were not right, and the result was a lot of wasted potential.

Players put terrific pressure on themselves, and should not have to spend time worrying about being thrown out on account of a couple of bad games. Such a scenario can push a player into a downward spiral where, knowing management is lining him up for the chop, he loses even more confidence in himself. Early in my rugby career in New Zealand I went through a bad patch after coming back from a head injury, until Kevin Horan, my coach at Marist St Pats, had a quiet word in my ear. He could see, he said, that I was trying too hard. I was a good player and the ability hadn't gone away—all I needed to do was relax. It was the perfect advice. My self-belief was boosted, and I quickly found my form again.

There are generally 33 players in a squad. Even with a few injured, there are still going to be some who don't get on the pitch, and the better the team, the better the quality of the guys being left out. At Perpignan, though, in the early years of Marcel Dagrenat's reign, there was a rattling turnover. The year I left nearly half the squad was changed, despite the club having made it to the final of the European Cup, something that hasn't been repeated since.

More recently, the club seems to have learned the lesson and there are now only four or five new players arriving every year. However, Dagrenat still seems to think of players primarily as units of merchandise. In an interview with *Midi Olympique* in October 2005, he declared, '*Les joueurs sont notre capital ... quand on a un capital, on le fait fructifier*' ('Players are our capital ... when you have capital you make it yield a profit').

The subtext is that investments that are underperforming need to be jettisoned. This may make sound business sense, but amount to short-term thinking when it comes to rugby. In 2003 Dagrenat brought in several high-profile foreign internationals, of whom perhaps the best known was Daniel Herbert. As a Wallaby centre, Herbert had been capped 68 times between 1996 and 2002, and had been a key member of the squad that won the 1999 World Cup. In addition, he had played 124 games for Queensland.

You don't play that much top-class rugby without incurring a few aches and pains, and Herbert arrived in France with a dodgy knee. The club knew about this, and it was agreed that for his aerobic fitness he would avoid the kind of long-distance running that might inflict wear and tear on aging joints, and replace it with low-impact cycling or rowing. However, this quickly became a sticking point. After Herbert had played, and played well, Dagrenat reasoned that his knee was obviously fine, so he could train alongside everyone else. Olivier Saïsset, the coach, presumably thought that as Dagrenat was not standing by the original agreement to give Herbert special dispensation, there was no reason for him to do so either.

Herbert, unhappy but feeling cornered and not wanting to look as though he were avoiding work, did the training. After a few games, followed by heavy running sessions during the week, his knee had flared up to the point where he had to have time off. After it settled down, he came back and played a few more games, before tearing his hamstring.

At this point, there were already rumblings of discontent emanating from the president's office. Herbert was being paid upwards of €15,000 monthly, and the return on the investment wasn't turning out to be as high as had been expected. Dagrenat was already looking into the possibility of having the Australian declared unfit to play rugby, which would mean the next two and a bit years of his contract would be null and void. Then, as Herbert was coming back from the hamstring injury, he started having problems with his neck. A disc had slipped. The problem deteriorated and in April 2004 it was agreed that he needed an operation.

Dagrenat then set in motion a series of procedures to ensure the club would not have to pay out any more money for a player he now saw as a lame duck. On the day Herbert was preparing to go into hospital for his neck operation (which would fuse two vertebrae together), he was told the club had not processed the necessary paperwork. This was no administrative oversight: Dagrenat told him that he would allow the operation to go ahead only if Herbert agreed to leave the club, giving up the last two years of his contract without any insurance payout or indemnity. Herbert, he said, wasn't fit to play rugby. He had known this when he arrived, and had acted in bad faith when he signed his contract.

Now, I know Daniel Herbert—not all that well, but well enough—and like any of us he has faults (the man is an Australian, for God's sake), but bad faith is not one of them. And it is worth noting that he had had an X-ray of his spine as part of the obligatory medical inspection performed by the club before signing new players.

Determined to prove Dagrenat wrong, Herbert sought the advice of France's top medical specialists and was told that, if all went well, he would be back playing rugby in five or six months, leaving him able to play out the last 18 months of his contract.

He duly had the operation in June 2004. Before the surgery, the right side of his upper body had been virtually paralysed, and for long periods he had been unable to move, or even eat. When he came around from the operation, the right side was better, but something had gone wrong—now his left side was stricken. He battled on. Despite having been barred from using club facilities, he devised a training schedule with the help of his old Queensland coaches, and trained twice a day for six months to get into the sort of shape he needed to return to competition. If he had come for the money, he was staying out of pride, fuelled by the kind of stubbornness that made him a great player.

In November 2004 he felt confident enough to tell the club he was ready to play again. In order to do this, he had to be declared fit for work by a *médecin du travail*, a doctor employed by the French state to decide objectively whether employees were physically able to perform their jobs. He took along fellow Australian Anthony Hill, a kind of camp mother to stray antipodean rugby players. Herbert was still shell-shocked by the way things seemed to work in France but Hill was a veteran, and they were armed with the opinions of the French specialists.

Once they had presented their case and the doctor had made his inspection, he started writing down his findings. Hill saw that he was declaring Herbert unfit to play rugby. He asked the doctor what he thought he was doing, given that all the evidence pointed the other way. The doctor sighed, got up and walked around, then told them that he had had Dagrenat on the phone that morning, and had been told that it was in his best interests to signal Herbert unfit. Dagrenat had reminded him of the influence he had in Perpignan, and was sure the doctor would understand.

At six-foot-six and 130 kilograms, Hill also has not inconsiderable powers of persuasion, and the two men had the advantage of being on the spot. The upshot was that the doctor declared Herbert fit to work.

This would have led to a long stand-off had Herbert's neck not started playing up again just a couple of months later. Medicine is an inexact science, and while the disc between C5 and C6 was all right after the vertebrae were fused, the one between C6 and C7 started causing trouble. From the outside it looked as though Dagrenat had been right all along. Now, after talking to the same specialists, Herbert agreed that he was unfit for rugby. It must have been a sickening blow, and just when he needed support from the people he was playing for when he received the injury, they put the boot in.

There was now no chance of Herbert playing again, and the French state, which had effectively been paying his salary for nine months through work accident insurance, washed its hands of the affair and sent him back to the club, who were legally obliged to offer him some sort of job for the duration of his contract. Dagrenat now made an offer it was impossible to accept: he proposed that Herbert act as his personal secretary, and on game days put ice into buckets, for which he would be paid the princely sum of 5 percent of his previous salary. There would be no negotiated settlement.

To avoid being considered in breach of contract, Herbert was unable to look for any other work until his contract was up, but he decided to fight in the courts, in what turned into a protracted affair. In July 2005 he received an insurance payout of around €200,000. He continued to fight for a payout from Perpignan, and in November 2006 the tribunal awarded him €181,000 in unpaid salary, excluding image rights. He appealed to get the image rights as well, and the club finally settled out of court for an undisclosed sum between €181,000 and €400,000. The upshot was that Herbert ended up with a total of nearly €500,000, nearly three times what he would have been prepared to accept had Dagrenat not been so pigheaded about the whole thing.

This is not the only instance of shifty behaviour on the part of the Perpignan president. He is said to have told player Pascal Meya he would ensure that he, Meya, didn't get a job in the region if he didn't give up the last year of his contract. When that didn't work, he reportedly menaced Meya with a smear campaign in the local press. He tried to get rid of former New South Wales Waratah Ed Carter by saying he would report Carter's girlfriend to the authorities as an illegal immigrant; the club was to have looked after her immigration papers, but stalled when they realised they could be a source of leverage. He has used his contacts to look into players' bank accounts to see how they're spending their money, and engaged in other blatant manipulation.

As well as the financial cost of defending lawsuits, the club's prestige has suffered. The rugby world is small, and word gets around, making potential recruits wary of signing up with a club where this kind of thing goes on. The club's sporting results are still relatively strong, but there is a certain sense of stagnation: it is now three years since Perpignan have made it to a final.

I would like to be able to say that Dagrenat was the only president who operated like this, but it is not the case. At the end of the 2004–2005 season, for example, an outstanding young flanker, Yannick Nyanga, found himself in a difficult situation. When Nyanga, who was born in the Republic of Congo and starting playing for Béziers at the age of 14, signed a two-year contract, the president, Olivier Nicollin, gave him his word that if the club were relegated he would be released without any fee so he could continue playing top-level rugby. Despite Nyanga's best efforts—he played so well he was picked for the French team—Béziers did go down.

However, Nicollin reneged on his word when he realised he could make money by selling the last year of Nyanga's contract. He proceeded to set the dazzlingly high price of €300,000 on a transfer, virtually pricing Nyanga out of the market, and making him very nervous about the possibility that his promising career was about to be nipped in the bud —or, at the very least, stalled for a season in the second division. In the end he was bought by Toulouse, probably for considerably less than €300,000, but some of the money would have come out of what Nyanga would otherwise have been paid.

When you tell this kind of story to grizzled rugby players of an earlier generation, you get the same sort of reaction you get from wide-eyed five-year olds after the first reel of *Bambi*:

a shocked loss of innocence. As Herbert has said, 'You shake hands with someone in the rugby world, and think it means something.' But the modern rugby player is not much more than a piece of meat in the eyes of men like Dagrenat.

Are rugby players naïve to think we can and should be protected from the uglier side of capitalism? After all, we are at the cutting edge of the free market: there are not many other industries where workers move so freely across borders to ply their trade. And rugby is a violent sport. Maybe it's only normal for bad behaviour to spread to the management side? Perhaps it is the entrepreneurial equivalent of eye-gouging?

In a magazine interview, Dagrenat described his detachment from the game. 'If USAP get to the final,' he said, 'I can happily watch it at home on TV ... What motivates me every morning is the economy of the club.' This is disarmingly transparent: he doesn't get any pleasure from the game or the club, but just wants to make sure there is plenty of money.

This isn't quite as worrying as the case of the American multi-millionaire Malcolm Glazer, who bought the football team Manchester United in 2005 for nearly $1.5 billion, largely to offload some of his business debts. But it does raise some questions. Dagrenat has enough money not to need any more, so he's not doing it for the cash; indeed he has reformulated the job description of president to make it impossible for him to be paid a wage. The game itself doesn't mean much to him, he shuns the limelight, and he has at least an inkling that, despite the success that he has brought to the club, he is not well-liked. 'In the rugby world,' he said in the same interview, 'everyone is friendly with each other, everyone kisses each other. No one kisses me. I don't know whether they like me or not, but it's not my problem.'

In late 2005, when it became clear that Dagrenat was introducing several shareholders loyal to him, who would tip the balance and give him influence over more than 50 percent of the club's holdings, several Perpignan officials launched a counterattack. They could, they said, no longer stand by and watch the values of the club they loved being eroded by a man who had no obvious regard for these values. The spat ended with a compromise: the two different sides now hold a total of 49 percent of the shares each, while a block representing supporters and former players holds a swing vote of two percent.

Dagrenat's best defence of his tactics remains the results of the team, and he still has a large number of supporters on his side, who are happy to see their team looking better off than it did before he arrived. The interesting question is whether Perpignan is a forerunner of a new rugby? Is USAP the canary in the coalmine?

In the week leading up to the game I try to train normally. The injury I sustained at Toulon is mysterious: the medical staff can't find anything conclusive on the MRI and scanner results, and the arm works all right 90 percent of the time. However, the physios test it with various exercises and strongly advise against my playing.

Nourault overrules them; he likes pitting players against their former clubs, knowing it gives them extra motivation.

He's right: I feel optimistic and desperately want to play against Perpignan. I decide to try out my arm in the opposition training on Wednesday. It's not great and I miss a tackle because I simply can't hold on, and then we start going backward in the scrum, and as my arm is stretched out and away from my body the pain is excruciating. I can't keep the necessary grip for my binding. Didier Bes is standing next to me as I pick myself up, and I give him an earful, for no good reason other than frustration. It is clear that the arm is not right—it will eventually be diagnosed as a ripped pectoral tendon—so once again I am watching from the stands.

It is a must-win game, and not simply because we are playing at home. We are twelfth equal with Toulon, and Pau are playing Agen in Pau. If Pau win and we lose, they will leapfrog ahead and we will be last equal.

David Bortolussi draws first blood with a penalty after only a few minutes, but after that it is one-way traffic. The ball is greasy, so Perpignan don't use their possession out wide in a way that might really have us in trouble after our Samoan winger Ali Koko collects a yellow card, but they attack intelligently. Nico Laharrague kicks four penalties and Christophe Manas scores a try without our firing a shot. The Catalan supporters, whom I used to love when I was playing there, are crowing, and it is really starting to annoy me. A man sitting right in front of me stands up and waves his scarf at us with a big grin on his face every time they score. I am surprised by how much I want to throttle him with it. At halftime the score is a glum 3–17. We will need a miracle to turn it around.

Eight minutes after the break, our supporters finally have something to cheer about. We work a move on the short side: Bortolussi slips through on a diagonal run and manages to offload in the tackle of the cover defence, flipping the ball up to Rickus Lubbe, who turns on the gas and heads for the corner. Bortolussi converts, and at 10–17 things are looking more respectable.

We wait for the inevitable counter-thrust, but incredibly it doesn't come. The game see-saws back and forth, but another penalty from Bortolussi and we start to think the unthinkable. It is 13–17 and they're under pressure. Ovidiu Tonita, their Romanian number eight, gets a yellow card and we capitalise again, with three valuable points putting us within striking distance. They are not going to roll over just like that though, and they press into our 22 as the seconds tick away. We defend courageously, but we won't be scoring from there.

With less than a minute to go, they set a scrum in a good attacking spot just 20 metres out. It looks as though it's all going to end in tears … but then they are penalised. I don't know what for, but who cares? We kick to touch up towards the halfway line, win the ensuing line-out and send the ball wide. There isn't much on and we are still nearly 50 metres out, but as the ball comes back across the field, the referee blows his whistle: offside against Perpignan. The siren marking the end of the game sounds almost immediately, but since the stoppage is a penalty we can play it. Bortolussi lines up the ball just inside their half, on the right side of the pitch. He is known as *La machine* because of his metronomic ability to put the ball between the posts, but he has only recently come back from injury and this is on the outer edge of his range. I am so beside myself I can't watch, but the television replays we see afterwards show that he hits it well, and even before the touch judges standing under the posts raise their flags he is punching the air and jumping up and down, celebrating what has to be the greatest comeback since Lazarus. 19–17. The crowd goes wild. I don't even care that I didn't play.

9

Europe, the All Blacks, the World

Rugby has been played in Agen since 1908, and Sporting Union Agenais has won the Bouclier de Brennus eight times since 1930, most recently in 1988. Agen's 30,000 inhabitants are proud to call their town the prune capital of France. As with many other small towns in the first division, if there were not for the rugby team there would not be much going on. It is beautiful country though, with a well-deserved reputation for good eating, and the rugby team is very good. This is the club that has come closest to breaking the hegemony of the triumvirate of Toulouse, Biarritz and Stade Français in the French championship in recent years, losing 22–25 against Biarritz in extra time in the 2002 final.

The irony of this result was that it came just a few months after Agen had lost 59–10 to the Welsh club Ebbw Vale in the junior European Cup competition, the European Shield. Even the most ardent supporter of Ebbw Vale would agree that this was an unexpectedly large win for the Welsh side, but what happened that day so shocked European rugby officials that Agen were suspended from European competition the following year, the only time this had happened in the history of the competition.

Confronted by a busy calendar, Agen had decided they were going to concentrate on the French championship. Qualifying for the next round of the European Shield would simply add to the pile-up of games to be played, so they decided to throw the game. The problem was that simply losing wasn't going to be enough: Ebbw Vale had to score a barrowload of tries to go through, which meant the French side had to make a meal of it, and they did, waving the Welsh through as though they were trying to free up a traffic jam. They then unashamedly owned up to their ploy in the press, and seemed surprised that disciplinary action was taken. (The penalty was later reduced from a two-season disqualification to one-season following an appeal.) They had cause to regret their action: by finishing second in the championship they would have qualified for the Heineken Cup, but they missed out because of the suspension.

You may be appalled by this exercise in cynicism. Or perhaps you will just shrug your shoulders and figure they made the right calculation, since they got as far as the final six months later. The reality is that this kind of attitude towards the European Cup is not unusual in France. Agen lacked the necessary subtlety that might have allowed the authorities to swallow it: a few yellow cards for repeated technical infringements would have given them much the same result. But every year, when the European competition rolls round after two months of week-in, week-out championship games, one or two clubs will look at the list of wounded, look at the depth of their squad, assess their chances of winning the competition, and quietly pull the pin.

There is obviously a difference between not going all out to win a game and actually throwing it, but it's only a difference of degree, and both run contrary to the nature of any competition. But the clubs know that a full-scale campaign will, at best, tire the players by adding to an already heavy workload, and, at worst, lead to the loss of players through injury, and so the risk has to be worth the potential reward.

This is not to say that the European Cup is systematically written off. It is a great competition for the players because it allows them to come into contact with different rugby cultures, and games tend to flow more because there is less at stake. The kind of negative play that is often seen in the French championship is left behind, and there is more emphasis on attack.

French clubs have a proud record in the European Cup, with Toulouse winning it three times and Brive once, and there have been two all-French finals in recent years. But you need to have strength in depth. Bourgoin, for example, had a bad run in the Heineken Cup in 2004–2005: they lost 0–34 to Treviso at home (the first time a French club had lost to an Italian one in France, and it was a pounding), and topped that in the next round by losing 17–92 to Leinster in Dublin. The reason given for these woeful performances was that Bourgoin (who made it to the semis of the French championship that season, so they weren't there by accident) had put their money into quality rather than quantity of players, and there was a big drop-off in standards when a few key players were rested or injured.

Apart from the three big clubs, and perhaps Perpignan, the rest of the clubs look at the European competition as cake, compared to the bread and butter of the championship. Everyone would like a slice of European success, but only the rich can consistently afford it.

In 2003–2004, Montpellier won the Parker Pen Shield, which sounds quite glamorous but isn't. We qualified by losing our first-round game against Glasgow and slipping down a level. Our rivals were Italian teams who hadn't made it to the Heineken Cup, and had also been knocked out of the second-tier competition. Still, it was fun to win.

It wasn't a great success as a concept though, and no longer exists. Today there is only the European Challenge Cup, the junior brother to the Heineken and with a similar kind of set-up—a four-team pool, with a round robin of home and away games. The winners of each of the eight pools move through to the quarter-finals.

At the start of the year, when we were drawing up our team goals, we discussed the emphasis that would be placed on Europe and decided we would aim to make it to the knockout rounds. This struck me as a little overambitious, given the standard of the other teams. Catania, a Sicilian club, was fresh up from Italy's second division so they probably weren't too flash, but Worcester, even though they had been in the English Premier division only as long as we had been in the

French version, were not going to be easy. And Connacht, the smallest of Ireland's four provincial clubs, would be highly motivated as well. Both Worcester and Connacht could realistically hope to qualify for the Heineken Cup by winning the Challenge Cup, and were sure to take it seriously.

Montpellier, after ten hard games in two and a half months, arrive at the doorway to the European season limping and wheezing like a sick man whose car has broken down half a dozen miles away. Nourault decides this may be a good moment to give the usual starting team a break and let those who have been kicking their heels have a run. It's a good decision. At this stage of the season, after the win against Perpignan but before the game in Agen, we are on 15 points, a nose ahead of Pau. They have 13, while Toulon bring up the rear on 11. We can't afford to lose any more players, and this gives the guys who haven't had much game-time an opportunity to show their talent, and perhaps force their way into the team.

South African Rickus Lubbe and I, the two old crocks, are left off the list submitted to the European Rugby Cup authorities. It will be months before I can play again, and Rickus is being rested. Unfortunately, we don't have the luxury of making the changes in the orderly way you might expect: pretty much everyone who's been playing regularly gets a weekend off or is on the bench, and this doesn't help organisation. A full-strength team, well-prepared and with an eye on the title, might just have had a chance to make it through to the next round.

The mix and match outfit that gets slung out on the field acquits itself reasonably well at Worcester, before going down 18–36 (after 15–15 just before half-time). But we then lose at home to Connacht 13–19, despite putting out a stronger side. The home game against Catania is the one bright spot: they are very ordinary, but we play well enough and keep our heads to win 74–12, which indicates how dreadful the result is when we go to Sicily and lose against them 34–37 a few weeks later. (It seems the more Latin your blood, the more 'home and away' you are.)

We are soundly beaten 10–43 in Ireland, and then lose 21–31 to Worcester at home, so Catania, who beat Connacht in Sicily in their last game, finish ahead of us, and we are dead last. Ouch. So much for qualifying for the next round. However, the beauty of the European Cup is that, even if this cuts at our pride, the wound isn't serious, and while it stings for a bit it soon goes away because we have bigger things to worry about.

The week before the game in Agen we train very well, particularly in opposition. It seems the European Cup experience, even if it not successful in terms of results, may have been useful: our continuity is better, with players getting away good passes in contact. Being less worried about the result gives us the freedom to try things that we might not otherwise, and if we can continue with this confidence in the championship it will add a dimension to our game that has been lacking.

'You play the way you train' is a coaching cliché with which most sides get ear-bashed all the time because it's generally true, but the French are such mavericks that form on the training field is no indication of what will happen on the day. I don't travel to Agen because of my arm, but from what I gather I don't miss much. Agen have had a scratchy start to the season—they are only three points ahead of us before the game, on 18—so perhaps we might sneak a win? A bonus point?

Er, no. Within a couple of minutes of the kick-off they score a converted try, then a quarter of an hour later another one. Dio dots down in the middle of a driving maul from a line-out, and Coco converts with quarter of an hour to go to half-time, but they reply in kind a few minutes later. 7–21 at the pause.

Rupeni Caucaunibaca, their flying Fijian winger, is always a handful (provided he's interested—not always the case) and he assures them of the bonus for four tries shortly after we return. He has a mazy running style, seemingly effortless acceleration, and a swivel-hipped change of direction that would make Elvis envious. All of these attributes combine to make him a nightmare to tackle, particularly if he has a few yards in front of the defence to turn you inside out. Despite the dance routine he's no will-o'-the-wisp, and occasionally mixes it up by simply running over the top of you. Great to watch from the stands, less fun close up. Anyway, it's now 7–28. Coco pulls a penalty back for us but then François Gelez kicks one himself, converts another try and rounds it off with a final penalty. It's 10–41, and definitely no bonus for us.

The result is not much of a shock, and by the time I find out that we have lost heavily I have set up headquarters in an Irish pub, and this eases the pain. I've dragged Marion along to watch England play New Zealand: the All Blacks are on course for a grand slam of the British Isles. Lack of foresight has me also watching the game with Nico Grelon and Drickus Hancke, who are injured too, so I have had to sit through France v. Tonga and Wales v. South Africa to keep them happy. This means nearly six hours of rugby, a considerable investment in what passes for stout in Montpellier, and one stroppy French girlfriend. Happily, the ABs squeak home against the English.

England v. New Zealand hasn't always produced great rugby over the years—historically the Springboks have been New Zealand's leading rivals for world supremacy, although of course the English are, at the time of writing, the current world champions. However, most Kiwis would agree that the one game that New Zealand must not lose is against England.

There is an element of chippiness involved, but it's more than that. New Zealand is often said to have come of age as a nation on the blood-soaked hills of the Dardanelles during the disastrously organised Gallipoli campaign of 1916. New Zealand then numbered less than a million inhabitants, and the Gallipoli campaign landed 8450 men on the Turkish shoreline, of whom 2721 were killed and 4752 wounded. During the whole of World War I, 58,000 New Zealanders were killed or wounded—in a war that took place on the other side of the world.

This may sound strange to self-assured Europeans with thousands of years of history behind them, but New Zealand is a young self-conscious nation with a tendency to judge ourselves by what others see in us, and the massive sacrifice involved during World War I validated the idea that we weren't just a far-flung outpost of the British Empire. We were as good as the Brits, and maybe even better, a country full of courage and resource and natural grit, and big enough to stand on the world stage.

The seeds of this national identity had been sown a decade earlier, when a team representing New Zealand had gone to play rugby in Britain. In 1905 'The Originals', as they came to be known, played 35 games, including five tests, losing only once, 0–3 to Wales. They wore a black jersey with a silver fern, and for the first time were referred to as the All Blacks. The story is told that, in a headline, a newspaper intended to describe the tourists, who were quickly making a name for themselves by allying ferocity with grace, and whose forwards were as skilled and fleet-footed as the backs, as 'All Backs!' but someone slipped in an 'l'. Unfortunately, no one can find a copy of the newspaper, so the more prosaic explanation that the name was a reference to their gear is now generally accepted.

Wherever it came from, the All Blacks beat England 15–0, scoring four tries to none. The men from the distant island colony had beaten the mother country—who had, after all, invented the game—and impressed the British sporting public with their skill and strength. Best of all, they elicited admiring comments from British writers about positive aspects of New Zealand that were reflected in the team's performance: natural, healthy living conditions made them strong and fit, and the egalitarian society made them adaptable, broadminded and scornful of convention.

All of this tallied neatly with what New Zealanders thought of themselves. New Zealand had measured itself against Britain (most particularly against England, the seat of power) and was proud to have proved its worth. From then on, New Zealand has felt that its place is on top of the rugby world. Losing to *anyone* is disastrous; losing to England is the world turned on its head. The first lines of the traditional haka run: 'Ka Mate! Ka Mate! / Ka Ora! Ka Ora!—'It is death! It is death! / It is life! It is life!'

It is impossible to grow up as a boy in New Zealand without knowing that you are supposed to play rugby and aim to be an All Black. Even before I started, I wore a pair of black pyjamas, with the silver fern over my heart. I was nine when I played my first competitive season, relatively late for a Kiwi kid. We played in bare feet at about eight o'clock on Saturday mornings on the Wanganui racecourse. The pitch was sandy, and in the cold winter mornings it should have been illegal to play without boots, but we loved it.

If the All Blacks have become the personification of New Zealand values, they are also the point of reference for all other sports played in the country. Even the monikers of the national teams in other disciplines are a kind of name check: the basketballers are the Tall Blacks; the soccer team the All Whites; the cricketers the Black Caps; the netballers the Silver Ferns; the yachtsmen steer a boat called *Black Magic*. Athletes, rowers and cyclists all compete in black.

People often wonder how a small country like New Zealand manages to stay so consistently at, or very near, the top of world rugby. There is a raft of different reasons. For example, a large number of the current All Blacks are of Pacific Island origin, and the explosive style of play of these men has allowed the team to keep ahead of the rest of the world in pure physical firepower. But what ties it all together is that the country sees rugby as such a big deal. The older generation, brought up in the rugby tradition, is keen to encourage younger players and pass on what they know.

Innovation has always been part of this tradition. In 1905 The Originals were the first to have specific positions for players, rather than simply lumping large men into the forwards and skinny ones out the back, and each new wave looks for a way to improve. The pyramidal structure put in place by the New Zealand Rugby Union means the whole country is geared towards acting as a feeder system for the apex—the All Blacks—and there is no damaging club v. country tug-of-war over players. Rugby going professional was, paradoxically, inimical to New Zealand's domination, because it levelled the playing-field: players in other countries now had the incentive to put in the same amount of effort.

Of course, New Zealand has gone through bad patches and lost games. And we have won the World Cup only once, in 1987, while our close rivals the Australians have won it twice. But New Zealand has a positive record against every other country in world rugby. Only the Springboks come close—the All Blacks have won just 55 percent of games against them.

I spent my last school year and then three university years in England, and the culture shock was considerable. It would be dangerous to draw conclusions from the rugby I played

147

in the rarefied atmosphere of Eton and Oxford—I didn't do the hard yards in a club, which would have been a better indicator of what English rugby was really like—but I was struck by the attitude of team-mates and coaches. In England, we were 'playing games', which was a healthy activity, and if you won that was great but if you didn't, well, that was all right, because it was the taking part that was important.

I had been brought up on competitive sport, which wasn't quite win-at-all-costs, but nearly. You would be criticised for cheating, for example, only if you were penalised—that is, if you were caught. Sportsmanship meant shaking hands at the end, and wearing the same mask whether you won or lost. In my first match for the Eton First XV, I was threatened with never being allowed to play for them again because I rucked a player who was lying all over our ball. The referee, a Scotsman, didn't blink, but the coaches considered this kind of behaviour deplorable.

Every boy had his own room at Eton, and there were no communal changing-rooms. Just before our first home game, I was stunned to discover that we were supposed to meet the visitors' bus, pick up our opposite number, and escort him to our room to get changed. I couldn't quite bring myself to do this. Once, after we had played Marlborough, a player whom I had been marking refused to shake hands with me, saying loudly, 'I would have enjoyed that game if you hadn't been cheating all the time.' He hadn't left the ground all day in the line-out because I had been jumping off his shoulder, so I felt this was something of a compliment. But what would we have said to each other if I had had to lend him a towel?

Oxford was a big step up from this in every way, but there was still dilettantism in the way things were done, not helped by the fact there was only one official game on the calendar: all the others were friendly matches. The Varsity Match against Cambridge is an anomaly in world rugby, a throwback to the glory days of gentlemen amateurs, when the two universities could field some of the best players in the British Isles. In the professional era it has become something of a sideshow. That said, it is a sideshow that packs 50,000 into Twickenham on a Tuesday afternoon in December, and attracts a television audience of a million people.

The players take the game seriously, but it is the sense of occasion that predominates. The Varsity Match is the last remaining bastion of rugby that bears some resemblance to the intentions of Dr Arnold, principal of Rugby School, and his fellow educators from the nineteenth century: an amateur ethos that is about training young men for life, where the rigour of competition is important, but winning is secondary to larger ideals. I had plenty of fun in my three years with the Oxford team, and made a number of lifelong friends, but the relaxed atmosphere away from the ruthless pursuit of excellence that I had known in New Zealand did not do my rugby any good. I emerged feeling I had gone backwards.

My first tour with Oxford took me to Japan and Hong Kong in 1992. Japan was, and still is, a relative minnow in the rugby world—it is currently sixteenth behind Romania and in front of Georgia on the IRB rankings—so I was astonished to find massive interest in a touring university side. The last of our three games was played against Japan's national Under 23 side in front of 40,000 people. (In Hong Kong, no one outside the expatriate community had seemed interested.)

Rugby's spread around the rest of the world is less obvious, but there are now 95 countries listed on the IRB world rankings. In Sri Lanka there is a 100-year-old tradition of rugby, and schoolboy games can attract crowds in their thousands. In 2005, 40,000 spectators saw the Madagascar Makis beat the South African amateur side at the national stadium in Antananarivo. In Georgia, 65,000 people watched their country play Russia in the 2006 European Nations Cup tournament. Japan has enough money to attract big-name players to its national competition, but poorer countries make do with the resources they have. The Georgians used to make scrum machines out of old Soviet tractors, while in Madagascar children in poor urban areas can be seen using scrunched-up plastic bottles as balls. Finland is ranked 95th of the 95 unions, but has bragging rights to the world's only annual Arctic rugby tournament.

10

Politics

Biarritz are the current French champions and one of the 'big three', along with Toulouse and Stade Français. The town of Biarritz is tiny—30,000 people—but it is part of the larger agglomeration of BAB (Bayonne, Anglet and Biarritz), which makes up the urban centre on the French side of the Basque country. Since 1998 Biarritz Olympique has been known as Biarritz Olympique Pays Basque—Biarritz Olympique Basque Country—which has caused some consternation in neighbouring Bayonne, where the feeling is that Biarritz are plastic Basques with a lot of money but not much soul. Towards the end of the season someone, probably a Bayonne supporter, steals the 'y' from the stadium sign, so it reads 'Biarritz Olympique Pa s Basque' (Biarritz Olympique *not* Basque).

The town is a former Viking settlement—the Scandinavians landed here in the ninth century and stayed to exploit the fisheries—and its name is said to be a corruption of the original Bjornihus (Bjorn's house) which became Biarnitz, and finally Biarritz. Not that this gives Bayonne anything to crow about as far as Basque names go: it used to be Bjorhamn, then Baionam, then ... well, you get the picture.

Biarritz have taken spectacularly well to professional rugby, largely thanks to the massive sponsorship of Serge Kampf, who may be French rugby's biggest spender through his massive IT and consulting company, Cap Gemini. Serge Blanco, the brilliant French fullback of the 1980s, has also been very helpful. Although head of the Ligue Nationale de Rugby, the administrative body for French professional club rugby, he is more than just a cheerleader for Biarritz Olympique, leading to occasional accusations of conflict of interest.

The result has been that Biarritz, who won the French championship only twice in the last century (in 1935 and 1939), have won it twice in the last five years—in 2002 and 2005—and are odds-on to do it again this year. They were semifinalists in the Heineken Cup in 2004 and 2005, and this year they made it to the final before going down 19–23 to Munster.

So once again we know this won't be easy. Our next game is in Paris, so that won't be any better—we are nearly halfway through the season and we have only 15 points. Happily we are not alone—Pau and Toulon are just behind us on 13 and 12 respectively, Narbonne and Bayonne just ahead on 17. All five teams are at home this weekend taking on the big boys: Pau v. Paris, Toulon v. Perpignan, Bayonne v. Castres. Narbonne have the easiest time of it with a game against

Agen. Depending on the outcome of the other games we could find ourself in a hole if we lose or out in front if we win.

We start by playing into the wind, and from the kick-off Biarritz dominate, using the wind to get into our territory and then looking to score quickly. Actually, it's a little too quickly: they seem to have their eye on the win and a bonus, but they rush and end up making uncharacteristic mistakes. Their knock-ons and kicks directly into touch mean we keep our head above water for a while. But only for a while. In the space of ten minutes their powerful little winger, Philippe Bidabé, scores two tries, Dimitri Yachvili converts one and pots a penalty as well, and it is 0–15, until Coco kicks a penalty for us.

A few minutes later, Mika gets yellow-carded for a high tackle on Biarritz's Argentinian centre, Federico Martin-Arramburu, but Yachvili misses the subsequent penalty and we hold them out, despite being a man down. At half-time it's 3–15, but they look as though they are cruising and will pick up speed in the second half to make sure they get their bonus. We have the wind but fail to make good use of it, and Yachvili makes it 3–18 with another penalty. This is almost exactly the same score that Perpignan led by before we stormed back to win, but I wouldn't be putting any money on that happening again.

Which goes to show what I know: with less than half an hour to go, our winger Lolo Arbo breaks and feeds our other winger, Seb Kuzbik, who barrels over. The try is converted: 10–18. Ten minutes later we kick another penalty, and at 13–18 everyone is thinking of the Perpignan game—can we do it again? With quarter of an hour to go, we have the momentum and Biarritz don't look much like champions. Ten minutes to go and Lolo is well set up by centre Alex Stoica in a two on one. It's now 18–18, with the kick to come. Coco pushes it wide but we still have plenty of time.

As the seconds tick down to the full-time siren, we are still in Biarritz's half. A scrum 40 metres out from their line will probably be the last play of the game. The referee blows for a penalty against us at the scrum. The Biarritz captain, Thomas Lievremont, grabs the ball, takes a quick tap penalty from next to where the ball was put in, and makes a few metres before being tackled by Mika Bert. This is exactly what he was hoping for in taking the penalty quickly: by panicking our defence into tackling him before he can make the requisite five metres (the opposing team has to be ten metres back from the mark where the offence was committed —should the penalty be taken quickly the opposition must allow the ball carrier to advance at least five metres) he gains another ten. The referee whistles for a new penalty near the halfway line, bringing it inside the range of his kicker. This time he gives the ball to Yachvili, as the siren sounds to finish the game.

It is a similar scenario to the Perpignan game, but the boot that will be kicking the ball has the wrong-coloured socks. Yachvili reacts well under pressure. He has played some of his best games for France when the heat was on, while he can look ordinary in less important games. This time he doesn't flinch: 18–21, and the Biarritz players are semi-apologetic as they shake hands, knowing they got away with a win from what was, by their standards, a very poor performance.

At the after-match function, a whisper goes around the Montpellier camp—more among officials and supporters than players—that a great injustice has been perpetrated. Strictly speaking, if Lievremont wanted to take a quick tap he should have taken it from behind his scrum, not from the middle where the ball was being put in. This may sound like nit-picking, but it's important because it would have given us an extra second to get back to an onside position, and we would have been less inclined to panic. So the referee, Christophe Berdos (one of two full-time professional French referees, along with Joël Jutge), should have taken Lievremont back to the mark, where he could play it quickly, or have waited until the scrum had properly broken up and played it on the original mark—that is, in the middle of where the scrum had been and where the offence occurred.

Without the extra ten metres, Yachvili would have been kicking for goal from about 60 metres—not impossible, but pretty unlikely. We would have had a morale-boosting draw and the two points that go with it, instead of a loss and only one bonus point.

Berdos was looking at the scrum and had his back to Lievremont, and it all happened very quickly, so I can understand the slip and I don't think there's any point in getting too steamed up about it. However, quite quickly there is a full-blown conspiracy theory going that we should have had the penalty from the scrum (and referees admit that they are often unsure about what happens in the scrum), that there was an incident just before the scrum where we should have had a penalty, and so on and so on. We wuz robbed.

The conspiracy theory gets juicy when you consider a couple of interesting facts. First, as already mentioned, Serge Blanco, president of the LNR, is a Biarritz man. Any pretence at neutrality was scotched when he was caught giving an energetic pep talk to the team at half-time in the European Cup semifinal against Stade Français in 2005. This was relayed to the television audience by a camera, of which Blanco didn't seem to be aware, in the corner of the changing-room.

Add a pinch of speculation: Berdos has never refereed the final of the French championship. The LNR have a good deal of influence over who referees the final of the French championship, and Berdos, a young man, is naturally ambitious for higher honours.

Finally, throw in a hint of conjecture: Berdos is said to have refereed a game between Toulouse and Biarritz eighteen months earlier that ended with a last-minute penalty for Toulouse, which meant Biarritz lost a game they would otherwise have won. (Actually, he didn't. Didier Mené refereed the game in question, but once the conspiracy juggernaut gets rolling facts get crushed under the wheels.)

Stir over the heat of a narrow home loss, and it's a rich, aromatic brew. However, of the other lowly ranked teams, only Narbonne won their game against Agen, which means we don't feel quite as bad as we might have otherwise.

Thierry Pérez sounds off in the press the next day, although he's clever enough to do so without adding in all the gossipy hearsay that swept across the after-match. I have the opportunity to talk to Nourault and him about the incident in Paris on the Monday after the game. The occasion is the annual *Nuit du Rugby*, a sophisticated bunfight put on by the LNR, Provale (the French union of professional rugby players) and Canal+ after a day of meetings between rugby's various groups. I am there with Lolo Arbo: we are Montpellier's two representatives on Provale.

I put it to Nourault and Pérez that they shouldn't be going public with their criticism: it can give rise to a kind of victim mentality, and legitimise the feeling players often have that the referee has made a mistake. If the club hierarchy starts doing it, you can quickly slide into a situation where players are thinking, 'That's not right,' rather than concentrating on whatever is coming next. Pérez and Nourault's argument is that if you allow bad decisions to occur without making some noise from time to time, referees may unconsciously go against you when a call is 50:50. And it is true that we are a small club and don't carry much weight; referees are more inclined to hear what internationals have to say, and this may not even be conscious.

The fact is, though, that referees have a tough job. Even with the advent of television replays, a decision about, say, whether a try should be awarded is not always obvious. And for a referee on the field, making a call in real-time, with vision often partially obscured, must be incredibly difficult. It's amazing they get it right as often as they do. In France, they do this in an environment that is almost always hostile: the slightest perceived error and the home crowd will give a referee hell. It is not unknown for a referee to be assaulted by irate spectators after a game.

A referee's job is not made any easier by the number of different interpretations open to him. Take a ruck situation where a player from the defending team has tackled the player with the ball, and is now on the wrong side of the ruck and slowing up the recycling for the team in possession. One of the attacking team arrives, and seeing the problem he rucks the man on the floor, and the ball is freed up. In a split second the referee has to make a number of judgments. Is the defending player making an effort to roll away? If not, he should be penalised. If he's lying all over the ball and the defending team have already been warned, a yellow card may even be justified.

On the other hand, is the attacking player simply trying to free up the ball? Or is he gratuitously jumping on his opponent, trying to hurt him? Again, depending how he sees the situation, the referee can let play continue, whistle for a penalty, or even reach for a yellow card.

Often the differences are quite subtle, and one referee will react in a completely different way to another. What is certain is that a referee's decisions have a big impact on the way a game is played. If a referee blows his whistle for the slightest misdemeanour, you may end up with a stop-start affair, which never goes beyond two phases before a penalty is awarded. But if he lets small misdemeanours go and the teams perceive a *laissez-faire* attitude they can exploit, an incident can quickly end up in a boil-over because one lot thinks the others are getting away with it, and decide to discourage them by taking matters into their own hands.

As if this weren't enough, both teams—coaches as well as players—are trying to put one over. From the minute a referee walks into a changing-room to check studs and discuss finer points of law with coach and captain, there are insincere smiles on all sides. Sometimes the chicanery starts even earlier, with press campaigns about how an opposing team cheats in certain situations, and how the referee will have to watch out for certain players, who habitually spend the afternoon offside.

A few years ago the recognition that scrums can be dangerous, and require specialist front-rowers to minimise the risk of serious injuries, led to a new law imposing simulated scrums if there are no front-row reserves left. This was well-intentioned, but open to abuse: if your team spent the afternoon in reverse in the scrum, you just needed a couple of props to go down and your problems were solved. You could bring on a back-row reserve in place of the 'injured' front-rowers, thus gaining an edge in mobility and ensuring you won your own ball in the scrum because there was no longer any competition allowed.

Predictably, this happened quite often. However, the referee had to apply the letter of the law, even if he suspected that teams were not acting in its spirit. And it was almost impossible to decide if someone was faking. Were a referee to tell a prop there was nothing wrong with him, and at the next scrum the player buckled and ended up with a serious spinal injury, the referee could be criminally liable. So this year the law has been changed. Now, if there are not enough specialists for the front row, scrums will still not be contested, but no replacement can be brought on in their place. Curiously, since the new law was put into practice the situation has not arisen.

A referee also has to literally watch where he steps. As he waits for a ball to come out of a ruck or maul he will often stand on the field's open side, on the advantage line between the defence and the attacking team. This means he can see what's happening in the battle for possession, judge the offside line, and be well-placed to get to the next phase. It is a logical position, but it can also be useful for the attacking team because the referee can be used as a screen, blocking the opposition's view of the ball-carrier as he runs into the defensive wall. If you run on an angle at the referee, the player who should be lining you up for the tackle will be partially unsighted as you come towards the contact area, and as the referee steps aside he can block you for a crucial split second, giving you an advantage.

In theory, it should be easy enough for the referee to stay well clear of the action, but if he momentarily checks the offside line, and is then confused by a number of dummy runners coming at him, or perhaps a scissors move—where the ball-carrier cuts with a support runner—he may not know quite where to put himself. And bear in mind that all this is happening very fast. If the ball or the ball-carrier touches him, the referee has to blow his whistle for a scrum to the team in possession, but if he interferes with the defence it's just bad luck. Hence, if a defender feels he is going to be at a disadvantage, he may be inclined to push the referee into the oncoming traffic, on the grounds that he is in the way, and the defender is simply trying to make his tackle. Not much fun for the ref.

Before getting to *La Nuit du Rugby*, Lolo and I have spent the afternoon with the other players' union delegates. I used to think of the union as a useful advocate in any run-ins with your club—for example, Daniel Herbert was represented by it during his legal battle—but in fact it is much more than that. Provale was the prime mover behind last year's *convention collective*, an agreement that guaranteed minimum wages for professional players: €2375 a month for players in the Top 14, with the minimum wage for second-division players fixed at half this rate, exactly the minimum wage for all workers in France; an eight-week break between competition in one season and the next (this doesn't include friendly games or training); six weeks' holiday a year; and at least one day off a week. It has also set up an agency to help retiring players get back into the working world through training and career orientation.

Provale has acquired a sufficiently important role in the French rugby landscape that the traditional clubs v. country wrangle is now a three-way Mexican stand-off—clubs v. country v. players' union. This complicates things, but it is good news for the players. At this meeting, for example, we talk about the possibility of playing games over the Christmas and New Year period, something that has been mooted by the clubs. Their argument is that the calendar is so full we can't lose weekends in the middle of the season without doubling up international games and club games on other weekends, or having to jam three games into ten days, playing Friday, Wednesday, then Sunday. But the players consider the Christmas break sacrosanct. Few live in the same town as their extended families, and it is the one time of the year where they can get together with their family and relax for a few days. Although we have a month's holiday in between seasons, this doesn't correspond with summer holidays for schools and most working families as we are back training by July 14. So, much to the disgust of the clubs, the Christmas break is voted non-negotiable by a large majority.

These kinds of decisions about the calendar may sound boring, but they have quite an impact on how the championship works. Every time an international game is played at the same time as a championship round, the big clubs, which have the highest concentration of international players, are disadvantaged, and the smaller clubs have more chance of pulling off an upset win.

Obviously, the smaller clubs like the idea of doubling up international games and club games (though they don't want to be seen promoting it) because it redresses the imbalance caused by differences in resources. The big clubs hate it because they feel they are being penalised for employing expensive international players. And the Fédération, representing the national side, wants to have the top players available for training and game preparation as much as possible. There is currently even more urgency in their demands because of France hosting the 2007 World Cup: a good performance at home will be a big lift for rugby.

Because the French system, like the English, is not centralised around a national body and side as it is in New Zealand, South Africa and Australia, there is always a certain amount of tension between club and country as the players are the subject of a tug-of-love, and 2007 looks like being particularly knotty. There hasn't yet been an instance of one of the big three clubs missing out on qualifying for the semifinals because they lost a game against one of the also-rans while their best players were on international duty, but if this happens screams of rage will echo round the rugby world, and steps will no doubt be taken.

At the players' meeting we also talk about a medical study taking place on the high number of games played in France, and whether they are dangerous for the long-term health of players. At what point can you be said to be playing too much rugby? Players regularly play more than 30 games in a season—internationals occasionally as many as 40—and with the ever-increasing intensity of the modern game this is worth thinking about: more games and less recovery may start to push players towards performance-enhancing drugs.

It is suggested that the union enforce a maximum number of matches for any one player over the course of a season, but this would be complicated to enforce: coming off the bench for ten minutes at the end of the game, for example, is obviously not as hard on the body as playing the full 80. And you could end up with the ludicrous situation of a player making the final with his team, only to discover that his quota of matches had run out and the union wouldn't allow him to play the most important game of his life.

Enforcing any kind of ruling is difficult: exceptions can always be made, and sometimes the player himself may want to play. At the start of this season, several clubs found that players who had been on tour with the French team were not allowed to play the first game of the championship under the rule laid down in the *convention collective* that requires eight weeks' break in competition from one season to the next. This was despite the fact they had legitimately played friendly games in the lead-up to the start of the season because they were non-official. And the players wanted to play—or at least said they did. (It is difficult to say no.)

Bourgoin followed the rules and didn't play their internationals and lost narrowly at Brive, while Biarritz, Toulouse, Perpignan and Narbonne all played men they weren't supposed to—arguing that they were obliged to because of injuries—and won. They were fined a few thousand euros, which for most of them amounted to being stoned with *profiteroles*. An exception was Narbonne, the poor cousin, who were proud to have Julien Candelon play for France but could ill-afford the resulting €10,000 fine. The players' union now hopes that any infringement of the *convention* will result in a sporting sanction—the loss of championship points—which will carry more weight.

The players' union also has the option of calling a strike. It has never come to that, but before the last game of the previous season there was muscle-flexing and the LNR backed down just a couple of hours before kick-off, when the union threatened a strike that could have been ruinous for everyone concerned: the last round of the season was being played simultaneously by all the clubs and was to be televised.

A strike would have had serious repercussions for the relationship between Canal+ and French rugby. In 1981 TF1, the private French terrestrial channel, was televising the final of the French Rugby League championship live when, after only four minutes, a massive brawl broke out and the referee called the game off, leaving an hour and a half of dead air to be filled. Legend has it that the sport was never again televised. This isn't true, but its reputation certainly suffered. Rugby has worked hard to build a positive media image, and to let down Canal+ would be to shoot itself in the foot. For the players, a strike remains the nuclear option—a kind of mutually assured media destruction. Strike action by professional sportsmen is not unknown, but seldom ends with a victory for the players.

For all the occasional disputes between the clubs, the players and the Fédération, the relationship is still a healthy one. Most of the key figures are former players themselves, and know how to settle their differences over a beer. I run into Serge Blanco, Franck Belot, the director of Provale and ex-captain of Toulouse, and Jacques Delmas, the coach of Biarritz, at about three in the morning in a Biarritz nightclub after our return game, and they are looking as though they get on all right.

For the Stade Français game in Paris I am still out with the ripped tendon, but I go up to watch. Stade Français have a fascinating past. In 1892, in the first-ever final of the French championship, they lost 3–4 to Racing, but the following year they won the championship, and they went on to win it eight times between 1893 and 1908. Then in 1927 they lost to Toulouse in the final, and the next 60 years were spent in the wilderness—until Max Guazzini took over the reins in 1992, amalgamating the by then third-division club with the nearby Club Athlétique des Sports Généraux (CASG) in 1995, and installing Bernard Laporte as head coach the same year.

In the next three seasons Stade Français won their division and gained entry to the next, and in 1998 they beat Perpignan in the final and were, once again, French champions, 90 years after their previous title. They won again in 2000, 2003 and 2004, and have twice made it to the final of the European Cup.

Bernard Laporte became the French coach in 1999, but retains close links to the club. He was followed as coach by George Coste, who was ousted during the season. The players then ran the show themselves for two months, and re-markably won the championship. Then came Australian John Connolly, who seemed to have problems adapting to the French mindset. Nick Mallett, the former South African coach, followed in 2003–2004 with more success, no doubt aided by an understanding of both the language and the national psyche, acquired when he played club rugby in France during the 1980s. Fabien Galthié, the former French captain, is the current coach.

The Parisians put out a side close to full strength, but have the luxury of leaving a few of their usual first-choice players on the bench. They shouldn't have too much trouble beating us, and their only real worry is scoring four tries to ensure they come away with the maximum five points. Within five minutes they have scored a converted try, and it looks like being a long, uncomfortable night for Montpellier. We hold our own for a while and even make a few holes in their defence—particularly from counterattacks—but we can't finish. After David Skrela has added a penalty, Jérôme Vallée cops a yellow card and Stade Français score again almost immediately. It is 0–17 and we've been playing only 25 minutes.

Montpellier were annihilated here last year 82–12, which was in some sense revenge for the 49–25 kicking we gave them when we played them at home. Let's hope we're not going down that road again. David Bortolussi kicks a penalty, so we go to the break with three points on the board.

Shortly after the restart they turn over possession to us in our half. We use it quickly on the short side, and Seb Logerot, our young utility back who is playing on the left wing, sets off on a darting run, turns his marker inside out and sprints all the way to the line. It is a peach of a try, and when Bortolussi converts it's 17–10. A couple of minutes later he kicks a penalty: 17–13.

The score against Perpignan was 17–3 at half-time before we turned it around. Surely that can't happen again? For a short while it looks, incredibly, as though it might, but then reality kicks in. Bubu gets a rather dubious yellow card, and in the ten minutes we are a man down Stade Français score twice, pocketing the bonus and putting the game out of reach.

With a little more than ten minutes to go, Jérôme boils over with frustration about another debatable call, and insults the referee to his face. Cue yellow card, which, because it is his second, becomes a red, and he is off for the rest of the game. Again Stade Français score twice, and wrap the game up 45–13. We spent just over 30 minutes of the game playing with 14 against 15, and during those 30 minutes they scored five of their six tries.

11

Food and Fire

First thing after the Christmas break we play our return match against Castres. I am injured again. If you are starting to worry about the fragile physique of the author, you're not alone. I hope you won't consider it giving the game away if I tell you that I do get to start a few more games during the season.

This time around I watch the game on television. By the time I switch it on, five minutes after kick-off, we are already seven points down. Uh-oh. Then Lolo Arbo burgles an interception: 7–7.

Our scrum starts to dominate in Meeuws' absence—even ex-All Black props get injured—and Coco kicks a couple of penalties: 7–13. Castres score again, but we are still in it at 14–13, driving a line-out into the in-goal, for what must surely be a try. But Dio, our hooker, seems to put the ball down on someone's foot, not grounding it properly, and then it spills forward, and the referee gives them the scrum.

Castres recover while we go to sleep for 20 minutes, letting three tries in and effectively losing the game.

When the half-time whistle blows it is 35–16, we are a man down after Jérôme Vallée has been yellow-carded, and any chance of a win has vanished. In the second half the game loses its structure, as often happens when the result is a foregone conclusion. Castres, having already scored four tries, have pocketed the bonus point for attack and are now just going through the motions. Another interception, this time from Seb Logerot, and then a well-constructed second try for Arbo mean that, with 20 minutes to go, we too can start to think of a bonus point. But a quarter of an hour from the end our tighthead prop, Antony Vigna, collects a red card for a wild swing of a punch that doesn't even connect but is right in front of the referee, and at 14 against 15 we just don't have the fire-power.

Antony is, in one sense, a prop of the old, old school. If Gorgodzilla looks like a grizzly bear, Antony is more like Big Ted, a roly-poly type who has made no concession to weight-training programs or dietician's directives over the course of his career. He is a good friend of mine, and his dedication to *foie gras*, cheese and extra helpings of all the good things French cuisine has to offer, combined with an enduring obsession with progressive rock from the 1970s and internet-based role-playing games, make him a particularly endearing character. Even if he is, by some distance, the least athletic person in the team (for which I am grateful, because otherwise I am the backmarker), he is a very effective player, who uses his bulk intelligently. All the shortcuts—or, as an old coach of mine used to say, 'the fat man's tracks'– are well-trodden paths to him, and the dark arts of the front row are an open book. However, he is not usually given to punching people without reason.

Antony's action is a sign of our collective frustration that we should have let slip a winnable game so badly that it became a 54–28 hiding, coupled with the fact that he got clattered high and from the side while standing quietly on the side of a ruck minding his own business. Still, we try to accentuate the positive. It was, after all, an away game against a good side, and 20 minutes of good rugby is better than none at all.

The home and away thing is, of course, not the only surprise for foreigners new to France and its rugby. One of the first things that struck me was the food. This, after all, is France, so food is important. For my first game at Racing Club we met four hours before kick-off to eat a three-course meal together, followed by coffee. I enjoy eating, was brought up to eat everything on the plate, and the food wasn't bad, so I tucked in and finished whatever was put in front of me. I may even have asked for seconds. It was only later, as we made our way out to the ground, that I realised that my digestion was never going to have time to cope with all that food between now and when we started the warm-up.

Adrenalin does funny things to the body, and I have played enough rugby that I need only walk into a changing-room, smell the liniment, and hear the sound of steel sprigs on concrete floors, and a Pavlovian response kicks me into so-called 'fight or flight' mode, even if I'm not playing.

Adrenalin shuts down your stomach and sends all the blood to your muscles and brain, which is ordinarily quite a useful thing, but not when you have just got through three courses with all the trimmings and coffee, and are starting to wonder whether you will shortly become reacquainted with the chicken and pasta you thought you'd seen the last of an hour ago.

I don't know how everyone else coped. Maybe they were used to it, or maybe they hadn't made such pigs of themselves as I had. In any case, my French wasn't up to discussing the problem and I had to start worrying about the game. My alimentary canal, though, wasn't going to be ignored, and as we started going through the drills there was a succession of perps, parps and hoots that would have put an oompah band to shame. Contrary to belief, the French enjoy toilet humour at least as much as the English, so if there was no sympathy I had at least made some of them laugh. By half-time everything had calmed down, but it was not a performance I would want repeated.

The other thing about pre-match food is that the menu is always the same. *Always.* That was my first taste of ham and *crudités*, followed by chicken and pasta, topped off with yoghurt or *fromage blanc*, and if I'd known it was going to be the same meal before every game for the next nine years I might have held off.

The quality of chicken and pasta varies, of course, depending on where you are. Italy is at the top of the table. Some parts of France are better than others—there is a little place just outside Castres where the chicken is always roasted with thyme and lemon juice—but the food is generally trustworthy.

England and Ireland, too, are all right. In fact, England was the one place where the infernal cycle of chicken and pasta was broken for me: once, in Gloucester in November 2002 (trust me, you remember these things), for some inexplicable reason we broke with tradition and had bacon and eggs as brunch before an early game.

Scotland and Wales, on the other hand, are infamous among French rugby players for being gastronomic hellholes. Admittedly, sampling has not been exhaustive, but the chicken always seems to be boiled an unearthly pink and borderline unidentifiable, and while pasta is not an easy dish to cock up, they seem to manage it.

'You are what you eat' is an old saw, and as professional sportsmen we are often reminded of the importance of diet. Most clubs have dieticians who intervene on a regular basis, and Montpellier is no exception. Over the years we have all heard the speech about complex carbohydrates, and branch amino acids, and fruit and vegetables, and no alcohol and certainly no tobacco. Everyone nods piously and asks a couple of token questions, but the reality is that the message falls on stony ground, in France anyway. In every club in which I have played at least a third of the squad are regular smokers and pretty much everyone boozes, although not to Anglo-Saxon proportions. Everyone eats pasta, even though, as All Black legend Colin Meads recently pointed out, if pasta is so good for rugby players, why aren't the Italians world champions?

Just recently our dietician tried to get across the message that, physiologically speaking, we should be eating big meals at lunch but lighter dinners. Laurent Arbo made the comment afterwards that this was a message that would be hard to get across, given the social importance of a good meal and everything that goes with it at the end of the day. As he said this, he was miming popping the cork on the evening bottle. So there is still work to be done.

Another thing for which France is justly famous, but perhaps less proud of, is its bureaucracy. The state seems to be everywhere, and for anything to be done all sorts of mind-numbing forms have to be signed in triplicate, and various pre-conditions satisfied. The trick is to get someone who knows how the system works—or, better still, the people who run the system, as I saw early on with Racing Club. My new coach, who had used a translator for contract negotiations, picked me up when I arrived, and predictably proved to speak excellent English. The '*je ne parle pas anglais* but if I have to I know a few words' line wasn't the only French cliché that went according to type. We dropped my gear at a hotel and then went to the offices of the Fédération de Rugby to start sorting out my licence. I was arriving in mid-season, after the cut-off date for signing new players, but he didn't seem fazed by this. Brandishing a box of chocolates for the secretary who would be looking after my dossier, he said, 'Here in France we know the rules, we understand the rules, but'—with a Gallic shrug—'we break the rules.'

Unfortunately, this kind of efficiency wasn't shared by

everyone at Racing and I spent the whole of my first year without a work permit—not because I couldn't get one, but because I had been reassured that I didn't need one.

Perpignan, my next club, was the same happy mix of annoying formalities and well-intentioned corruption. Shortly after getting a car from the club I picked up a parking ticket, and knowing by then how things worked I decided to mention this to one of the helpful club officials. He was embarrassed by my question (I suppose I was hinting that I wanted something done about it), not because I was implying that he might be able to help me with something dishonest, but because it seemed to him to be so self-evident that parking tickets should not be paid off but dealt with through the proper channels—that is, by someone who knew the right person to talk to. He was genuinely put out by the fact that, as he explained, he wasn't able to help because his usual contact had recently quit and the new guy was less helpful. The new man was from somewhere else, and didn't understand the way things worked.

In February, the week before our return game against Bourgoin, I have another close-up view of the bloodthirsty nature of French rugby players and decide not to get involved. Coming back from injury (still) I have to tog out with the Bs. The captain is our young hooker, David, who is 21 and a fiery little bastard hell-bent on proving himself. He's not a bad player, but today his tactical decision-making leaves a lot to be desired. I make a quick calculation and realise that I was playing for the Wanganui Under-14 rep side around the time he was born, and can't decide whether I find this amusing or terrifying.

I am playing alongside Drickus Hancke, the new lock recently arrived from South Africa and ex-captain of Eastern Province, who is also feeling frustrated. As we roll up to another line-out and David makes another debatable call, I hear Drickus mutter under his breath, 'That's right buddy, throw the dice.' I keep trying to make helpful suggestions based on the wisdom of my considerable age, but keep being told, '*Non, ce sont les consignes*' ('It's the game plan').

This does little to improve my mood. We are playing against the second team from Auch on a Sunday, and it's been a long week. Training with the *Espoirs* on Wednesday is a grim affair well out of town on a dodgy potholed pitch, and culminates in a game situation against *les Reichels* (the Under 21s). If the *Espoirs* are, as they are sometimes described, a swarm of Killer Bs when playing against the first team, the Under 21s are like a school of piranhas against the *Espoirs*: if you look at them individually they are not particularly intimidating, but as soon as you have the ball in your hands you have about six of them gnawing at your leg. And there seem to be about fifty on the pitch.

Anyway, this particular Sunday afternoon we are beating Auch (whose first team is in the second division) but there is nothing very impressive about the way we are doing it. We are under pressure in the scrum but nothing serious. We are comfortably clearing the ball, but David is unhappy because the props are boring on him and he makes the executive decision that I should *relever la prochaine mêlée* ('lift up the next scrum')—that is, drop my binding and reach through and punch one of their front-rowers.

I have done this a couple of times, but only on special occasions when we are really getting pasted. I am not about to do it in a Sunday afternoon B game that we will win at a canter, just because someone's pride is being dented. I don't want anyone to get hurt—least of all me, particularly as it would be well-deserved: no one takes kindly to getting popped in a scrum while they are defenceless, and there's a good chance that it would kick off a *bagarre générale*.

All-in brawls are much more fun to watch than to participate in. What I try to do in these situations is keep my back to our side and make sure I don't get outflanked by anyone. The sneaky prick who blindsides you tends to do much more damage than anyone fighting face-on, and my reach tends to make sure no one gets close enough from in front to land one. Wading valiantly into the fray like some latter-day knight in search of honour, glory and justice for all may seem like a good idea when the adrenalin is pumping and the blood starts singing in your ears, but really it's a mug's game. In the unlikely event that you connect with your target you will probably get a red card, but there's more chance of getting clubbed yourself, particularly if you're on your own—and you probably will be. The best you can reasonably hope for is to flail away for a bit, firing warning shots across people's bows, and taking a couple of light grazes that will show up well at the after-match to remind everyone that you don't mind getting stuck in. This strikes me as not much of a reward for a hell of an effort and considerable exposure to danger.

If you're really getting pummelled, grab the guy nearest you and pull his head as close to yours as possible, while holding on to him so he can't head-butt you, and snarl something suitably belligerent that will make him think twice without encouraging him to go berserk. (Suggestions of cuckoldry are best avoided in France, being the one insult guaranteed to goad the target into a blind rage.) That way he can't hit you, and his mates are unlikely to try because they may miss you and hit him, and with any luck it will all be over quickly.

Whatever you do, don't go down. Kicking people in the head is an absolute disgrace and contrary to all the unwritten rules, but you never know just how crazed some of the opposition may be. Sometimes your team-mates can be just as scary. I have a lasting memory of a *générale* in Perpignan, when we were playing against Bourgoin, and one or two faces on our side with big grins obviously revelling as boots went flying in, and Sebastian Chabal racing in to swallow-dive into the middle of the fracas.

While everyone probably prefers to play in games that don't descend into brawls, it is difficult not to be nostalgic about the brawls after the fact. Generally people are no more seriously hurt than they are while playing the game normally, and you can have a beer afterwards and talk up your own performance outrageously with your mates. Some people will think that sounds mad, but most people who have played rugby in France will understand.

Soon after I arrived in France I was genuinely moved by something that happened to me in what could have been a very ugly situation. Racing Club were playing in Montpellier in a cup game. I tackled a guy who was running straight at me across the chest with my shoulder—the sort of thing that had happened a lot in New Zealand and that I considered perfectly legal. However, I timed it particularly sweetly so his feet went flying out from under him and he spilled the ball forward and landed flat on his back with a satisfying grunt, and my tackle may have looked a bit high.

I fell next to him and was surprised to have one of our players jump on me almost immediately. I understood when I felt a hail of kicks thud into his body—he was covering my head with his torso because he had seen a horde of nutters descending on me. He must have taken five or six solid blows to the back, but he just got up and said, '*Ca va, mon ami*?' As I dusted myself off I saw it was our hooker, Carlos Martos. I haven't seen Carlos for nearly ten years now but I would happily buy him a beer any time he likes. Without getting too bleary-eyed, I find it beautiful that someone, particularly someone I didn't know well, would do something so selfless for me. (Footnote: The referee, after roundly remonstrating with everyone involved, penalised me.)

The return match against Bourgoin turns out to be one of our better games. My miserable outing with the *Espoirs* is not enough to get me back into the team, so again I am watching from the sidelines. Bourgoin score one beautifully worked try from a set piece, but they are without Benjamin Boyet, their linchpin at fly-half, and Papé seems below his best before going off, and by squeezing them in scrums and line-outs we prevent them building anything. With half an hour to go, it's still close at 23–20, but a converted try and a penalty allow us to pull away to a comfortable 33–20 win.

12

'Should I Ever Need You'

You can see the bell tower of Bayonne's Gothic cathedral from the middle of the rugby field. Historically, *l'esprit de clocher* meant that anyone who lived within earshot of the church bells was supposed to uphold the honour of that town in the traditional sport of *la soule*. *La soule* is one of rugby's ancestors, a game played between two villages on holy days and fêtes, and written evidence of it dates back to the twelfth century. Each side aimed to manhandle a ball made of leather or an animal's bladder into their own goal, be it a wall, a tree or a body of water. The exact origins of the game are murky, but there is a suggestion that it was linked to pagan fertility rituals: unlike rugby or football or most other modern sports where you go forward to attack the opposition's goal, in *soule* you wanted to take the symbol of the sun or the harvest or the child-bearing properties of their village back to yours.

That seems to have been the only rule. As to how you got the ball or bladder there, you could kick it, throw it, carry it, but of course the thing was to get hold of it. The sport was often bloody. With no rules to police, and no one to police them anyway, injuries were commonplace and deaths not unheard of. Once the game had been won, the recipient of the *soule*—probably an innkeeper or the local noble—was obliged to put on food and drinks for the victors as recognition of their valour on behalf of the village.

These bacchanalian festivities were not well-regarded by the *bourgeois élite* in place after the French Revolution. They preferred order and good sense from their workers, and over the course of the nineteenth century *la soule* was gradually stamped out. The spirit of the bell tower, though, lives on. A hardy few are even attempting to revive the ancient game, and in recent years matches have been played around France, although more in the spirit of organised fun than for village honour or the harvest gods.

Britain had similar games of 'folk football' through the Middle Ages, while in Italy Florence had the famous *calcio*, which, despite being a sport where you could handle the ball, has now lent its name to their football championship. In fact, ball games with goals were played all over Europe—and the world. The Chinese had *tsu chu*, and the pre-Columbian South Americans had *tlachtli*, although handling was not allowed in either game.

As far back as 800 B.C. the Greeks were playing *episkyros*, while Julius Caesar kept his troops fit playing *harpastum*. So the idea that William Webb Ellis was the first person to pick up a ball and run with it is romantic but misguided. There can be no doubt, however, that the modern game was refined in the English public schools and universities, where various forms of football were played. Rugby split from Association Football in 1863, and the Rugby Football Union was founded in 1871. The following year the game arrived in France via English merchants and sailors, and the first club, Le Havre Athletic, was set up by Britons in 1872. The same year saw the founding of the English Taylors Club in Paris— Brits again. Racing Club de France and the Stade Français were formed by French students in the 1880s and the two clubs competed in the first-ever final of the French Championship in 1892 (Racing 4, Stade Français 3). The referee was a certain Pierre de Coubertin of Olympic Games fame; he would also referee the first full French International against New Zealand in 1906.

It was under de Coubertin's aegis that rugby was played at the Paris Olympics in 1900. It was then played in three more Olympics and the reigning champions are the United States, who in 1924 in Paris beat the French 17–3 in the final. (Romania was the only other team entered in competition.) The game was a vicious affair, with players knocked out and sent off, and apparently two Frenchmen simply walked off at half-time, sickened by the violence. At the end of the match the crowd rioted, and some of the American spectators were set upon. The whole affair was considered not very Olympic-spirited, and rugby disappeared from the games.

Until 1899 the French championship had been open only to Paris clubs, but that year provincial teams were allowed to compete. Stade Bordelais beat the Parisians of Stade Français 5–3 in the final, and the power base of French rugby shifted south to what is still the rugby heartland. If you draw a line across the middle of France from La Rochelle in the west to Lyon in the east, of the thirty clubs in the professional divisions (Top 14 and Pro D2), only the two Paris clubs, Stade Français and Racing (now Racing Métro), are north of the line.

Rugby grew quickly in popularity, cemented by the French accession in 1910 to what then became the Five Nations. However, in 1931 France was suspended from the tournament following suspicions of professionalism, excessive violence on the field, and the introduction of rugby league, the amateur code's professional cousin. League drew spectators and players away, and the 15-a-side game slumped, until it was given an unlikely shot in the arm by Marshal Pétain during World War II. Certain rugby union officials close to the Vichy regime exercised their influence to eliminate the competitor by having *le jeu à treize* banned, its assets stripped and its grounds taken over, with players given the choice of playing union or nothing at all. Although rugby league was unbanned after the war, it never received compensation and has struggled ever since.

The English, though, can't afford to feel smug about French rugby's unsavoury connections. Just before the war, George Orwell wrote that 'a bomb under the west stand at Twickenham on international day would end fascism in England for a generation.'

Why did rugby take off in France when cricket, say, did

not? The other major nations of the rugby-playing world—the foundation members of the International Rugby Board—are all 'home' nations (Britain and Ireland) or former British colonies with similar values and a shared cultural heritage. The English public schools and universities where rugby was codified into a sport were a far cry from the popular enthusiasm of the *Midi*, where rugby was taken up *en masse*. In England the game had developed under men—such as Dr Arnold at Rugby School—who wanted to formalise elements of education that couldn't be learnt in the classroom. Strength, stamina, teamwork and physical courage were seen as important to a class of young men who were to make up the officer class of the British Army, and run the vast empire that Britain had acquired. The idea behind this 'muscular Christianity' was that military virtues were framed by discipline and respect for rules. In this context, rugby was considered character-building. Baron de Coubertin, when he encouraged Parisian students to take up the sport, was thinking along the same lines: he had been inspired by what he had seen during his numerous trips to England.

But in the South of France, the attraction was not so much the building of character as the expression of identity. The Olympic creed—'It's not the winning, it's the taking part'—reflects de Coubertin's idealistic view of sport as generating moral virtues simply through participation. Try telling that to a Frenchman playing in a derby game between Quillan and Limoux, Bayonne and Biarritz, Lourdes and Tarbes, or any one of dozens of small towns bristling with parochial pride, and full of old scores to settle with their neighbours or their big-city cousins. They would sweat blood—and didn't mind spilling a bit—to ensure victory. Rugby clubs around the world all treasure their pride in the jersey, but the deeply rooted nature of the French population in the south made it particularly fertile ground for a game that was a vehicle for expressing the better qualities of their menfolk in an inclusive, egalitarian group that drew upon the special skills of individual members. The combative, physical nature of the game lent itself to a reinforcement of bonds that were almost tribal.

A couple of weeks before the return game against Bayonne, I call Nourault and ask him if he will be wanting to take me. If not, I plan on having a weekend off. The game with the *Espoirs* did little to help me back into the team, and I tell him I don't plan to spend the rest of the season—in all probability the rest of my career—playing second-string rugby. He says the other locks are playing good rugby, and should he ever need me he'll let me know in advance.

The good news is that this means a weekend off. The bad news is the phrase, 'Should I ever need you...' I tell him I feel great, having been able to spend a couple of months doing weights on my legs, and that I am not so old I am ready for the knacker's yard. And I performed pretty well in a recent friendly game against Castres. 'Of course, of course,' he laughs ominously. Shit. I used to be pretty high up the food chain. In my first year, despite carrying various niggling injuries, I was rolled out every weekend, bar one when I was too sick to play. Last year, despite complications with my knee that demanded constant running repairs, I was assured of a starting spot. I hadn't realised how vertiginously steep the downhill slope would be.

It's no consolation, but I am not the only one feeling frustrated. Our Argentinian flanker Martin Durand is the one guy in our team of genuine international class. *Midi Olympique*, the French rugby newspaper, recently conducted a poll among international rugby writers as to who were the best players in the world, and Martin placed equal with Schalk Burger and Joe Rokocoko, and just ahead of Carlos Spencer. No one else in Montpellier comes close to rubbing shoulders with those kinds of names. Yet Martin has played only a handful of games and has spent more than his fair share of time in the *Espoirs*. His form has not been as good this year as it was last year, when he was quite extraordinary, and he has had problems with his back, but he has had a gutsful and is apparently applying for a transfer.

The return game is billed as a must-win affair for both sides. Although we have managed to build an eight-point cushion between us and Pau, in thirteenth position, we are still twelfth on 25 points. Bayonne are just ahead of us on 26. Logically, there is no reason we shouldn't win. We won here last year in similar circumstances, and if we were 30 points better than them in September surely things haven't changed that much?

Bayonne look jittery at the start, making several unforced errors, but we are unable to do anything right so after an initial period of 15 minutes, where both sides feel each other out, Bayonne slowly take control. Individually and collectively we are disastrous. The score of 16–0 at half-time becomes 44–0 with ten minutes to go, and we look like finishing the game without even firing a shot, until our reserve halfback, Harley Crane, comes off the bench to play flanker after our promising young back-rower, Louis Picamoles, goes down with a dicky knee. Crane takes a tap penalty, and runs through virtually unopposed to score from 30 yards out. Bayonne are just going through the motions now, and at the death Anthony Vigna bustles over for a score, Coco converts and the score is a slightly less humiliating but nonetheless highly embarrassing 44–14. Not having been involved myself, I won't pretend I lose any sleep over it. If you looked closely, you may even have seen the flicker of a smile when I heard the result.

It had been hoped that the return game against Bourgoin was a turning point but it now seems a distant memory. The home-and-away mentality explains some of the gap between the September and February results, but we are talking about a 60- or 70-point difference, and you can't attribute all of that to a change of venue and a bus ride.

Much of the blame for our sloppy performance is, therefore, laid at a convenient door. An article in *Midi Olympique*, published the day before the game, had said Montpellier were to get a new coach next season and this is said to have *destabilisé* the team.

The rumour mill about the coach has been in full swing for a while, and is probably good news. Nourault seems to have run out of ideas—or rather, he has spent the last few weeks casting around for new ideas, done the rounds of what might work without really giving it a chance, and, having reassured himself that he was right all along, has come back to the dead-end street we were going down in the first place.

Alain Hyardet's is the name most often mentioned as a replacement. Hyardet was successful with Béziers, although he then had a disaster at Montferrand, where he was sacked early in his second season because the squad was underperforming. By all accounts he wasn't solely to blame, but the spectacular success of his replacement, Olivier Saïsset, didn't do his reputation any good. The gist of the *Midi Olympique* article is that Hyardet will be coming to replace Nourault, and there will be several new signings across the board. This is what really starts tongues wagging—the mercenary is intensely conscious of the precariousness of his situation, and that anyone can be swept out by the arrival of a bright new broom who will inevitably want things done his way.

To try and calm everyone down, on the bus going to the game Nourault and Pérez talk to the team, saying nothing is finalised and you can't trust the press, but they are looking at signing new players, and coaches are being interviewed as Nourault will be taking a step back into a more managerial role. Predictably, this fails to calm anyone: it is effectively confirming what was said in the paper. There is a widespread feeling that the presence of smoke tends to indicate flames somewhere underneath, and everyone is wondering whether their arse is going to get burnt.

However, most of the guys are signed until at least the end of the next season, and there is widespread agreement that we need a new coach. So, why all the fuss? This sort of thing happens all the time in professional sport, where results are paramount; it is, after all, a business (of sorts) and the bottom line is that anyone underperforming gets chopped. Seeing the speculation in print, I suppose, brings it out of the realm of idle gossip and crystallises fears. It is one thing to stand around griping about the coach and the way we play—in fact, it's almost part of the job description—but you need to be careful what you wish for, because you might just get it.

The truth is that we are a conservative bunch. 'If it ain't broke, don't fix it' is the mindset. But the team itself rarely gets to decide when it is 'broke'. There is a natural loyalty to your fellow players that makes you view with suspicion the idea of new recruits. New 'in' means old 'out' and you might be one of the old. In my first year at Perpignan, when we were hoping to qualify for the Heineken Cup, I remember one of the players saying that we would be better off *not* qualifying, because qualification would mean that the club would have more money and, being ambitious, would sign up flash new players and we would end up being surplus to requirements. I was a key part of the team at the time and I thought this was rubbish, but he was right. We did qualify, as Perpignan have qualified every year since then, and four years later only two of that group are still playing for Perpignan.

13

Davids v. Goliaths

Our return game against Toulouse is played the same weekend that France play England, depriving Toulouse of their six French international players. There is a good deal of wailing and gnashing of teeth on the part of coach Guy Novès that the game is being played at all, but it has already been delayed once because of a clash with the Six Nations program, and there is simply no more room in the calendar unless we play on a weekday.

It is worth pointing out that Toulouse are missing merely their *current* internationals: in fact there are still twelve players in the starting line-up with international experience: nine for France, and one each for New Zealand, Ireland and Argentina. Not too shabby, then. At the same time, Toulouse have suffered over the past couple of months from what seems to be fatigue, with most of their squad on call for international duty of one sort or another, as well as the European Cup and French Championship. They have lost a couple of games they would have normally expected to win, particularly a shock home defeat against lowly Bayonne. So we think there may be the sniff of a chance.

The French king Henri IV was, apparently, rebuked by his confessor for his sexual liaisons outside his marriage to the queen. His response was to order that the priest should be given nothing to eat but partridge. *'Toujours perdrix'*— 'Partridge again'—was the lament of the man of god when confronted with the same rich feast night after night. I have eaten enough chicken and pasta to know what he was talking about: professional rugby has you playing so many games throughout a season and over the course of a career that playing top-class sport in front of a crowd of thousands becomes a humdrum affair.

However, the match against Toulouse is my first game back after four months out with the ripped tendon in my arm, and even though I am only on the bench I revel in the whole thing as though coming to it for the first time: the training session the night before in atrocious conditions, where we don't drop a ball through the 45 minutes; the comfortable intimacy of sharing a room with a team-mate; the slow build of adrenalin as we get closer to kick-off; the precision of the line-out drills in a nearby park the morning of the game; the uncanny silence of the bus ride to the stadium with everyone in their own thoughts; the feel of the ball in your hands and the smell of the grass underfoot during the warm-up; the first sharp thuds of contact with flesh and bone as the intensity of preparation increases; the rapid sentences, full of expletives, that are spoken earnestly by the group's leaders in the changing-room as the minutes tick away. In between, players' backs are slapped, bums tapped and encouragements murmured, small gestures of affection that would probably be inappropriate anywhere else but which I find strangely moving. Several guys tell me how pleased they are to see me back.

As always, we gather in a tight circle with our arms over each other's shoulders and look each other in the eye as a few final words are said, the referee's whistle blows and we file out, steel sprigs clicking on the concrete floor, towards the tunnel, and the noise and colour of the arena. As I take my seat on the reserve bench, 'Carmina Burana' is at full throttle on the loudspeaker system and the drums of the Toulouse fans are thudding a slow martial beat. I love every minute of it and the game hasn't even started yet. It makes me realise how much I have missed it, and how much I will miss it when I stop.

Believing you can beat Toulouse in Toulouse is a triumph of optimism over experience, particularly for a 'little' team like ours. The problem is that if you don't believe, if you go there simply out of obligation and think more along the lines of damage limitation, you will get slaughtered. They can put 50 points on you without even playing particularly well. I remember going to Toulouse with Perpignan the year we made it to the final of the European Cup. They put 40-odd points on us and we didn't even feel we had played badly. Last year the tally was 60 points, all done without even making it hurt. Unlike other teams that beat you up before sending the ball wide, so you have physical bruises to go with your psychological ones, they were able to score several tries from first phase without having a finger laid on the ball-carrier. The irony was that we scored four tries ourselves, largely through driving mauls from line-outs, and so came away with a bonus point for attack and considered it a good day at the office.

For most of the first half the two teams seem evenly matched. Toulouse break through a couple of times, but don't seem able to finish as easily as usual, and you can feel that their confidence is brittle. After half an hour they do score, but at the break they are only 5–0 up and we feel anything could happen. Perhaps they will finally cut loose, or perhaps the slight edge that we have in the scrums and line-outs will pay off.

In the ten minutes after half-time they kick a penalty and score an unconverted try, but we don't let go of the game as we have on other occasions. With 30 minutes to go I come on, and am so excited to finally be back playing that twice I go rushing up in defence with an over-eager, big swinging arm and bounce off tackles.

Eventually, I settle down and start enjoying the game. Our defensive line is swarming over them, and Rickus Lubbe, our South African centre, is having a great game containing Jauzion. I latch on to their number eight as he goes to ground, and get my hands on the ball, but am turned side on as their forwards arrive. My leg is jammed under him at an awkward angle and I get hammered as they try to clear me out. For a moment I think my knee has given way: a bolt of lightning shoots through my leg and the joint bends in a way nature never intended. But as I gingerly get up it seems to be still working and we get the penalty. Over the last 20 minutes we really turn up the heat, until a couple of uncharacteristically bad throw-ins in their half from Olivier Diomandé, who has come on as replacement hooker, put paid to any chance of a win. Still, in the last minute we finally scramble over the line from a tap penalty and need only the conversion to secure a bonus point. But Coco swings it wide, and we have to settle for 13–5.

Afterwards in the changing-room we are almost euphoric, and at the after-match function various Toulouse fans ask us to sign flags and jerseys and programmes, which, if scant reward for the evening's efforts, is a mark of respect and a welcome dose of flattery. I run into Slade McFarland, who has recently arrived as a replacement for the injured William Servat, and was on the bench for Toulouse. The last time I saw him was in 1991, when we were kids playing for the New Zealand Under 19s. He is talking to a sponsor, a man from EADS, the giant multinational behind Airbus, and one of several financial heavyweights that pour money into the rugby club that has the biggest budget in the world. (Ordinarily one or two English clubs may have been able to lay claim to this title, but the salary cap in place in the English championship, even though widely acknowledged as a farce, makes it impossible to get any idea of real figures.)

By this stage of the season there is a yawning gap between the big teams and the little teams. The clubs qualified for Europe, all with budgets over €7.5 million, have between 50 and 62 points and are jostling for position for the semifinals and next year's Heineken Cup qualifications. The minnows like us have only half as much. Along with Narbonne, we are on 25 points, just ahead of Pau on 21 in the red zone of 13th place, while Bayonne, largely thanks to their surprise win over Toulouse, have breathing space on 31. Toulon, the back-marker, are already coming to terms with the fact they will be back down to the second division next year: they have only 12 points. Between the two poles are Brive and Agen on 37 and 43 respectively.

The direct correlation between money and success is hard to miss, although luckily there are one or two anomalies that keep it interesting: Narbonne, who have the smallest budget, €5.8 million, and don't look to have much future in the élite of French rugby in the long term, keep pulling it off against the odds, while Montferrand, at second place on the money table with more than €10 million, are the serial under-performers of the competition.

'Professional sport' is in one sense an oxymoron. A funda-mental principle of any sporting contest is that it take place on a level playing-field, but when one side has two, or even three, times as much money as the other the odds are heavily weighted in their favour. The worst of it is that the circle is as virtuous for the 'haves' as it is vicious for the 'have-nots': the more money you have, the more likely you are to be suc-cessful, and your success will attract more money still. This can jeopardise interest in the competition: if the outcome of a game is predictable, why bother watching?

The hope of watching David sneak a victory against Goliath still has people coming to watch obvious mismatches, and the home-and-away thing adds a bit of spice in France, but the gap between big and little teams is growing into a gulf, and there is only limited interest in watching Goliath smashing David to a pulp again and again. Since I have been playing in France the first division has shrunk from 24 teams to 14 in an effort to ensure a quality spectacle for the punters, without whom there would be no sponsors, no money and no competition. But the best games are the relatively rare occasions where Goliath is up against Goliath (or, occasionally, David against David).

Rugby is particularly vulnerable to accusations of predictability in terms of results: the rules of the game have been engineered to produce numerous scoring opportunities, and thus high scores, so the better team have more scope to make sure the scoreboard reflects their superiority. The Rugby World Cup is a typical example. It may be difficult to predict the eventual winner, but you know it will be one of a small handful of top teams. In fact, you can fairly accurately predict the semifinalists simply by looking at the draw; with one or two exceptions, pool games are rarely as interesting as their equivalents in the FIFA World Cup.

This is problematic for the future of the sport, and there have been various suggestions as to how to fix it, at least at club level. The salary cap is one option, but the English example seems to show this is not worth the effort. The smaller clubs stick to it simply because they don't have any more money, while the big boys easily circumvent the problem by providing 'jobs' for their players with major sponsors, much the same as during the bad old days of shamateurism. In essence, Joe Blow signs a contract with his club for £50,000, and this is his salary as a club professional. The club is concerned that Joe might want a little more to be going on with, particularly since another club has offered him £60,000, so they have a word with their sponsor, Acme Cleaning Products, who find Joe a particularly well-remunerated position doing next to nothing for £30,000 a year. So Joe is on £80,000, but only £50,000 shows up on the club's books, allowing it to comply with the salary cap.

The same kind of system is already in place in France, where it is referred to as 'image rights': the sponsor may use your photo for marketing purposes, or you may have to attend a corporate bunfight to add a little sporting glamour to the otherwise dull proceedings. This has a double benefit to the club: it avoids the heavy taxes for employees, and ensures the money is not considered part of the *masse salariale*, which is not allowed to be more than 55 percent of a club's overall budget.

This means published figures for club's budgets are not entirely trustworthy. Biarritz, for example, reckon they have a budget of €8.5 million, just €2 million more than Montpellier. I guess it is possible to assemble the sort of all-star team that, like the Real Madrid of Beckham, Zidane and Ronaldo, is nicknamed The Galactics, on just €8.5 million and a love of the Basque country and its climate, but I have my doubts.

Another option is the draft principle along the lines of American football or basketball, where the bottom-placed clubs get first choice at the new talent. This is probably unworkable for several reasons. Players are not yet paid enough that you can oblige them to move from one part of France to another, and clubs would be discouraged from bringing up players through their *centres de formation*, training academies, if they run the risk of losing them at the end. (Currently clubs have to pay a fee to the feeder club if they sign a player out of a *centre de formation*.) And it is notoriously difficult to make the right choices about young players who are yet to be exposed to top-level competition.

One of the things that puzzles me about the people who have been indirectly paying me for the last nine years is why. Why do they do it? What is in it for the sponsors? In the unlikely event that I were ever to become rich enough to be sitting on the sort of money necessary to invest in professional sport, I could think of plenty of other things I would want to spend it on before distributing largesse to a bunch of hairy-arsed schoolboys running around in shorts. Still, there's no getting around the fact that more and more people are pouring money into the game, and they can't all be idiots.

In the spirit of investigative journalism I go along to one of the sponsors' monthly lunch parties in Montpellier, and find there are a number of different reasons, depending on the size of the business and the money it can put into the club. At the lower end of the scale are businesses that simply buy season tickets, which allow them to come to games and have access to after-match receptions. Montpellier suffers from having a stadium well past its use-by date so there are no corporate boxes, but the club has cunningly decided to spend a lot of money on excellent food and drink. If sponsors come for the rugby, they stay on late for the *foie gras* and other delicacies served by the Brasserie du Corum, washed down by unlimited quantities of wine and beer in a party atmosphere. Often the businesses are relatively small and the owners simply enjoy going to the rugby and having a knees-up afterwards, and they can take along a client or whomever they feel like and slip the season tickets into the communications budget, thereby making the whole thing tax-deductible.

Bigger outfits are happy enough with the rugby and the party, but they also come for the schmoozing. Rugby's egalitarian atmosphere means potential clients can be met in an informal setting and useful alliances made while discussing whether Montpellier should have kicked for goal, or taken the scrum, or the referee who has it in for us, or indeed anything from the vast panoply of rubbish that people talk about after a game. 'Jobs for the boys' is a common theme in business all around the world, but perhaps even more so in France, where cultivating *le piston*—the contact—is an art form. Here in Montpellier, the Agglomeration is the major sponsor, and they are also responsible for spending a massive envelope of taxpayers' money on roadworks and building projects, so rubbing shoulders with the people from the Agglomeration can be well worth your while if you can provide anything they might want to buy.

The really *big* sponsors—the ones who put hundreds of thousands, or even millions, of euros into the clubs every season—have a variety of reasons for spending on rugby. For *les mécènes*, the corporate philanthropists, it seems to be a hobby that doubles as a useful marketing ploy. Serge Kampf bankrolls Biarritz and the French Barbarians. Pierre Fabre at Castres, Max Guazzini at Stade Français and the Michelin family at Montferrand are all multimillionaires in their own right, and can afford to dabble in a sport that has high media exposure without being as expensive as football. They probably consider the emotional return on their monetary investment justification in itself. This is not to say they are simply rich dilettantes—I suspect you don't get to the top of the pile by splurging on a whim—but they are not particularly concerned to get a concrete return on their investment.

This is not the case for Orange, the France Telecom Group, which sponsors a number of rugby teams, as well as football teams, and must justify their spending. Working out how much the space on the front of a jersey is worth must be a hell of a job, and quantifying the returns on sponsors' money far from simple. There are people who are paid to note the amount of screen-time a particular sponsor's logo gets. How much attention viewers pay to a logo, consciously or unconsciously, while watching a game must be almost impossible to gauge, and what it is worth compared to an equivalent amount spent on conventional advertising is anybody's guess.

Then there are the *collectivités*—the towns or regions who spend taxpayers' money on professional sports teams because they consider sport a drawcard and see the team as standard-bearers for the town. In Montpellier the prime mover behind the massive taxpayer funding of the rugby club is the former mayor and current head of the Agglomeration and the Languedoc-Roussillon region, Georges Frêche. Something of a benevolent dictator, Frêche has said that the rugby he played as a young man taught him important values, and he wants to encourage the youth of Montpellier to learn the same thing. He clearly feels that the best way of promoting the game in the region is by implanting Montpellier in the élite of French rugby. Not only has the Agglomeration been paying the lion's share of the club's budget, it has also stumped up most of the €60 million for the construction of the new stadium. While this has obviously been of massive benefit to the club, allowing it to make giant strides over the last five years, having most of your money dependent on political goodwill is a precarious state of affairs. Frêche is coming to the end of his tenure, and there is no guarantee his successor will be as enamoured of the oval-ball game.

The danger of finding a black hole in the middle of your budget is very real in French rugby. Over the nine years I have been playing in the country, four clubs have been relegated for financial reasons, and every year there is talk of money trouble dogging one or more of the élite clubs. Toulon, Grenoble, Colomiers and Bègles-Bordeaux have all paid the price for miscalculating what was coming in and what was going out. When this happens it leaves the club in ruins. Players depart *en masse*, and new management comes in to pick up the pieces. The road back is not an easy one. This year, Toulon made it up to the first division after five years in the second division, only to discover that this time round they were too cautious with their money, and by not investing in the necessary talent they didn't have the fire-power to compete at the top level.

There is every chance that this will continue to be a common theme in the coming years. As the gulf between first and second divisions becomes unbridgeable, there will be a yo-yo system of clubs coming up, getting hammered for a year *à la* Toulon, then going straight back down. Lyon look like being the one club that might be able to put together the kind of long-term project necessary to survive in the top flight, largely because they are a major city and benefit from the kind of heavyweight financial backing that is unavailable to smaller clubs—unless a moneybags turns up and decides to throw money at it until the required results arrive. And even then, money on its own is no guarantee of success: it needs to be intelligently spent, which is not always as straightforward as it sounds.

14

Winter Blues

Every year, Montpellier seem to go through a lean period over the winter months from November to March, and this year has been no exception. But unlike other years where, if there has been cause for concern, it has never been more than superficial, this time the cracks run deep. The reason seems to be twofold. Unlike previous years, where we set ourselves the limited goal of avoiding relegation, this year we have set our sights higher—between sixth and eighth place—so the fact we are still languishing near the bottom in twelfth means that, by our own standards, we are underperforming. This, together with an influx of new players impatient with a structure that doesn't seem to be working, has led to a widespread questioning of the system in place.

Over the last couple of years, the move from second-division semi-professionals to first-division professionals has cut a swathe through the ranks of Montpellier's old guard. Of the squad of 33 who won the second-division championship, only ten are left. As semi-professionals, tied to Montpellier by links other than rugby and feeling implicated in the future of the club—and therefore less likely to rock the boat than the 'mercenaries' like me who have replaced them—they became victims of their own success. If Montpellier had stayed in second division, most of them would still be playing for the club.

Of the twenty-three who no longer play for the club, only four retired. Two became assistant coaches: the talented Catalan centre Pat Arlettaz, who runs the backs, and Didier Bes, the former hooker and captain, who resembles an amiable garden gnome on steroids, and is in charge of the forwards. Both play an important role, not only as coaches but also as surrogate group leaders.

The clear-out of old players has left a vacuum at the heart of the group, and although the captain, Jérôme Vallée, himself a survivor of the old team, is a good player and a good bloke he lacks the stature to pull everyone together. He seems to want a democracy-style chat-fest where every player has a say, but when the inevitable happens and everybody starts talking at once he blows up. This affects his own performance and he often reacts badly to pressure, trying to take on all the responsibilities of running the team—calling line-outs, making tactical decisions—when he is not the best qualified for the job. His status is not helped by the lingering suspicion that he was appointed captain because he is such a genuinely hard worker and nice guy he would be unlikely to question the authority of the coach. Recently, as the rumblings of discontent have grown louder, this has started to change and he has been forced into confrontation with Nourault.

During the course of a season, the leaders, and the underlying attitude of the group itself, may change for a variety of reasons. Leaders may be injured or dropped, lessening their legitimacy in the eyes of everyone else. New arrivals may assert themselves, forming a new hub of power as different individuals form alliances to make up new sub-groups. If this is starting to resemble a David Attenborough documentary on silverback gorillas, it is fair to say that there are a number of similarities—apart from the obvious physical ones. The group is a complex and interesting structure, relatively impenetrable to an outsider, that has no obvious hierarchy apart from the captain and the coach, and both these positions are unstable, particularly in clubs performing below par.

The single most important part of any squad is the coach. He answers to the club president, who hired him and will almost certainly eventually fire him, but while in place he calls the shots. He is responsible for recruiting players, training them, and picking the team to play on the day. A good coach should have good managerial skills; good communication skills—listening to what his players think, as well as telling them what to do; an ability to motivate different individuals in different ways; and be someone the players feel they can trust, and for whom they want to play well: ideally, a sort of father figure. He must know the game well enough to be able to analyse problem areas in the performance of individuals and the team, and be able to coach both specific and general skills. And he should have a vision for the team that he can impart to them. He needs to have an eye for talent and an ability to plan for the future, and he should be prepared to innovate. Given the demands that will be made on his time, the need for a good work ethic goes without saying. Running a professional outfit has become too much for any one man, so he must also know how to delegate.

The problem is that this is a hell of a lot to ask of anyone; there will always be a gap between the ideal and the reality. In my experience, French coaches suffer from a desire to run everything themselves. One of the problems of the professional generation is this tendency towards shrinking the traditionally generous spirit of rugby. The importance of the team used to be paramount, whereas now power-sharing is seen as a kind of weakness, or at the very least a loss of control. Coaches want to centralise decision-making because they know it's their head on the block, and understandably they prefer to make their own mistakes, rather than be fired for someone else's. This makes for a strange relationship between the coach and his players. Although he's in charge, everyone knows that he is the one more likely to pay for poor performance, simply because it is easier to fire one man than thirty. Hence the players retain a certain power over him.

It is difficult to say whether France is exceptional in this way, but the revolutionary culture is still alive and well in its rugby teams. Over nine years I have had four different coaches. One—former French coach Jacques Fouroux—was fired during the season. One—Saïsset—almost went while I was there but then went a short time afterwards, despite taking the team to a European Cup final and, the following year, to the final of the French championship; he was given notice the day after the final. And my current coach, Didier Nourault, looks increasingly unlikely to survive the growing clamour for his head. In every case, the impetus came from the players.

A relationship with the coach is tricky to handle. I try to have a close dialogue so I get regular feedback about how he sees my game, and I can tell him what I think about the training sessions and how the team is shaping up. Perhaps because I'm older—closer in age to the coach than to some of the younger players in the team—I look for the kind of relationship you might have with a colleague. As a rule, though, players tend to see the coach as a boss-teacher hybrid. This means the relationship quite often spills into a conflict situation, us against him.

What I see as my adult, open-dialogue style of doing things does leave me open to accusations of arse-kissing, and until I was recently disinherited I was known as being one of Nourault's three or four 'sons'. But at least you know where you are—or you think you do until things go pear-shaped, which they invariably do at some point. When this happens, I tend to fall back on the age-old tradition of spoilt children who stick out their bottom lip and pout: I stomp around in a black cloud of ill-humour until I get back in the team. Not pretty, I know, but it does seem to be effective. It's not the sort of thing you could get away with in England or New Zealand, where your lip is supposed to remain stoically firm come what may, but the French seem more ready to accept the temperamental shenanigans of their men.

The mercurial nature of the French means the psychological aspect of the team is extraordinarily important. I still find it astonishing that the same team can play so well one weekend and cravenly badly the following, for no apparent reason. Although it's the fault of individual players, the onus falls on the coach to come up with some form of social engineering that will lead the team to fulfil its potential. So every year we have team-building exercises. I have rock-climbed, abseiled, bungy-jumped, canoed, mountain-biked and done community work, all in the name of team-building. I count myself lucky. Other teams have been on military camps, overland treks and one year, at the end of a long day's march, the players from one team were given live chickens, a knife and a box of matches and told to sort dinner out for themselves.

The jury is out on how useful these things are. A couple of years ago Montferrand were taken on a gruelling week-long trek through the Massif Central, bivouacking wherever they could. Their coach, Alain Hyardet, said it was a great success and he now knew whom he could count on in the team as the difficult conditions had brought out the best in certain people. He was, he announced, going to construct his group around these guys, whom he saw as the real leaders.

This sounds like bollocks. If you were to give me a compass and map and send me off into the great outdoors with a handful of unfortunate team-mates under orders to follow me, I could virtually guarantee we would be hopelessly lost and shivering in a ditch with hypothermia within twenty-four hours. But why would this exclude me from a leadership role on a rugby field? All it would show is that I'm hopeless at hiking.

Anyway in February, as the team looks like it is starting to unravel, Nourault decides we need a bit of team-building. This is unusual because it is the sort of exercise usually done during pre-season training, but he is canny enough to know that he is losing his grip on proceedings, and his only hope is that the team will start to grow up and take more responsibility for itself. The plan is to divide us into five crews who will race catamarans on the Mediterranean (with the help, mercifully, of qualified skippers), interspersed with three hour-long sessions with a sports psychologist, and some fitness training.

None of this sounds unreasonable. We start off with a serious-minded regatta before lunch and everyone plays along, steering or grinding or whatever, according to their designated role, and we agree it is good fun, although it is bitterly cold on the water despite the winter sun. But the boys have figured out there isn't actually much to do—the skippers are capable of sailing the boats more or less on their own—so it is suggested a few drinks may keep out the cold when we go back on the water that evening. In the interval between dinner and the session with the shrink, stocks are laid in for the night.

The sports psychologist is a vast improvement on the previous year, when we had to suffer the New Age idiocy of some pony-tailed, leather-trousered charlatan and his mishmash of eastern religions, power crystals and coloured lights. This year the psychologist is a young woman and not unattractive. She goes over what is well-trodden ground for most of us—mental imagery, relaxation techniques, and so on.

Concentration levels are not high, and the hour sprawls into an hour and a half as her role devolves into one of crowd control over a bunch of catcalling kindergarten children. Afterwards we have an exhausting fitness session, then more psychology before dinner. By this point some of the lads are lying on the floor asleep, and the poor woman can't get her video to work, and she asks if anyone can show the team how to do the haka, which she considers the pinnacle of pre-match preparation. I am reluctant, but I can't help feeling sorry for her and am about to oblige when Harley Crane, a fellow Kiwi, points out that it wouldn't be right. Like all New Zealanders, we consider the haka special, sacred even, not the kind of fairground attraction that should be performed for a laugh, and certainly not something to be shared with Frenchies, who would tend to take the piss out of it.

After dinner we are back on the boats, supposedly to go racing until three or four in the morning, although the clanking of bottles in the overnight bags hint at what the team has designated as its real priority. The coach has arranged a midnight snack a few miles down the coast before we turn and head for home, but by the time we're halfway there all the boys are munted, having played drinking games, sung songs, and shouted insults at each other over the boat's radio. Fake 'man overboard' calls, cancellations of the 'race'—to which only the skippers are now paying any attention—national anthems, dirty jokes: everything comes washing over the radio.

When our skipper thinks he may have a problem—something is bumping against the hull of the €650,000 boat for which he is responsible—he tries to get in touch with the safety boat carrying the organisers so they can come and have a look. However, he is shouted down by a chorus of hoaxers. 'Jean-Pierre here. You seem to be being attacked by a ten-metre shark, WATCH OUT! FOR GOD'S SAKE, WATCH OUT! AAARRGGGHHH...' 'Okay, we're sending in the scuba team. Standby for Operation Rainbow Warrior. I repeat, standby for Operation Rainbow Warrior.'

Any attempt to suggest the situation is serious just leads to an increase in volume. When we arrive at the rendezvous point, the crews reel in and quickly start throwing food around. A couple of senior players mash cheese into each other's hair. Other players urinate into the marina. And watching over the whole thing with a sickly smile, because he doesn't know quite how to rein in the chaos he has unwittingly unleashed, is Nourault.

We would never have got this out of hand at the start of the year. Last year Nourault roared with fury when he saw Olivier Diomandé, our Muslim hooker, eating chips he had been given by the well-intentioned but not very nutrition-minded catering staff because he couldn't eat a side order of peas that had been sprinkled with bacon. The general feeling was that this sort of thing was a bit much, but everyone kept their heads down. However, Nourault's credibility has waned over the last few months, and rather than supporting him we have made an unspoken decision to cut him adrift. He can feel it, and knows he no longer has the authority to lay down the law. When we stagger into breakfast the next morning, he is genuinely solicitous: 'Everyone sleep all right? Not too tired?'

The final hour of psychology passes smoothly enough because everyone is too knackered to backchat. As we shamble off home, I can't help thinking the whole thing has been a complete waste of time, but the following weekend we play probably our best game of the season to date, so the management consider the expedition an unqualified success.

Perhaps they're right. If pushed, I would say that recreational team-drinking is a good thing: it provides the social lubricant that helps work relationships become friendships, and the better you get on with people the more likely you are to play well with them. There was also an element of group muscle-flexing that was no doubt beneficial. Fighting for your right to party is not exactly textbook mental preparation for professional athletes, but if you're all in it together maybe it doesn't matter what you do.

Each team forms its own sense of identity around a hard core of a few influential players, who tend to have formed tight bonds to the club itself over, if not a career, at least a few years. They are the temple guardians, experienced, charismatic players who set the tone for the approach to the season. Players who arrive from elsewhere try to fit in with the way things are done because it is the basis of the team's *esprit de corps*, and, although it might not be what you're used to, no one wants to look as though they're being difficult, and adapting is part of the life of the professional player.

Here in Montpellier, for example, the backs—known disconcertingly as 'The Sect'—have their own monthly meeting over dinner. Among other things they discuss the state of the team, and vote on their choice for 'zero of the month', generally a forward. It is supposed to be a secret affair, and the minutes are solemnly noted down. From time to time, some of the forwards try to find out where the meeting is so they can steal the minutes, or spray shaving foam on the backs' cars. If this sounds futile and childish, you have to remember that we are grown men being paid to run around in shorts after an inflated pigskin. Our whole existence reeks of childishness and futility. And this kind of thing has the merit of bringing players together in a relaxed atmosphere away from the eyes and ears of the coaching staff. And it is a tradition, which is important for such a young club.

New players, however, will subscribe to a system only as long as it seems to be working. There is too much at stake for the mercenary to sit back and go with the flow when the flow looks like it is leading up you up a certain creek without the proverbial paddle. The club has brought in experienced players who are highly conscious of the stain that a drop into the second division would represent on their curriculum vitae.

As the grumbling gets louder, people move from quibbling about the direction the ship should be taking to calling their agent and trying to make sure there is a place for them in a lifeboat somewhere. Once this happens, things can quickly go wrong. The mercenary has a limited stake in the future of a club; what is of paramount importance to him is that he looks good enough to get a decent contract next time the meat market opens. This sounds ugly and to some extent it is, but it comes to this only when a player feels he has exhausted all his options.

Initially, a player pours his guts into a new club. You want to believe it can work, and that you have value to add. But if by March things are shaping up badly, looking after number one becomes your first priority. Top-flight players with long-term contracts at successful clubs are less likely to find themselves in this position, but for the journeyman plying his trade in the clubs inhabiting the lower regions of the competition it can be an annual event.

The self-centred, short-term focus of the mercenary can exacerbate an already difficult situation. Whispering campaigns blaming captains, coaches, players—basically anyone in range—can lead to a vicious circle of resentment. It is late February as I write this, and I already suspect one or two of my team-mates of looking to the lifeboats, a bad sign. It doesn't really apply to me any more. Given that I am coming to the end of my contract, I won't be going anywhere and am pretty sure I will be retiring—although I change my mind about that weekly.

By now you may have a dark view of the hired rugby player, and it is true that I have not been painting a pretty picture. But I should point out that when I look around the changing-room I can't see a single player whom I think of as lacking in honour or courage, or any of the other noble qualities rugby demands of its players. Certainly the 'pride in the jersey' formula is a little hollow these days, when it is not unusual for a player to represent four or five different teams in the course of his professional career. But that does not mean the core values of self-sacrifice, shared responsibility and team spirit have been jettisoned: it now comes down to self-respect—pride in what you do and how you do it. Being able to look at yourself in the mirror is perhaps more of a guideline than having pride in your team's colours, simply because as a newcomer you can't possibly draw on all the history of a club within the first weeks or months of arriving. But as a rugby player you know about the spirit of rugby; even if you occasionally lose sight of things because you're worried about a potential dent in your pay cheque, you still know that the best way of getting something out of rugby—money, pride or whatever—is by putting into it everything you have.

For us, the important thing in these shaky times is that the group's leaders keep the faith and make sure we stay positive. For the two years I have been here these leaders have stayed largely the same: Olivier Diomandé, our hooker from the Ivory Coast, a tireless workhorse who has stayed loyal to the club despite interesting propositions from other clubs; Michel Macurdy, a lock who has occasionally been converted to number eight this season, and is probably our most intelligent reader of the game; Jérôme Vallée, who is growing into the captaincy; 'Bubu'—Sebastian Buada—our ballsy little half-back, an instinctive player rather than a tactician, who gives it everything; Alessandro Stoica, our Italian centre, always well kitted out in designer clothes, sunglasses and fast cars; and the very experienced winger Laurent Arbo, top try-scorer in the history of the French first division.

I am a backbencher, yapping when I feel like it, but deftly sidestepping anything that looks like having heavy responsibility attached: I was captain of Racing Club the year we went down and it was no fun at all. Coco Aucagne should also be in this list of leaders, given that he plays in the key fly-half position and is the only man in the team who has played for France. However, he is so modest he doesn't seem to want to put himself forward, which is a shame because he has much to offer, and we need someone capable of taking proceedings on the field by the scruff of the neck.

All these men have a place in the starting line-up as of right, something else that has been causing tensions. There are no real stars at Montpellier so no one is irreplaceable, and the large number of games that have to be played, plus the fact all 30-odd of the squad are at a similar level, would point towards a policy of rotating players. But too many guys feel they are not being given their chance. This sort of thing happens all the time, but if the team is winning you just shut up and take it. When it is underperforming and you're still not getting a chance, you get irascible.

Worse still, if you're really not playing at all, you have to go down and spend some time in the *Espoirs*. There are some very good young players in the *Espoirs*, mixed in with a few who will never make it to the first division, and the games can be of a reasonable standard. And at least you don't feel the constant pressure to perform.

But really it is a living death for established players—a taste of the anonymity and ordinariness to which you will return after your time in front of the crowd. It is difficult to play well because the team patterns and lines of running are very different to what you are used to. Even if you do play well, it is only what is expected of you. And if you play badly—because you haven't been able to motivate yourself to get involved in what is typically a scrappy affair in front of a couple of people who happen to be passing by, on a potholed, muddy field that looks as though it has been used to grow potatoes, and run by a referee who seems to have no more than a passing acquaintance with the rule book—then you look and feel like a fraud.

The one moment of the week when you can try to stake a claim on your rightful place in the first team comes during the contact sessions, when the As are pitted against the Bs—or, as the English-speaking members of the team call it, the Attack of the Killer Bs. This is when the first team are recovering from the weekend's game, and thinking about the coming weekend, and are really not interested in the rough-and-tumble of full-blooded opposition. After all, they have nothing to prove: they're already where they want to be.

The Killer Bs, on the other hand, have all the motivation in the world, and aren't about to let slip their chance. Even though I think of these sessions as ridiculous, unnecessary and of little use to the first team, if I am stuck in the Killer Bs I, like everyone else, fly into the session with as much determination as I would on a Saturday game, and the end result is that these little half-hour sessions are often won by the B team.

Tensions can run high during these sessions, and at the end of one I find myself, not entirely blamelessly, in a scuffle with Mika Bert, a lock who has been being groomed for the big time and now, aged 26, has broken through and is playing some excellent rugby. Regrettably, this means that he has taken up one of the spots that used to have my name on it, and as I had been doing some of the grooming I am a little put out by his bad manners. To make things right, we have to perform the little ritual of *le bisous de l'amitié*, two henpecks on the cheek. This is the flipside of a French habit that I usually enjoy as it permits you to kiss fragrant, attractive young French women whom you've only just met. Sweaty, unshaven second-rowers whom you've been handbagging a minute before are less agreeable, although the ritual does oblige you to be more sincere than the usual handshake and cursory nod.

15

Countdown

André Lestorte is no longer president of Pau, and I don't hold any grudges against the team itself, but by the time our return game against them comes around it looks as if the dreaded thirteenth place is reserved for either us or them, and I'd sooner it was them. There are still just a handful of points separating us—they are on 21, while we are on 25. It is now mid March, just ten weeks before the end of the season, and a loss would put us in a very uncomfortable position.

We dominate proceedings and score a couple of good tries, including a peach of an effort from our talented fullback, David Bortolussi, who runs in a chip-and-chase from inside our own half. Again, Beauxis is kicking goals from everywhere and he keeps them in touch, so we go to the break leading 20–12.

It is difficult not to think that the whole thing is running according to script and with luck we'll manage a bonus point for four tries. But all the hard work of the first spell is undone within ten minutes of the start of the second. A converted try and a penalty and we are staring the unthinkable in the face—Pau are beating us 22–20 at home with just half an hour to go. Knowing this game is do-or-die for both teams, busloads of their supporters have turned up, and the Montpellier crowd, never particularly vocal, is being swamped by chants of 'Sec-tion!' Clap-clap-clap. 'Sec-tion!' and Pau's green and white flags are waving furiously. We reserves—I am on the bench again—have been buggering about, thinking we don't have any worries, but suddenly everyone is tense, gnawing at fingernails, tut-tutting at the referee and swearing softly to each other. With just under half an hour to go, I am relieved to get on the field. Out in the middle you have less time to think about the consequences; you just slip into doing what you know.

Pau aren't creating anything, they are just living off our mistakes, so we tighten up the game and go back to rolling mauls, forcing a penalty, which Coco kicks, and then we drive over in the corner from a line-out, and from the restart we head up field again. Pau are panicking now, giving away silly penalties as they feel the game sliding away from them, and Christophe Laussucq, their halfback, cracks and punches our prop, Clément Baiocco. The referee doesn't see it but the touch judge does, and Coco puts the penalty over again: 31–22.

Now that their team is losing, Pau's backs, realising they have to take chances, start to operate with more menace. They run back a sloppy missed touch-finder from inside their half, and a well-timed grubber kick is gathered by Cassin, who scores. Beauxis converts. 31–29. Christ. Twenty minutes to go. At least the crowd are getting their money's worth. Play see-saws back and forth, each side kicking long and hoping the other will make a mistake.

Ten minutes to go. Seb Kuzbik, our big powerful winger, breaks down the left flank and scores, and Coco converts. That's the bonus point and surely the game. As Kuzbik was sliding in to touch down, one of Pau's defenders had come across and spitefully dropped his knees into his back, so the referee awards us a penalty on the halfway line. Once Coco has converted the try he slots this one as well: 41–29.

Pau are not finished yet, and after we take the kick-off Bubu sets himself up for a kick that will relieve the pressure. Patrick Tabacco, Pau's tall back-rower, leaps to charge it down. The ball bounces kindly into his arms and he is away, beating our cover defence to score his second try. Beauxis converts, and with the score at 41–36 we spend a nervous last couple of minutes down in their end before the final whistle releases us from purgatory. Pau come away with a bonus point but so do we, and with the four points for a win that should be enough.

A week later, I am again in the starting line-up for the return match against Brive. In fact, I'm starting to feel pretty good, and am thinking more and more seriously about playing another season. The day before the game I am interviewed in the local paper and asked if I am retiring. I leave the door ajar, replying that I am 95 percent certain this will be my last year. When you're enjoying playing rugby, winning games, having fun with your mates and the money is piling up nicely in the bank, you can't think of a better job. What's so good about the real world anyway?

Things start to go wrong pretty much as soon as these thoughts form. That night the neighbours decide to have a party, and one of the guests accompanies the Gipsy Kings on the bongos until three in the morning. It doesn't get much worse. I am a bit grumpy the next day, but after all it's the best job in the world, so let's get on with it. Then it does get worse: I hear a rumour that Samuel Chinarro, a Brive lock, is in contact with Montpellier about next year. As I am the only lock without a contract for next year, it's my spot he would be taking. Still, there's probably nothing in it. Idle chit-chat. Happens all the time. Agents trying to talk up the value of their player, that sort of thing. As I say, let's get on with it.

We start well, and I get the impression Brive are not very interested—they're in ninth position on 38 points, well out of the danger zone. Pau are still thirteenth on 24, while we're eleventh on 30. Agen, in eighth place, are on 48, ten points ahead of Brive, and then it's another four or five points to the European clubs—realistically, an unbridgeable gap. So Brive haven't much to play for. After four minutes it's 3–0 to us. Here we go...

Then we make a couple of mistakes and they kick a penalty to touch 15 metres out. No danger there though: we defend well, particularly at home. Famous last words: they get a clean take and the most ordinary-looking maul spins off—helped by my incompetence as I try to pull them apart but succeed only in splintering our defence—and Chinarro, the would-be Montpellier lock, plunges into the in-goal to score.

Sweet mercy, what have I done to deserve this? After ten minutes it's 7–3 to them. We really need to win this game because our last few matches are against heavyweights, apart from Toulon whom we play at home, and if we're not careful we will be scratching around in the basement again, despite having worked so hard to get out. We bounce back quickly with a penalty, and then Murphy Taele crashes it up in midfield after a scrum. I come in to clean out, and collect his boot in my face as he's wiggling around on the ground with his feet in the air, like a dying insect.

Bubu picks up the ball and darts 20 metres through their non-existent defence to touch down, but I don't see any of this because I am looking at the blood on my hand that seems to be coming out of my eye. Surely not. This is ridiculous. Oh well, at least we're winning now. I go off to have my injury looked at. It will need a stitch but isn't as bad as it might have been.

I get back on just after Coco kicks another penalty and we are starting to look reasonably comfortable. I find the rhythm easy, and after the initial panic I relax and start to enjoy it. Both teams are trying to play an open game and we are often a little too ambitious, attempting miracle passes that don't connect. Brive kick another two penalties, Coco drops a goal, and at half-time it's 19–13. We dominate without managing to score, and with 30 minutes to go I am hauled off. Shortly afterwards, Brive's young lock, Denys Drozdz, gets a yellow card and we strike almost immediately: a try for Seb Kuzbik. That wraps it up, 24–13, with neither side able to score in a strangely flat last 25 minutes.

The return match against Clermont-Ferrand, scheduled for the end of January, had to be put off because of flooding, and we finally play it at the end of March. The delay is a blessing: by this time the atmosphere in the team has changed considerably for the better. We have managed to string together a few wins, and a conscious effort has been made to bind the group together. A system of fines has been instituted for people who arrive late at training or team meetings, have their photograph in the paper, or allow their cellphone to ring in team meetings. If a ball is dropped during a team run, everyone does ten press-ups. And after home games the team gets together in the changing-room, has a few beers, and nominates contenders for the 'wig of the week' award. Anyone guilty of a cock-up has to wear a long blond wig at the after-match function and to and from training sessions during the week. If this seems contrived, it is nonetheless effective, and gives everyone the opportunity to have a laugh and let off some steam while atoning for various sins, real or imagined.

I come off the bench at half-time, when the score is 15–10 to us. Our backs played well and after only 15 minutes we were 15–0 up, but just before half-time the Springbok winger Breyton Paulse got a bit of room on the short side and sprinted 60 metres for a try that could destabilise everything we have painstakingly put together. Shortly after the break,

Laurent Arbo scores from broken play and all the steam goes out of Montferrand. Having hoped for a semifinal berth, they are now looking to hang on to sixth place to assure themselves of qualifying for the European Cup next year, so they have plenty to play for, but they seem to go to pieces.

Aurélien Rougerie, the French winger and their usual captain, is out injured so that may have something to do with it, but given their talent and experience—Argentinian, Italian and French internationals sprinkled through the team, along with former All Black flanker Sam Broomhall, Welsh Lion Stephen Jones at fly-half, Paulse on the wing and so on—it is little short of a disgrace. Admittedly, Canadian Jamie Cudmore gets an ill-deserved red card with 15 minutes to go, but by the end the only people who seem to be trying are Tony Marsh, the Kiwi who played in the French midfield for a few years up to 2003, and Jones, who is leaving at the end of the season to go back to Llanelli. That may be a little unfair on some of them—God knows I've slogged my guts out in losing teams often enough—but the end result is a stunning 42–13 landslide. We score five tries, the fourth one when we atomise their scrum (a man down without Cudmore) five metres out from the line on their put-in, thus collecting a bonus point.

I have a word with Tony Marsh afterwards, and ask him what is going on. He tells me it's the same story they've had at Montferrand for the last six years. Over that time they've changed the coach four times. The team never has time to settle into a pattern, and I suspect their policy of buying stars doesn't help, because all stars tend to think of themselves as individuals, and naturally want to keep the habits that have allowed them to become successful. The French have a culinary image for the idea that different elements may come together to form a successful whole: *Est-ce que la mayonnaise va prendre?* Montferrand's experience shows that even the best quality ingredients don't help if the chef doesn't know how to make mayonnaise, or doesn't have the time. I also talk to Jamie Cudmore, who tells me that life for Montferrand is, in fact, too easy. Everything is on a plate, nothing has to be fought for—there are no contact sessions with the Killer Bs, for example—and it is easy to get soft in such a cosy environment.

16

My Beautiful Career

After the Montferrand game, we have a weekend off while the semifinals of the European Cup are played. We take advantage of this to play the annual foreigners' cricket match organised by former Sydneysider Anthony Hill in Narbonne. Anthony is a year younger than I am but he wrecked his back last year playing for Montpellier and was forced into retirement. He now owns and runs a bar in Narbonne. Take one Australian former rugby player, give him unlimited access to beer, and a slipped disc that means he can't exercise, and nature inevitably takes its course: this former professional athlete now sports a silhouette to rival Homer Simpson. But he does have his uses, and cricket day is worth circling in your diary.

We are told to arrive at ten-thirty in the morning, but when we get there well after eleven people are still dribbling in. What French rugby journalists refer to as 'the Foreign Legion' looks more like a shambling mob of irregulars after a night on the booze. Some of the boys have managed to find one-day cricket outfits in the appropriate colours, and Dwayne Haare, who seemed quite keen on taking my head off last time I saw him, is wearing a wig to go with his beige slacks, and a mud-coloured shirt that is obviously a tribute to the Kiwi one-day teams of the 1980s and '90s.

Anthony manages to pry us away from the bar about one o'clock and we head out to convert a local rugby field into the hallowed turf of the Melbourne Cricket Ground or the Basin Reserve, or whatever you fancy. As there are more New Zealanders than any other nationality, it is decided the contest is New Zealand v. The Rest of the World. I am startled to find myself opening the batting, and even more startled when I remember how hard that little red cricket ball is, and see the speed at which South African Breyton Paulse is chucking the thing down. I had boosted my confidence with a few pre-match drinks, but I feel it slipping away as I realise that I forgot to put a box in and, aided by an unpredictable pitch, the ball is zipping around and my bat is not always where it ought to be. Mercifully, the ordeal is soon over and I can head back to the bar. The rest of the day is a blur. For the record, New Zealand won but it was close.

Our return match against Narbonne comes a couple of weeks later, and there is a little more riding on the outcome. Still, there doesn't seem to be much pressure. We are still in twelfth place but there is now an eight-point gap between us and Pau, while Brive, Bayonne and Narbonne are four points, two points and one point ahead respectively. We haven't won an away game yet, and this is probably our last chance. I am on the bench. The reserves have arranged a sweepstake for the first player to get on—€10 each in the pot, €70 for the winner—so there is more than usual enthusiasm about stretching and warming up in case Nourault looks over.

We start well, recovering our own kick-off, and before a minute is up Coco slots a drop goal and we are up 3–0. Then he misses a couple of penalties he would normally put over. He gets the next one though—6–0—and we are dominating them in the scrum to such an extent it should be the platform for a comfortable victory. Jason Hooper, who anchored the Kiwi batting line-up with the kind of raw but efficient agricultural style that you would expect from a prop, gets yellow-carded this time, and once again Coco does the honours.

It's now 9–0 and Narbonne are struggling. However, we seem to be going for miracle passes that don't quite go to hand and don't manage to develop an insurmountable lead. Cédric Rosalen, Narbonne's kicker, misses a penalty attempt and then makes up for it just before half-time, so as we go to the break they are still in touch.

In the second half, Narbonne get their act together quickly. A well-worked try by Lionel Mazars and another Rosalen penalty to go with the conversion mean that after quarter of an hour they have the lead and momentum: 9–3 has become 9–13. A minute later their fullback, Nicolas Nadau, attempts a drop goal from the halfway line. It's so far out it looks impossible, but the ball sails between the posts. 9–16.

By now I am bouncing around on the sideline like a jack-in-the-box, trying to catch Nourault's eye and get on to claim the €70. Saving the day would be nice as well. Montpellier finally react and start exerting a bit of pressure, but Coco misses another penalty. David Bortolussi goes off the bench to pick up the €70 and a few minutes later is handed the kicking duties. This time it goes over: 12–16. Five minutes later he does it again: 15–16.

Ten minutes to go and things are getting interesting. Neither side seems to have a knockout punch, but Rosalen kicks a penalty to make it that much farther for us to go: 15–19. Five minutes left and we have to score a try or kick two penalties to win. With a couple of minutes on the clock we are awarded a penalty about 20 yards out. If we go for the posts we will still be a point short, and they will kick-off deep to us and let the clock run down, so we elect to kick for touch and hope to drive over from a line-out about five metres out.

Unfortunately we cock it up and they clear to touch. There are still a few seconds to run and we have possession. We launch a final attack, lining up our giant Samoan prop Philemon Toleafoa in the hope that he will go rampaging through to the line. But the move is telegraphed and there are already four guys in orange and black ready to leap in front of the juggernaut. Phil can see them coming and is already trying to calculate the best angle to run. While he is doing this he takes his eye off the ball, and when it arrives he spills it. The final whistle blows. We get a bonus point, but again it could have—should have—been more.

After the game, I bail up Nourault and say I hope the reason he didn't use me was that he wanted to keep me fresh for the game against Toulon. He says they haven't yet decided who will play in that game, but Sam Nouchi will certainly be starting, and I will be starting in the game after that because it is against Perpignan. This means I will almost certainly not even be on the bench for the Toulon game. Before Perpignan, I won't have played for the best part of a month.

I try to bluff Nourault by saying that I don't want to look like a fool against my old club, and I'd rather not start if he doesn't give me a chance against Toulon. Some hope. He calls my bluff: I don't play against Toulon, and when Perpignan rolls around I'm warming the bench again. Worse still, the two games after that are Agen and Biarritz, and Sam used to play for both these clubs.

After my injury in Toulon, the club recruited Drickus Hancke from South Africa and he has proved to be an excellent player, younger and more dynamic than me and a good workhorse. He is now first choice for the five jersey, so Sam and I scrap over who gets to sit on the bench. Drickus is a good guy and we have become great friends, so I can't resent him his success. He has adapted well to the team, something Alex Codling never managed because he spent too much time making comparisons between his experiences in British rugby and the way things are done in France: inevitably these comparisons were unfavourable to Montpellier. To give Alex his due, he wasn't necessarily wrong, and his bad back injury wouldn't have helped his mood, but he was so negative the other players cut him adrift, rather than helping him integrate. This weighed on him as well, and he ended up in a difficult position.

Current club gossip revolves around who is doing what next year. As things have been better for a while and we look relatively safe from relegation, most of the team look like staying, although a few have been entertaining offers from other clubs. Clement and Dio have received serious offers from Harlequins in London, and would like to go. The hitch is that they are still under contract. Even though Dean Richards, the Harlequins' director, is prepared to pay out the contracts, Thierry wants to hold on to the players and won't let them go for anything. Fair enough—he is acting in what he thinks are the best interests of the club. Still, it's a shame for both of them. Dio, now 32, probably won't get another chance to move and it is a great opportunity for him. Clement is young enough, but he has recently broken up with his girlfriend, who works at the rugby club, so they still run into each other regularly and he could do with a change of scenery. He is one of those sturdy, uncomplaining soldiers you can see standing dutifully at the front of any battle line, and it would be good to see him get a break.

Toulon, when they arrive, are awful. They are missing a number of their more experienced players, have just changed coaches, and are dead last by a distance. They have nothing to play for, and away from their home turf they just aren't interested. Their line-out is shoddy, their scrum is in reverse, and to some extent it is a credit to them that they manage to hold out for 20 minutes before we cross their line, although David Bortolussi has already slotted a couple of penalties. When we do cross, however, the floodgates open, and it's 27–0 at half-time, before turning into a full-scale rout in the second half. We do well to keep our shape sufficiently to pile on the points, and the final score, 65–0, reflects the gulf between the two teams.

Just to keep things interesting, though, Pau beat Perpignan. After their victory in Toulon the week before, this puts them on 34 points, still in thirteenth place. We are in eleventh place on 40, with Bayonne on 37.

What makes the final straight particularly tasty is that we now go to Perpignan, play Agen at home (Agen are on fire at the moment, having beaten Castres in Castres the week before, and look like qualifying for the European Cup, so they will have everything to play for), then Biarritz, and finish with a home game against Stade Français. Three probable semifinalists, and one European contender: we should win at least one of these games, but we may not win any. If this happens and Pau win two, they will be ahead of us. Bloody Pau—they've had their heads under water so long you would have thought they'd have the decency to be dead by now, but I'm beginning to wonder whether they might do Glenn Close's bunny-boiler trick in *Fatal Attraction* and come screaming out of the bath with a knife.

The brighter news is that the win against Toulon has resulted in a cash bonus. After the game against Bourgoin, Thierry Pérez calculated that 19 more points should mean we were safe, and put up €100,000 for the players to divide among ourselves should we score 19 points over the coming six matches, which we have now done. It is ironic that we're not yet safe, but obviously Thierry can't go back on his word, so all we have to do now is work out how to divvy up a hundred grand. I suggest we establish a tradition whereby we give it all to the guys who are retiring (that is, me) as a golden handshake. Unfortunately, everyone seems to think that I'm joking.

I have had a hell of a time deciding whether I want to keep playing. At some point it was suggested that, given the club's key role in the process, I ask them whether they are at least interested in offering me a contract for another year. When I approached Nourault—who has jockeyed his way back into a good position for next season and will probably end up coaching again—his response was on the cool side of luke-warm. I gathered it was not likely to get any hotter. A well-mannered guest knows when to leave and so I will make my exit with dignity, at about the exact moment that the door gets slammed in my face.

17

Going the Distance

We go to Perpignan for our return match at the end of April, when the championship is getting close to delivering its verdict. Perpignan are almost certain to play the semis, while we are still holding out in eleventh place but feeling the heat. We have little hope of winning, but a bonus point at this stage would be very useful.

I'm on the bench, and now we're here I'm not terribly unhappy about it. It will be a hard game, and aged thirty-four there is no use kidding myself: I haven't played enough rugby over the last few weeks to be competitive against a top side for more than half a game.

Nourault's pre-match speech annoys me. He talks about it being a 'must-win game', which we all know it's not; next week against Agen at home will be a genuine must-win. You can only say you're playing must-win games and then go and lose them a certain number of times before the concept becomes meaningless. He follows this by saying, '*On a rien à leur envier*—essentially 'They are no better than we are'—which just shows a lack of humility as Perpignan are placed third on 69, while we are eleventh on 40. Of course they're better than we are. There must be something more constructive to say. Why can't we talk tactics, or at least have something genuinely motivational? The players are rolling their eyes at each other, and not for the first time I decide that Nourault has run out of steam.

As is often the case, Pat Arlettaz speaks after him and finds the right tone. He used to play for Perpignan himself and knows what a cauldron we are about to be thrown into. He talks about the pride and the culture, and the influence that the Catalan crowd seem to have on the game, and points out that this is simply background noise—the quality of a team's spirit comes from the inside, and we have our own strengths we can rely on.

It is a funny feeling going into a stadium where I have been so many times before and then not turning left to go into the home changing-room, but turning right and walking down the corridor to the visitors'. It is not the first time I've been back: the year after I left we played well and lost narrowly. Despite being booed when I held up play for a couple of minutes because I couldn't get a contact lens back in, I received an ovation from the crowd at the end of the game. I got a little misty about it: it's good to feel appreciated.

Although Perpignan supporters are famously one-eyed, they don't follow their team blindly. If they feel the players are not giving it their all, they will let them know, and are not afraid to boo them if they think the occasion calls for it. I once returned after a 40-odd point away loss against Stade Français to find a note on my car: 'Shame on you all! What must the Catalans who live in Paris have thought?'

As we check out the pitch beforehand I run into a few Perpignan players I know. It's good to see them. To be honest, I can't help feeling jealous. I know they will be thinking to themselves, 'This might be sticky for a while, but we will win.' At least, that's what I used to do when I was there. This may sound complacent, but it's not: it's just the confidence in your own abilities and those of your team-mates that comes from success. At Montpellier we have done some good things, but we have been conscious of the sword of Damocles hanging over our heads, and knowing the least slip can lead to disaster is stressful and prevents you getting into a rhythm.

When I came to Perpignan after playing for Racing, I felt as though I had started going out with a celebrity. Intrinsically you are the same person, but overnight you are transformed from a nonentity into someone of interest because everyone is watching. I have played in front of bigger crowds than the 14,000 who pack themselves into Stade Aimé Giral, but they have never made the hairs stand up on the back of my neck the way the roar of the crowd does when you come out of the tunnel here. After experiencing the unbelievably enthusiastic support of the Catalans, Montpellier felt a bit of a comedown.

The game starts in extraordinary fashion when Laurent Arbo burgles an intercept and scores before a minute is up on the clock. Nearly a quarter of an hour passes before Perpignan reply with a try from Manas: 5–5. The tit-for-tat session continues. Julien Laharrague drops a goal for them, Régis Lespinas drops one for us; Guillaume Bortolaso scores for them and Mathieu Bourret converts; Seb Kuzbik scores for us and David Aucagne converts. Unfortunately, the symmetry is broken when Laharrague scores a try and Bourret converts with ten minutes to go—we don't 'tat' their 'tit' and at half-time we are down 15–22.

In the first quarter of an hour of the second half they put the result out of our reach, having no doubt been reminded, during the team talk at the break, of what had happened in Montpellier. (What we thought of as our glorious comeback, they perceived as their collapse.) Their young kicker Mathieu Bourret slots a penalty, Nicolas Mas scores a try, then Greg Le Corvec scores another, which Bourret converts, and suddenly it's 15–37 and could easily hit 50.

With just over 20 minutes to go I come off the bench, at the same time as Perpignan's former All Black Scott 'Razor' Robertson. I hurtle around trying to be useful. After a few minutes I run into Razor in a ruck and he says, 'Jesus, you've got another three years in you,' which we both know is a lie, but it's nice to hear from an All Black and my ego needs massaging today. A few minutes later Perpignan push us off our own ball at the scrum, and run a simple move on the short side for Jean-Philippe Grandclaude to score: 15–42.

They have now scored six tries; their five-point haul for the victory, plus attacking bonus, is assured, and they take their foot slightly off the throat. We react well. We have quite a lot of ball now but are having trouble breaking through their defensive lines, so Coco puts a clever little kick in behind them and Seb Logerot scores in the corner. That makes it three tries for us, and with quarter of an hour to go there is a real possibility we may pocket the attacking bonus ourselves if we can score again.

But if Perpignan are not that bothered about increasing their tally, they are proud enough not to want us to score. Their defence allows itself the luxury of giving penalties away: they know we want the try and three points is no use to us. So we go to line-outs deep in their 22 again and again, and every time they step across into the gap and disrupt our jumpers, making it impossible to get the clean ball we need to set up a maul. It's very frustrating, but I have to admit that it is cleverly done: they manage to get their jumpers up at the same time so it looks reasonably legitimate, and the referee lets them get away with it.

We should probably belt them to discourage the practice, but you need to feel very punchy to start laying about you at Aimé Giral. And besides, we are convinced that we can score a try if we just get one clean ball. But it's too scrappy, there's no platform, and they are killing even our ruck ball.

At one point Colin Gaston, who has been a pain in the arse all afternoon, leaves his long legs poking through to our side as he lies under a pile-up, and kicks the ball just as Seb Galtier goes to pick it up. The referee whistles for a knock-on against us. Seb jumps on Gaston's legs in frustration, the two packs square up, and for a moment it looks as though a brawl is finally going to kick off, but no one is willing to put the flame to the tinderbox. In the end they hold out (or we miss out, depending on your point of view), so we are left hoping we won't end up ruing another lost opportunity to garner a point.

After the game I am looking forward to catching up with the Perpignan players, but I find that Montpellier are eating apart, consigned to the club-rooms of the *école de rugby*, just behind the main stand. Perpignan is the only club in the first division where this happens. It is a shame. As Serge Simon, a former French prop who is now president of the players' union, once said of rugby: '*C'est un jeu ou on peut se mettre des marrons et puis aller boire des bières ensemble après*'—'It's a game where we can slap each other around and then go and have a beer together afterwards.' These days, given the high stakes of professionalism, it is less easy to wind down than it used to be, and relations between opposing teams are also less convivial. Even so, most players know each other by name and there is a mutual respect that develops; getting to know opposing players after a game is part of the camaraderie.

The argument against it is, of course, economic. The Perpignan players need to eat in the same room as the club's sponsors so that the people who put the money into the club get some face-to-face contact time with the people they are effectively paying. The more sponsors the club can get into the room the better, and opposition players would just take up space where there would otherwise be paying customers. In certain circumstances it is worthwhile cramming the other team in. In Perpignan, Biarritz, for example, eat with the sponsors, because Biarritz have plenty of famous international players, and the sponsors get to rub shoulders with the stars. Lowly Montpellier have no shoulders worth rubbing, so we get shunted off backstage like the hired help—which, in a sense, we are.

The home game against Agen is crucial. We are now so close to the end of the season that we will have little chance to redeem ourselves if we make a mistake and the other teams take their opportunities. The relegation battle has become three-sided: Bayonne are behind us on 37, and Pau behind them on 34. We appear to be in the most comfortable position on 40 points, but after Agen we play away to Biarritz and then at home to Stade Français.

Both teams will be peaking, as we play them the week before they play crucial matches. A coincidence of the calendar means that while we are playing Agen, Pau are playing Biarritz at home, while Bayonne host Stade Français. Biarritz play the final of the European Cup in two weeks' time, so they are resting some key players, while a few others are on the bench. They don't need the points as they have already qualified for the semifinals. There is also a suggestion that they wouldn't be unhappy to see Pau stay up ahead of Bayonne; geographically speaking, Biarritz and Bayonne are virtually the same town, but when it comes to rugby they have a not very friendly rivalry.

Fortunately for Bayonne, Stade Français have also decided to rest a few players, which evens things up, but again, could make things uncomfortable for us: both Pau and Bayonne are unlikely to win their next round games, which are away, but the last round will see them at home against Castres and Montferrand respectively, and they may well win. Luckily, Agen have also decided to send out a mixed bag. A good performance should see us win, and that would put us out of danger.

I am slated to be on the bench, which suits me well enough. This season is the first when I have spent so much time as a reserve, and if it was initially hard to swallow I am now used to it and looking forward to the game. However, as we arrive at training I do a head count and realise there are too many players. There should be 24 of us, but I make it 25. Montpellier always carries two additional, non-playing reserves, invariably a front-rower and a utility back, in case someone breaks down at the last minute. I used to think this was unnecessary, but it is surprising the number of times they are used. Jérôme Vallée has been out with an injury for some time, but he is hoping to play. Jharay Russell and Seb Galtier are there as well, which is one more back-row reserve than we need, but if Nourault thinks he is taking a risk by starting Jérôme, perhaps he will cover two back-row slots and use Michel, who is playing number 8, as the lock reserve. This will mean I get the flick.

As we are warming up, Nourault calls me over. He starts in by saying that he has decided to play Jérôme, but I know what's coming next, and walk away before he has time to finish explaining. I could probably have handled this if Jérôme were at peak form, or there was another reason that I felt justified his selection, but we have been doing all right recently without him, he hasn't played for weeks, is carrying a back injury, and there are other guys capable of assuming his role. And provided we win this will be the last important match of the season—and of my career. The last two will just be runarounds. Fuck it. That, gentle reader, is professional rugby for you.

After this little drama, and high stakes in the build-up, the game itself is an anticlimax. We are wound up for a battle royal, but most of Agen's heavy artillery are at home or warming the reserve bench. Philemon bowls over a few players for a brace of tries in the first few minutes, David Bortolussi converts both and then adds a penalty on the quarter-hour mark, and Alex Stoica scores a couple of minutes later. With the game not yet half an hour old, Lolo Arbo scores to make it four tries, Bortolussi converts, it's 29–0 and the season is effectively over. They won't come back from this, and we have a five-point victory.

Just to make sure, Antony Vigna also scores, and Bortolussi converts again. At half-time it is 36–0, and Agen still haven't fired a shot. After making a few changes in the second half, they score three tries, but by then it's too late, and we round it off with a converted penalty try to make the score 44–19. Both Pau and Bayonne win as well, so mathematically we can't be sure we are saved, but Pau are playing Stade Français in Paris next weekend and they have no chance of winning there, especially after the Parisians lost in Bayonne.

Biarritz lies about 600 kilometres from Montpellier in the Basque country on the Atlantic coast. The long bus ride takes it out of us and claims one victim: Martin Durand has a niggle in his back flare up after more than six hours of travel, and by the time we arrive he is unable to play. I don't feel too flash myself, having acquired something resembling a groin strain after getting up from my usual position on the floor of the bus. (Trying to squeeze my two-metre frame into a bus seat is like squaring the circle, and I prefer to stretch out in the corridor, even though it means I collect an occasional shoe in the face.) Hell, if I can't even take a bus ride without injuring myself, it really is time to hang up my boots. Happily, it warms up all right at training and shouldn't bother me the next day.

Meanwhile, though, I am rooming with Antony Vigna, which is something of a disaster. Nearly all rugby players snore—most have broken noses—but Antony is a stand-out performer, with a strong deep roar interspersed with snuffling noises. When he was playing for Grenoble he was the only player allowed a room of his own, having been boycotted by the rest of the team. It's not the first time we have been lumped together so I know what's coming, and in my panic to get to sleep before he does I get myself so worked up the opposite occurs: when he starts his hibernating bear routine I am wide awake.

My grogginess the next day fits right in with the mood of the team. As we are now saved from relegation we have little to play for, and the pre-match team talk is full of ominous signs. Thierry Pérez asks us to *éviter le ridicule*—avoid being ridiculous—and Pat Arlettaz stoops to the old 'pride in the jersey' motivational speech. The idea of a bonus point is vaguely referred to but no one dwells on it.

Biarritz are using the game as a dress rehearsal for the European Cup final next week, so they have put out their top team. There is the slight hope that they may be worried about getting injured and therefore be tentative in contact, but they are too good for that: everyone knows that going into contact half-heartedly is, paradoxically, the best way to get injured. There is also the fact that one of our two away wins over the last couple of years was here, the week after they played the semifinal of the European Cup, but they put out a largely second-string side that day and are clearly not going to make the same mistake again. They are winding up, while we are winding down. We know it isn't going to be pretty.

And it isn't. Small-scale cock-ups that we might normally get away with are ruthlessly exploited, and the points pile up at an alarming rate. Twice, Michel calls throws to the back of the line-out, but he is shouting to Nico Grelon who is throwing in at the front; he doesn't take his mouth-guard out, the Biarritz crowd is singing, and the guys at the tail are surprised when the ball goes sailing over their head into open space because they haven't jumped. On both occasions Biarritz gather quickly, send it wide, keep the ball alive well, and score.

At one point we kick deep and arrive for the line-out. As we are organising ourselves they take a quick throw-in and their scrum-half, Dimitri Yachvili, romps 60 metres down the sideline to score. We look ridiculous but feel we are again getting a raw deal from the referee: on this occasion the line-out shouldn't have been allowed to be taken quickly because it was already formed. Heads go down or start yapping. Seb

247

Petit, our prop, takes it a step too far and gets a yellow card for questioning the referee's eyesight.

Despite a high tolerance level for occasional mistakes by the ref, I am also starting to feel frustrated. Towards the end of the first half, Biarritz chip a kick through a little too far and we are able to touch down in goal. I am standing on the 22-metre line, and there is a big hole in front of me. I am passed the ball, and as I bend down to do a sneaky little quick drop out to myself, I get cut in half by Serge Betsen, who arrives from behind me. Obviously he is offside and shouldn't have tackled me, so as I pick myself up I ask the referee, who is allowing play to continue, where the Biarritz flanker might have appeared from if he wasn't offside. Whistle. Penalty against my big mouth. Biarritz kick to touch, take the ball cleanly and start mauling slowly towards the tryline. I go to pull down the maul—legal if you are the first man in defence, and something I usually do quite well—but find they are so compact and well-structured that the bastards won't go down, and they score again.

They are a bloody good side. Things are going so fast I have lost count, but at half-time the scoreboard shows that they have scored six tries and are winning 43–0. (A few weeks later I will find it reassuring to watch them put 31 points, including five tries, on Toulouse in the second half of the final, which they win 40–13.)

They go a bit easier on us in the second half, bringing on reserves. I limit myself to a couple of well-chosen epithets directed at the ref, and save my breath for the running around: I haven't played the full 80 minutes for months and am not finding it easy. After they score their first try of the second half—about 20 minutes in—I go up to compete for a kick-off with Jérôme Thion. However, with his lifters under him he gets high, while I, knackered and operating under my own steam, barely get off the ground. My shoulder hits his rear, he hurtles to the ground, and as I fall I reach out and grab at him in a reflex action that makes his crash to the floor even uglier. Oops. I would feel very bad if he couldn't play the final next week because of me. The Biarritz forwards close in, but I think they can see that I am genuinely worried and that it wasn't deliberate. Thion, swearing, lies motionless for a while, but I drag him to his feet and luckily he stays up without further assistance.

After the game I feel low with accumulated fatigue and the heavy defeat. I have had a few hidings in my life but it is a while since I had 50 points put past me. Strangely enough, I feel I played all right: despite giving away a couple of penalties, I took the ball up about a dozen times without losing it, made a few good tackles, including one covering tackle on Thion that was enough of a thump to make him spill the ball forward, and my tight work wasn't too bad, even if I wasn't able to stop their maul from scoring. Normally, this would be enough for me to say that it wasn't my problem, the fault lay somewhere else and at least I had done my job. But this time, it isn't. At the after-match I am still pulling myself together. I darkly note that some match officials are laughing, joking and having their photographs taken with the Biarritz players.

18

The Slippery Slope

Stade Français have built a reputation for doing things a little differently. An example came under Nick Mallett. When the club reached the middle of the winter without being as well-placed as they would have liked, a break in the championship for the Six Nations meant they had a week without a game. Mallett might easily have used this as a training camp to try to whip them into shape after a disappointing start to the season. Instead, the South African took his troops off to the alps for a few days skiing, far from the muddy, and occasionally frozen, training grounds of the capital. Some skiing went on—by all accounts there was quite a bit of *apres-ski* as well—but Mallett let the team get on with pretty much whatever they felt like. Some observers—and even, I think, some of the team—thought this was crazy, but Mallett had read the situation brilliantly. The players came back refreshed and ready for the business end of the season, and went on to win the championship.

When rugby went professional, players could spend more time training, and this led to an improvement in player skills and levels of physical preparation. In addition, clubs became employers, rather than people organising what you did for fun, and because they were paying they wanted to see you sweat. This was fair enough, and by and large standards of play have risen considerably. However, if your work ethic is telling you that to get an edge you will have to train relentlessly—more than the other guys—the positive effects of repetition can easily slip into overkill: everyone else is working hard, and to do more than them you have to do a hell of a lot. Quite quickly, something you once enjoyed can make you wonder whether you want to get out of bed in the morning.

Enthusiasm is one of the keys to playing well, and if spending a week skiing allows a team to bond in a healthy way and forget about scrums and line-outs and rucking and mauling and tackling and catching and passing and kicking and all the rest of their normal activities, and they are mature enough to use the time to recharge their batteries, it is worth doing.

Enthusiasm is easy to have when you're young and recovering quickly. As the years wear on, rugby takes a toll on your body and, up to a point, your mind. Having to worry about creaking knees, a sore back, and that shoulder niggle that just won't go away, takes some of the shine off your enjoyment, even if it doesn't affect your determination.

And enthusiasm goes hand in hand with confidence, which is a massively important part of a player's mental ability.

When I was about twenty, having played for the New Zealand Colts I considered myself an All Black-in-waiting: it was just a matter of time, I thought, before I would be one of the world's best players. I was already in the ante-room. Now that I have played a couple of hundred first-class games and never got within shouting distance of an All Black jersey, this attitude strikes me as seriously deluded, but at the time it was a major asset. Going on to the field believing you are better than the other guy gives you a massive head start. Such confidence can't last, obviously, but while it does you are hard to beat.

When eventually you have to come to terms with the fact that there are people out there who are at least as good as you, and perhaps quite a bit better, it's character-building, but it isn't necessarily a good thing for your game. Instead of going out saying to yourself that you are going to prove you are better than the guy opposite, you wonder how good he is, and all the little things that may go wrong crowd into your consciousness. One of the hardest, but most vital, things in sport is to learn how to lose from time to time. All the things you thought made you so good have to be re-examined, and your failings identified and broken down. Only then can you build yourself back up to become a better player.

People find their confidence in different ways, and humility is good protection from falling too far, but if you want to compete with the best you have to rate yourself highly, and this means treading a fine line between confidence and arrogance—not swaggering around as though you own the place, but having faith in your ability to come out ahead of the other guy. The margin between individuals at the top level of most sports is very small. In a 100-metre final, all runners will probably finish within one or two metres of their competitors and it will be the one who gets his or her nose in front who wins. What is going on in your head can make all the difference.

Ending up with a big ego is rare in rugby, as in most team sports, because you are surrounded by fellow players who will let you know if you have an inflated idea of yourself. Commanders of Roman armies were allowed to parade through the streets of Rome after victorious campaigns, but the senate ensured that they had someone alongside them in the chariot to whisper in their ear, 'Memento mori' ('Remember you will die'). At the end of the English season, just before our return game against Stade Français, Jonny Wilkinson comes down to stay with Harley Crane—they used to play at Newcastle together. Wilkinson may be the highest paid player in world rugby, and the man who won the World Cup for England, but he still has to deal with Crano relentlessly roasting him about his dodgy haircut.

Mental maturity is supposed to come with experience, and French clubs tend to value experience over youth, often buying in older foreign players rather than giving younger home-grown ones a chance; there's a feeling that young players need to prove themselves over a number of seasons at lower levels. In New Zealand the attitude is quite different: if you're good enough, you're old enough. Indeed, thirty is considered the start of the downhill run, while in France there are plenty of players in their early thirties who are considered to be at their peak. The average age of the All Blacks' 2006 squad was 25.5, while for the French Six Nations squad it was 28.5.

I have personally benefited from the French emphasis on experience, but its importance may be an illusion: once a player has mastered the fundamentals, rugby is not very complicated. If you can handle the jump to a higher level, you will come into contact with better players and progress quickly. And often the younger you are, the more quickly you adapt. This year in Montpellier we have had the example of Fulgence ('Fufu') Ouedraogo, who has improved so dramatically at the age of twenty that, having started the season in the *Espoirs*, he is now one of our best players.

This is good news for the club, but fairly average news for the other flankers: as we are ringing the changes, some are on the way out. During one of the particularly flat training sessions we have before the last game against Stade Français, Didier Bes and Thierry Pérez have a long conversation on the sideline. Judging by Didier's sharp-edged gesticulations and Thierry's stony face, it doesn't look good for Didier, and during the period between the end of this season and the start of the next he is shunted off to coach the Reichels, the Under 21 piranhas. This is hard on him: the forwards have been solid in his domain of scrums and line-outs all year. If anything, it's been one of our strengths.

Meanwhile, Thierry announces that Nourault is staying on. Jérôme has earlier organised a 'democratic' vote on whether Nourault should coach us next season. The result was massively against, but Thierry has made his decision.

Alain Hyardet is confirmed as the replacement for Pat Arlettaz as backs' coach. Olivier Sarraméa from Stade Français, Argentinian Federico Todeschini from Béziers and Didier Chouchan from Biarritz are confirmed as new recruits. Again, this is good news for the club because they are good players, but less good news for the people whose places they will no doubt occupy, and there are one or two long faces when we hear the news.

The Georgian Mamuka Magrakvelidze has not had his contract renewed, and our fullback Fred Benazech has been 'let go', despite having another year on his contract. Everyone else will be back again to start pre-season in just over a month.

Except me, of course. As I go into what will be my last game of rugby I find myself unable to take in the enormity of the fact that, after 25 years, I won't be doing this again. This is coupled with the unpleasant realisation that I now have to find a 'real' job. Professional rugby looks a sweet deal when you are in your early twenties, and your non-rugby-playing friends are struggling to find work, or starting at the bottom of a career ladder. However, now I am in my early thirties and my friends have managed to work their way up the career ladder, I am the one who has to start at the bottom.

In the changing-room before the game, I try to drink in the atmosphere and ignore the void that lies ahead, but idle thoughts drift across my mind. I wonder whether I should go and have a massage. Lots of players do, but I have always thought it would send me to sleep so I've never bothered.

Now I'll never have the chance again. And it's free. Christ, I'm going to start having to pay if I want to go to the gym.

Come on, concentrate. You need to play well, to finish on a good note. I visualise things I will be doing in the game, make sure I have a mental image of doing them well, and busy myself with my boots. We go out to warm up, and I am reminded of how hot it is. All the games are being played at the same time, three o'clock on Saturday afternoon, so that no club has an advantage, but summer starts early in the south of France, and already it is well over 30 degrees.

After the warm-up we come back into the changing-room and pour water over ourselves in an attempt to cool down. Then we make our usual preparations. In my case it's Vaseline on the ears, Vicks VapoRub under the nose, and a strap around my left wrist to prevent the bone popping out. We huddle together for a few final words. It seems so unreal I can't register what is said.

Fred Benazech and I lead the team out with our arms around each other. We have played together for two seasons but it is only in the last couple of weeks that I have started to understand him. I have heard that at the Agen game he was misty-eyed in the changing-room: he had just that week heard the club wouldn't be keeping him on.

I had always thought Fred wasn't really interested in excelling. I once heard him greeted by a journalist as 'the greatest waste of talent in French rugby', which he seemed to take as a compliment. I have seen him throw out of the back of his hand, behind his own goal-line, a suicidal 30-yard reverse pass that was intercepted and a seven-point gift to the opposition, but I have also seen him run a ball back from 70 yards out through most of the opposing team and score an amazing individual try.

It's not, I've come to realise, that he's not interested: he has just held on to the simple joy of risk-taking, and rates this above playing a dour, safe percentage game. This is what commentators mean when they talk about French flair, and you don't see much of it these days. Playing this kind of game matters to him enough that, although he's nearly the same age as I am, he is going to play another year of rugby with a third-division club.

Determined to do something impressive in my last game, I run around like a rookie, and when a break in play allows me to look at the clock I see there are only seven minutes gone. How am I going to make it to half-time in this heat? The Parisians, seeing the game as a dress rehearsal for next week's semifinal, have their best side out and are in impressive form, while we are mentally at the beach having barbecues.

A couple of minutes later Fred goes off injured. It's still nil all, but it won't stay that way for long. We are using up a massive amount of energy just to hold on to our own ball. Scrums are such a struggle that after a couple, despite knowing I am needed at the next phase, I lurk on the wing, knackered, until I can catch my breath. I take up the ball a few times and have a hell of a time holding on to it in contact. Stade Française are in like robbers' dogs, low, strong and very hard to shift, and once I am penalised for not releasing.

After 20 minutes Skrela kicks a penalty. This is a turning point: Stade Français score twice in quick succession, and after 25 minutes the score is 0–15. They dominate every phase of play. I manage to pull down a couple of their mauls, but when I miss one they roll right over the top of me, and unlike the gentlemanly Biarritz pack, they really work me over, deliberately targeting weak points. Knees and ankle joints, where there is less flesh, are vulnerable, and even though I am wearing shin-pads my lower legs begin to look like as though someone has been playing noughts and crosses on them with a knife.

With five minutes to the break, David Bortolussi dots down for us to make it 5–15, but Stade Français score again, and then convert to make it 5–22. At half-time, as we are dousing ourselves again, it occurs to me that people die from heatstroke in conditions like these. How long will I have to stay on before Nourault pulls me off?

One of the big differences between the two teams is that we go to ground and waste time and energy having to recycle the ball, while Stade Français keep it alive, making passes out of contact situations. Partly this is because their players have good individual skills, but it's also because we haven't placed enough emphasis in training on passing in the contact zone. Hopefully, the lesson will be learned for next year.

I leave the field, mercifully, just ten minutes into the second half. Stade Français score again to put the game beyond any lingering doubt at 5–29, but then we manage a brace of rapid-fire tries, one by Régis Lespinas and another by Laurent Arbo, well set up by Seb Mercier, who shimmies through the opposition centres and runs 60 metres before offloading to Lolo. Just to drive the nail home, Stade

Français score another couple of tries, making it 17–43, but Lolo Arbo has the final word. As his second try is our fourth, we get a bonus point, making the whole thing look a little more respectable.

Meanwhile, Pau and Bayonne both lose their games, so Pau finish on 40 points and go down, while Bayonne end up on 43, us on 46 and Narbonne on 47. Castres, on 66, head off Montferrand, on 63, to qualify for the European Cup next season.

Ideally, the last game of a career would be one in which your team wins the championship, or at least the game, but I manage to convince myself the result was a good one for me because, coming on the heels of the Biarritz game, it convinced me I no longer have what it takes to compete at the top level. Against anyone other than the big three, I think I still hold my own (a bit like Montpellier), and were I to be lucky enough to be playing in one of these teams I might be carried for another season. But there is no room for margin of error in a small club. I might be able to find another club that needed someone like me, but it would probably be in the second division, and I don't want to spend another season just hanging on. As it is, my body has been giving me warning signs most of this year.

Despite being hammered, we do a little run round the pitch—not so much a victory lap as a 'we're still here' lap—clapping the supporters and being clapped by them. Nico Grelon and Philemon Toleafoa hoist me up on their shoulders, and I perch uncomfortably for about ten yards before

Nico says, *'Putain, il est lourd, l'ancien'* ('Fuck, the old man is heavy') and they put me down.

As the old man of Montpellier, I am intensely aware of how the game has changed since I was a young player. When I played my first game for Wellington in 1994, lifting in the line-out was still outlawed, tries had been worth five points for only a couple of years, and flankers could break off the side of the scrum. I remember this particularly because I was considered mobile enough in those days to be stuck on the flank, and for that first game, against Auckland, I had to cope with an All Black back row of Zinzan Brooke, Michael Jones and Mark Carter. Most of the time I hovered about a metre off the scrum, terrified they would rumble my cart-horse speed off the mark. All I got from the game was a ticket so my Mum could watch from the stands, and a memory that I plan to take with me to the grave.

Just a few years later I was heading back to Paris with Racing Club. We had won the semifinal that meant we qualified to go up to the first division. As we were celebrating we called the club president, Gerald Martinez, down to the back of the bus. He arrived with a big grin, certain we were going to get him involved in drinking games or similar mischief. In fact, we asked him for a bonus. The grin crumpled.

It would be hypocritical of me, one of the first wave of rugby's international mercenaries, to mourn the passing of the amateur era. I am grateful to have had the opportunity to make money out of what I enjoy doing. But I can't help hoping that rugby doesn't become a multinational corporation and lose its human touch. Winston Churchill once said,

'We make a living by what we get; we make a life by what we give.' In the years to come, I hope that rugby players—amateurs, professionals and mercenaries—make sure they give at least as good as they get.

Epilogue

It has been more than two years now since I ran out for that last time against Stade Français. I played in a pick up game of touch rugby recently—the first time I have been near a rugby ball for a couple of years—and straight away the buzz of adrenaline kicked in, followed by the almost unconscious mental calculations: where were the weak points in the opposition, who were the people I could rely on around me, and what could I do to help them? The brain picked up more or less where it had left off and like a gangly —if slightly flabby—Labrador I bounded eagerly after the leather oval, chasing it back and forth, full of work rate and faithful support of the ball carrier. Clearly, this couldn't last. After ten minutes, enthusiasm levels were ratcheted back considerably, and the decision was made to draw on experience rather than aerobic capacity. Still, after an hour I felt a vicious twinge in my calf as I tried to burst onto a ball that might have put me in a gap. I hobbled to the side of the pitch, regretted the lack of medical staff, and got a taxi home.

People always ask retired professionals if they miss it. By common consent, the universally approved response to the general public runs along the lines of 'No way, I've got so many things I want to do, there are plenty of exciting opportunities coming up and I'm looking forward to having my weekends back...' But in my experience, amongst themselves, every ex-player admits to his peers that life after rugby isn't easy. The structured lifestyle, the camaraderie, the pay cheque (in no particular order)—it's hard not to miss them as you try to adapt to the new reality of the rest of your life. The first summer is fun, a long break where you don't have to worry about being in shape for the coming pre-season. As your mates start making their way back from holidays, slogging and sweating to get up to full fitness, life seems pretty good. But then the games start again, the championship is soon in full swing, and you are an ex-player. What is a weekend for if it's not to play rugby?

Montpellier struggled through the 2007 season, missing relegation by a hair—but in 2008, boosted by several young players from the ranks of the Espoirs (three of whom now play regularly for France: 'Fufu' Ouedraogo, Louis Picamoles and Francois Trinh-Duc) they only narrowly missed out on qualifying for Europe. The team have moved to a spectacular new stadium, have already won away three times this year and are starting to look like they might become genuine heavyweights.

Even if it is only for a six-month stint, Dan Carter's arrival at Perpignan (where Marcel Dagrenat was ousted in a coup in 2007—having spoken to Carter, it seems highly unlikely that he would have signed there were Dagrenat still in charge) is an indication of the continuing pulling power of the north, and especially France. Since 2006, player's salaries have gone up by nearly 50 per cent again, so that average wages here are now around €10K a month, €25-30K is not unusual, and Carter himself, having signed the most expensive contract in the history of rugby (give or take €700K) is on about €100K a month. The arrival of a number of highly ambitious multi-millionaires on the scene—notably Mourad Boudjellal at Toulon—has ensured that paypackets just keep getting bigger as they compete for the services of the world's best players.

Here in France and around the world, the game is a growth industry: even if the rugby wasn't always brilliant, the 2007 Rugby World Cup was a phenomenal success in terms of audience and revenue. Whether the 2011 edition in New Zealand will work as well is another question, but clearly interest in the game is spreading beyond the traditional strongholds to a new public. Russia now has a professional competition, and the USA plan to start one within the next couple of years. New Zealand and Australia, who played a one-off Bledisloe Cup test in Hong Kong last year, are desperate to find new markets as the Super 14 and Tri-Nations model starts to look pale in comparison to the European competitions. This has led to some undignified crowing among the European rugby punditry, who enjoy watching South Africa, New Zealand and Australia, who have stuck it to them for so long (and still are at an international level), squirming as the economic reality of a small population base hits home in their domestic competitions. Admittedly, the southern hemisphere nations put a few noses out of joint by telling everyone else how to do things when they were in a position of strength in the early years of the Super 12, but the rubbish being talked about the purity of the European club model would be less hard to stomach if the playing field did not tilt so obviously in favour of the north. In any case, the relationship is symbiotic—if the south suffers, it will ultimately have an impact on the north as well. One interesting development is that a Bledisloe Cup test will be played in the USA in the next couple of years as Australia and particularly New Zealand look to tap the huge potential of the American market. If rugby takes off in the States, it will change the face of the game around the world.

The growing interest in rugby as a spectator sport and its ongoing professionalisation isn't all good news. The coach of one team that featured prominently in the Rugby World Cup told me that he fears rugby will become more and more like American Football. According to this theory, children will continue to play up until their late teens, but as the physical demands of rugby increase and a gulf develops between those who can make it as professionals and those who can't, there will be a big drop off in participation. In my home town of Wellington, numbers of adults playing rugby are down by about half from the 1980s—and about a third of those still playing rugby at senior level (over 19) participate in the 80/80 competition, where players' weights are limited. This is the kind of competition that could allow rugby to grow into new areas like Asia—Thailand hosts an annual international 80/80 competition, involving teams from places like Sri Lanka as well as New Zealand and Australia—while holding on to players who enjoy getting out on the field but struggle to keep up with the demands of the game at professional or semi-professional level. This kind of initiative is about the game at grassroots level, and it is vital. The real measure of a sport's success is surely in the satisfaction gained by the people who take part in it rather than the revenue generated by the people who watch it. The professional world is the shop window of the game, and it needs to reflect the fundamental ideals of rugby: we need to avoid getting so caught up in performance and the associated money-making that we forget about why we wanted to play in the first place. In marketing terms, the brand of rugby is strong precisely because its set of values are old-fashioned. An old coach of mine used to say that, up until the age of about 20, rugby develops character. After that, it exposes it. The game has a great future ahead of it, provided it stays faithful to the character it has developed.

About the author

John Daniell was born in New Zealand, and educated both there and in England. After studying English at Oxford University, he worked as a journalist for Radio New Zealand and Capital Television. His early rugby career included playing for England Schoolboys (1990), New Zealand Under 19s (1991), New Zealand Colts (1992), Marist St Pats (1992–97), Oxford University (Blue, 1992–94) and Wellington Lions (1994–96). In 1996 he turned professional, playing for French clubs Racing (1997–2000), Perpignan (2000–2003) and Montpellier Hérault (2003–2006). Currently a free-lance journalist, he has been published in *The Observer*, *The Sunday Telegraph* (UK), *The Evening Post*, *The New Zealand Listener*, and French publications *Rugby* and *La Semaine du Roussillon*. He lives in Montpellier, France with his girlfriend, Marion Chaulet. He has a daughter, Chloé.